THE
BIRDHOUSE
MAN

RICK DESTEFANIS

THE BIRDHOUSE MAN
Copyright © 2020 Rick DeStefanis

Excerpt from *Raeford's MVP*
Copyright © 2015 Rick DeStefanis

ISBN: 978-1-7331833-4-5

Acknowledgements

This story was written with the help of many people. Several are veterans and graduates of either the United States Military Academy at West Point or the Officer Candidate School at Fort Benning, Georgia. Some were Army Rangers and others were fellow paratroopers. Some were Green Berets (I know guys: You're not a f@#*#g hat!). All are friends and include writers and editors without whom this story would not have found its way to print in its current form. I am deeply indebted to all. Listed in no particular order are some of those people.

Robert (Doc Enz) Enzenauer, Brigadier General, Retired, United States Army, United States Military Academy, Class of 1975, 19th Special Forces (Green Beret), OEF2, FOB 195, JULY 2002-June 2003, Kabul, Afghanistan, 5/19th SFG(A), Colorado Army National Guard, OIF2, Camp Victory, Baghdad, Iraq, 928th ASMC Area Support Medical Company, Colorado Army National Guard, 004. MD, MPH, MSS, MBA, Professor of Ophthalmology and Pediatrics, Chief of Ophthalmology, Children's Hospital of Colorado, Aurora, Colorado. *Oh, yeah*, and one knee replacement—happens when you jump out of enough airplanes: All the Way, Doc, AIRBORNE!

Robert (Bob) Walker, Captain, Drafted 1966, OCS 8/1967, Fort Benning, GA. US Army Ranger, Republic of Vietnam 1968-69. Recon platoon leader for 2 months then company commander for the remainder of his tour. 2nd/39th Infantry, 1st Recondo Brigade, 9th Infantry Division (AO-Mekong Delta). Twenty-six decorations including four Bronze Stars with V devices, Soldiers Medal, Distinguished Flying Cross, three Silver Stars and The Distinguished Service Cross. Bob was my first boss at FedEx and I believe he can still wear his original set of dress blues. He is also a man for whom I hold the highest respect.

Lionel (Tony) Atwill, Lieutenant, OCS-6/1967, US Army Ranger, and Airborne School-Fort Benning, Georgia. Third Special Forces Group-1967, 1st Infantry Division, Republic of Vietnam 1968-1969, Recon platoon leader, 2/18th. Two Bronze Stars with V devices, Purple Heart Medal, Air Medal and Vietnamese Cross of Gallantry. Tony lived it and provided much of the vital detail for this story. He lives in God's country, smack in the middle of the Colorado Rockies. I am jealous.

Orlando (Orie) Illi, LTC, U.S. Army (Ret) retired from the U.S. Army Acquisition Corps after a 36 year combined Active Duty / Federal Civil Service Career. He was Commissioned from OCS in 1978 and retired as a LTC from the Faculty of the Defense Systems Management College (DSMC). He was subsequently appointed as a HQDA GS-15 where he served as Deputy Product Manager for the Army's Tactical Electronic Medical Records Program until his retirement from Civil Service. LTC Illi is a designated National Security Professional and attended training at the Department of State, FEMA, DHS and National Defense University on Inter-Agency National Security Coordination. LTC Illi was a Finalist for the 2009 Samuel J. Heyman Service to America National Security and International Affairs Medal and was inducted into the Army OCS Hall of Fame in 2019.

Jeremy Klages, Captain, United States Army, 1992-1997, United States Military Academy, Class 1992. Military Intelligence 1-6 Infantry, 3rd Brigade, 3rd Infantry Division, Germany (Balkan Theater), Task Force

Able Sentry 1994, Joint Task Force Provide Promise 1995, Army Achievement Medal, Army Commendation Medal, Joint Service Commendation Medal, Meritorious Service Medal. Jeremy provided some of the most detailed feedback and suggestions that made this story what it is. He is also an author and an outstanding writer in his own right. Check out the Kade Sims technothriller series by Jay Klages.

Carol Carlson, childhood friend, editor, fact checker and mother and daughter of military veterans. It's a fact: In the 1960s, we sat in the limbs of a mimosa tree between our yards and chewed the fat long before either of us reached puberty.

Ellen Morris Prewitt, friend, author, and an accomplished writer of Southern Fiction. Her input and suggestions always make me a better writer. https://ellenmorrisprewitt.com/

Chris Davis, friend, writer and an outstanding critic and story editor. I remember when Chris first came to work for me in my operation at FedEx in 1988. It was the beginning of what has grown to become a thirty-two-year friendship.

Todd Hebertson, friend, writer, and the best cover designer in the business. Email: mypersonalartist@hotmail.com or visit his website at: www.bookcoverart.webs.com.

Elisabeth Hallett, unmatched as a line editor, she is the last set of eyes on the manuscript before it goes to print. Elisabeth is another of those fortunate souls who live in God's country, the Bitterroot Valley of Southwestern Montana. Contact her at: soultrek@montana.com.

Author E.M.S., My All Everything! My formatter, guide, and general "keep me from screwing up" people, they are top-notch professionals.

Author's Note

This is *not* an adventure war story. It is a different kind of story about war and young army officers as told by a now aging veteran who fought in a war, and a young woman whose father fought in another. This is a story about the scars left on them and their families. It is a story about friendship and about men who made the ultimate sacrifice for family and country.

Although parts of this novel include actual events, locations, and military units down to platoon level, all the names of the men and officers included herein are totally fictional. Many of the men who fought these battles are still living today, and the fictional characters in this story are meant to represent their valor and sacrifice in the most honorable manner possible, while telling a story that could not be told otherwise. Additionally, while official military After Action Reports and other historical documentation were used to ensure close adherence to actual events, some artistic license was taken in the telling of this story. My goal is to keep alive the memories of my buddies and their valiant efforts to preserve the freedoms we enjoy as Americans. For your convenience, there is included at the end of this story a glossary of military terms and jargon.

CHAPTER ONE

Beyond the Ultimate Sacrifice

July, 1968
Near a Montagnard Village
Central Highlands, Republic of Vietnam

The North Vietnamese were here and Sam Walker's long range reconnaissance patrol was doing everything possible to avoid them. The young lieutenant knelt behind his Montagnard guide, who was point man for the team. The jungle was quiet and the midday sunlight filtered down into the twilight world of the triple-canopied jungle. All morning they had silently paralleled a trail on the Laotian border, finding enemy signs at almost every turn. The slack man, Robbie Knowlton, dropped to a knee and pointed out from beneath the undergrowth to a hilltop several hundred meters away.

"Out there, sir. See them?" Robbie whispered. "They're long bamboo huts kind of like birdhouses on stilts."

"That's it," Sam whispered. "That's the Montagnard village we're looking for."

The bronze-faced point man, Khul, turned and nodded. It was his village, one of the few whose people had refused to relocate to the security of the CIDG camps. The indigenous soldiers of the

Civilian Irregular Defense Group were an integral part of combat operations and Sam respected the Montagnards on his recon team. They were dependable and loyal—something that wasn't always the case with some of the South Vietnamese—especially when the chips were down, but these men had proved their grit.

Sam studied the huts with his field glasses. The village was six hundred meters away beyond a shadowy chasm, and only a couple of the huts were visible back in the tangle of vines and trees. The rest disappeared into the dense forest atop the hill. This village was home to the Montagnards on his team, but after scanning with binoculars for several minutes he found no visible movement. Something seemed amiss, but from somewhere far down the valley came the resonating whoops of Siamang Apes. This was a good thing. The monkeys were relaxed, likely because there were no large concentrations of North Vietnamese troops nearby.

Sam gazed back at his men scattered down the trail behind him. Slowly he motioned them forward. It would take time, an hour, possibly longer, to cross down into the deep ravine and climb out again. Besides his recon mission to locate a well-used trail hidden in this mountain pass, he was to deliver tools and medical supplies to the inhabitants of the little village. It seemed a pretty simple task until taking into account the thousands of NVA troops hidden in base camps throughout the highlands. Sam and his men were in the enemy's backyard.

The plan was for his medic, Lee Miller, to treat any villagers needing medical attention while Sam's Montagnard team members reunited with their families. The next day he hoped to get the hell out of these mountains, but six and a half klicks of jungle undergrowth still separated them from the extraction point. His only communications were with the Bird Dog flyovers every two hours where squelch was broken twice to indicate all was well. In the interim, he and his men were on their own and it was a situation where contact with the enemy could spell disaster.

Sam shot an azimuth to the village, not that it was needed with the Montagnard guide, but it was habit, a habit born of good military training. They started carefully down into the little valley. A step, two steps, stop, listen, another few steps. The entire team moved with the soundless stealth of the Indochinese tigers that populated these mountains. It was a game of chess where one lax moment could put a man's life in permanent checkmate.

After stopping at the rocky stream near the bottom of the little valley, they refilled their canteens and began the steep climb up through the canopied jungle toward the village. Sam studied Khul, his point man. The young Montagnard had increased his pace, obviously excited about seeing his wife and family, but that was okay. There should be no trouble now. They were well off the trail and getting closer to the village, well hidden back in the jungle. If there was going to be trouble they most likely would have already found it, but less than thirty meters from the first hut, Khul went to a knee and raised his hand to halt the column. Something wasn't right.

Sam eased up beside him. The little Montagnard's face, only minutes before bright with anticipation, was now rigid and sallow. His jaw flexed and his dark eyes, wide with fear, darted about. Slowly, he raised his M-2 carbine under his arm, but he remained otherwise unmoving.

"What is it?" Sam whispered.

"Something wrong," Khul answered.

The Montagnards built their huts on raised platforms, and the incessant buzzing of flies came from the nearest one. There was not a hint of a breeze, but Sam caught the momentary scent of what he had already begun to fear was there. Just before beginning to degrade toward putrescence, large amounts of blood emit a unique odor that speaks almost viscerally of death. It was faint but he had caught a definite whiff—enough that the hair on his neck was crawling.

Soundlessly, he deployed the men across the slope, and when they were ready he motioned them forward. Not a footfall was heard, not a leaf rustled nor a branch broken as they moved steadily up the hill into the village. There was only the incessant buzzing of the flies. Sam noticed spent brass scattered about and picked up one of the shells. It was 7.62 Russian—an AK-47 round. The NVA had been here. Khul scrambled up the ladder to the first hut, dropped to his knees and set his weapon to the side. He bowed his head, cradling it between his hands while trembling in silence. Sam climbed the ladder behind him.

The bodies of an elderly woman and two small children were there, soaked in blood and riddled with gunshot wounds. Sam placed a hand on Khul's shoulder. "We need to secure the village first, my friend. Then we will tend to the dead."

Khul nodded and followed Sam down the ladder. The patrol swept slowly forward across the hilltop and through the village searching each hut. The corpses of the elderly, the women, and the children were scattered throughout. At the center of the village, bodies of several old men had been bound to trees by their wrists. Eviscerated and mutilated, they had likely suffered a horrible and torturous interrogation before the eyes of the entire village. These were the fathers, grandfathers, and uncles of Sam's men who were now using their machetes to cut the ropes by which the bodies were suspended.

A deep anger ached in Sam's gut as he watched his young Montagnards go about the business of gathering the remains of their families. They had brought along several entrenching tools to give the villagers, but the men were now using them to dig graves. These innocent mountain people, armed with little more than bows and arrows, were of no consequence and presented no threat to the communists of the North Vietnamese Army. Yet, this was the Communist methodology for capturing the hearts and minds of the people.

Sam had seen it several times before—the killing of innocents for no reason other than what seemed the joy of slaughter. He had also grown to understand that this was a necessity for the communists because they never truly captured anyone's heart or mind. They simply eliminated them, leaving their remains as a form of intimidation. He had grown to hate them during his months here in Vietnam and he was fighting his own inclination to now become like them—a wanton killer.

It was late afternoon when they moved off the hilltop and deeper into the jungle. Sam had to put as much distance as possible between the village and his long range recon patrol. Should the enemy return to find the fresh graves, they would know the patrol was near and begin combing the area. He also avoided taking a straight-line path toward the extraction point. If they were following, a straight line of travel would tip off the enemy as to where they were headed. It was dusk when the men crawled into a bamboo thicket and established their night defensive position. Tomorrow they would break radio silence and head for the extraction site.

The jungle had grown quiet, until from somewhere back in the hills came the yelp of a dog. The NVA used tracker dogs when searching for American patrols, but Sam's tail gunner, the medic Lee Samuels, had dusted their back trail with powdered CS, probably the reason for the dog's yelp. A nose full of the powdered tear gas would not only prevent the dog from tracking for a time but also burned like fire. That dog was finished tracking for several hours. The question was if the enemy had more dogs.

Sam had to decide whether to make a risky night movement or wait till morning. The NVA were obviously on their trail, but the jungle was thick, with numerous rocky ledges and steep ravines, and the extraction point was still several klicks away. He waited and listened. There came the yelp of another dog. He had a decision to make.

CHAPTER TWO

Claire's Senior Thesis

September 2018
Boone, North Carolina

T he blond-haired boy held his chin high as if the old man sitting at the table weren't there. The boy's Lacoste shirt was pink, but the old man was certain it had nothing to do with the women's breast cancer movement and everything to do with the boy's sense of stylish, in-your-face masculinity. He could wear a yellow tie, a pink shirt or whatever it took to prove his ability to ride a trend at the cutting edge of cool. His hair was perfect and his jaw long ago squared by an orthodontist's artistry. The old man felt sorry for him.

Sam Walker was in his seventies, and many of his students over the years had been much like this boy standing before him. This one fit the profile—not quite one of the childish snowflakes of his generation, but not yet one with the manners and humility required to be a true man. Many men grew old without ever developing either. Sam smiled, but the young man continued ignoring him while looking over his shoulder—obviously waiting for someone.

Impolite imbeciles were common nowadays and seldom bothered him—no more than this kid did, now. At least that's what Sam told himself, but he was lying. He didn't care for aloof assholes who seemed incapable of at least a polite "Hello," or "How are you?"

Perhaps the boy thought that sitting behind a table selling birdhouses wasn't exactly a pinnacle accomplishment for a man, but it was what Sam had chosen to do since the death of his wife. It brought him a certain sense of peace. Caroline had been his everything since that war over fifty years ago. She was his anchor and it was her strength that had allowed him to cope with the memories. Now that she was gone, there was only time to mark until he was with her again. The arts and crafts festival was an annual event, and the park grounds were crowded with the local university students, many of whom were here only for the extra credit.

The young man again turned and gazed at the birdhouses. Sam shoved one toward him. It was one with his school colors—gold with black trim, and it had a little sign over the entrance that said, "Winners Only." It would appeal to someone like him. The young man picked it up and gave Sam a sideways smirk.

A girl wandered up beside him. She was pretty, with clear, blue-gray eyes that said she might be as bright as she was attractive. And she *was* very attractive, but Sam found himself caught in a moment of awareness. There was something more about this young woman, something in her persona that said she was much more of a woman than her boyfriend was a man. Sam attempted another smile but was pretty sure it came off more as a grimace.

The girl gazed across the row of birdhouses at him and her smile slowly faded. She seemed at first to stare him in the eyes, but he realized it wasn't his eyes. It was his cap—the one with the 82nd Airborne insignia. Her eyes clouded and she picked up a birdhouse, but it seemed more a means of distraction than one of interest. She ran her thumb across its weathered wood surface. After a moment she looked up. Her mouth opened as if to say something, but closed again. Sam studied her. Something had upset the girl.

"You want that one?" the young man asked.

"No," she said.

He looked down at Sam and bared his bleached teeth with a grin.

"Sorry, Pops. She's a finicky shopper."

Fighting to maintain his best poker face, Sam stared back at him, but the boy took the girl's arm and turned away. She pushed his hand away and refused to budge.

"That patch," she said.

Sam removed his cap and studied it before again looking up at her. "Yeah?"

"What does it mean?"

The young man nudged her with his elbow. "Claire, don't be so crude. What else could it mean?"

The girl turned to him with wrinkled brows. "Huh?"

"That AA on it means he's a member of Alcoholics Anonymous."

The young woman's face paled. "You're an absolute idiot, Brad. I can't believe you just sa—"

"Calm down, for Chrissakes. I was joking. I know it's an army hat or something."

Despite a momentary jolt of anger, Sam fought to avoid his *grumpy-old-vet-gonna-kill-you* persona. No sense in creating a scene at a campus arts and crafts festival. The girl looked gut-punched.

"It's okay," Sam said.

Her eyes moistened.

"Really. It's okay."

She tried a failed smile.

"This patch is the unit insignia of the 82nd Airborne Division. The 'AA' stands for 'All Americans' because when the unit was formed at the beginning of World War I it had at least one man from every state in the union. Later, when the division was re-formed at the beginning of World War II, this little crescent patch that says 'AIRBORNE' was added. It means we were paratroopers."

Junior's eyes bugged, "Sorry, sir. I didn't mean—"

"That patch," the girl said, "It's the same one that's on my grandfather's old army uniform. He was wounded in Vietnam. He was my...."

The young woman's bottom lip quivered ever so slightly as she tried to speak. A tear hung on her eyelid.

"Is he...?" Sam paused, not wanting to be himself crude and uncaring.

"He died back in the spring. He was my best friend. We...." Her voice again trailed into silence.

Sam's eyes locked with the girl's. "I can see that."

"Were you in Vietnam?" she asked.

Staring down at the table, Sam nodded. It was Game Day at Appalachian State and the rattling beat of the drums from the marching band echoed through the campus buildings. That along with the rippling pop of the flags at the convocation center across the street brought back the memory of graduation day from Basic Training.

He had been in the army nine weeks by then. There were lots of flags that day too, along with cottony clouds, sunshine, blue skies, and freshly starched uniforms. A brass band played the usual pomp and circumstance while the men marched across the parade field with button-busting pride, snapping salutes and pivoting on a dime. The people in the bleachers shaded their eyes and smiled. Some applauded. The popping flags, the drums, and finally becoming real soldiers—it was pretty heady stuff for a twenty-one-year-old, but it all went to shit after that.

"My grandpa was going to help me with my senior thesis this year, but he—" she swallowed hard and drew a deep breath. "He promised to tell me about when he was in Vietnam. It was going to be our project. I'm a journalism major, and he refused to talk about the war for years, but he finally agreed, and…." Her voice again trailed into silence.

"What was your grandpa's name?"

"James Robert Pearle. He was a sergeant."

"James Robert Pearle," Sam said. "When was he there?"

"I'm not sure," the girl said, "but I can get the dates for you if you want."

"What made him decide to tell you about his time in Vietnam?"

The young man cleared his throat and nudged her. She ignored him.

"I told him about my history professor's lecture on the war and I think it made him angry. He said he would tell me the whole story when I was ready. I turned in my thesis proposal to the dean and it was already approved when Grandpa had his heart attack."

"So the school year has started and this is your last year?"

"Yeah."

"What are you doing about your thesis?"

"A couple weekends ago, I took my recorder and drove to the VA Hospital down in Asheville. I tried to interview some veterans who were there for a post-traumatic stress session, but it got sort of crazy. Some of them got angry, and the staff refused to let me interview them after that. I suppose—"

"Sir, your birdhouses are very much over-priced."

It was a woman with a fat rock on her finger who had interrupted the girl. She was probably in her early fifties, carrying a gargantuan purse and wearing high-dollar diamond ear-studs to match her ring. Her perfume was an overpowering fragrance of eau de some chest-bared, long-haired European dude. She held a birdhouse and scowled at the price tag with her too-red lips screwed in a tight circle.

"I can buy birdhouses down at Blowing Rock for half this price."

"Don't go anywhere," Sam said to the girl.

"Ma'am, you can't buy *these* birdhouses there, because I don't sell them there. Each one is unique, handmade and hand-painted, and all the proceeds are donated to a local charity."

"Oh, really? And what charity might that be?"

Her lips were pressed flat now and slightly pooched as if she were a high school teacher about to catch a boy in a lie.

"Save the Montagnard People."

"That's an odd one. So, what's the least you will take for this one?"

"Twenty-five dollars."

"But this tag says it's fifteen dollars."

"I know, but there's a ten-dollar whiner's fee."

Her face flushed. With a loud huff she set the birdhouse down and stomped away. Sam turned to the girl and grinned. "Sorry. I had one of my 'grumpy old vet' moments."

She gave him a sad smile. "You remind me of my grandpa."

"You remind me of my granddaughter."

The boy tugged at her arm. "The game starts in less than an hour. We're going to miss the kickoff if you don't stop talking."

Glancing at the boy, she pursed her lips and exhaled through her nose.

"I suppose I need to go now. It was nice talking with you."

Sam had spent fifty years compartmentalizing and carefully storing old memories that were better left to crumble away in the attic of his mind. The last thing he wanted to do in his final years was sift through the horror of that time back in Nam. He had no desire to relive sights and sounds he had worked so hard to forget. Yet, here was a kid, a young woman, who actually gave a shit. She actually cared enough to want to write a thesis on it and learn about her grandpa's wartime experiences.

"Hey, young lady," he called out. "You know, perhaps I can tell you about Vietnam for him."

The girl stopped and turned back. "Really?"

"Come back around three. I'll be loading these birdhouses into my truck. It's a red GMC parked back there in the lot. Maybe I can answer some of your questions."

She pulled away from the boy. "I have to go to the dorm to get my recorder and notepad."

"What about the ballgame and the fraternity beer-bust tonight?" The boy stood with his arms spread wide and his mouth hanging open.

The girl pursed her lips, glanced at Sam, and back at the boy.

"It's Saturday for Chrissakes," the boy said, "and it's the first home game of the year! Can't you do that some other time?"

She exhaled in frustration as her cell phone began making a noise—something Sam was pretty certain her generation considered music. He remained silent while the girl thumbed out a text message. Both he and his offer for help had become a sudden sideshow to these youngsters' drama and the girl's cell phone.

"Who's that?" Brad asked.

"Megan. She's changed her mind. Her and Travis had another fight and she wants to go with me to the party tonight."

"Oh, that's just great," the boy said, rolling his eyes. "You'll have another of your guard dog chaperones with you."

The girl ignored him and turned back to Sam. "I'm sorry. There's been a change of plans. Maybe we can talk another time."

Sam gazed at her. She had seemed so mature and so intensely interested only moments ago, but now.... At least she seemed somewhat conflicted, but her decision was probably for the best. Had she truly wanted to know about her grandfather's military experiences, none of this trivia would have interfered.

"I am sure your grandfather would be happy to know how much you're enjoying your college years."

The girl's eyes softened and retreated beneath the shelter of her brows as she bowed her head. Deserved or not, his sideways jibe had found its mark, but it left him with a twinge of regret.

He tossed her a bone, if for no other reason than to avoid burning another bridge forever. "If you change your mind, I live on Janaluska Road up north of town."

The young couple disappeared back into the campus and Sam didn't know if he was angry, disappointed, or relieved. He so missed his beloved Caroline. She had always been his refuge when dealing with these kinds of people. She understood things about them that remained mysteries to him and she no doubt would have told him how he should have handled the situation, but it no longer mattered. He was old and on his own now, and when he was gone, it would be a mutual relief. These young people would no longer have to hear his antiquated opinions and he would no longer have to deal with theirs.

———————————

Sam had donned his grungiest coveralls and crawled beneath his pickup. It was Monday after the ballgame. A cold front had rolled in bringing with it clouds and a misty drizzle. Pissed off at himself for procrastinating, he had finished changing the rotors and pads that morning and was doing the last of the lubing on the chassis while lying on the cold concrete in his driveway. Sure, he was a cheap bastard. He'd admit it, but why pay some young grease jockey a few hundred bucks for what he could do in a morning?

He jerked the grease gun free of the fitting, smacking his sore thumb against the oil pan.

"Shit," he muttered.

He had cut the thumb while making the birdhouses and would have put it in his mouth to warm it and relieve the pain but it was covered with grease and road grime. It was strange, but he immediately thought of Khul, Dak, his old Montagnard friends, and all those who had suffered in ways so much worse than he ever had.

The pain in his thumb quickly receded.

"What are you doing under there?"

The young woman's voice caught him by surprise. He glanced out at two red tennis shoes standing beside his truck.

"I've fallen and I can't get up."

It may have been sarcasm, but those words were actually becoming a growing reality for him, and Sam wondered if he would be able to stand after he crawled from beneath the truck. After all, his clothes were damp, he was half-frozen, and, like most days, he was stiff everywhere but where he wanted to be.

"Seriously, what are you doing under there?"

He recognized the voice. It was the kid from the park.

"*Seriously*, I'm doing the simple crap most people pay big bucks for."

He wiped the excess grease from the last grease fitting and began scooting from under the truck.

"How did you find me?"

The girl held a canvas tote on her shoulder while she pulled a wisp of hair from her face. "I had Megan drive up and down the road till I spotted a red GMC pickup."

Sam braced against the side of the truck and strained as he pushed himself to his feet. Up at the road a blue Toyota sat idling in a pool of white exhaust vapor. He wiped his hands with a shop rag.

"Why aren't you in class?"

"We skipped."

"Y'all skipped. Well, that's just great. I'm sure that's something else your grandfather would be happy about."

A momentary flash of anger crossed the girl's face but it quickly morphed into disappointment. She lowered her eyes and turned away as she began walking back to the road. Since Caroline died, Sam had become an asshole. He wasn't proud of it, but life and age had led him down that road. He had never tolerated fools easily, and now he had begun ridiculing the very ones he had spent so many years trying to educate.

"Hey." She ignored him. "Young lady!"

She stopped.

"I was out of line. Come back and let's talk."

The girl slowly turned and walked back to him.

"Perhaps I'm being a little too judgmental." And they weren't even *his* words. They were Caroline's, and he couldn't count the number of times she had told him that very same thing.

"Let's start over. What's your name?"

"Claire Cunningham. What's yours?"

"Sam Walker."

She extended her hand. "I'm sorry for being rude Saturday, Mister Walker. I was just…I guess I wasn't thinking."

"It's Sam, and I get jealous when I'm preempted by cell phones."

"You and my Papa Pearle have a lot in common."

"Why do you say that?"

"He hid my phone from me one time for three days, until I promised to never again let it interrupt another one of our conversations. I suppose I'll have to add you to that list."

"Don't want to sound preachy, missy, but you'd do well to put everyone on that list—even store clerks, waitresses, and such. It's just plain rude to interrupt a conversation with a person to answer a phone without at least saying 'excuse me.'"

"You and Papa Pearle must have been cousins or something. So, when were you in Vietnam?"

She wanted to get down to business right away. Perhaps Claire Cunningham wasn't a slouch after all.

"I was actually there twice—for a short time in 1967 and again in '68. Don't you want to wait till you can sit down and take notes?"

"I'd like to go someplace quiet, but—"

"Tell you what. You and your friend go on back to class. I'll give you my phone number and you can call after your last class. We'll arrange something then. Okay?"

———————————

Later that day they made arrangements and the next Saturday afternoon Sam was picking up Claire at her dormitory. Another home game had the campus plugged full of cars and he stood beside his truck parked in a tow-away zone in front of the dorm. She came out the door and leapt down the steps two at a time while carrying a canvas tote bag.

"Sorry to keep you waiting. I was hurrying as fast as I could."

The canvas bag hung from her shoulder and a tiny film of perspiration lined her upper lip. She had indeed hurried. The whites of her eyes had reddened with tiny capillaries of stress.

"Have you decided where you want to go?" he asked.

"No. I mean…well, Brad said with all the people here for the ballgame, every place in town is packed and he's just hanging out at the frat house till they go to the game."

It wasn't a big thing, but it seemed she would have cared enough to find a place where she would be comfortable meeting with him. The word "patience" came to mind—another of the mantras Caroline had used to tame him over the years. His was wearing thin. If the term "to bite your tongue" was applied, he would have been the coyote gnawing his leg off to escape the trap. He said nothing as he stared back at her. She seemed rattled by his silence.

"Wait!" Claire said. "I know. We can drive up on the parkway to Thunder Hill Overlook. It's a fantastic spot where we can see for miles and…"

Her sudden enthusiasm fell into a drooping mask of disappointment. "Never mind—I can't expect you to drive all the way up there."

Sam drew a deep breath of patience and forced himself not to frown.

"Claire, whether or not I will drive up there should be the least of your worries. We just met last week and I'm a total stranger. How do you know I'm not some sort of creeper or whatever it is you young people call perverts nowadays?"

The sudden wild-eyed look of a lunatic filled her face. "Well, how do you know I'm not some sort of female psycho who preys on old men?"

Sam could only shake his head slowly from side to side. "If you were my granddaughter, I'd—"

"I'm not stupid. I have this." She reached into her canvas shoulder bag and came out with a jumbo can of pepper spray. Even the police didn't use cans with that potency. "Brad bought it for me. It's bear spray for when we hike the trails in the mountains. Besides, it's not like we'll be alone. There are always people up there at the overlooks."

Sam looked past her down the street. "Speak of the devil. Is that Brad coming there?"

She glanced over her shoulder, and he quickly plucked the can from her hands. She turned back—calm, but slightly wide-eyed. Her face was lost between surprise and innocence, and perhaps the slightest hint of fear. Sam smiled, cocked his head to one side and tossed the can back to her.

"I rest my case, missy."

Her lips squinched into a tight circle as she maintained eye contact while dropping the bear spray back into her bag. "And I rest mine, too. Papa Pearle would have said the same thing. So, where can we go to start the interview?"

"Oh, hell. Let's drive to the overlook. You're right. There are always people up there and we can get away from the football crowd. Have you had anything to eat today?"

"No, but I'm not really hungry."

"You sure?"

She shrugged. "I can get something later."

Sam read her better than if she had said it aloud. Like most college kids, she didn't have a lot of discretionary money for eating more than the meal-ticket food at the cafeteria. The girl looked down at the ground as if she were embarrassed.

"Can you drive?"

She looked up and grinned. "If it's got wheels, I can drive it. Why?"

He tossed her the keys. "Take us out to the Cardinal. I'll get us some hamburgers and fries for lunch. And when we get to the overlook, I'm not talking about the war without having a drink or two. That means you're the designated driver on the way back."

CHAPTER THREE

Plastic Soldiers

September 2018
Boone, North Carolina

They had to wait until nearly game time before getting seated at the restaurant and after talking a while the time got away from them. It was well after six p.m. when Claire pulled the pickup into Thunder Hill Overlook. She backed in and Sam stepped out on his side and Claire on hers. He gazed southeastward out at the rolling North Carolina hills. The air was cooling and a smoky blue haze hung over the hills that stretched for miles out to the horizon. Far below, vehicles wound their way through the valley roads, and a few early lights had twinkled to life. Yet there was no sound. The wind had calmed, leaving the mountains still and quiet.

"I take it you want to sit on the tailgate," he said.

Claire smiled as she set out her notepad and recorder. Sam opened the ice chest in the back of the truck, grabbed a glass and filled it with Old Forester. Sitting there on the tailgate, he sipped his whiskey and waited, but not without some small degree of apprehension. The war was something he seldom talked about, except when he had taught at the college. And the school more or less demanded he teach a bleached-out version that said little more than it was controversial, but even that was a hard lecture to deliver. Hopefully, this interview with the girl would be easier with a little bourbon.

Claire reached into her bag and came out with a bottle of something that was labeled as a "pomegranate infusion." He watched with curiosity as she twisted the cap and set it beside the recorder. She set the notepad in her lap and glanced over at him. Catching his stare, she paused. "What?"

"Nothing. I reckon a lady has to have her health drinks."

She smiled. "I like you, Sam."

"I like you, too, Claire, but you might not like me as much when we're finished with this interview."

The corners of her lips turned downward. "Why?"

"Depending on how much detail you want, we'll need to meet two or three times a week. And it's going to require a lot of hard work on your part even after the interviews."

She wrinkled her brows and nodded. "I know."

"Good. First of all, I want to know what you want. Do you want the PG-13 version of the war, the cleaned-up adult version, or the damned ugly truth? It's your call, but fair warning: That last version, the uncensored one, I've never told anyone—not my wife, my kids, or even my friends, but it's up to you."

He had always wanted to tell someone, anyone, the real truth about the war in Vietnam, but not even the love of his life, his Caroline, had heard his darkest secrets. It wasn't something easy to share, and a girl the age of his granddaughter wasn't the "someone" he had in mind. War and stories of war turned the lightest of hearts dark with the stark realization that there are no guarantees in life, and still darker when they learned of what otherwise normal boys became when faced with the real-life horror of something like the war in Vietnam.

Yet, here was Claire, and something about her, perhaps some sense of maturity, said she was ready to hear what he had to say.

She wanted to hear the truth about the war, and he was ready to tell her what most vets seldom talked about—not even with one another. But he wanted to tell her in such a way that he didn't let his buddies down, especially the ones who never came home. Only then would it be worthwhile.

"I want to hear the damned ugly truth."

"I suppose you know the truth is a pretty tough sell these days?"

"Yeah, I know. It seems objectivity and truth have both become things more relative to people's political persuasions than to fact."

"That's a pretty astute observation, little woman. I applaud you."

She grinned and pointed out toward the horizon. "Damn the facts! Full speed ahead."

"Well, at least you know you'll be sailing treacherous waters."

She had such innocent eyes—crystal clear and full of life—yet there was some fleeting essence of an underlying wisdom. This was his chance, probably his last opportunity, to tell someone what he had held inside for over fifty years, but why this kid? And what was it she really wanted to learn? Some sixth sense told him there was more to her need for this interview than met the eye. She acted tough but was she really, and what was it she really wanted?

Sam had always been able to read people well. Claire seemed above average and capable of extrapolating the grains of truth from any lines of bullshit someone might feed her. God knows he had fed enough bullshit to the curious ones over the years—if only to satisfy their morbid curiosity about the war, the men who died there, and the human wrecks who survived it. Perhaps this was what she wanted—a deeper understanding of what it's like to be a combat veteran.

Claire's cell phone warbled. She glanced at it and rolled her eyes. "It's Brad."

"Aren't you going to answer?"

"Sorry, I guess I'd better. Do you mind?"

"Not at all, dear, but please, don't be long."

"What? I can barely hear you with all the background noise. I know. Yes. Yes, like I said, I'm at the Overlook. No. I'm fine. What? That's good. No. Maybe tomorrow afternoon. I gotta go now. Y'all have fun."

She punched the button to end the call and looked up. "Sorry."

"No problem. That was pretty considerate of him to call and check on you."

"Maybe, but I really think it was because the game was a blowout and they're having their party now. So, where do we start?"

She reached down, pushed a button on the recorder, and picked up her ink pen. Sam looked out at the horizon and smiled. This girl was all business. He liked that, except he suddenly found himself unable to think. Here it was—his opportunity to speak his thoughts and say what he really wanted to say about the war, but it stared back into him as a giant shadow. He froze and cast a quick glance over at Claire.

She seemed to read the situation and without hesitation fielded the problem like a world-class shortstop. "Why don't you tell me first what you were planning to do, before you ended up going to the war?"

A flash of joyful déjà vu lit his soul as he realized this was something his Caroline had often done—lighting the path to understanding with a few simple words. He cast another quick glance at this girl who was so much like her it was uncanny.

"You know, my goal was to become a teacher back in the early sixties. Hell, I graduated right here in Boone from the same school you're going to now, except back then it was called Appalachian State Teachers College. I was a student teacher and thought I'd found my calling. Problem was, when I graduated I got a letter from the draft board saying I was reclassified 1-A.

"Back then, the Vietnam war was a remote event on the other side of the world. I had heard some about the politics that led up to it, but if America was behind it, then surely it must be for a good cause. Enlisting before the draft board called, I volunteered for OCS. That's Officer Candidate School. You know the old Mountaineer spirit. I went for it all."

The girl's soft features suddenly hardened and she cast a wary glance his way. "So, you were an officer?"

Her reaction was strange, but Sam decided not to press her for now. "Yup. A brand new second lieutenant and after OCS and Airborne school, I went on to Ranger School at Fort Benning. While all that was going on, I made it my business to learn everything I could about Indochina and Vietnam. Problem was, the more I read, the more convinced I became that the Great and Powerful Oz was running a smoke and mirrors scam on us.

"We can talk more on that later. Anyway, whatever was happening in the political world slipped by me, because for the moment, I was drunk with the glory of completing OCS and earning a commission in the United States Army."

July 1967
United States Army Ranger School
Fort Benning, Georgia

Ausbin Langston was one of the first officers Sam met at Ranger school. Tall and too stern, he seemed aloof. Like Sam, Ausbin was a brand new second lieutenant, except he had graduated from the military academy at West Point. He wore his class ring with pride, and Sam found himself somewhat awed. Yet from the start Ausbin displayed a certain weakness. He tried almost *too* hard. It was as if he were attempting to fulfill some iconic image of himself and having to live up to a higher level of expectation than his fellow officers—the ones who weren't Academy grads. It seemed for a while that he might become a Roman candle and simply flame out.

Sam had learned early on that it was okay to stand out in the military, but doing so at the expense of your fellow soldiers was certain to draw the kind of attention no one wanted. His TAC Officer at OCS told the platoon that "If you have to tell someone you are an officer, you're not." Those words returned to him as he watched Ausbin. It was his turn to be the leader for the day and he was drawing that same kind of attention from the trainers. The Army Ranger School trainers were hardcore combat veterans—NCOs who knew how to lead men.

"Ranger," an instructor shouted, "you're leaving your men behind."

It was the team obstacle course, and young Lieutenant Langston looked over his shoulder while yelling at his men. "Move, move, let's go!"

Of course, no one wanted to be a slacker, but there was a reason it was called the "team" obstacle course. The trainer slowly shook his head side to side.

"Teamwork," he shouted. "You can't separate yourself that way and expect your men to function as a team."

Sam sat on his bunk that night in the officers' barracks. It was the first week of Ranger School and Ausbin was there as well, lying on his back staring up at the ceiling. Ausie was a nice guy, but the barrier the young lieutenant had built by separating himself from the others was palpable. An officer had to separate himself from his men by necessity. It was an inherent part of being an officer, but Ausie didn't seem to understand the lesson couldn't be taken too literally—especially when you separated yourself from your fellow officers.

It was a basic element of leadership that you develop a relationship of trust with your men. This was how you gained their respect, but it wasn't gained if you sat astride your "high horse" and waved a saber while everyone else crawled through the mud.

"You okay?" Sam asked.

Ausbin cut his eyes toward him before returning his gaze to the ceiling. Even while lying on his bunk it seemed as if he were at a rigid parade rest. His eyes were a hard and unflinching brown, his jaw firmly set.

"I'm fine. What makes you think something's wrong?"

Sam lay back on his sheets and folded his hands beneath his head, leaving the green wool blanket at the foot of the bed. The fan at the end of the barracks rotated slowly, pulling a mild draft of night air through the open windows and across the bunk beds. Wearing only boxers and a cotton T-shirt, he relaxed as the cool air took the stress and the heat of the day from his body.

"You've seemed stressed and frustrated the entire week."

"Nothing I can't handle. It was part of daily life at the Academy."

"Oh, really?"

Ausbin cut his eyes over at him.

"What do you mean by that?"

"Maybe you're trying *too* hard. Maybe you just need to dial it back a notch. You know?"

An acidic grin crossed Ausbin's face as he continued staring at the ceiling.

"You know, my father started his business in Pennsylvania. That's where I grew up. He built it from nothing into a multimillion dollar concern. And he didn't do it by '*dialing it back a notch.*'"

Sam said nothing. He was tired and not ready for a contest of wills. The fire guard would switch off the lights in a few minutes.

"My father has more pull around this country than some senators, and he has a reputation for being a straight-up honest man. The last thing I will do is disappoint him."

By the time they completed the final phase of the Army Ranger Course down at Eglin, Ausbin seemed to have figured things out.

They returned to Benning and celebrated graduation day with celebratory drinks across the river in Phoenix City. Afterward, they packed their duffle bags for the trip back home. Both had thirty-day leaves before reporting to their next duty station with the 173rd Airborne Brigade in the Republic of Vietnam.

"Hey," Ausie said, "I'm thinking about spending my last week of leave at my parents' beach house in Hawaii. Why don't you join me? We can drink pineapple drinks and chase hula girls before going over. What do you say?"

This was the first time Ausbin had said something that was even slightly affable and it caught Sam off guard. It was a tempting offer.

"Really?"

"Well, I know I'd be slumming, hanging out with an OCS dreg and all, but—"

Sam gave him a sideways smile. "You can kiss my OCS ass—"

"Oh hell, I'm just messing with you. We can have a great time. What do you say?"

If it weren't for that grain of what Ausbin thought was truth, Sam would have instantly said "yes," but he hesitated. After weeks eating, sleeping, and training together, Ausbin only now had decided to become friendly. It seemed odd.

"I don't know."

"Tell you what, let's trade telephone numbers. I'll call you in a couple weeks and we'll talk. You can decide then."

Sam agreed. At least he would have some time to think about it, and so would Ausbin. Besides, a week in a beach house before going to Vietnam might be the best and last vacation he ever took.

———————————

October 1967
Oahu, Hawaii

The two men lounged on the veranda of the Langston family beach house in Hawaii, soaking up balmy Pacific breezes and massive doses of liquor and sunshine. Ausie was the apparent beneficiary of an unlimited bank account—ordering the delivery of fat steaks, lobster, and trays of tropical fruit, along with a parade of young women. But with his ever-present air of superiority he could still be a bit of a pain in the ass at times. Sam refused to be the great one's junior adjutant and refused to be cowed.

"I thought you rich dudes went to Harvard or Yale."

Ausie grinned and sipped his glass of gin and juice. The palms rattled gently with the onshore breeze, and down the hill beyond the beach the blue-green waters of the Pacific glittered in the afternoon sun. Hawaii was a million light-years from the war and damned near paradise in Sam's eyes. He drank in the elixir of the steel guitars, girls' hips quivering in grass skirts and the intoxicating odors of tropical flowers and cocoa suntan oil. It seemed for a while as if he had only imagined that somewhere out there across the Pacific there was a war.

"I thought you dudes from down south all got drafted after flunking high school."

Sam laughed. "Reckon I fooled them. Actually, my old man owned a small furniture store in Boone and worked his ass off so I could go to college, so I figured I'd better study and make good on his hopes."

Ausie gazed out toward the beach where vacationers lounged on towels while children chased balls, squealed with glee, and splashed in the surf. Sam studied him from the corner of his eye. Ausie seemed preoccupied—likely thinking about the war but unwilling to discuss it. And Sam wasn't without his own concerns, but to discuss them here in paradise seemed almost a desecration of sorts. Regardless, the thought hung as a dark ogre peering from the back of his mind: In a few days he would be in a combat zone with a platoon of men who would look to him as their leader.

The temptation was too great. He had to ask. "Have you thought much about this war we're heading into?"

"It's a regional conflict," Ausie answered. "I wouldn't get all worked up over it."

Sam remained silent, but gazed at him.

"What?" Ausie said, his brows arced.

"What about the First Cav in the Ia Drang Valley and the French at Dien Bien Phu?"

"Oh hell, the French haven't won a real war since Napoleon, and that little bastard lost more than he won. Besides, Vietnam is divided into two countries now, and the south has its own army."

"History has a way of repeating itself," Sam said.

Ausie laughed. "Didn't they teach current events at that hillbilly college you attended? We aren't the French, and the First Cav kicked the enemy's ass in the Ia Drang Valley."

"I don't think you're giving the French soldiers their just due, especially for what they faced in Indochina."

Sam reached for the bottle of Old Forester beneath his chair.

"You hillbillies like your bourbon, don't you?"

"Keeps me semi-sane. So, what if it grows into a lot more—I mean something like a real war?"

"We have superiority in every way—air power, weaponry, everything. We'll stomp their asses back into the 19th Century where they belong."

Ausie's confidence was likely a product of his military academy training, but Sam was hard-pressed to accept what seemed like blind trust in the system. "And what if it turns out not to be that simple?"

"Oh hell, in that case I suppose we'll win some ribbons and medals."

Sam grinned, but it was only to hide the doubt that plagued him. Ausie displayed the same ego and devil-may-care attitude that had been the earmark of some other army leaders. Sam had read about several of them in his studies—Patton, MacArthur, and of course there was another flamboyant general named Custer. Things hadn't worked out so well for him.

"I wish I had your confidence," he said.

Ausie laughed. "Follow me, shake-n-bake, I'll take care of you."

It would have been easy to get rankled, but Ausie would have reveled in it, and Sam wasn't allowing that to happen. He laughed instead and said, "So, the question still stands."

Ausie turned up his gin and juice and drained the glass before responding. "Which one is that?"

"I would have figured you for a Yale or Harvard man. I mean, your family obviously has money, so why West Point?"

"When I was a kid, I had this old Uncle Dorsey, my mother's brother. He jumped into Sainte-Mère-Église, France, with the 82nd Airborne the night before D-Day. I looked up to that man. He was my hero. I also had a box of little plastic soldiers. I would put them in a line in our flowerbed and attack the Germans, but we were always smart about it. We would parachute in and flank the Nazis like Dick Winters did at Normandy.

"And when I was in junior high I began reading about all the great battles and military leaders—Chamberlain at Gettysburg, Lee at Chancellorsville, Patton, Rommel. I read everything I could get my hands on. By the time I reached high school my mind was made up. I knew what I wanted to be and I pitched a real bitch when my dad said he could get me an acceptance to Yale. I told him I wanted to go to West Point. I suppose I won."

"You sure?"

Ausie shrugged. "You know, after talking with you, I'm beginning to have my doubts. The shit over there begins looking real when you're one of the little plastic soldiers. It makes you think. Have you ever wondered about those poor bastards over at Pearl Harbor back in 1941? Do you think they felt the same way we do now—I mean before December 7th?"

Sam sat up in his chair and killed his glass of bourbon. "You mean soaking up the glory of these islands—fat, happy, and contented?"

Ausie's face had grown dark. "Exactly, but then they woke up that beautiful Sunday morning getting blown to bits, burning alive, and drowning."

"Yeah. They were probably a lot like us. They thought they were in paradise, too. And I have to admit this *is* somewhat of a surreal experience. Only difference now is we already know what's coming next. They didn't."

"So, you really think Vietnam is going to be *that* bad?"

Sam glanced over at him. "You're kidding, right? Didn't you listen to our trainers at Ranger school?"

"I know it's going to be bad *at times*, but I also think hyperbole is the favorite teaching tool for all military instructors."

"Well, you're asking the wrong person. Regardless of how powerful you think our military is, you should ask the French. I think they were pretty confident themselves."

A long silence ensued. This was the first time Ausie had truly shown a more humble side of his rigid military persona. When he'd had a few drinks, he could almost be a nice guy. After a while Sam noticed he was looking over at him.

"So, what's your story?" Ausie asked.

"Not much to tell, here. I really had no big plans. I graduated college and lost my deferment. That's when I decided to join the army and become an officer before they drafted me. Figured officer chow might be better and there would be something to do besides get shot at, but—*did you know* everybody who comes out of OCS at Benning is trained as an infantry officer?"

"Ha! Bastards fooled you, did they?"

"Damned recruiter was a devious sonofabitch. Said I could do whatever I wanted—just had to ask. Reckon I should have asked more questions."

"Do you have a girlfriend back in North Carolina?"

"I did, but I sort of broke it off when I enlisted."

"So, you guys weren't that serious, huh?"

"Oh, we were pretty serious. Hell, she was broken-hearted. Suppose I was too, but I didn't let on. I told her if she hadn't changed her mind when I got back, we would pick up where we left off. She's in her last year of college now. You have a girl back home?"

"Yes, except she's from upstate New York. Her parents own some hotels and a resort in the Catskills. I met her while I was at the Academy. We're engaged."

Ausie continued gazing out through the palm trees, but his lips had tightened and he seemed perplexed. Sam studied him for a moment. "You don't seem all that enthused when you say 'engaged.'"

"It was her idea."

"Well, I suppose that explains the parade of women you've had coming through here."

"I'll walk the straight and narrow when I get back home."

"I hope so. It'd be pretty ironic to survive the war only to go home and get your ass shot by a jealous wife."

"That's what I like about you, Sam. You have a way of distilling complex issues down to their simplest terms."

The week at the beach house was like none Sam had ever experienced. They ate pig roasted over open pits, listened to the pounding war drums of the Pacific Islanders, and ate freshly harvested pineapples so luxuriously sweet they vied with the girls who came to visit each night. And the week passed so quickly it seemed but a quick dream in the night.

The screened door on the veranda slammed shut, and Ausie showed up one morning, not with drinks, but with two cups of steaming hot coffee. It was time. The young officers packed away their flowery shirts and sandals and donned starched khaki uniforms and spit-shined Corcoran jump boots. The balmy Hawaiian breezes had stilled that day as they stood in line waiting to board a silver Flying Tigers DC-8 bound for Vietnam.

CHAPTER FOUR

Life in the Rearview Mirror

September 2018
Boone, North Carolina

"What happened to your girlfriend? Did you ever see her again?"

Claire gazed at him with the eyes of a girl who wanted a fairytale ending.

"She wrote me letters—at least one a week. And yes, I did see her again, but I'll tell you about it later."

"So you really sort of knew what you were getting into when you and your friend left for Vietnam?"

"You know, Claire, life always looks different in the rearview mirror. It's already happened and you see it more clearly in terms of black and white. But when it's happening, it's in vivid color and everything looks different. The bastards in Washington...sorry, I mean, those people—"

"Mister Walker, you can't keep doing that."

"Doing what?"

"Talking to me like a child. I've been around these college boy macho-wannabes for four years and I've heard it all. If you were telling this to another vet, would you be sorry for calling a bastard a bastard or a sonofabitch a sonofabitch?"

"No, but—"

"Then don't do it with me. I want it unfiltered because I want to hear the truth about the war as you and the other men who were there saw it. I really want to understand what it was like to fight and face the things you must have faced."

Sam sipped his bourbon and grinned. "So, you don't think it's just a lack of vocabulary?" He tried intentionally to lighten the conversation, because there was something more she wasn't telling him. There was something she knew or something she had experienced perhaps through her grandfather, but she wasn't sharing it. It was as if she was searching for answers beyond those required for her senior thesis.

"No. It's your expression without alteration about what you faced and how you felt about it. Now, tell me about the bastards in Washington."

"Governments seem to never tell people the entire truth. I believe ours had everyone fooled at first. Even knowing what happened with the French there in Vietnam, they made us believe we could stop the communists and we did, for a while, but as the truth was revealed, many so-called activists used it for misguided political purposes. They used it to glorify the communists and to vilify the American soldiers who went to Vietnam believing we were doing our duty. To this day I hate that bitch Jane Fonda. Say what you want, but the communists and their American activists in this country have successfully conspired to rewrite the history of the war in Vietnam."

"That's a pretty strong indictment of our system of government."

"Call me a grumpy old vet if you want. Maybe I don't know what I'm talking about, but I won't change it to mollify the politically-correct sycophants who want us to become another France."

"Another France?"

"They're about appeasement, love and let live, no flag-waving allowed—the most liberal damned nation on earth. The Germans demonstrated the fallacy in that belief system twice in the twentieth century, and we had to bail the French out both times."

Claire gave him the dubious glance of the unconvinced while Sam tipped up his glass and finished his drink. He might lose her after that harangue, but the bourbon was good tonight, and for once he was outside the confines of a classroom and speaking his mind.

"If you ever get the opportunity, you should visit the American Cemetery in Normandy. You will see what I mean."

November 1967
Tan Son Nhut Airbase, Republic of Vietnam

It was a jarring juxtaposition. For everything Hawaii had been with fresh tropical breezes, flowered leis, and buxom hula dancers, Vietnam outside the barbed wire appeared to be a land of poverty and filth. Mopping the sweat from his face, Sam gazed about at the shimmering heat mirages rising from the tarmac. This was certainly a place where the heat of hell would take no better than a participant's trophy. And the Vietnamese versions of the hula girls were outside the fence wearing red vinyl skirts and painted round eyes, shouting something about "number one boom-boom" in high-pitched nasally voices. Already it seemed that home was a world away.

Helicopters thundered overhead, and the odors of diesel fuel and rotting garbage permeated the air as Sam walked with Ausie across the tarmac at Tan Son Nhut. They were boarding an OD green bus with heavy wire guards over the windows—something the driver said would keep the locals from throwing grenades inside.

"Don't worry," he shouted back as he closed the bus door. "It's not too far out to Long Binh, and the road is heavily patrolled by the White Mice and our MPs."

"White Mice?" Ausie said.

Sam shrugged, but the driver gazed into the mirror and answered. "That's the Vietnamese Military Police. They're those little pricks out there in the white helmets. They get their nut screwing with drunk G.I.s."

The bus passed a guard bunker and exited through the gate, heading down a road that soon became lined on both sides with clusters of makeshift shelters.

"It's hot as hell," Ausie said. "My damned khakis are soaked."

"All that wasted starch—that's just tragic," a soldier said. Sam couldn't help but laugh. Ausie ignored him. It was another young lieutenant who had joined them, Ted Salter. Salter, like them, was bound for the 173rd Airborne Brigade via the 90th Replacement Battalion at Long Binh. He too seemed enthralled by the sensory overload as he stared out at the Vietnamese countryside—litter, naked children, rivers, and palm trees—sort of like paradise gone to hell.

The bus bumped, rocked, and swayed as the driver wasted no time dodging potholes. Blowing his horn, he swerved around the crowds of rickshaws, bicycles, and motorcycles that were using the smoother parts of the road. He again shouted over his shoulder. "Don't worry. The engineers check out these shell holes every day for undetonated rounds."

"Shell holes?"

The bus sped on, hitting the craters with bone-jarring jolts.

"Hey. Check this place out, guys," Salter pointed out the window. "Dude there has a beer can house."

"A beer can house?" Ausie gazed over Salter's shoulder.

"Yeah. It's flattened beer cans. See? It's a tin can palace courtesy of Miller High Life, Schlitz, PBR...." He continued looking back, but his voice trailed off as the shelter disappeared behind them. A house made of beer cans should have said something more to him, but Sam was overwhelmed by the sensory overload.

"These women all have black teeth. What's that about?" Ausie asked.

Sam and Salter shrugged.

"Betel nuts," a soldier sitting nearby said. "They chew them for the narcotic effects. Makes their teeth black."

Sam and the other lieutenants gazed out the windows at children holding their arms out, palms up, and fingers curled—begging. Behind them, the squalor of their little huts was exceeded only by the flotsam in the roadside ditch. The stench, something Sam would describe as an eau du diesel mixed with excrement and rotting animal carcasses, made his eyes water.

Ausbin wrinkled his nose. "Do you guys smell something dead?"

Salter's eyebrows folded together as he glanced at Ausbin then at Sam. "So, where did you hook up with this MENSA candidate?"

Ausie fixed him with a hard stare and gripped the seat in front of him, putting his Academy class ring on display for Salter. "Do you have a problem, asshole?"

Salter laughed.

"Where are you from, Ted?" Sam asked.

"Texas, why?"

"So, you Texans are accustomed to smelling cow shit and such. Why don't you give my city boy a break?"

Salter glanced over at Ausie. "Aw, hell, man, I was just messing with you."

Ausie said nothing, and Sam turned to look out the bus window. They had crossed a river and come along a less populated stretch of flat ground surrounded by flooded ditches and rice paddies. The distant tree line was shadowed and dark, and as he gazed out, the water erupted a few hundred feet away.

Something had landed in the muddy rice paddy sending vegetation and buffalo dung skyward in a magnificent shower of mud and shit. A moment later the sound of the explosion reached them and the bus shuddered and swerved—first to the left then back up on the road. Another explosion directly in front of the bus sent a shower of dust and gravel skyward, shattering the front windshield.

"What the fuck?" someone yelled.

A soldier in camouflaged jungle fatigues bolted forward and stood beside the driver. "Stop!" he shouted.

The driver looked up at him. "Are you crazy?"

"Do what I'm telling you. Stop, now."

The bus ground to a halt, and a moment later two more explosions shattered the road just ahead. More gravel, smoke, and a cloud of red dust blossomed skyward.

"Now, do as I say," the soldier said. "Keep your foot hard on the brake and start giving it gas. When I tell you, let off the brake and give it all the gas you can."

The driver's face dripped with sweat as the soldier opened the bus door and stood on the bottom step gazing out at the far tree-line. Sam watched and listened.

"What the fuck is he doing?" Ausie said.

"We're sittin' ducks," Salter added.

Sam listened. A moment later there came the *thoomp-thoomp* of the mortars firing more rounds.

"Now!" the soldier yelled. "Go, go, go. Give it all the gas you can."

The engine in the floor behind them whined and the bus lurched forward ever so slowly. The soldier closed the bus door and stood beside the driver. He turned and looked back at the passengers. "Get down," he yelled. "Lay on the floor."

Sam, Ausie, and Salter dove to the floor as the bus slowly picked up speed. Moments later the mortar rounds exploded behind them and another cloud of dust and smoke billowed skyward. From outside came the metallic clacks of shrapnel peppering the bus. Sam glanced at Ausie. His eyes were squeezed shut, and Salter was watching him. A moment later Ausie's eyes sprang open.

Salter grinned. "Welcome to Vietnam."

Ausie's face was white. "Jesus H. Christ, didn't that scare the shit out of you?"

Salter shrugged. "Yeah, it did, but—" Salter stopped talking and glanced up.

Sam felt the presence of someone behind him. The bus motor whined at full RPMs as it bounced along at breakneck speed. He cut his eyes upward. The soldier in the camouflaged fatigues was standing over them.

"Y'all can get up now, sirs."

Sam extended his hand and the soldier pulled him to his feet. The first thing he noticed was his eyes. The soldier stared through him as if he weren't there. He stared as if he saw something well out beyond the horizon, something no one else could see.

"Damned good call back there," Sam said.

The soldier wore the wing and dagger shoulder patch of the 173rd Airborne on his fatigues.

"I see you're with the 173rd."

"Long Range Reconnaissance Platoon, 503rd Infantry, sir. Specialist 4th Class Moore."

Sam grinned and extended his hand. "My pleasure, Specialist Moore. We're all new lieutenants headed for the 90th Replacement Battalion, but we have orders for the 173rd. This is Lieutenant Langston and this man here is Lieutenant Salter."

The soldier didn't shake hands, but gazed at them for several seconds, saying nothing.

"How much longer till we reach Long Binh?" Ausie asked.

The soldier glanced in Ausie's direction. Only the slightest twitch crossed his left eye, but he stared through him, out at whatever it was that no one else could see.

"It's okay, sirs," the soldier said. "Listen to your men. Don't try to be heroes. You might make it."

He turned, walked back up the aisle and sat in his seat.

"What the fuck?" Aussie whispered. "That guy is seriously whacked-out."

It was the first of November and the 90th Replacement Battalion was like none Sam or his fellow officers had experienced. "Hurry up and wait" was the common description for everything the Army did, but there was no "wait" here. They were rushed building to building, getting pushed into already crowded orientation classes and led through the warehouse to draw jungle fatigues, boots, helmets, socks, and a list of essential in-country wear.

"I get the feeling we're being put on the fast track," Salter said.

The three lieutenants were gathered beneath an awning outside the officers' quarters. Sam and Ted were smoking cigarettes. Ausie stood behind them gazing up at the sky. The afternoon clouds had blotted out the sun and the three of them were waiting. They had been told to pack their gear and be ready, because they might ship out that afternoon. It was only their second day in-country.

"I think you're right." Sam motioned with his head toward a lieutenant coming their way. He had three brown envelopes in his hands.

"Gentlemen, roll your mattresses and fall out here with your gear. Two trucks will arrive shortly to take you to Bien Hoa to catch a flight."

"Where are we headed?" Salter asked.

"Dak To, to the 173rd Airborne. There'll be thirty enlisted men going as well. They'll already be on the trucks when they arrive.

These are your orders. There will be someone to meet you when you arrive at Dak To."

He handed them the envelopes one at a time. "Langston, Salter, Walker."

The lieutenant paused and pressed his lips tightly together. "The 173rd has taken a lot of casualties up there the last few months. Good luck, gentlemen."

The men boarded a C-130 for the flight up to Dak To. Trading small talk to relieve the growing tension, they tried to ignore the anxiety that gripped them all. Ausie and Ted soon discovered each had been on a championship high school football team. Of course, Ausie's was a private boy's academy near Pittsburgh while Ted's was a typical Texas big small-town team. Sam said he was too busy deer hunting to spend his afternoons sweating and getting screamed at by some red-faced football coach. Besides, he figured running cross-country track in the mountains gave him a decided edge over the flat-landers.

None of them had found time to sew unit insignia or rank on their new rip-stop jungle fatigues, but all three had attached their shiny brass infantry insignia and butter bars to their collars. Sam admired his new jungle boots. Green nylon uppers with drain vents on the black leather lowers, they were much lighter and more comfortable than the Corcoran jump boots. Of course the rucksack stuffed with fifty pounds of gear negated the difference. Sam had lost track of time when the aircraft banked sharply. Instinct said it was show time.

An airman in gray coveralls came down the aisle, shouting. "We will be landing at Dak To in five minutes. Have all your gear ready. We will be on the ground for only a couple of minutes. When the ramp drops you will disembark rapidly. Do not hesitate.

Do not waste time. Stay to the rear of the aircraft, and follow the directions of the ground-guides, and clear the airstrip quickly."

Sam felt his ears pop as the aircraft spiraled downward. The airman plugged his headphones into the bulkhead and began talking to the cockpit. He smiled and gave them a thumbs-up as he gazed at the three second lieutenants sitting beside one another. After removing the headphones, he bent toward them.

"Dak To is quiet right now. We're lucky, but we can't waste time. We'll get rockets or mortars if we stay on the ground too long. Can you guys help me get these men off the aircraft as fast as we can?"

"Sure thing," Ausie said.

"Let me know when, and I'll move them to the rear of the aircraft," Ted said.

A few minutes later the C-130 crunched down on the airstrip, braking hard and vibrating as the props were reversed. It seemed like only seconds before the ramp began dropping and the airman shouted over the noise to move the men toward the back of the aircraft.

"Let's go, men. Move. Now!" Ausie shouted.

Sam grabbed his gear and pushed past the few already standing as he made his way to the rear of the aircraft. "Come on, guys," he said. "Grab your gear and let's get moving. Follow me."

The C-130 lurched sideways and spun, throwing everyone off-balance, and just as they regained their feet, it lurched to a stop. The ramp lowered the remainder of the way as the plane's four turboprops maintained a high-pitched whine.

"Go! Go!" the lieutenants shouted.

And the young paratroopers responded, shuffling rapidly down the ramp with their ruck sacks and duffle bags. A Spec-4 and a buck sergeant stood at the back of the plane shielding their eyes against the spray of sand and dust kicked up by the props. With their free hands they motioned the men off the airstrip. Ausie pushed his way to the front.

"Where is the 173rd Airborne Brigade HQ, Sergeant?" he shouted.

"Sir," the young sergeant shouted, "we'll all go down that road there to those tents and buildings. The Sergeant Major is expecting you guys."

Sam followed Ausie and Ted, but his gaze was fixed on the mountains to the west. Looming dark and ominous, these mountains would soon be his home—and his neighbors would no doubt be the hordes of enemy soldiers that inhabited them. Just beyond were Cambodia and Laos, refuges and staging areas for thousands of NVA troops—well-trained soldiers who had been fighting this war long before the United States and Sam Walker decided to come here. The Vietnamese had already vanquished the Japanese and the French, and several times over the centuries, the Chinese. Ted stopped and looked back.

"What're you looking at?"

Ausie stopped as well.

"Those mountains," Sam said.

Ted grinned. "The emerald palace beckons."

"Yeah," Sam said, "but I wouldn't be smiling. It's what's under that triple-layer canopy that worries me."

"Lions and tigers and bears, oh my!" Ted said.

Ausie rolled his eyes. "You learn that shit at the Benning School for Boys?"

Ted spun and pushed up into Ausie's face. "We're all in this together, you smug asshole, but just for the record I did my training at Texas A&M. So lose the attitude."

Sam grabbed him by the shoulder. "Ease off, Ted. He's just giving you some of what you've been giving him."

Ted pushed Sam's hand from his shoulder and turned back to Ausie. "Just remember, asshole, we may not be hot-shot Academy boys like you, but someday when your ass is in a bind you may need us."

"I was just kidding," Ausie said. "I know A&M has a cadet corps of sorts."

"Why don't you guys give it a rest? This shit is the real thing and we need to stick together."

The rumble of artillery came from back in the mountains and the three lieutenants stopped and stared out at the horizon.

"Hey! You assholes catch up with the rest of the men. Hurry up and—"

It was a sergeant coming up the road toward them, but he stopped mid-sentence when he saw their rank. "Sorry, sirs. I didn't realize you were—"

"Shouldn't you salute us then, sergeant?" Ausie asked.

The sergeant grimaced. "I suppose I can if you insist, sir, but we don't normally salute officers out here in the field 'cause it identifies you for the gook snipers."

Ausie's face paled and he glanced around. "I didn't know this was considered the field."

"For god sakes," Ted said, "please don't salute me, Sarge. I'm good." He extended his hand. "Ted Salter."

"Mac Owen," the sergeant said.

"I reckon you're right, Sergeant Owen," Sam said. "We better catch up with the rest of those assholes. The sergeant major won't be too happy if he thinks we're slackers."

"And, sirs, I wouldn't be arguing and bumping chests in front of the enlisted men in the future. I mean, just saying, it's not a good example."

"Thank you, Sergeant," Sam said. "Recommendation well taken." He turned to the others. "Let's go, assholes. We better double-time and catch up."

September 2018
Boone, North Carolina

"It's getting late and the game is probably over," Sam said. "Maybe you can catch up with your boyfriend and still have a good time this evening."

"I want to get all this down on paper and organized while it's fresh in my mind. I'll catch up with him tomorrow after his hangover wears off. When can we meet again?"

Sam raised the tailgate and opened the driver-side door. Claire stood beside him.

"I thought you wanted me to drive," she said.

"Your arms are full, dear. I'm just getting the door for you."

"Oh, thank you. I wish Brad would do more of that."

It was tempting to suggest she find a boy who had better manners, but Sam resisted. Perhaps Brad too had some unseen qualities. God knows, with time, Claire certainly had revealed hers.

"It's pretty much up to you when we meet again. You have my cell phone number. Just let me know."

Claire drove the pickup down the steep grade, taking the curves like an experienced driver.

"You drive well."

"I'm from a little town down west of Asheville called Maggie Valley. My mama let me start driving her pickup when I was fifteen. Do you want me to drive you home?"

"No. Go to your dormitory. I'm in good shape and my house isn't that far up the hill from the school."

"I get out of my last class at 2:50 Monday afternoon. Can we meet then?"

"Sure. I'll pick you up in front of your dorm around 3:15. How's that?"

"That's great. I really want to thank you for doing this, Mister Walker. I mean—"

"Claire, it's something I probably need more than you do. We will consider it a mutually beneficial project, so your thanks are appreciated but not necessary, and it's 'Sam,' not 'Mister Walker,' unless of course you want me to begin calling you 'Miss Cunningham.'"

Sam glanced over at her. Her face glowed in the dashboard lights, and it occurred to him that in many ways she was an old woman in a young woman's body. *But, what was it that made her seem that way?* She smiled, while keeping her eyes focused on the highway. It was an honest smile, but one nonetheless hiding what Sam was growing to believe was a deeply wounded heart.

CHAPTER FIVE

Into the Emerald Forest

October 2018
Boone, North Carolina

C laire was waiting in front of her dormitory that afternoon with the canvas bag on her shoulder. Sam pulled the pickup to the curb as she waved goodbye to a couple of girls and hurried to meet him.

"Your friends?" he asked.

"That's Megan and Toni. Megan is the red-haired girl. She's my roommate, except she mostly stays at her boyfriend's apartment off-campus. It makes for a lot of nights sleeping alone. Her parents came in town this week, so she actually slept in our dorm room last night. It was nice. We stayed up late and talked."

Sam had sensed a certain degree of loneliness in Claire, but loneliness seemed odd for a young woman in college. Sleeping alone every night in a dorm room might explain some of it.

"Where to?"

She shrugged. "The Overlook again?"

"Works for me, and I'll treat you to supper somewhere when we're done."

"I want to ask a couple of questions while we're riding."

"Shoot."

"Why was there friction between Ausie and Ted? I mean I get it that Ausie went through West Point and Ted and you went through OCS and ROTC, but what's the difference?"

"Now, *that*, Claire my dear, is a loaded question. I suggest you get out your recorder and turn it on, because this will take a minute or two."

Claire started the recorder.

"West Point is the four-year United States Military Academy that trains career Army officers. Those that graduate there have a lot of pride in their West Point education and traditions. Naturally, a few of the 'ringknockers' let their pride show too much around their fellow officers, mainly those who come out of the Officer Candidate School at Fort Benning.

"Ausie was that way when we first met. You see, Army OCS also trains officers. It's an intense and grueling six-month test of endurance, persistence, and to some degree intelligence, but it's only a six-month school. That's where I was trained. A third or more of the officer candidates don't make it. It's that difficult, but those that do have one advantage over the West Point guys. OCS officers come from the enlisted and NCO ranks. They know what the Army looks like from the bottom up, and that's a perspective that can't be taught."

"So, are you saying that OCS officers don't make careers out of the Army?"

"Well, actually, many do."

"Did you?"

"No. I became a school teacher."

Claire nodded thoughtfully and glanced down at her notes. "So, the last time you said that you, Ausie, and Ted had arrived at Dak To and were going to your brigade headquarters to report in."

November 4, 1967
173rd Airborne Brigade HQ, Dak To

The brigade Sergeant Major eyed the three young lieutenants as he accepted their orders. Although it was considerably cooler in the highlands, the inside of the command tent was hot and dusty. Sam glanced about. Several radios lined a table. Their volume was turned down low as they hissed and squawked with chatter from the field units. Behind the radios on the tent wall hung several large topographical maps. The acetate covers on the maps had that familiar plastic odor and were marked with red, blue, and black grease pencil notations, arrows, and other symbols.

"Welcome to the 173rd Airborne Brigade, gentlemen. None of our officers are here right now, but we were expecting you. The general is out on aerial reconnaissance with one of the regimental commanders. The XO and the others are over in the troop area at a pre-mission briefing. I'm going to give you a quick overview of the situation here around Dak To and Ben Het before sending you down to the supply hooch to draw weapons and ammo. First, I want each of you to tell me a little about your background and training. The general will want to know."

He pointed at Sam. "You go first."

"Sam Walker, Sergeant Major. I'm from Boone, North Carolina. Graduated from Appalachian State Teachers College. No training or previous assignments other than Basic and AIT at Polk, OCS, jump school and Ranger school at Benning."

"You play sports or have any hobbies?"

"Played baseball and ran cross-country in high school and college, and I did a lot of deer hunting in the fall."

"What's your story, Lieutenant Salter?"

"Ted Salter, Sergeant Major. Denton, Texas. Played football in high school. Shot a few wild hogs for fun, but that's about it. I am ROTC trained out of Texas A&M. My other training is the same as my two friends. Reckon I'm green as a gourd, but like them I'm ready to learn whatever I need to become an effective platoon leader."

The sergeant major didn't so much as crack a smile as he turned to Ausie.

"I am Second Lieutenant Ausbin Langston, Sergeant Major. I am from Pittsburgh, Pennsylvania, where I was quarterback for my preparatory school football team. We won the private school state football championship two years in a row. I also played baseball and enjoyed tennis when time permitted. I am a graduate of the United States Military Academy and completed the Officer Basic Course, Airborne and Ranger training at Fort Benning. I have also traveled to Europe and—"

"Thank you, Lieutenant Langston. The first thing I want you men to do is take that brass insignia off your collars and put it in your pockets. Enemy snipers will pick you out of a crowd wearing that stuff. We will get you some black insignia to wear. When you get to your units, I also encourage you to have your RTOs put their radios inside their rucksacks and tie the antennas down the side where they aren't quite so obvious.

"Gentlemen, we've had our noses bloodied a few times back in the summer—lost a lot of good men. One of the primary problems was the little bastards popping out of spider holes behind us and shooting our officers and RTOs in the back. If you have a notion of leading from the rear, you may want to keep that in mind. There is no rear. It's a 360-degree battlefield."

The sergeant major stood and walked over to one of the topo wall maps. He was lean and rangy. An NCO's NCO, he moved with ease but appeared hard as a rock.

"I am not going to sugarcoat our situation here. We're in a pretty bad fight with these bastards and it's getting worse every day." He pointed to the map. "Here we are. And over here about ten miles away is Ben Het. The 4th Battalion of the 503rd is up there now conducting search and destroy operations while we build a forward operating base. Most all our other battalions are scattered west, south, and southwest of here.

"Gentlemen, we are facing the equivalent of a full division of well-trained and experienced North Vietnamese Army regulars. Most have been fighting in Indochina from ten to fifteen years. Up here to the northeast are the NVA 24th and 174th regiments. Here along these hills and mountains to the west, south, and southwest are the 6th, the 66th, and the 32nd NVA regiments. They are supported by the NVA 40th artillery regiment. Make no mistake, gentlemen. The enemy is a formidable opponent and they are here in numbers, dug in, and loaded for bear.

"Intelligence reports the NVA have bunker complexes surrounded by trenches on just about every major terrain feature in the AO. According to a recent Chieu Hoi, their stated mission is to take Dak To and annihilate those of us who are here to defend it. They think they have the makings for another Dien Bien Phu. We intend to kick their ass back across into Cambodia and Laos before they can do that. Problem we face is most of the AO is double and triple canopy jungle and the ground cover is probably thicker than anything you have ever experienced. My best advice is that you listen to your platoon sergeants. Most of them have been here long enough to know what needs to be done.

"Now, I want you to head down to supply. You will check in your duffle bags and personal belongings there. Anything you want to keep with you will need to be removed, but remember: you'll be humping it wherever you go from now on. Here is a sheet listing everything you'll need to draw. Oh, and one more thing: I don't know if the colonel has decided exactly which units you will be assigned to. We have lost several officers in 4th Battalion, two KIA and one wounded. You will be assigned by the battalion commander once you arrive in the field."

Sam glanced at Ted and raised his eyebrows. They both turned and looked over at Ausie. He was poker-faced. At that moment it came to Sam that the three of them were all wondering the same thing: which of them would be next on the casualty list.

"Better get a move on, gentlemen. Come back here after you draw your equipment. I'll find a hooch for you to stay in tonight. We expect to hear from your battalion commander this evening. In the morning we'll get you on choppers to join his unit out in the bush."

The three lieutenants wore their rucksacks and lugged their duffle bags as they walked side by side down the dusty road.

"You know, we're probably making history here," Ausie said.

Sam glanced over at him and grinned. Ausie shrugged. "What?"

"I don't mean to bust your bubble, big boy, but in another hundred years this whole war will probably be a footnote in history. Hell, we'll be lucky if our own descendants remember us."

Ted turned and walked backwards, laughing as he talked. "Good grief, Sam. Do you have to be such a dick? Ausie's gonna be the next General Patton if you don't bust his bubble."

Sam shrugged. "Just trying to keep things in perspective for you fellas."

Ausie threw his hand in the air. "Wait. Wait. How's this?" His voice dropped a few octaves. "We're not going to just shoot these sonsofbitches, we're going to rip out their living goddamned guts and use them as vines to swing through their stinking jungles. We're going to murder these lousy commie bastards by the bushel-fucking-basket."

Ted's face was one of unmatched glee as he looked at Sam. "Well, there you go. Our boy even sounds like Patton. I rest my case."

"Oh," Ausie said, "and by the way, Ted: fuck you."

And Ted, never to be without the last word, threw his hand into the air as he shouted to no one in particular, "Never fear, for we are here, united against evil, for we are The Three Musketeers."

"You know," Sam said, "for a while I was thinking we might all be crazy, but you two clowns have successfully erased all doubt. I am now certain."

After a breakfast of C-rations, Sam, Ausie, and Ted made their way to the LZ. Sam leaned against his rucksack and pressed his green towel against his face, wiping the sweat from his eyes. By late morning the clouds were billowing high overhead as both the heat and the humidity climbed. What had been a cool and comfortable morning was fast becoming another miserably hot day.

The three lieutenants sat on the LZ with a couple dozen enlisted men, most of them new replacements. From somewhere out in the jumble of hills came the rhythmic thumping of approaching helicopters. They were the Slicks, UH-1 Huey helicopters, coming to pick them up and deliver them to their units before noon.

"You ready for this shit?" Ted asked.

Sam pushed his hand beneath his helmet, scratched his head and shrugged. "Ready as I'll ever be." He was doing his best to act casual, but his mind raced with an adrenaline high.

One of the enlisted men walked up and stood in front of him. It was a PFC that Sam swore couldn't be a day over fifteen years old.

"What can I do for you, troop?"

"Sir, they told us in orientation that the unit we're going to has been in contact almost every day, and we're replacing men who were killed or wounded in action. There must be thirty of us out here on this LZ. I mean—that's a lot of men. Do you think they were just trying to scare us?"

"What's your name, trooper?"

"PFC Pender, sir."

"Well, Private Pender, I don't think they were trying to scare you, but if you weren't already scared and you are now, that's probably a good thing. Just don't let your fear get the best of you. Let it make you think better and faster. We're all out here trying to act tough, but you can bet we're all scared, scared as hell. Just listen to the old heads and do what you're told."

The PFC eyed him carefully and gave a solemn nod. "They told us not to salute you officers while we're in the bush, sir, so—" he shrugged and nodded his head. "Thank you, sir."

The thundering beat of the choppers grew louder.

"You're welcome. Now, go on back over there and stay with your stick. We'll be boarding in a few minutes. And good luck."

The soldier turned and walked back toward his group.

"I'm impressed," Ausie said.

There was the usual hint of condescension in his voice, but Sam refused to be baited.

"With what?" Ted asked. "You mean that a dumb-ass OCS officer could handle—"

"Oh, for God's sake! Will you two give it a rest? We're getting ready to go into battle and you're still acting like a couple of high school jocks."

His two colleagues gazed at him for a moment before turning away, and Sam realized he had tipped his hand. They saw now that he was on edge. He drew a deep breath and exhaled. He had to do a better job of maintaining a calm façade in the future.

The men shielded their eyes from the spray of grit as the first of the helicopters hovered past and landed. More followed while the men stood and helped one another shoulder their rucksacks. The door gunners on each ship motioned them forward and the troops bent low as they ran beneath the churning rotors.

The first thing Sam noticed was the bullet holes, lots of them, everywhere in the metal skin of the chopper. He was already sober to the reality of what was coming, but this brought it home with sudden clarity as he sat with his body covering at least two of the holes.

The turbines whined and the RPMs rose as the helicopters lurched and scooted forward. Nose-down they crossed a line of sandbagged bunkers and concertina wire. The main rotors clacked loudly and the air cooled rapidly as the formation rose above the hills. They were headed west toward Ben Het. Sam, Ted, and Ausie were each on choppers with groups of enlisted men, all on their way to join the 4th Battalion out in the bush.

Sam gazed out across miles of untracked mountain jungles and became lost in thoughts that took him from this place on the backside of the world to the rambling hills of North Carolina. Home was where his mother and father awaited his return. Home was where Caroline was—broken-hearted and trying to figure out what she would do with her life. He had left heaven for hell, no doubt.

And only minutes had passed when the chopper dipped toward an open valley along the edge of the mountains. Up ahead he spotted what looked like an LZ that had been rapidly clawed from a hilltop—a jumble of brush and trees scraped aside. Green smoke was drifting in a stream southward into the trees. The wind, the whining turbine, and the thundering rotors prevented verbal communication, but the door gunner gave him a thumbs-up. This could only mean one thing—a cold LZ. He was rapidly growing to understand the small pleasures of war.

Its main rotor again clacked loudly as the first chopper came in fast and tilted nose up before straightening and setting down. An NCO in dusty fatigues and a flak jacket motioned the troops off the choppers. Sam jumped and motioned for the others to follow. Within moments the second, third, and fourth choppers had come and gone, and a strange silence settled over the LZ as the sounds of the helicopters faded into the hills. From somewhere on a nearby ridge came the echoes of small arms fire—a steady *pop, pop, pop, pop* sound, followed by a momentary silence then the thud of an exploding grenade.

"Sirs," the sergeant said, "Captain Hollister is waiting for you at the company CP. Hang tight here while I get these men assigned and I'll take you there."

The sporadic sounds of a firefight not yet fully developed continued on the distant ridge while Sam and Ted knelt in the thick cover adjacent to the LZ.

"Where's Ausie?" Ted asked.

Sam glanced about. "Hell, I don't know. I saw him go into the trees over that way.

Ausie had disappeared with his group of newbies, but the LZ was small and he couldn't be far away.

"I sure hope he makes it okay," Ted said.

Sam gave him a sidelong glance. "I thought you two hated one another."

"Nah. I just wasn't going to let the haughty prick think he was better than me. I really sort of like the guy. Besides, I think you're right about him trying to prove himself for someone."

"You're right. He's a nice guy, just a little uptight about looking good for his dad."

From somewhere down in the jungle came a loud moaning. The lieutenants glanced at one another as the moaning gradually grew louder. After a few minutes, the voices of men grunting and cursing accompanied the moans. As they drew closer, the crashing of brush and the hacking pings of machetes came up from the jungle below. A moment later the sergeant that first met them came running along the edge of the LZ.

"We've got a bunch of wounded coming up here for a dust-off, sirs. They probably need your help."

Another paratrooper came running across the LZ. "Sarge, we got activity over yonder. Doggy and Mick just came in from the

LP. They think we got gooks moving up the ridge toward us."

A grenade exploded down the hill from where the paratrooper had just come. A second explosion followed, punctuated by the echoing clatter of multiple automatic weapons.

"Shit. Okay, get back over there and hold them back. The old man said the dust-off is inbound in ten mikes. I'll see if he can get a gunship up on the net."

The sergeant turned back to the officers. "Sirs, if you will, leave your rucksacks but take your weapons and bandoliers and see if you can help those guys down there bringing up the wounded."

The sergeant glanced around. "Where's your other lieutenant?"

"Over that way," Ted said. "He took a bunch of the replacements into the trees."

"Okay. I'll find him. You two get going."

Sam led the way, pushing into a solid wall of undergrowth. The hill quickly fell away into a steep ravine. Below from no more than fifty or sixty meters away came the moans of the wounded along with the grunts and curses of the men climbing the hill. The wall of green was all but impenetrable as Sam slid on his rear down the slope. The sounds, all but the moaning, suddenly ceased. Sam caught a sapling and froze. Ted fell over him, and slid to a stop.

"It's okay," Sam called out. "We're coming down to help you."

"Shit," a soldier muttered. He was barely five meters away, but still hidden in the wall of green just below.

Sam and Ted pushed down through the jungle and found the men. Eight of them struggled with two makeshift poncho litters, carrying bloodied and pale paratroopers. One of the wounded was moaning loudly, while the other was ghostly silent. A medic between the litters held two plasma bags. Three more bloodied and bandaged soldiers struggled up behind them. Another soldier carried the corpse of another paratrooper over his shoulder. Sam was mesmerized by their eyes—wide, unfocused, yet fiercely determined.

Ted replaced a man on the corner of the closest litter. "Go back there and help that man with the leg wound." He turned to Sam. "Get the other corner and let's get this one up to the LZ first. We'll come back for the other one in a minute."

"How far is it up to the LZ?" the medic asked.

"No more than fifty meters," Sam said. "You're almost there. Give me that plasma bag. We'll be back in a minute to help you with that one."

Within minutes the last of the wounded were at the edge of the LZ, and the medevac chopper was approaching. In the jungle on the other side of the ridge a full-blown firefight had ensued. The dust-off flared to land as green tracers streaked overhead. Sam grabbed the corner of the poncho and started toward the chopper door.

The crew chief leapt to the ground and ran past to help one of the walking wounded who had collapsed. An RPG streaked over the helicopter and crossed the LZ, disappearing into the jungle on the other side. A moment later a second RPG streaked at a lower angle across the front of the chopper, missing the cockpit by inches. It exploded in the trees at the edge of the LZ. Sam felt a sting on his back beneath his flak jacket as he lifted the wounded trooper into the chopper. He ignored it as the adrenaline kept him focused on the task at hand.

Ted ran across to the edge of the LZ, where he stood spraying the jungle with his M-16. The sergeant appeared again, running toward him across the open ground. He all but tackled Ted, dragging him to the ground as green tracers snapped through the air, only inches above them. The sergeant lay on his back and held his sixteen over his head, spraying the jungle below while Ted changed magazines.

A moment later the chopper lifted from the LZ and tilted eastward as it climbed out through a spray of more green tracers. It again became quiet—almost eerily quiet. No one moved. They waited, and after a few minutes it seemed the enemy realized they had missed their chance and pulled back—at least for the moment.

The sergeant pulled Ted to his feet. "Sorry, sir. You were giving them an easy target standing up that way. You gotta stay low or you won't last any time out here. Go over there with the other LT and y'all get your rucks. Oh, and see if you can find your other officer. I'm gonna go down here and check on my men to see if any of them got hit. I'll be back in a minute."

Sam followed Ted and Ausie, pushing through the wall of vegetation behind the sergeant. How in hell the sergeant hoped to find the company CP in this thick undergrowth was a mystery. Everything looked the same in the twilight of the canopied jungle. After a few minutes the sergeant stopped and called out. "Coming in, sir." They eased ahead.

An RTO, a medic, two riflemen, and the CO were lying on the jungle floor in a place with no recognizable features other than a three hundred and sixty-degree wall of smothering palms, ferns, and other vegetation. Sam, Ausie, and Ted traded quick introductions with their new CO and the captain pulled a map from the cargo pocket of his trousers, unfolding it.

"Gentlemen, I wish we had time for better introductions, but we've stirred another hornets' nest up here and we've got to get ready for a counter-attack." He pointed to a cluster of circular brown gridlines on the map. "Delta Company is engaged over here on the south side of the hill. Alpha Company is still moving to secure positions to the north—up here. They got hit earlier this morning while they were moving down the ridge. They had three men KIA and five more wounded—two seriously. We're providing flank security for them and covering the LZ as well."

The captain glanced at Sam. "Lieutenant Walker, I want you to go with Sergeant Ingram, here." It was the sergeant who had met them on the LZ. "He's your platoon sergeant and I'm assigning you as platoon leader for First Platoon. Your call sign will be Bravo-Red-Six. Sergeant Ingram has been with the unit since May of this year and he will help orient you to your command."

Sam reached out to shake hands with his platoon sergeant but pulled up short and grimaced. It felt as if he had torn a muscle in his back when he lifted the wounded soldier into the chopper.

"You okay?" the CO asked.

"Yes, sir. Just a little pulled muscle in my back."

"All right. Any questions?"

"Are there any other friendly units in the AO?" Ausie asked.

"We have two battalions from the 4th Division. One is just west of us here covering our flank and Alpha Company's flank. They were in heavy contact earlier this morning, but it's been quiet over that way for the last few hours."

"Is that it?" the captain asked.

"Where is the battalion CP?" Ausie asked.

"This is it. The old man is somewhere up there." The captain pointed up through the treetops. "He manages the mission from his Loach where he can have a better view of the terrain and see what's happening. I'm the senior commander on the ground. Lieutenant Salter, you'll be Second Platoon leader, call sign Bravo-White-Six. Your men are deployed up the ridge on the south side of the LZ. My first sergeant will be back here in a bit and get you hooked up with them. Lieutenant Langston, you will stay here with me. You're going to Alpha Company. Let's go ahead and move out."

Sam glanced at Ted and Ausie. Their brief liaison as "The Three Musketeers" was about to end. "Good luck, my friends."

"Same to you," Ausie said.

"Stay low," Sam added.

"You ready?" Sergeant Ingram asked.

"Yeah, ready as I'll ever be, but you better take the lead if you don't want to take the scenic route."

Ingram grinned. "No problem, sir. Follow me."

Sam and his platoon sergeant joined the rest of their men on the LZ and listened to the radio as the battalion consolidated its position on the hill. The surrounding mountains echoed with the constant chatter of small arms and the *karoomphs* of impacting artillery rounds. Later, Sergeant Ingram took Sam and the RTO along the eastern perimeter checking on the men and introducing them to their new platoon leader.

Sam quickly noticed a difference between these soldiers and the replacements he had flown with from Bien Hoa. These men were lean—not a pinch of fat on them, and though they were the same age as the replacements, they had the faces of older men—tanned, hardened, but with tired eyes.

He got their names and most mentioned hometowns scattered from Florida to Oregon. Many were white, some black, and one was full-blooded Arapaho. Two were Puerto Rican and another was from the Philippines. The thud of his heart gradually grew in Sam's ears as a sobering reality settled in his gut: These were *his* men now and he was responsible for them.

"How many men do we have, Sarge?"

Sergeant Clyde Ingram was a twenty-four-year-old E-6 from Tuscaloosa, Alabama.

"First Platoon has twenty-eight troops total—counting the four replacements we got today, plus yourself, sir."

"Any issues that need immediate attention?"

"We've been up here on this hill since this morning and we're about out of water. Most of our canteens are going to be dry by tomorrow. Other than that, we're in pretty good shape."

"Morale?"

Ingram shrugged. "Pretty damned good—considering."

"Considering?"

"We've been told we're facing an entire NVA division up here and we're just a brigade. The men know they're in for a hell of a fight and we don't have numerical superiority. I can tell you more if you want."

"I get the picture. Give me a sit-rep on this operation. I received one from the brigade sergeant major, but I want to hear what you have to say about it."

"Sir, the enemy is here ready to fight and they know their shit. They all think they're damned Audie Murphy and they don't engage us till we're right on top of them. I'm talking between five and twenty meters. This keeps us from using our air support and artillery. The terrain is also working in their favor. I mean we can't see them most of the time, even in that close. And while they have us pinned down, they have other units maneuver around and attack our flanks.

"It's a pretty shitty situation, but we *are* wising up to them. It just hasn't made it a whole lot easier. Their bunker complexes are deep with interlocking fields of fire and connecting tunnels. Hell, we've had direct hits on them and thinking we've wiped them out we start to move up, only to have more of the little bastards come up from a tunnel inside. And they're coming up out of holes behind us, too."

"Sarge, right now you're light years ahead of me, and after meeting with the men today, I know you have their respect. We will work together to maintain that respect."

Ingram cut his eyes up at him, but only nodded. Sam felt like an idiot. It was going to take more than words to earn this platoon sergeant's respect.

"What about the old man?" Sam asked.

"Captain Hollister is one of the best officers I've served under. He's a West Pointer who knows his shit and he takes care of his men, but he ain't no pushover."

"What about you?"

"What do you mean?"

"You talk like a man who's at least had some college."

Ingram raised his eyebrows. "You mean I don't sound like your average country nigga, right?"

Ingram smiled, but Sam was now feeling he had broached a subject better left alone.

"Lighten up, LT. I'm not Bobby Seale. My mama and daddy were medical professionals in Atlanta, and I went to the University of Alabama on a football scholarship, but I quit after my freshman year when I got my girlfriend pregnant. She's my wife now, but it got my ass sent over here to Nam."

"Who's Bobby Seale?" Sam asked.

"He's one of the dudes that started the Black Panthers."

"Oh, yeah. I've heard about them."

The RTO, who had been lying in the thicket beside them, called out in a low voice. "Sarge, it's the old man." He tried to give the handset to the sergeant.

"Glasspack, give the handset to the LT."

Sam cast a quick glance at Ingram. "Glasspack?"

"I'll explain later," he said.

Sam took the handset. "This is Bravo-Red-Six, Over."

The assault on the hill had been successful and the perimeter was well established, but the NVA were moving up on all sides. A dozen more casualties were being carried back to the LZ and medevac choppers were inbound. The two battalions from the 4th Division laagered in place in the nearby valley, while the 4th battalion of the 173rd continued securing the hill and clearing another LZ.

Sam got permission to take a patrol down the ridge to a blue line one hundred meters to the east to fill canteens. Sergeant Ingram stayed behind with the remainder of the platoon on the hill.

With nightfall less than two hours away, there was little time to waste. Spec-4 Tom "Blackie" Blackmore was on the point with PFC Nick Riganti walking slack. Sam and his RTO, Glasspack Baker, were next, followed by four men lugging nearly twenty canteens apiece. A ninth man walked drag.

Each step taken was slow and deliberate as they pushed silently through the dense undergrowth toward the stream. Mosquitoes, leeches, and wait-a-minute vines added to the miserable heat and humidity, but the fear of coming face to face with the NVA made all else seem nothing more than minor distractions. Each step and each parted palm frond was a moment of tension. With the sun getting lower in the sky it was tempting to move faster, but Blackie was letting nothing divert his attention. It was clear why the CO said he was the best point man in the battalion.

One of the men in the rear bumped his canteens causing them to rattle. Everyone froze. They waited with their weapons at the ready. The jungle remained quiet. The sweat trickled down his neck and the mosquitoes buzzed incessantly, but Sam moved only his eyes as he searched the shadows. After a couple of minutes, Blackie silently signaled and the column continued moving.

Sam had measured the pace and by his estimate they should be nearing the stream. Blackie and Nick both dropped to a knee. After nearly two minutes when they hadn't moved, Sam eased up beside Nick. They made eye contact and the slack man pointed to his ear and raised his hand tapping his thumb and fingers giving the sign of someone talking. He pointed up ahead. Sam heard nothing. They waited.

After another minute Blackie rose to his feet and motioned for them to follow as he moved ahead. The stream was there—barely fifteen meters wide, shallow and rocky. Sam eased up between the two men lying on the bank beside one another. They could see no more than twenty meters in either direction. He motioned for the men with the canteens to come forward.

Time was stuck in eternity as the men filled canteen after canteen, passing them back to the others to cap. The enemy had to be close, and Sam sweated as much from the tension as from the stifling jungle heat. Parachute cord was laced through the cap-loops of as many canteens as one man could carry. Iodine tablets would be added when they returned to the ridge. And when the last canteen was filled, Sam breathed a sigh of relief as they backed into the undergrowth away from the stream.

Everything was done with hand signals—not a word having been spoken since leaving the ridge. The jungle was now growing duskier and the sounds of the approaching choppers grew louder. They were the dust-offs coming to pick up the Alpha and Charlie Company wounded. Sam motioned for Blackie to take the point and move out. The loud clacking of a helicopter's main rotor indicated the first dust-off was landing up at the LZ, but there came the hollow *thoomp, thoomp* of mortars firing behind them just across the creek and less than forty meters away. Within seconds the rounds impacted on the ridge above with thunderous *karoomphs*.

Sam snatched two frags from his harness and motioned for Blackie and Nick to do the same. Turning back, the three men quickly retraced their steps and crossed the creek. The sharp nasally voices of the enemy mortar teams were now less than fifteen meters away but they were still hidden in the dense cover. The enemy had cleared the jungle canopy overhead for their mortars and Sam pointed to the grenades in his hands and to those Blackie and Nick each held. He gave them a throwing motion then threw his thumb over his shoulder to indicate a quick retreat.

They pulled the pins on their first grenades and threw them simultaneously. Without hesitation they yanked the pins on the next grenades before the first ones landed. Throwing them as well, they ducked beneath the creek bank for cover. The first explosions were followed by the agonizing screams of enemy wounded only to be drowned out by the next series of detonations and an unexpected jarring blast—apparently the detonation of an 82-millimeter mortar round. Shrapnel turned the surrounding jungle into salad as leaves, sticks, and dirt rained down everywhere.

The three paratroopers hugged the bank of the stream and Sam glanced left and right to make sure his men were okay. Chunks of shrapnel splashed into the creek, and the moans of the wounded came from the NVA mortar positions. There was likely more of the enemy around and nightfall was only minutes away. He motioned for Blackie and Nick to follow and the three men sloshed back across the creek to join up with the rest of the patrol. It was dark when Blackie called out to the men near the LZ and led the patrol inside the perimeter.

CHAPTER SIX

An Up Close and Personal War

October 2018
Boone, North Carolina

Sam's nightmares returned for the first time in years. He had awakened from three in the last week. The worst was when he was verifying his KIAs. Some were recognizable only by the personal effects in their pockets, while there were others whose faces he had seen only moments before as living, breathing boys but were now non-responsive, waxy-gray corpses. These had stuck with him all his life. He awoke with a start and looked at his hands. It took a moment before he realized he was holding his bedsheet and not a bloody fatigue shirt, and he was home in his own bed. He used the sheet to wipe the perspiration from his face.

Rolling over, Sam looked at the bedside clock. It was 6:45. Claire had called the night before and said her Wednesday class was cancelled and Megan was dropping her off for breakfast there at 8:00. After starting the coffee pot, he stood in the shower and let the hot water burn his face in an effort to purge the memories from his mind. The nightmares had left him exhausted and he didn't really want to talk about the war today. Perhaps she would give him a break. His well-intentioned project had grown into this ugly specter staring at him from the past.

After starting the bacon, he sipped his first cup of coffee as the knock came at the door. Claire was there smiling, her canvas bag slung over her shoulder.

"Come on in, little lady. I've got breakfast going. Pour yourself some coffee." He busied himself putting the biscuits in the oven.

"Can I help you with something?" she asked. She shot a second glance at him. Apparently she had noticed.

"Restless night," he explained. "Stir those grits into that water on the stove when it boils, add some salt, pepper, and butter, and turn the burner down low."

Claire said nothing, but she had the grits going in a few seconds and went to the refrigerator and found the eggs. After cracking several into a bowl she turned the bacon and poured Sam another cup of coffee.

"Do you take sugar in your coffee?" she asked.

"No. Black is fine."

He studied her for a moment. "You know your way around a kitchen, don't you?"

"Before Papa Pearle passed away, I went home every weekend and fixed breakfast for him."

"So, you don't go home on the weekends anymore?"

"Once in a while. No reason to, now."

"Why is that?"

"There's no one there."

Sam said nothing, but glanced over at her. Avoiding eye contact, she turned and looked out the kitchen window at the town down below. He followed her gaze. The fall colors were still a month away, but a few of the leaves had begun turning. It was that "in-between" time, not quite autumn but no longer summer, somewhat like their relationship and the awkward moment he now felt.

She was most certainly holding something back, and he wanted to help her, but restraint was the better part of good judgement. He said nothing. She would open up when she was ready. After a few moments Claire turned and glanced at him. The void left after her last statement begged to be filled. *Why was there no one there?* He gave her what he hoped was a reassuring nod.

She sighed. "My mother passed last November. They said it was a heart attack, but it wasn't. It was a broken heart. She still loved my father. We found him down at Myrtle Beach the summer before, living on the street. Mama begged him to come home, but he wouldn't."

Claire tried to hide it, but her eyes had moistened.

"What happened? Why did your father live on the street?"

"He was in the Army in Iraq. He was a lieutenant and an IED blew up under two of his vehicles. Two of his men were killed. Two others lost arms or legs. He survived, but…" Claire didn't finish as she turned instead to the stove. It was all suddenly clear. His suspicions were correct. Her thesis wasn't the only thing driving her to seek his help.

"It sounds like post-traumatic stress," Sam said. "Has he been to a VA hospital?"

"Mama tried several times. He would go in but always ended up leaving. He just didn't care enough about her or me to get the help he needed. She tried, I tried, but…"

"When was the last time you spoke with him?"

"We went back down to Myrtle Beach last fall when it turned cold, but we couldn't find him. We tried to find out if he'd gone back to the hospital, but the VA wouldn't give us any information except to say he wasn't there. We came back home and a couple of weeks later Mama had a heart attack and died."

Claire stifled a sob. "She wasn't sick or anything. She just died, and she didn't deserve what he did to her. She was there for him all those years, and he broke her heart. We waited for him, but…"

She didn't finish, and Sam pushed the skillet off the burner and put his hand on her shoulder. "I'm sorry," he said.

Stepping closer, she bowed her head and grasped his extended arm. "I don't mean to be—"

"It's okay. You've been through a lot in the last year. I think we just need to relax today, maybe go for a drive and talk more about this later. Vietnam can wait, too."

Claire hung her head. "No. I want to work on my thesis. I have to submit the outline by the end of November. Besides, it will take my mind off all this."

"We'll see," Sam said. "Go sit at the table and drink your coffee. I'll finish cooking breakfast."

When the food was ready, Sam set the table and together they buttered the biscuits.

"So, your father wasn't wounded in the IED explosion?"

"He had a severe concussion and some minor shrapnel wounds. When he came home he was okay at first, but he changed. He began getting angry with me and Mama for no good reason. He just wasn't the same person, and the Army ended up diagnosing him with a traumatic brain injury and gave him a medical discharge. After that he got even more sullen and detached and got fired from his job. He left home the first time when I was fourteen."

"Maybe we should go back to Myrtle Beach and try to find him."

"No! The last time we saw him he yelled at us and called Mama a 'nagging cry-baby.' I never want to see him again."

Sam sipped his coffee and gazed at her. Claire fixed him with a red-eyed glare and poked her fork aimlessly at her breakfast. "I really need to go down to Maggie Valley later today to check on the house. I haven't been home in nearly a month."

"How do you get down there?"

"I usually pay Megan or one of my friends who have a car. I can't afford insurance or tags for my mother's old pickup."

"Let me drive you. I think you need company today, and I'll try to talk with you more about Vietnam."

"It's over two hours down to Maggie Valley. I can't ask you to do that."

Her words didn't match the hopeful look in her eyes.

"I went to a lot of trouble to cook your breakfast, so eat. We'll get on the road shortly."

November 1967
The Hill South of Ben Het
Republic of Vietnam

Sam hoped destroying the enemy mortars might give the battalion a much-needed reprieve, but bright flashes along the top of the ridge lit the nighttime jungle, followed by the *karoomphs* of the impacting rounds echoing up and down the valley. These were accompanied by the whistling of inbound rockets as more explosions lit the night sky. So much for hope. It was going to be a long night.

Captain Hollister was huddled with the platoon leaders when the barrage began. Except for the flashes of the incoming rounds, the inky blackness of the nighttime jungle offered zero visibility. The CO spoke in a barely audible voice. "We need to make this quick, so you can get back to your units. You were damned lucky this afternoon, Lieutenant Walker. The NVA seldom leave their big mortars without infantry to protect them."

"Yes, sir. I figured as much. That's why we chunked the grenades and hauled ass. I don't think they knew what happened until we were halfway back up the hill."

One of the other platoon leaders slapped his back. He flinched as the pain there reignited.

"Good job, Sam." He couldn't see him, but Sam recognized Ted's voice.

"By the looks of things, it didn't make much difference," Sam said.

"Regardless, I'll be submitting you, Blackmore, and Riganti for bronze stars with V devices," the captain said. "That was a pretty ballsy move, and your action likely saved some lives while we were medevac'ing the casualties this afternoon."

The CO paused as a nearby radio handset scratched quietly. Turned down low, it broke squelch as the platoon RTOs began calling in sit-reps from around the perimeter. "We've got a lot of movement around the ridge, sir," the RTO whispered.

"Get on the command net and let's see if we can get Spooky to start dropping some flares," the captain said.

"Gentlemen, I expect the little bastards are going to hit us hard tonight. Get back to your men and remind the new men to use grenades so they don't give away their positions."

Dawn broke in a dripping wet wall of white fog. It had been a long night with numerous probes, but the expected all-out enemy attack had not materialized. Sam sat in the foxhole with his RTO, shivering in the cold mountain air. His poncho liner was soaked by the mist. The visibility in the undergrowth, barely ten to fifteen meters without the fog, was down to less than five. Glasspack was scraping the last yellow crumbs from a can of ham and eggs.

"Where'd Sergeant Ingram go?" Sam whispered.

Glasspack grinned. "He's takin' a dump, LT, and that's a helluva lot better than what he did last time."

"What do you mean?"

"We was gettin' hit pretty hard the other day. The gooks were just outside the perimeter, shootin' at us with RPGs and AKs, so he just shit in the bottom of our foxhole."

"Still, isn't as bad as you, Glasspack." It was Ingram in the bushes and totally invisible although no more than four or five meters behind the foxhole.

"Glasspack," the platoon sergeant said as he emerged from the fog, hitching up his trousers, "do you want to tell the LT or should I?"

Sergeant Ingram eyed the young radioman. Glasspack grinned, hunched over and ripped off a world class fart.

"You see," Ingram said. "That's exactly what I'm talking about. Dude does on-command farts. And sometimes he sounds like a Chevelle Super Sport with glass-pack mufflers—thus the name."

"Except, I don't do them so much anymore since the accident," Glasspack said.

Sam wagged his head in resignation. "Somehow I know I shouldn't ask, but what accident?"

"He's talking about the time when we were at LZ English and the CO ordered him to fart for the whole company. Tell him, Glasspack. Tell him what happened."

"I shit in my pants in front of the whole goddamned company! So there. You happy, Sarge? Now the LT thinks I'm a fucking idiot."

"Don't take it personal," the sergeant said. "It's a great story. Besides, the shits are kind of a regular thing around here."

Ingram jerked his rifle up and fired a burst into the undergrowth. A ChiCom grenade thudded into the dirt and skidded into Sam's chest. He grabbed it and threw it back down the ridge.

"Move," Ingram hissed. "Let's go."

Glasspack detonated his Claymore and grabbed his rifle.

"Go!" Sam said. "Follow the sarge."

The three paratroopers scrambled on their bellies away from their foxhole as enemy bullets kicked up the dirt behind them. A moment later another grenade exploded, showering them with dirt and debris. Ingram pulled the pin on a frag and tossed it back toward their previous position. Glasspack threw one down the ridge.

Two NVA soldiers lunged from the misty undergrowth firing

their AKs, but their aim was high as they stumbled and fell over the three paratroopers. Sam fired his sixteen into the belly of one, while Glasspack held the other by the throat as both men struggled for one another's rifle. Sergeant Ingram began pulling pins on frags and tossing them one after another into the surrounding brush. Sam pressed his sixteen to the chest of the enemy soldier fighting Glasspack and fired. From up and down the perimeter came the rattle and pop of sixteens and AKs, punctuated by the explosions of grenades.

Sam's ears were deadened and ringing from the grenade blasts and the world had again become a surreal rush of adrenaline and confusion. He glanced about. Someone was shouting at him, but he couldn't see them. It was as if he had somehow become disembodied. He touched his head. It was still there. The voice came again to his deafened ears and someone tapped his arm. It was Glasspack tapping him with the radio handset. "Sir! Sir! It's the old man. He wants a sit-rep."

Sam took the radio handset and spoke into it, not knowing if he was shouting or speaking in a normal tone. "Bravo-Six, this is Bravo-Red-Six, we're hand-to-hand down here." He sucked down a deep breath. *Gotta remain calm. Gotta remain calm.* He keyed the mic again. "Suggest you secure your position. Some of them have gotten past us. Over."

"Roger, Red-Six. We've got TAC inbound. Can you have your boys mark their positions with smoke?"

"Roger, Bravo-Six—" An enemy soldier burst from the cover and lunged at them. He had no weapon and fell before Glasspack or Sam could fire their weapons. Ingram, who was behind them, froze. The soldier was soaked in his own blood and didn't move— apparently succumbing to his wounds. Only then did Sam feel the most virulent form of cold fear he had ever experienced as he saw the smoking ChiCom grenade gripped in the soldier's hand. The pin had been pulled.

Rolling on his side, he shouted, "Grenade!"

Hunching his shoulders and curling, Sam realized he was too close and about to leave this world in the same fetal position in which he had entered. He gritted his teeth and waited. A second elapsed, then another. He refused to move.

"It's a dud, LT. Get the fuck out of there," Ingram said.

It took no thought, and there was no hesitation. It was an almost instantaneous reaction as Sam found himself running like an ape on all fours as he passed his RTO and platoon sergeant. The tracer rounds continued cracking and streaking through the undergrowth, clipping leaves and limbs, and thudding into the dirt. Desperate calls of "Medic" came from both directions along the perimeter.

"LT," Glasspack said, waving the radio handset. "It's the old man. He's calling for you again."

From somewhere high overhead the subtle roar of the F-100s echoed amongst the clouds. The jets were on station and ready to make ground support runs.

"Sarge, do you agree that we pop purple smoke?"

"I'm not sure they'll see it in this fog, LT, but we don't have much choice. The TAC air might keep more gooks from reinforcing the ones who are already on top of us."

The platoon sergeant pulled the pin on a purple smoke canister and tossed it a few feet to his front.

Sam punched a fresh magazine into his M-16. "Glasspack, tell the old man we're popping grape and tell the FAC to have his people deliver their ordnance to within a hundred meters. Stay with me. I'm going this way to check on our men."

He turned to Ingram. "Sarge, you go that way."

Sam found the first defensive position after crawling fifteen meters. It was the black kid from Chicago, Calvin Castleman. He was in the hole beside one of the new replacements, a kid named Mooney, from Iowa. Both were dead, shot through the front of their helmets. The safeties for their Claymore detonators were still in place. The enemy had apparently done the same thing here, bursting out of the undergrowth at point-blank range. Only these hadn't aimed high. Sam continued crawling along the perimeter.

Matt Hoback and his squad leader Sergeant Rob Dobbins were still alive in the next hole, but Rob was hit, shot through the side of his chest and in one arm. Both men were bug-eyed and Rob was drenched with blood. Around them were the corpses of a half-dozen enemy soldiers.

"I got his bleeding stopped, LT, but he's hit pretty bad." Hoback was trying to whisper, but his voice cracked with tension. "They were all over us before we knew it."

"You got a purple smoke?" Sam asked.

Hoback nodded rapidly.

"Pop it and toss it right there in front of your hole. We've got—"

Glasspack slapped Sam's helmet with the radio handset. "It's the old man, LT. The fast movers are inbound."

"Make room," Sam said.

All four men squeezed into the foxhole as the first jet thundered past. The explosions weren't as jarring as Sam expected and he looked up. It was napalm, swelling into a huge boiling black cloud and spewing tentacles of flame in all directions. The searing heat was instantaneous as streams of the flaming gas splashed down everywhere, miraculously missing them by only meters.

By midmorning the fog was gone, and Sam was still crawling along the perimeter with Glasspack checking on the men. Sporadic gunfire continued along with the occasional thud of a grenade. When they met back with Sergeant Ingram they added the toll. Three of their men were KIA, seven wounded, three seriously. He wrote each of their names and serial numbers on his notepad. Afterward, he helped the medics bandage the wounded and wrap the bodies of the dead in their ponchos.

They carried them up to the LZ where the wounded were taken first. When the last medevac landed, the dead were loaded onboard and Sam watched as it rose into the sky and slipped away back across the hills, the thumping of the rotors a fading requiem that ended in silence. That was it. That was "good-bye" to men he had scarcely gotten to know—his men.

Sergeant Ingram was up the ridge talking with the captain while Sam stood staring out at the hills. His mind was a blank haze, and his ears were still ringing. A few minutes later the platoon sergeant walked back down to where he stood.

"The old man wants to meet with you, sir." He held up a couple of bandoliers of ammo. "He gave us some extra ammo. I'm going down to distribute it to the men."

Ingram paused and gazed at him. "You did good this morning, LT, damned good."

Their eyes met and Sam nodded. "Thanks, Sarge. I reckon we all did. I expected the count to be a lot worse."

"I think it will be before this is done," Ingram said.

He turned and walked down the hill. Sam watched as the platoon sergeant disappeared into the broken timber.

"You okay, Sam?"

He turned. It was Ted Salter.

"Tough morning, Ted. I lost three men. Three others are in bad shape."

"Yeah, I heard your platoon sergeant telling the captain. He also said you did some damned fine soldiering down there. Did he tell you the captain wants to see you?"

"Yeah. How about you? Did y'all get hit, too?"

"Not like your platoon. I think ours was just a diversionary attack. They chunked a few grenades into the perimeter, but that was about it. One of my guys got a piece of shrapnel in his jaw, but he wouldn't let us medevac him. Hardcore little bastard spit it out in his hand and put it in his pocket."

"We've got some tough ones. One of my squad leaders had six dead NVA around his hole this morning."

"Better get going before you miss our boy, Ausie. He's up there at the CP with his CO talking to the old man."

October 2018
On the Way to Maggie Valley, North Carolina

After a while Sam's memories drove him into silence. They had been so carefully stored away for so long he had not remembered some of them until now. He focused on the highway, while attempting to push them back inside to that one special place he reserved for the worst of his wartime experiences. It was a vault that even Caroline had allowed to remain closed, but Claire had found the combination and Sam worried.

"How old were you then?"

Startled, he looked around. He had almost forgotten there was someone with him. Claire's eyes had reddened.

"Twenty-two."

"You were so young. I'm twenty-one, and I just don't understand how you went through that and...."

Her voice faded, and Sam shrugged. He was ready to talk about something else, but she at least deserved an answer. "I was considered an 'old dude' by my men. Most of them weren't more than a year out of high school and not even twenty yet, but it didn't matter. After a few weeks and a few firefights, those of us who weren't killed forgot about ever being young."

They drove on for a few more miles before Sam glanced over at her. She returned the glance. "Claire, I see some of that same sort of maturity in you."

"What do you mean?"

"Like my men back then, you have matured out of necessity. I believe with the recent losses you've had, you've developed a level of maturity that exceeds your years."

He meant it as a compliment, but Sam felt a tinge of guilt for switching the focus to her. Several minutes passed before she again turned to him. "You think I should try to find my father, don't you?"

He could feel this young woman's heart as if it were his own. She was a minefield of unexploded emotions where reckless words could cause lasting damage. Sam thought about the young enlisted soldier that first day when they were waiting for the helicopters at Dak To. The right words had come to him then, but it seemed more luck than wisdom. Claire stared at him and waited.

"I think you are sad and angry, and justifiably so, but you are too close to your losses at the moment to understand that you *really do* want to find your father."

Her eyes grew wide with anger and her lips parted, but Sam kept talking. "You don't have to answer me right now. Just give it some thought, and we'll talk about it later."

"I don't think so," she said. "Not about that."

She turned and looked out her side window at the mountains. Sam said nothing more. It was going to take time and perhaps some gentle persuasion, but he first had to know more about her father. He had a source with the Veterans' Administration in Washington, but he wouldn't contact him without Claire's approval. He punched on the radio and handed Claire his cell phone.

"If you don't mind, find the playlist that says 'Rock Love Songs' and play it on shuffle."

She dutifully pushed the buttons and the voices of Tony Williams and The Platters leapt from the speakers singing "The Great Pretender."

Oh-oh, yes I'm the great pretender
Pretending that I'm doing well
My need is such I pretend too much
I'm lonely but no one can tell

It was one of Sam's favorites. It always made him think of the time after he left Caroline and went to Nam. He had been "The Great Pretender" back then. After a minute he noticed Claire was looking his way. He cut his eyes over at her.

"What?"

"That song."

"Oh, no. No way. You put it on yourself," he said. "You put the playlist on shuffle, right?"

She didn't answer as she looked straight ahead. A single tear trickled down her cheek, but she gave a gentle sigh. Her face was now noticeably more serene. It was times like this that Sam felt the hand of Providence in his life, and he understood what Claire was now feeling, because he too had felt it long ago. Along with Caroline, it was old songs like this one that helped heal a soul that had been shredded by the ravages of war.

CHAPTER SEVEN

Leaving Purgatory for Hell

October 2018
Maggie Valley, North Carolina

T he house was stuffy and stale inside as Sam helped Claire open windows and turn on ceiling fans. He stopped and stared at a wall of framed photos. A young soldier wearing a second lieutenant's gold bar was in one. In another there was a younger version of the man in jeans and a T-shirt standing beside a beautiful woman. He was cradling a little girl in one arm. The woman looked very much like Claire. She stepped out of the adjacent room and stopped.

"This photo here, is this you with your mother and father?"

She smiled. "I was two years old then."

"Your mother—I can't believe how much you look like her now."

"Yes, I've heard that before. They used to call me 'Mini-Connie' because of it."

Sam glanced about as they walked through the house. "Are you coming back here to live when you graduate?"

"I don't think so. I was thinking about selling this place, but…"

"You think your father may come back someday and want to live here, right?"

"Damn!" She slowly wagged her head. "I must be an open book." Claire's face clouded again, more so this time it seemed with self-directed frustration.

"Not really. I had a wife who was a lot like you, and now a daughter and a granddaughter. They taught me a lot. I learned that most women tend to think with their hearts, while most men tend to think with their…well, let's not go there right now."

"That's Brad's problem. He's badgered me to the point of frustration. He says I'm going to become a nun when I graduate."

"He's pretty much the norm for guys his age, and I admire you for your…ugh."

"It's not difficult. He's fun to hang out with, and it's low stress, but he's just so immature at times. Actually, I've already decided to move on. I just haven't told him yet."

"Hmmm. You ladies can be such heart-breakers."

"I'm sure he'll get over it." She paused. "I still can't get over how young you were when you were in Vietnam. And having some of your men killed right off, that had to be just…."

"Like I said before, we had to grow up fast."

"What did your men think about the war? I mean from a political perspective, did they feel it was justified?"

"Remember, we had no internet and very little news-talk television back in those days. Most of what we learned came from our parents and the newspapers. The only ones who were more naïve about the war than us young officers were the eighteen- and nineteen-year-olds we led. I believe that's why the most profound and lasting effect of that war for many Americans was that it instilled a virulent distrust for government."

"Do you think that's a bad thing?"

"If you had asked me that right after the war, I would have said it was a very good thing, but in recent years it's become an irrational epidemic of political anarchists ripping the fabric of our country to shreds."

Sam paused and took a deep breath. This argument had been a personal one for him. It had rolled around in his head ever since the war, tethered only by his training as a United States military officer. He truly believed what he said, but perhaps he had spoken a little too forcefully.

"Questioning governments and authority is always good, but to attempt to destroy one that has probably saved the world at least three times during the twentieth century is insanity. Yeah, our history has not always been a proud one, and our politicians have screwed us and others royally many times over the years, but this country is still the best the world has known."

"So, you and your men were fighting for your country?"

"Careful what you say, Claire, dear, lest we draw the ire of the modern intellectuals and be accused of jingoism. But to answer your question: yes, up to that point in 1967, there were many of us who actually believed what we were being told by the people in Washington. Regardless of that, if there was ever any doubt, we still fought for one another, because when it gets down to it that's almost all any soldier fights for."

The front doorbell rang, followed by a loud knocking. Claire stared wide-eyed at Sam and shrugged. When she opened the door, a little woman with tinted amber hair and white tennis shoes stood on the porch. She gave a concerned smile but turned to look over the top of her eye-glasses back at the road. She seemed satisfied that no one was out there watching.

"Well, hey Missus Simpson. How are you?"

The woman turned back. "I'm just fine, Claire, honey. And how are you?"

"Good, I reckon. Will you come in?"

"Oh, I don't know." She craned her neck and looked past Claire to where Sam stood in the foyer behind her. "I suppose you're fine with your friend there."

"That's Sam. He's a Vietnam War vet who's helping me with my senior thesis."

The woman eyed him for several seconds before turning her attention to Claire. "Well, I suppose he looks okay to me. I just stopped by to tell you what happened the other day."

"What was that?" Claire asked.

"Well, it was actually a few months back. I just haven't seen you around lately to tell you."

"Oh?" Claire said.

Missus Simpson glanced around again as if to make sure no one was lurking in the shrubs.

"There was a man." Her voice had dropped to a pseudo whisper. "He had long hair and a beard, and he was a-goin' 'round peekin' in all your windows. So I called the sheriff. A deputy came out, but he left, so I called the sheriff later. He said it was the man who owned the house, Mister Cunningham. I reckon it must'a been your poor daddy, but it sure didn't look like him, and I ain't seen him since."

"When was this?"

"Oh, I'd say maybe early August."

Claire thanked the old woman and closed the front door. She turned to Sam. Her face was ashen.

"Maybe the sheriff will know where he is," Sam said. "You should give him a call."

"I suppose so. I mean…at least he tried to come home."

"I think your neighbor was a little concerned about me."

"Oh, that Missus Simpson is such a busybody. I suppose that's why Mama always called her Missus Kravitz."

"Who's that?"

"She was the nosey neighbor character in some TV show Mama always watched."

By midafternoon they finished checking the house and were on their way back to Boone. Claire seemed lost in somber thought as she rode in silence. Her phone call to the sheriff had been for naught. Her father had shown an ID and said he had lost his house key. They released him. There was no further information on the report.

Sam didn't know what to say. He really didn't want to talk about Vietnam anymore today, but she needed a distraction.

"Get your recorder out and I'll tell you some more about my experiences during the war."

She removed it from her bag and set her spiral notebook in her lap as she gazed expectantly at him.

November 1967
The Hills South of Ben Het
The Republic of Vietnam

The first two weeks with his new unit were worse than Sam could have imagined. The area south of Ben Het was crawling with enemy troops and this was not the hit-and-run war he trained for or expected. The battalion had been in contact with the enemy almost every day, experiencing incidents ranging from sniper fire to all-out firefights. He was losing men he barely knew, and nothing he did seemed to make a difference. He and his men were all subject to the orders of their commanders, the whims of the enemy, and the terrain around them. A meager stream of replacements kept his platoon barely combat-effective.

Another sunrise found Sam and his entire platoon pinned down on another slope west of Ben Het. An NVA .51 caliber machine gun on a rise to their right was making splinters of the trees all around. With Glasspack's help, Sam had just delivered coordinates for a fire-mission. Streaming from a bamboo thicket several hundred meters up the hill were thirty or forty NVA soldiers, forming a skirmish line and advancing toward them. Second and Third platoons were flanking the enemy machine gun on the right, but if they didn't hurry, Sam's platoon was going to be cut to pieces and overrun.

"Shot out," Glasspack shouted.

An RPG exploded in the treetops, showering shrapnel down on the men.

"I'm hit!"

The shout came from the jumble of timber to his immediate front. Sam couldn't see who it was, but Doc Cashen crawled forward, under a fallen tree and over another until he was out of sight. A few seconds later the artillery smoke round burst a couple hundred meters out and directly in the path of the oncoming enemy.

Sam shouted at Glasspack, "Tell them to fire for effect—six rounds HE."

"Incoming artillery, danger close," Sam shouted. "Keep your heads down."

He glanced about. It was wasted breath. No one was about to raise his head with the enemy machine gun making toothpicks out of the trees all around them.

"LT!" Glasspack shouted. He held the radio handset to his ear and listened. Sam waited. "It's Rosario, the old man's RTO. They're pinned down, and Bravo-White-Six is calling for you."

Bravo-White-Six was Ted.

Sam crawled up beside his RTO and took the handset just as the first of the 105 rounds exploded, sending showers of logs and shrapnel boiling skyward. The concussion from the blast was a sledge-hammer blow that knocked the air from his lungs, rendering him instantly deaf. Two more rounds, then another shook the ground and filled the air with smoke and dust. All were pin-point accurate, but Sam was momentarily dazed as he looked over the fallen tree toward the bamboo thicket. Everything in the draw including the attacking enemy soldiers was totally obliterated.

"Bravo-Red-Six, this is Bravo-White-Six. Talk to me, Sam. Over."

Ted must have been screaming into his handset, but Sam could barely hear him.

"Bravo-White-Six, go ahead Ted."

Sam shook his head, trying to clear the cobwebs.

"You guys okay? That damned artillery had to be close."

"Roger, White-Six. Just a little deaf right now. Over."

"We're in some deep shit over here, Sam. We're bogged down. There are three bunkers just above us and we're trading grenades with them. Over."

"Can you disengage? Over."

"Negative. We're close up under them and we'll take more casualties if we try to pull back."

"Bravo-Six, Ranger-Six, Over."

It was the battalion commander calling for Captain Hollister on the company net.

"Go ahead Ranger-Six."

"I've got two gunships inbound in about five mikes. Can you have your men mark those bunkers with smoke?"

"Ranger-Six, Bravo-Six, that's a negative. My men are too close to them for air support."

Sergeant Ingram scrambled back over the tree and landed between Sam and Glasspack. "Sir," the platoon sergeant shouted, "did you call in that damned artillery?"

"Yes, I did. Are any of our men hurt?"

"Why?" Ingram shouted.

"Why, what?"

"Why did you call it in?"

Ingram turned to Glasspack. "Dammit, Baker, you're supposed to know better."

"You guys were about to be overrun by forty gooks," Glasspack shouted. "If the LT hadn't called in that arty you'd all be dead by now."

"I didn't see any—"

"They were coming down that draw up there," Sam said, pointing up the hill. "Answer my question, Sarge. Are our men okay?"

"Yes, sir. I mean other than Mickey. He got some shrapnel in his thigh from an RPG, but Doc has the bleeding under control. Sorry, sir, I didn't—"

"Forget it, Sarge. Second and Third Platoons are pinned down over on our right beneath several bunkers. I believe if you can take two squads up that draw to that bamboo thicket you can flank that damned machine gun. It's sitting just above and to the rear of those bunkers. If you take it out, you might be able to move down and take out a bunker from there. I'll keep the rest of our men back here and we'll do our best to distract them while you get in position. Speak your mind. Do you think it's doable?"

"Yes, sir. With some luck." Ingram turned to crawl back up the hill. "Let me get up there and—"

"Hold up, Sarge." Sam pressed the handset to his ear. "Bravo-Six, this is Bravo-Red-Six, Over."

"Go ahead Red-Six. Over."

"Bravo-Six, if you can hold off those gunships, I believe I can maneuver some elements to relieve White-Six, Over."

"Bravo-Six, Ranger-Six. I roger that last transmission. Let's see what your man can do. Alpha is moving into position to assist but he's still two klicks away. I'll hold the gunships till you give the word. Over."

From somewhere back to the east came the steady beat of their rotors as the gunships approached.

Sam turned to Sergeant Ingram. "I'm thinking that fifty-one cal is going to turn and start looking for those gunships when they get closer. It may be the break we need. If he does, watch for me to bring the rest of our men up there on your right. Good luck, Sarge."

"Sure gonna need it, LT." With that, he climbed over the fallen tree and crawled on his belly across the dirt into the broken timber.

Sam had just given another order that would put men under his command in direct danger. They would obey, because they were paratroopers. Even his experienced platoon sergeant, Clyde Ingram, would follow his order. The sergeant would take them forward into the jaws of the beast. Sam couldn't help but second-guess himself. How does one man order others into such a terrible conflagration? He told himself that it was the best option, but he closed his eyes for a quick prayer.

A moment later the horrendous huffing and cracking of the .51 caliber rounds suddenly ceased. It was the break he had hoped for. Sam gazed skyward and slowly raised his head as he peered over the fallen tree. Up the hill near the bamboo thicket Sergeant Ingram was motioning his men forward. It was time for him to begin moving his men forward as well, but he could see none of them. They were burrowed beneath the fallen timber that lay all about.

"All right, men," he shouted, "follow me, but stay down. We're going to move up the hill into that ravine on the right."

No one answered.

"You ready?"

Glasspack gave him a rapid nod.

"Let's go."

The enemy in the bunkers continued a non-stop fusillade down the hill toward Ted Salter's Second Platoon. Sam crawled forward with Glasspack, and four of his men appeared from nowhere as they followed. If he could get close enough to take out the first bunker, the rest might go like dominoes. His eyes darted everywhere in the broken timber, searching for that one spider hole, that one tunnel opening, anything he might have overlooked. The smoke and dust felt like sandpaper in his throat, making him cough while sweat dripped from beneath his helmet, burning his eyes.

The .51 caliber began firing again. Sam stopped and gazed up the hill. The tracers were shooting out over the bunkers, skyward across the valley. The enemy gunner was firing at the two Cobra gunships circling in the distance. He motioned his men forward, and they continued crawling on their bellies through the jumble of timber and craters. When he stopped, he was less than five meters from the side of the first bunker. Inside, an enemy machine gun was steadily firing down the hill toward Second Platoon.

The crunching thud of several grenades came from the hill behind the bunkers and the enemy .51 caliber stopped firing. A head popped up out of the ground behind the bunker. It was an enemy soldier less than ten meters away looking up the hill toward the machine gun that Sergeant Ingram and his men had just destroyed. He raised his AK-47, but Sam raised his M-16, aimed carefully and fired. The enemy soldier's head exploded.

"Damned good shot, sir," Glasspack said.

"Let's go," Sam shouted. He crawled forward, but one of his more experienced men sprinted ahead and tossed a white phosphorus grenade into the hole where the enemy soldier had appeared. Another tossed a grenade from the side into the gun port on the front of the bunker. They dove for cover as smoke and dust belched from the bunker openings.

"Get inside and make sure more of them don't come up from a tunnel in there."

Another of his men scrambled forward toward the second bunker only to double-up and fall backward. It was one of his squad leaders, Sergeant Washington. Sam crawled up beside him. He had talked with Washington a time or two. Always smiling, the gregarious young NCO had challenged him to a poker game when they got back to Dak To.

Darrell Washington was a light-skinned black guy with a freckled face. He was from Baltimore, and his light brown eyes gazed down at his torso. Sam realized the young sergeant was holding his own gray intestines in his hands.

"Medic!" Sam yelled, and he helped Darrell who was trying to push his intestines back into his abdomen. The blood spilled down from inside his chest cavity, and Darrell locked eyes with him. It was hopeless, and Sam held him in his arms as his eyes faded and lost focus.

More of his men crawled up beside him and Sam motioned with his head. "See if you can get a grenade in that bunker up there and kill that sonofabitch."

They crawled forward, tossing grenades while he held Darrell and waited for the doc to arrive. He knew it was too late, but he couldn't turn him loose. After a while he heard a voice—disembodied it seemed. Someone was calling him. "Sir. Sir. LT. Lieutenant Walker. Sir."

Sam looked around. It was Glasspack.

"He's dead, sir. We need to keep moving."

"Give me the handset."

"Bravo-White-Six this is Red-Six. Over."

"Go ahead Sam."

"Have your men stand down, Ted. We've taken the first bunker and are moving against the next one."

"Grenade!" someone shouted.

It arced high and landed in the timber to his left. The explosion sent more dust, sticks, and shrapnel spraying in every direction. A moment later another grenade exploded in the brush behind the bunker, followed by bursts from several automatic weapons—M-16s.

"Hold your fire," Sam shouted to the men around him.

Behind the second bunker he spotted a soldier. It was Nick Riganti, one of the men who had gone up the hill with Sergeant Ingram. He crawled atop the bunker and threw a grenade inside. Sam motioned his men forward.

Four hours later the AO was secure and an LZ cleared for the dust-offs. Sam had three wounded and Sergeant Washington KIA. It would have seemed miraculous except for the casualties taken by Second Platoon. Ted Salter had six of his men KIA and eleven more were wounded, including himself. He'd taken shrapnel from a ChiCom grenade in the chin and shoulder.

Captain Hollister sent the first medevac out with the most seriously wounded. The Third Platoon leader, Lieutenant Johns, was amongst them. A second chopper was approaching as Sam knelt with Ted beside the small LZ. They gazed over at the boots protruding from beneath the ponchos wrapping the dead. They would be loaded out after the wounded.

"I'll be back in a few days," Ted said.

He was shirtless with a bloody field dressing strapped around his chin and another tied to his shoulder.

"Damned if you boys don't look like shit."

It was Ausie coming up the hill with the lead elements of Alpha Company. They were just arriving. Stopping, he looked Ted over carefully. "How bad are you hit?"

"Just a couple small pieces of shrapnel. Not too bad."

"I don't know what I'm going to do if I have to keep coming to rescue you fellows."

For once, Ted Salter seemed unwilling to engage. His eyes were fixed on the bodies of his men wrapped in their ponchos. Sam gazed up and narrowed his brows. Ausie was only trying to provide some jocular relief, but his timing was shitty.

"That's okay, Lone Ranger," Sam said. "You're a day late and a dollar short, again. We've already kicked Charlie's ass off this hill. Where have you been the last few hours, anyway?"

"I swear we came as fast as we could, Sam. I had my guys two abreast with machetes, but that was some of the thickest crap we've come through yet. We could hear you guys catching hell over here and we even redirected twice, but we were bogged down in the vines, briars, and bamboo."

There came the thud of mortars impacting on the far side of the hill. Captain Hollister motioned for Ausie to continue his advance.

"Sounds like duty calling," Sam said.

October 2018
Appalachian State University
Boone, North Carolina

Late Wednesday afternoon Sam pulled the pickup to the curb in front of Claire's dorm. Their round-trip to Maggie Valley had made for a long day with a lot of driving and she was showing emotional strain after hearing the news about her father.

"Everything's going to work out, kiddo. Just hang in there."

She gave him a sad smile and Sam motioned with his head.

"Someone's waiting for you."

Brad was sitting on the steps out front and Claire cast a knowing glance over at Sam. Over the course of their road trip to Maggie Valley that day he had learned more about this gentle young woman and her family than she had admittedly shared with anyone. She was proud, but in need of some help—both with guidance and her finances.

She needed her mother's pickup truck, but she couldn't afford the insurance. Sam intended to remedy that situation, but hadn't yet told her. What he had promised was to help her paint the outside of the house as soon as the weather warmed in the spring. The siding and trim were in danger of rotting if a new coat of paint wasn't applied soon. His only hope was that his seventy-three-year-old body would hold up during the job.

And there was her father. Sam wanted to help Claire search for him but not without her agreeing.

"Before you go, I want to ask you something," he said.

Brad stood, ran his fingers through his hair and began walking down the walk toward the truck. He was wearing what Sam had come to realize was his signature smirk.

"I have a friend with the Department of Veterans Affairs in Washington. Would you mind if I contacted him about your father? With all the HIPAA laws, I'm not sure he can tell me anything, but we go way back, so he'll help if he can. What do you say?"

"It's not going to change my mind about him, Sam, but if you want, I suppose I really *would* like to know if he's been admitted to a VA hospital somewhere."

She leaned across the seat and placed her hand atop his. "I have a lot of transcribing to do and research on these battles you've talked about. I'll call you Friday afternoon."

She opened the door and stepped out as Brad walked up.

"So, are you and the birdhouse man going steady now?" he asked.

Rolling her eyes, she closed the truck door and walked past him. Sam watched as he followed her like a little pooch up the walk to the dormitory doorway. Brad was again shouting apologies and saying he was only trying to be funny.

Dumbass kid had no idea how wonderful this young woman really was, and he'd blown it. Sam thought of his own Caroline and how he'd nearly done the same thing with her fifty years ago, but she never gave up on him. Perhaps he was judging Brad too harshly. After all, it was a different generation. He put the truck in gear and glanced back again. No, he wasn't being too harsh. The kid was a twenty-four-karat dumbass.

CHAPTER EIGHT

The Professor

October 2018
Boone, North Carolina

Friday afternoon Claire called and came by after class. She had discovered Sam's framed medals and ribbons in his home office. "What's this one?" she asked. Sam pulled on his glasses and gazed over at the one she was pointing to.

"That's the Silver Star."

She walked over and sat in the chair by the window and began looking at her cell phone. He was glad she had become distracted. Although he was proud of every one, he really didn't like talking about them. Most of his decorations represented circumstances where some of his men were killed or wounded. The medals were as much theirs as they were his.

She looked up from the phone, back at the display case and over at him.

"What's wrong?" he asked.

"Nothing. I mean, I just googled your medals. You've got two Bronze Star Medals with V devices, a Silver Star, the Distinguished Service Cross, a Purple Heart..." She glanced down at the cell phone and back at the display case. "Excuse me, *two* Purple Hearts, and what's this one? It's not shown here."

"That's the Vietnamese Cross of Gallantry."

"And that one?"

"The Air Medal."

She gazed at him, steady and unblinking—almost childlike. "How long were you in the army?"

"A little over two years."

Her lips parted and her eyes widened. "You got all these medals in just two years?"

"Actually, most of them came during the time I was in Vietnam. It was an ugly war, dear. Not that all wars aren't ugly, but Nam had its own particular class of ugly."

"Sam…" She paused and gazed at him. "I feel I hardly know you at all."

He smiled and shrugged.

"What did you do after you got out of the army?"

"I spent part of the first year doing physical therapy down at the VA Hospital in Asheville."

She stood and gazed around his office at the shelves crammed with books.

"And after that?"

"I taught school."

Her jaw dropped after she read the inscription on a plaque. She stopped and turned toward him. "Oh no, I am such an idiot! *Professor Walker.* I've heard them talk about you in the history department at school. You retired a few years ago, I believe it was my freshman year, and they said I had missed the opportunity to study under one of the best history professors ever. I had no idea. I'm so sorry. I would never have asked—"

"You didn't. I was the one who suggested it. Remember?"

"But?"

"Just don't mention me by name, and you will be fine. Also, I will not look at your paper. I will make suggestions for reading materials, but it needs to be solely your work."

"Oh my God. I feel I should call you Professor Walker."

"I prefer Sam, now…but thanks."

"Okay. I've been trying to complete my list of readings. The dean gave me three, and I'm supposed to add a minimum of three to the list."

"I'm pretty sure I already know what's on their list. If *Street Without Joy* isn't one of them, I want you to read it. A memoir like Caputo's *A Rumor of War* would also be helpful. And I want you to read one titled *Dereliction of Duty*. It was written by a guy named McMaster. It's well documented and footnoted. McMaster graduated from the U.S. Military Academy and holds a Ph.D. in history from the University of North Carolina. He's about as close to an impeccable source for the truth as you can get."

Claire finished making her notes and looked up. "The last time we talked you had just been in another battle near Dak To." She glanced down at her notes. "I mean west of Ben Het."

"Are you sure you want to go through my entire tour of duty? You may end up with a hell of a long opus a little over a month before you have to submit your outline."

"Yes. I do. I think it's important."

Claire walked into the hallway and glanced up at a photo on the wall. "Oh my! You were a hunk back in the day."

Her face flushed and she shook her head. "Sorry, I didn't mean—"

"Don't be silly. Old age is an insidious condition only the fortunate get to experience."

"Well, your hair *is* gray now, but you still have those lady-killer brown eyes."

"Ted Salter always said I had the heartless eyes of a cougar."

"Well, he was wrong about the 'heartless' part. Who's the girl there with you? She's pretty gorgeous herself."

"That's Caroline. We were down at Myrtle Beach my senior year when that photo was taken, and she was the only girl brave enough to wear a bikini when they first came out."

Claire wrinkled her brows as she studied the picture. "Myrtle Beach, really? It looks more like some quaint village on the outer banks."

"Yeah, there weren't any high-rises, golf courses, or much else other than some beach houses back then. Let's get on with the task at hand. We'll talk more about those things later."

Claire glanced down at her notes. "So, you had been in Vietnam a little over two weeks and already you had seen so much terrible stuff. I read a lot more this week about the 173rd Airborne and the battles around Dak To. Were you near the battle on Hill 875?"

November 19, 1967
Firebase Sixteen on the Cambodian Border

Three days later, Bravo Company was ordered to move to a nearby LZ and airlifted into Firebase Sixteen. Upon arrival, Captain Hollister brought his platoon leaders together while the NCOs distributed fresh supplies and ammo to the men. Ted Salter had already returned from the hospital, and Ausie was moved over from Alpha Company to replace the wounded Third Platoon leader in Bravo Company. The three musketeers were together once again. The sun had risen in the eastern sky and everyone's nerves were raw with anticipation as they met with the CO.

"Gentlemen, as you know, 4th Battalion has received orders to move as rapidly as possible to relieve 2nd Battalion on a hill three klicks southeast of here. They are surrounded by several hundred soldiers from the NVA 174th Regiment and taking heavy casualties. When we get there, we will clear an LZ to take out their wounded and move to clear the hill of the enemy. Our company is the first to arrive here on the firebase and we've been ordered to move out as soon as we resupply."

Sam gazed across at Ted and Ausie. Despite a couple of stitches on his chin, Ted looked rested, but Ausie was a hollowed-eyed wreck. Just that morning they had gotten their updated numbers. Bravo Company was down to ninety-eight men. The battalion, with 21 KIAs and 94 wounded, was down to fewer than 280 men. Sam did his best to maintain a poker face while he wondered how in hell this exhausted and motley crew of paratroopers was going to relieve anyone.

"Sam, I'll be there with you, but I want you to take the lead," the CO said. "Put Blackmore and Riganti out on point. Ted's platoon will have the flanks and Ausie's platoon along with the weapons platoon will complete the diamond. This will give us three-sixty security, but suffice to say a single rifle company will be ripe pickings for an NVA ambush. Keep your wing men out far enough to keep us from walking into a kill zone. We have to move fast, but don't be reckless. I'll change azimuths every five hundred meters or so to keep the dinks from setting up an ambush in front of us. Questions?"

"Where's the rest of 4th Battalion?" Salter asked.

"The 335th Aviation has been shot up pretty bad while supporting 2nd Battalion on that hill. They're doing their best with the few choppers they have left to get the rest of the battalion in here. That's going to take at least four more hours. We can't wait that long. Those men over there on that hill need us."

The captain glanced around at them. "Okay, we'll move out at 0945 hours."

Sam felt the clock ticking that morning as they headed down a narrow trail almost due west from Firebase Sixteen. Another unit of the 173rd, men just like his, was about to be overrun and Sam's platoon was leading the first of the relief force. The thick scrub soon became nearly impassable bamboo, which quickly graduated into the eerie twilight of double- and triple-canopied jungle. The CO said there were several hundred NVA on the hill surrounding 2nd Battalion, but there were likely many more between Firebase Sixteen and the hill. It wasn't exactly a suicide mission, but there was the distinct possibility that Bravo Company could end up in the same fix as 2nd Battalion, if not worse.

Despite the risks, Blackmore and Riganti pushed ahead rapidly. These two soldiers weren't regular army. They were draftees, but volunteered as paratroopers, and like most airborne troops they didn't hesitate when given an order. They led the company toward Hill 875. Sam could only speculate what motivated men like them, but he was pretty certain their motivation was the same as his. There were paratroopers out there. They were in trouble and fighting for their lives, and were the roles reversed they would be doing the same thing—coming to their aid.

The stuttering cracks of an AK-47 stopped the column in its tracks as everyone dropped and hugged the ground. Several men returned fire, spraying the jungle. After a moment it was quiet again. Sam raised his head and glanced around. He had to stay focused.

"Anyone hit?" he shouted.

No answer.

"Move out."

There was no better option. They had to keep moving if 2nd Battalion was to be reached before nightfall. A while later they came upon an array of trenches and several abandoned enemy bunkers. It was an enemy base camp that had been destroyed by artillery or air strikes. Equipment, body parts, and several enemy dead were scattered about. The stench of the decomposing bodies turned Sam's stomach. His men emerged from the bunkers with mortar rounds and other abandoned NVA armaments. Sam glanced back at Captain Foster.

"Blow them in place," the captain ordered. "Make it fast. We have to keep moving."

The sun was beginning to sink into the hills as they approached the base of Hill 875. More enemy bunkers were barely visible in the undergrowth and strewn along the trail were abandoned ammo, haversacks, and enemy helmets. Blood trails appeared, now coagulated, dark and sticky. Someone had been in a hell of a fight along this trail.

Blackmore stopped and raised a hand. Sam eased up to where he stood beside the trail. There were the carefully stacked bodies of a dozen or more uniformed NVA soldiers. The flies and the stench were horrendous.

"Move out," Sam whispered. He turned back to the man behind Glasspack. "Pass the word, nobody touches the bodies. They're booby-trapped."

Whether or not they were, he had no idea, but there was no time to examine them now and he didn't need any dead souvenir hunters. A few meters up the trail, Blackmore stopped again. The occasional staccato of automatic weapons rose and fell up on 875, punctuated by the thudding whumps of grenades. Sam again eased up beside Blackmore and Riganti. They stood staring down at a body. It was an American. The ground around him was littered with hundreds of shiny 5.56 millimeter brass casings. His bloodied M-16 was still clutched in his arms—jammed. Sam knelt and copied the information from the soldier's dog tags into his notebook.

Glasspack tapped him on the shoulder and pointed into the undergrowth. On the right, Captain Foster and the first sergeant were kneeling beside two more bodies, copying the information from the dog tags. Foster's eyeglasses rested on the end of his nose, and his usually stern façade had been usurped by one of tight-lipped sadness. Sam felt his agony. These were the bodies of their Airborne brothers—men who had gone down fighting.

A few minutes later Blackie made contact with the perimeter of 2nd Battalion and the company moved up the hill. In the previous two and a half weeks Sam was certain he had seen the worst of death and carnage wrought by battle, but here the bodies of the dead were stacked amongst the wounded and it was difficult to tell which were alive and which were dead.

Discarded equipment and weapons were tossed about everywhere. The trees that remained standing were scarred and splintered, but many were scattered about like giant toothpicks, shattered and broken. The jungle was now a barren landscape of destruction. Those of the wounded who were able to sit upright stared out from under bloodied gauze bandages with the eyes of the forsaken.

The stench of feces, urine, and decomposing bodies along with the acrid odors of burnt gunpowder and napalm was nearly as overwhelming as the sight of the dead and wounded lying intermingled. Sam was left with a numb lump in his throat, but he had to keep going. He couldn't stop now. He had to keep his men focused on the task at hand, yet he was struck mute and frozen with paralysis.

"You guys got any water?" a medic asked. "We've been out for two days."

Sam was jolted back to the moment. Realizing he had been momentarily mesmerized by the surrounding nightmare, he looked toward the medic. His fatigues were soaked crimson with the blood of his buddies.

"Yeah, sure," Sam said, giving him one of his canteens.

Sergeant Ingram called out to the other men. "Share your water with these men," he said.

Sam opened another of his canteens and helped a wounded soldier to drink from it. Captain Foster knelt beside him. "Are you okay, Lieutenant?"

"Yes, sir, but what the hell happened here?"

"One of our own aircraft dropped a five-hundred pounder on them. It hit the CP, killing the captain and most of the officers."

The medic, who was helping one of the wounded sip water from the canteen, looked up and motioned with his chin. "It hit that big tree up there and blew up right over us. I think we got maybe forty or fifty KIA from it."

"My God..."

"Sam," the CO said, "I need for you to take your men and move up the slope to fill in the gaps on the perimeter. I'm staying here to start a crew clearing an LZ so we can get the wounded off this hill."

Ted came up with Second Platoon on the left while Ausie brought Third Platoon up on the right. Sniper rounds cracked and zipped continuously and no one was standing upright as the three platoons began crawling up the hill. Behind them came the sputtering buzz of chainsaws as the CO began clearing the LZ.

When First Platoon was in place, Sam lay beside Glasspack and Sergeant Ingram watching while Ausie finished placing his men on the right. He noticed Ingram studying Ausie. The way he eyed him you'd have thought Ausie was a bamboo viper.

"That's Lieutenant Langston," Sam said. "They brought him over from Alpha Company to replace Lieutenant Johns."

"I know who he is."

"So you've already met him?"

"Not exactly."

His silence now revealed almost as much as his tone of voice just had. Sam waited while the platoon sergeant lit a cigarette and sucked hard on it. "Gotta get me one more smoke before dark."

After a minute or two, Ingram snuffed the cigarette and looked over at him. "I'll shoot straight with you, sir. I had my doubts about you. I mean—we always do with new lieutenants, but you've done damned good since you got here. And from what Sergeant Pierson says, Lieutenant Salter is doing real good with Second Platoon, too."

He went silent again.

"I take it you've heard some unfavorable scuttlebutt on Lieutenant Langston."

"It wasn't just scuttlebutt, sir, but maybe we just need to let it go. I'm not sure it's appropriate for an NCO to bring this sort of thing to an officer."

"Is it something that could get our men hurt?"

"I don't know for sure, sir. I suppose it could. I mean...." He paused. "Sir, can I speak freely—in confidence? I just don't need to catch shit from anybody."

"I can't promise you anything, Sarge, but I'll do my best to maintain confidentiality."

"His platoon sergeant, Tucker, told me he accidentally overheard a conversation between that new lieutenant and the old man while we were back at FB Sixteen this morning. He was telling the captain how it was good to finally be reporting to a fellow Academy grad and how Bravo Company was already loaded with ninety-day-wonder platoon leaders, but he would get Third Platoon whipped into shape."

"What did the old man say?"

"He told him Captain Porchette over in Alpha Company might be an OCS graduate, but he was also one of the finest company commanders in the 503rd, and that you and Lieutenant Salter were doing outstanding as platoon leaders. Then he told him that Third Platoon didn't need whipping of any kind, just good leadership."

Sam couldn't help the sardonic smile that crossed his face. Poor old Ausie was doing it again—stuffing his spit-shined boot in his mouth, all the way up to his knee.

"Sir, I don't mean to be disrespectful, but I don't think it's something you can laugh about. That kind of John Wayne attitude is what gets men killed out here."

"Sorry, Sarge. I'm not really laughing about it. I've known Lieutenant Langston since jump school, and he *is* a bit pompous about his West Pointer status, but he's a good officer. Just the same, I'll keep an eye out in his direction."

Near dusk there came a thundering explosion down the hill near where the CO was clearing the LZ. It was an enemy mortar. A second and third followed and the chainsaws went silent as construction of the LZ was halted. From down the hill came calls for a medic. Sam listened to the radio. The captain had been slightly wounded, and several of the men from weapons platoon had been killed. It now seemed Bravo Company had done nothing more than crawl inside the trap with 2nd Battalion.

At 2100 hours that evening, the lead elements of Alpha Company arrived and began moving up the hill to reinforce the perimeter. They were followed at 2220 hours by Charlie Company. The enemy's B-40 rockets, recoilless rifle fire, and mortars made for a long night, but the situation seemed under control for now. Regardless, only brief snatches of sleep were taken by the exhausted troops.

November, 21, 1967
Hill 875
Dak To, Republic of Vietnam

Dawn broke over Hill 875 that morning with the air still and pregnant with tension. In a few short hours the paratroopers of the 173rd Airborne were once again going to assault the hill. Were it not for the shrieking F-100s and thundering airstrikes on the slope above, the surrounding silence might have been equally unsettling. The 4th Battalion troops were organized along the line of departure for the final attack. Bravo Company was at the center. Jump-off was scheduled for 1100 hundred hours.

Sam's First Platoon was in reserve behind Ausie's Third

Platoon, which was twenty meters forward on the right, and Ted's Second Platoon twenty meters forward on the left. Ted and Ausie had crawled back to Sam's position and the three platoon leaders huddled behind a fallen tree. Sergeant Ingram and Glasspack were down the line somewhere checking on the men.

"Where's the captain?" Ted asked.

"He went back down the hill with a detail. They're still trying to clear an LZ."

"We won't be able to use it till we kick these bastards off this hill," Ausie said.

"Yeah, I'm ready to get it over with," Ted said. "This waiting is getting on my nerves. Besides, the little bastards are probably so far underground right now we're not hurting them with those airstrikes."

Ausie nodded as another bomb exploded up the hill, followed by the shriek and thunder of a jet's afterburners as it climbed skyward. The fluttering whir of shrapnel passed overhead and afterward came the muted snaps and thuds of spent steel dropping through the overhead.

Sam remained silent. He'd been fighting fever, dizziness, and nausea all night.

"You okay?" Ted asked.

Sam opened his mouth to speak but quickly turned about and blew his guts out on the jungle floor, retching and coughing as the dizziness returned.

"Dammit, Sam! You okay?" Ausie asked.

"I don't know. I think maybe I've gotten some kind of bug or something."

"Have you been taking your malaria pill?"

"Every damned week."

"Well, you look like shit."

"Thank you, Ausie. I'll accept that as your professional diagnosis."

"No," Ted said. "I mean, he's right. You *really* do."

The jungle tilted sideways and spun in a blurred carousel of green before righting itself and coming to a stop. "I really do what?"

"You really *do* look like shit. You need to go back down and catch a medevac when they come in."

Sam uncapped his canteen and took a sip. He waited. His two fellow officers sat staring at him. The water stayed down.

"We're going up this damned hill in a few hours and I intend to be here with my men when we do. If I'm not better by tonight, we'll see."

Glasspack crawled over the fallen tree and rolled in amongst the platoon leaders.

"Your platoon leader is sick," Ted said.

"Yeah, I know. He's been puking all night."

"Well, keep an eye on him," Ausie said.

Glasspack gave him a thumbs-up.

"Did you and Sergeant Ingram tell your men that our platoons are only twenty meters out in front of you and not to get too jumpy?" Ted asked.

"Already done, sir." The voice came from the other side of the fallen tree. Sergeant Ingram's head appeared. "Y'all do the same and make sure your men know we're back here behind you."

"Where's your esprit de corps, Sergeant?" Ausie said. "We're well-trained paratroopers, not Keystone Cops. I will, however, take your suggestion under advisement."

Ted knew him well enough to know Ausie was again exercising his obtuse sense of humor, but Ingram scrambled over the log. "Advisement, my ass! Tell your men what I said so we don't have any more friendly fire accidents."

Ted raised his eyebrows and gazed at Ausie. A vein had popped out on his neck.

"...*Sir!*" Ingram added.

Sam raised his hand between the two men. "I think we're all pretty frazzled right now. Let's take a time-out. Ted, you and

Ausie better get back with your units. I'll address this with Sergeant Ingram."

For once, Ausie seemed willing to swallow his pride. The two platoon leaders slithered over the tree and into the undergrowth. Sam gazed at his platoon sergeant. The dizziness and nausea had diminished. "Sergeant Ingram."

"Sir."

"Next time you address an officer will you please lead with "Sir or LT" and not tack it on at the end?"

"Sir, I'll take that under advisement."

"Seriously, Sarge, we rookie lieutenants need your guidance, but you've got to respect the rank."

"I'm probably getting to sound like a broken record with this, sir, but again, permission to speak freely?"

"Fire away."

"Sir, I've seen a lot of cherry lieutenants over here, and most of them I can deal with, but that Langston gets under my skin big time. If I had to take orders from that prick, I'd tell you to just go ahead and bust me back to private and send me down to the LBJ."

"No, you wouldn't, and you know it. You want to be right here with your men so you can help figure out how to keep us all together and get the job done."

Ingram slowly shook his head side to side. "I suppose you're right, LT. We're just a bunch of thrown-together draftees, replacements, and shake-n-bake sergeants and officers. For what it's worth, we *are* the army, but all that esprit de corps bullshit is for another time and another war. All we have out here in the bush is one another and what we do for one another is all that matters. It's the only reason 'duty' becomes something rational."

Sam wasn't particularly surprised by his platoon sergeant's observation. Clyde Ingram had always seemed a cut above average. He gazed back at him and nodded. "You know, Sarge, someday when we aren't wearing these uniforms, you and I might have a pretty good conversation about the army and this war."

A man came up the hill behind them, a runner from battalion.

"The assault time has been changed, sir. We go at 1430 hours."

"Good enough," Sam said. "We'll pass the word."

The waiting was already grinding on raw nerves. Now this—another five hours to think about just how bad it was going to be when they stood up and began pushing forward up the hill. Another five hours of random sniper fire. Another five hours sweating with this godawful fever and nausea. Sam felt like a dog dying from distemper.

CHAPTER NINE

A Quick End to a Fast Start

October 2018
Boone, North Carolina

"I have some news for you," Sam said.

They were on their way to breakfast. A light rain was falling, and Claire was still wrestling with her canvas tote bag and rain jacket as he pulled the pickup away from the curb. The campus was dreary and relatively quiet that Saturday morning. She gave him an expectant glance.

"Your father visited a VA Clinic in Pensacola, Florida, just last week."

She stared at him a moment and her face slowly drained of color. Sam was immediately aggravated with himself for breaking the news so abruptly.

"He's okay. He just went in and saw a doctor. They refilled his medications and treated him for dehydration. He was released the same day."

Staring straight ahead, Claire whispered something, but her lips barely moved. Tears began streaming down her face.

"I can't take you into the restaurant looking like that. They'll swear I kidnapped you."

"I don't care. I don't want to go down there."

"To the restaurant?"

"No! To Pensacola."

"Who said anything about going down there, and if you don't care, why are you crying?"

She looked down and shook her head.

"There was no address on his medical report other than your home in Maggie Valley."

"No, I can't just—"

"Listen to me, Claire." Sam reached over and put his hand on hers. "Whether or not you *want* to go is irrelevant. This is something you *have* to do. No matter how you feel about your father, or what happened to your mother, you have to do this for yourself."

"But what if he—"

"No!" Sam caught himself and forced his emotions inward. "Sorry. I didn't mean to raise my voice. No excuses. No matter how you feel about him, you have to go. If you don't, you'll regret it for the rest of your life. What you do after that, I'll leave up to you, but you've got to do this. How about we make a plan? I'll help you any way I can. Fall break is coming soon. We can pack our bags and head that way after your last class."

Claire sat a while before giving the slightest nod of her head. The windshield wipers beat a dreary rhythm as Sam drove down a wet highway streaked with the glare of daytime headlights. She glanced over at him. "Would you mind if we went somewhere other than Cracker Barrel this morning?"

"Do you have some place particular in mind?"

"Why don't we double back and go to The Local Lion? My mom always loved to go there when she came for a visit. She said the chocolate espresso donuts helped when she was depressed. I like their orange glazed ones. I could eat a dozen right now."

"Then The Local Lion it is, but I want to ask a favor."

The problems she faced with her father explained a lot, but Sam couldn't help but wonder if there was something more he was missing, perhaps something between her father and grandfather. The father-in-law relationship would be an obvious explanation, but Claire's intense feelings against her father seemed to indicate there might be more.

"Sure," she said, "if I can. What is it?"

"Do you have any of your grandfather's old military papers—a DD-214, orders, letters, or anything like that?"

"Yes. Before he died, he gave me a folder with a lot of his old letters and army documents. Why?"

"I thought that since your grandfather and I were both in the 82nd around the same time we might have crossed paths and it could be that I just don't remember him. I mean the odds are pretty good, considering the 82nd was pared down to a light infantry brigade a couple months after we got to Vietnam. I'd like to look at his papers if you don't mind."

"No problem," she said in a subdued voice. "I'll bring the folder next time we meet."

Claire wiped her sleeve across her face.

"Hang in there, kid. Things will get better. You'll see."

She gave him a sad smile and turned on her recorder.

"Tell me about the attack on the hill."

November 21, 1967
Hill 875
Dak To, Republic of Vietnam

"LT," Sergeant Ingram said, "I'm going over on the left with our men behind Second Platoon. If I might suggest, you should move over to the right with our men behind Third Platoon. That way we can fill in the gaps and give the support where we're needed."

"Will do, Sarge."

"I already briefed them this morning to keep one eye looking down for spider holes and the other up in the overhead for snipers. A dude from 2nd Battalion said the gooks had entire squads of snipers up there in the canopy."

The word came at precisely 1430 hours that afternoon. "Move out!"

Second and Third Platoons came to their feet and began advancing with recon by fire, shooting at anything and everything that looked like an enemy hiding place. Over on the left, Sergeant Ingram was shouting for First Platoon to begin moving as well. Sam eased up in front of the men lying on either side of him. "Okay, men. Let's move out. Remember, watch the ground for spider holes and the trees for snipers."

The undergrowth was thick and afforded only occasional glimpses of the first line of troops just to his front. They had moved less than fifteen meters when Sam heard an enemy machine gun open up—and another. Somewhere up ahead he heard Ausie shouting for his men to keep moving. A rocket arced and hissed down through the trees, exploding somewhere on the left. Loud snaps and pops cracked all around. Leaves and limbs had begun shattering and falling everywhere in the undergrowth when something delivered a hammer blow to Sam's left bicep.

He nearly dropped his sixteen, and glanced down at his arm. It was hanging limp, and there was a tiny hole in the sleeve of his fatigue shirt. His arm was numbed by the impact. He turned to tell Glasspack, but the young RTO was lying on his back, unmoving. Dropping to his knees, Sam crawled to him. There was a tiny hole under his left eye, and only then did Sam realize the back of his head was missing. Riganti crawled over to them.

"Dammit LT, they got Glasspack."

"Get the radio and his grenades," Sam said, "and catch up with me."

Sam was now moving on the raw instinct instilled by his

training as he turned and continued forward. Holding his M-16 at the ready with his right hand, he broke into a more open area. Green tracers were crossing in two directions. An enemy machine gun had the entire skirmish line pinned down with enfilade fire coming from the right. None of the men in the first line of attack were visible. Riganti crawled up beside him and they lay behind a fallen tree.

"Give me cover fire," Sam said. "I'm going to try to move ahead and see if I can find any of Third Platoon."

Sam raised his head as bullets splintered the topside of the fallen tree. He ducked and grabbed Riganti. "Wait!"

There came a pause in the enemy fire.

"Now!"

He leapt over the log, landed on his belly and crawled rapidly forward. After crawling only ten meters he dropped into a shallow ravine atop two men. Both were conscious but badly wounded. They were trying to apply field dressings to leg and hip wounds. Sam went to work cinching the bandages tight.

"Where's Lieutenant Langston?"

One of the men pointed up the hill. "He got out ahead of us, sir. Last time I saw him he was up there about another ten or fifteen meters. That machine gun opened up on us and I got hit. I fell down in this draw."

"Give me your frags and stay put."

Both men handed him their grenades. Sam climbed to the top of the ravine. Machine gun rounds were cracking barely ten inches above his head. If Ausie was still alive, he had to be right up against the enemy machine gun to the front, but the fire coming down the hill from the right was chewing up everything over a foot high. With his head flat against the ground, Sam began crawling.

A few meters ahead he spotted jungle boots protruding from beneath a fallen tree. Crawling and reaching forward, he grabbed one of the boots and pulled it. There was no response. He pulled harder and began drawing the man back to him. It was Ausie's RTO. His chest was riddled with machine gun rounds.

The enemy machine gun to the front continued firing. It was no more than five or six meters away. He crawled forward under the fallen tree and through the pool of blood. By now the feeling was returning to his left arm as lightning bolts of pain shot through his body.

He spotted Ausie. He was lying on his back and pointing to something just above his head. The barrel of the enemy machine gun protruded from the undergrowth no more than eighteen inches above him. Only then did Sam realize his friend had no weapon and apparently no grenades. Ausie's M-16 lay off to one side. A mangled mess, it had apparently been struck by the machine gun fire. Sam crawled up beside him, and handed him two frags. Neither man spoke, but Sam found with his injured arm he couldn't pull the pins on his grenades. He held the spoons tight and extended the grenades toward Ausie, who pulled the pins. The machine gun paused firing and the voices of the enemy soldiers came from the trench only a few feet away.

Sam nodded and both men threw their grenades over into the trench. The explosions blew the foliage away and Sam leapt over into the machine gun nest. Something ripped across his back searing him from shoulder to shoulder. It seemed as if someone had slapped him with a red-hot branding iron.

He started up the trench, but an enemy soldier appeared and raised his rifle. Using his one good arm, Sam shot from the waist and emptied half of a magazine into the soldier. The dizziness returned and he went to his knees, but from behind him came the stutter of another M-16. He looked back to see Riganti and Ted Salter tumble over into the trench.

"You okay?" Ted asked.

"Yeah, sure. Just lost my footing." He tried to stand and the world went black.

October 2018
Boone, North Carolina

Claire had stopped eating her donut as she stared across the table at Sam. "You were shot twice?"

"Yes, but neither of those wounds was life-threatening. The first one got a little bit of my left bicep and armpit. We figured it was the same round that killed Glasspack. That was a bad day and for years I did a lot of second-guessing about it before Caroline brought me to my senses. The second round laid me open across my back and caused me to get about a hundred stitches, but it was the wound I didn't know about that got me in trouble."

"It really wasn't a pulled muscle in your back, was it? You got hit by shrapnel that first day when you arrived, didn't you?"

"I suppose it was a combination of being high on adrenaline, as well as being stupid and in denial. For a moment after the RPG exploded that day I thought it could be shrapnel, but I figured getting wounded would be...I don't know...maybe, more dramatic. Besides I had on a flak jacket. That's why I chalked it off as a pulled muscle.

"Turns out it was a piece of shrapnel smaller than a BB that penetrated the jacket and hit my shoulder blade. Later when the wound went septic over the three weeks we were in the bush, it gave me blood poisoning."

"What happened to you?"

"The infection damned near got me. They sent me to Japan first, then back to the States to Womack Army Hospital at Fort Bragg. I was kept on an IV of antibiotics and later had some surgery on my back. By Christmas I was almost completely recovered, and they assigned me to the Third Brigade of the 82nd Airborne there at Bragg."

"What happened to Ted and Ausie?"

"They both got through it alive and took the men up the hill the next day. Ted received the Distinguished Service Cross for carrying me back down the hill and going back twice more to get two of Ausie's men who were wounded."

"Did you get a medal?"

"A Purple Heart and The Silver Star for taking out the machine gun."

"Did you ever get to talk with them again?"

"As a matter of fact, I regained consciousness briefly that afternoon there on the LZ as the dust-off was coming in. Ted and Ausie were both there. Ted was saying something about how I would miss all the fun we were having, and how he was pretty sure I would be back. Ausie told Ted not to worry, that I was too gung-ho to stay away. I remember telling them 'Like hell I will. I'm never coming back.' They laughed. I don't remember much after that, but they were right."

"What do you mean?"

"I'll tell you later. Right now, I can't stand it any longer. I've got to get one of those orange glazed donuts you're eating. Those things smell like a cake Caroline used to make."

CHAPTER TEN

Starting Over

October, 2018
Boone, North Carolina

Sam fumbled for his cell phone on the bedside table and glanced at the screen. It was 6:30 a.m. and there was an incoming call from Claire.

"You're up early this morning, little lady."

"Hey. Yeah. I thought I would check with you before getting ready for class."

"Well, you'll be happy to know, to my amazement, I am still here, above ground and still breathing."

"That's not funny, Sam."

"Sorry, kid. So what's up?"

"Do you want me to go online and make our hotel arrangements?"

"Sure, but use my credit card. I'll text you the info. And make sure the rooms are non-smoking. What time do you get out of class tomorrow?"

"Can you pick me up at the dorm around 3:15?"

"Sure, that'll work. You know it's a ten-hour drive if we drive straight through, right?"

"We can swap off driving, if that's okay."

"Works for me. Don't forget to bring your grandfather's army papers."

"Okay."

Sam glanced again at the clock. *Why had she called so early?* She actually seemed excited about this trip to Pensacola.

The pickup was gassed-up and his overnight bag was in the backseat when Sam stopped in front of Claire's dorm that afternoon. This trip was fraught with tension. He could feel it. She would not admit it, but despite whatever blame she felt her father bore for her mother's death, she not only wanted him, she needed him. Sam hoped the trip would turn out well, but there were so many things that could go wrong. When she came out the door, Claire looked nonetheless excited as she trundled down the sidewalk with her luggage.

He got out to help her. "Three bags—really? Are you planning on spending the winter down there?"

She grinned. "It's a woman thing."

Within minutes they were on their way south.

"You might as well turn on your recorder and get out your notebook. We've got a long trip ahead of us."

"You know my list of questions for you is growing?"

"Would you rather do a Q&A session today?"

She shook her head. "No, not now, except for one thing I want to ask you. How could Ausie and Ted joke so much after all that happened—I mean like when they teased you about coming back to Vietnam? I would have wanted to cry."

"The human condition demands some form of humor amidst tragic pathos, lest we become insane. It doesn't mean we can't cry. It merely provides another release for those pent-up emotions. I actually saw men do both after particularly tough engagements."

Claire remained silent, while Sam drove southward and allowed her to contemplate what he had said. After several minutes she turned toward him. "I want to hear what comes next. Last time you said you ended up getting assigned to the 82nd Airborne Division at Fort Bragg. I'll bet you were happy you didn't have to go right back to Vietnam, right?"

"Oh, most assuredly. I actually felt guilty about it, at least for the first month or so, but as things have a way of doing in life, my feelings of guilt were soon rectified."

January 1968
Fort Bragg, North Carolina

It was the day after New Year's when Sam first met his men. He had missed first call that morning while over at Womack for his final physical therapy session. The men had already finished PT and the daily three-mile run. They were at breakfast. At Sam's request the platoon sergeant called for a platoon formation when they returned from the mess hall. Why he was nervous about meeting his new command was a mystery, but he felt like a rookie lieutenant again.

His new Stateside fatigues still had their deep olive-green color. They were starched and perfectly creased, and were it not for the Combat Infantryman's Badge sewn over his pocket above his jump wings he would have looked like a brand new second lieutenant. And technically speaking, he was. He had served less than a month in a combat zone, gotten himself shot to hell and was medevaced back to the world. Now he was starting over. He drew a deep breath as he walked down the steps outside the barracks.

The azure sky was cloudless and the morning air crisp and cool with bright sunshine as his men fell into formation that January morning. A string of Hueys from the 17th Cav thumped by out beyond Smoke Bomb Hill. Platoon Sergeant Henry Evans called the men to attention, executed a perfect about face, and saluted him with precision. "All present or accounted for, sir!"

Sam returned the sergeant's salute. "At ease, men."

He studied them carefully. For a Stateside unit, they weren't exactly what he had hoped for—especially from an elite unit like the 82nd Airborne. A couple hadn't bothered to shave and others wore fatigues that looked as if they had slept in them. Several had hair creeping dangerously close to coming over their ears and one wore an afro that bulged out in fuzzy wads from under either side of his ball cap. What gave Sam hope were the jump wings, CIBs, and Ranger patches many of them wore. Most of the men in his platoon were combat veterans.

"I thought I was joining a platoon of paratroopers, not Spanky and Our Gang."

Several men grinned. Others smirked.

"How many of you served in Vietnam with the Hundred and First?"

Nearly a dozen men raised their hands.

"How many of you served with the 173rd?"

Ten others raised their hands.

"How many of you served with other units over there?"

Two more raised their hands.

Sam nodded. "How many of you have not served overseas?"

Only a few raised their hands.

"Gentlemen, I feel I am fortunate to have been given command of a group of men such as yourselves. Most of you have already been to hell and back, and stared the beast in the eye." Several pressed their lips tightly together as they gave knowing nods. Sam paused and began again. "Stateside duty can be a huge adjustment. I know this, because I am now facing that same adjustment. It's not an easy one, but it *is* necessary.

"Right now, Third Brigade is beginning our field training month. We need to get ourselves and our equipment in good order, because next month we go to ready alert status. How many of you have taken leave or received a pass in the last month to spend time with your families?"

Nearly two-thirds raised their hands.

"Sergeant Evans, I want to begin a rotation for those who didn't get leave time to receive some or else get a three-day pass in the next month. No more than three men at a time. Anyone living over a thousand miles away will get an extra day. That will begin day after tomorrow."

They glanced around at one another, nodding. Some grinned.

"In the meantime, I am giving you twenty-four hours to bring yourselves up to the standards and expectations of Airborne troopers. This will include your barracks, your uniforms, your equipment, and your personal appearance. I expect you to be clean-shaven every day. I expect your hair to be high and tight. You don't have to wear whitewalls, but I expect you to meet the standards set forth by the army. You will sign out your individual weapons and present them along with full field gear for inspection at oh nine hundred hours tomorrow."

The platoon took the sudden posture of a meerkat clan staring at a circling honey badger.

"Gentlemen, this doesn't have to be difficult. I simply expect you to maintain readiness and maintain your personal pride until your military commitments are fulfilled. I will work with you. I want you old heads to help out the new guys to make sure they are ready for the inspection. If you are missing any gear or uniform parts, inform Sergeant Evans. Anyone failing to pass muster will be restricted to barracks until a follow-up inspection the next day. This also includes anyone who finds it necessary to go on sick-call tomorrow. If you have questions or concerns pass them up to Sergeant Evans.

"Sergeant Evans, dismiss the platoon."

"Platoon, aten-hut! Dismissed."

Despite a month in military hospitals and an additional week of intense physical therapy, Sam was still a little shaky on his feet. He had to rebuild his strength, but the cup of coffee and two pieces of toast at the hospital that morning left him feeling hollow. He glanced at his watch. He had little more than thirty minutes until the 1000 staff meeting with the CO. The officers' club was too far away, but there was a small PX and grill just up the street.

He ordered two hamburgers, a large order of fries, and a chocolate shake, then glanced about. His eyes locked on a table near the window. He didn't expect it would be simple—taking this new command—but Sam had hoped for at least a few days to get his feet on the ground. It was one of his platoon members, Spec-4 afro, sitting at a table near the front window. Their eyes locked and the soldier leaned back, giving Sam a contemptuous grin. This wasn't the place or the time to confront him. Sam turned to face the counter.

The soldier's voice rose above the others in the little grill. "Wha'cha gonna do, LT, send me back to Nam? I done already been there."

The soldier left him with no choice. Sam turned. The trooper had removed his ball cap and was using a pick to shape what was damned near a perfect Diana Ross afro. There were more than a dozen other enlisted men in the little grill. All had gone silent and were staring at the Spec-4 and the lieutenant. Sam had to meet this challenge or lose face. He walked over to the table where the specialist sat. The patch over his right pocket said his name was Pegues.

"Specialist Pegues, is that correct?"

The soldier glanced down at his name patch. "Shows you can read, LT."

Sam lowered his voice to where it was barely audible. "How much time do you have remaining on your enlistment?"

"Five months, three days, and a wakeup, LT," he said with a toothy grin.

Sam nodded carefully and locked eyes with him. "I may not be able to send you back to Vietnam, Specialist, but I sure as hell can send you to Leavenworth to pound rocks in the hot sun for a year. So, which do you prefer, a few more months playing army here at Bragg or a year at Leavenworth?"

Pegues's smile faded into a grimace and his eyes lost their teasing glint.

Sam now lowered his voice even further—to a tone he hoped sounded more like a psychotic voice grinding rocks in hell. "I suggest you get your ass back down there with the rest of the platoon—No! First, take your young ass next door to that PX barbershop and get yourself a regulation haircut. I want you looking like the paratrooper you'll claim to be when you get back home on the block. Then, you can go back to the barracks and help the rest of the platoon prepare for tomorrow's inspection."

Sam had moved to within a foot of the young soldier's face and was now staring down at him. Pegues suddenly shoved his chair backward. Sam remained rock steady, not so much as flinching as he maintained his steady glare. It was another failed ploy by the soldier. The soldier's eyes faded to submissive uncertainty.

"Okay, if you'll just let me get up from here, I got your—"

"I believe you meant to say, 'Okay *sir*.' Is that correct, Specialist?"

"Yes, sir. That's what I meant."

The only sound in the grill was the sizzling of the burgers.

Sam's new CO was Captain Robert Calvert, a decorated OCS officer who had already served a tour in Vietnam. Sam prided himself in his ability to quickly and accurately read people, and Calvert was the real McCoy—just a regular guy who did his duty without fanfare or bullshit, and one who knew how to lead. Frank "Hard Dick" Hardrick, on the other hand, was different. He was a first lieutenant and the platoon leader for First Platoon. He was from Connecticut, or as he proudly proclaimed, *the suburb of the Big Apple*. He also wore his black hair high and tight and seemed to look down his pointed nose at the other officers. There was something about him Sam didn't like.

Upon their introduction, Hardrick said he was looking forward to his tour in Nam and wanted to hear about Sam's time there. He was hoping to get orders later in the spring. It was tempting to tell him to be careful what he wished for, but Sam gave him his best poker-faced nod. Tom DeGrass was the weapons platoon leader and Doug Stone was Third Platoon leader. Stone was quiet and the only other West Point grad in the company beside Hardrick. Despite being only a few months out of the Academy and having not yet been overseas, Stone seemed to have his head screwed on tight. The company XO slot was the only open position.

The staff meeting was two hours of the usual administrative bullshit and it was lunch time when they headed for the mess hall. Hardrick hovered at Sam's shoulder as they walked.

"So, you've already done a tour in Nam and you're still a second lieutenant. Why is that?"

Sam cast a glance over at him. Hardrick wasn't smiling and it was tempting to tell him to fuck off.

"That's why we call him 'Hard Dick,'" Stone said. "He's always fucking around in other people's business."

"I'm just curious, and maybe we can learn something that will keep us out of trouble when we get over there. Did you have some problems?"

"Yes, I did. Three weeks into my tour of duty I got my ass shot up pretty bad on a hill south of Dak To."

"Are you happy, now, Hard Dick?" Stone said. "It probably wasn't the answer you thought it would be either, right?"

"Damn," Hardrick said. "You were with the 173rd back in November—Operation MacArthur. I heard all about it. You guys walked into a buzz saw. Were you on Hill 875?"

"Lieutenant, I don't mean to be short with you, but right now I just want to relax and have some chow. Maybe I can fill you in on the details some night over drinks."

The three lieutenants walked through the double doors and headed straight for the chow line. Crowds of soldiers sat about at the tables laughing and talking loudly, but as the officers made their way across the mess hall, the boisterous conversations quickly faded to a few sideways comments as the soldiers eyed them.

"What the hell is *their* problem?" Hardrick mumbled.

"They're all looking at you, Sam," Stone whispered.

Sam glanced about. A couple of the soldiers seated nearby had been at the PX grill earlier that morning. Some of his platoon members were also seated with them, while at a table near the back several black soldiers were sitting with Spec-4 Pegues. His hair was trimmed high and tight. He looked down at his tray and didn't raise his head.

"I met with my men this morning and put them on notice."

Hardrick gave a humored "*humph*" and grinned, but said nothing. The officers went through the chow line and made their way back into the officers' mess. Out in the main mess hall the raucous sounds of laughter and conversation returned.

"Believe me, young Lieutenant Walker," Hardrick said, "you *will* have an uphill battle with these dregs. I've levied so many Article-15s my men simply shrug when they get one. It's not easy when none of them give a shit."

Sam cast a sidelong glance at Hardrick. This pompous little asshole was the same age and had no business calling him "young lieutenant" even if he did have a few months of time in rank on him. He felt his face flush, but held himself in check. It was that "anger" thing again—something that had troubled him since his return from

Nam. Gritting his teeth, Sam swallowed hard and fought the urge to grab Hardrick by the throat and thrash him about like a rag doll. He instead looked over at Stone and hoped for a reprieve.

Stone caught his drift and nodded. "His people have been fined so much that they're all broke and they bum money and cigarettes from my men."

It wasn't the reprieve he hoped for, but it was at least a distraction.

"So, you haven't had to give any Article-15s?" Sam asked.

Stone shrugged. "I think the last Article-15 I administered was nearly three months ago, and it was for a minor infraction—just some extra duty."

Sam looked across the table at Hardrick and raised his eyebrows. Hardrick's lips were turned down at the corners as his eyes met Sam's. "It's only a matter of style," he said. "My people know I don't tolerate bullshit, and if they step out of line, an Article-15 is automatic. You should take note. You've inherited the worst bunch of losers in the company—maybe the battalion. Some tough discipline might help."

Sam said nothing.

"And that's why we call him Hard Dick," Stone said.

January 22, 1968
Fort Bragg, North Carolina

After three weeks in his new assignment, Sam had found his twenty percent—the core group in his platoon that would create eighty percent of his problems. And it seemed there was one primary cause—drugs. Several of the men returning from Southeast Asia were users. Opium-laced Thai sticks was one of the favorites, along with hashish and marijuana, but the real problem came from those strung out on heroin.

Smack, horse, or whatever nickname they chose for it, it had them treading a narrow ledge above the abyss. Their military service, their roles as paratroopers, their decorations, life itself, all took a backseat to their next fix. They were shells of their former selves, not quite ready to wash up bleached on the shores of life, but well on their way.

"Gentlemen, most of you have impressed me with your willingness to bring this platoon up to a standard expected of the Airborne. I appreciate that. Yet, we still have one major obstacle to overcome."

Sam glanced out over the formation. All his problem children were present—by design. Sergeant Evans had swapped them out with more dependable men who were now pulling duty in their place around the base. Most of these men were here because their families couldn't afford college or they had made bad decisions that left them with no recourse other than joining the military. It was a shame, but there was no excuse for the problem they now faced and he wouldn't mince his words.

"We have a drug problem."

His eyes searched the formation. Most of the ones with the problems averted their eyes, except for one, Corporal Parks, one of the squad leaders. Parks had him fixed with a challenging "don't give a shit" stare. Sam locked eyes with him, calm, dead-eyed, and unblinking. After a few seconds Parks, like the others, stared straight ahead. Parks was a young black kid from Memphis who had returned from Nam only weeks earlier. He had already earned a Bronze Star with a "V" device and an Oak Leaf Cluster. He had potential, but he was one of the hopheads.

"You can deny it. You can hope I won't catch you, but there is only one thing that will keep you from coming to grief over it. That is to come to me. You have my word. I will give you one free pass with no redress and the opportunity to go for treatment over at Womack. However, choose not to come to me and I catch you, or go for treatment and return to your old habit, and I will have no choice but to hold you accountable to the Military Code of Conduct. And make no mistake about it, I will.

"I will not have you endanger the lives of my other men who are doing their duty. And just for the record, I already know who most of you are, but I will not force you. You must choose your own paths."

One of the users, a pimply-faced kid named Matt Whittington from Virginia, came to him that afternoon. Matt had been with the 101st and seen some brutal combat. He insisted he was only "chipping."

"So, you think you can beat it without any help, right?"

Whittington grinned. "Not a problem, sir. I got this." The young PFC turned and looked out the window at the vacant parade grounds. The grass had long since faded to a winter brown, and the sky was gray overcast with the threat of snow. It was pretty obvious he was only hoping he could beat his addiction, and his life would come back to center. Hope was good, but hope alone could not defeat addiction.

"But that wasn't my offer, Matt. You go for treatment, and we can start over. Otherwise, I have to do what's best for all the men in our platoon."

Whittington agreed, but his reluctance was worrisome, and Sam felt as if he had strong-armed the kid. Corporal Parks came several days later and also agreed to go for treatment. Despite Sam's doubts, everything seemed to be working out for the best until word came from the brigade surgeon: Whittington had snuck out one night, got caught and failed his drug test.

A court martial was the only remaining recourse. Sam hated to see this young vet go that route, but he wouldn't have his other men put at risk. The brigade had returned from a training exercise and would go on ready alert status the first of February. That was only a few days away and the drug issue had to be resolved quickly.

CHAPTER ELEVEN

About Face

February 1, 1968
Fort Bragg, North Carolina

I t was a Thursday, like any other day, except the CO had called for an oh five hundred hours staff meeting—again, not something particularly alarming since it was Third Brigade's first day on ready alert status. This meant that the 82nd could deploy anywhere on the planet within eighteen hours and it was Third Brigade's month in the hot seat. They would be first to go. The CO no doubt wanted to make sure all SOPs were in place and well-communicated. Sam sat in the captain's office sipping coffee and waiting as the other officers filed in.

When everyone was settled, they waited expectantly while Captain Calvert studied a dispatch. His face was dark, his jaw set hard, and by the look of his eyes he'd been up for a while, perhaps all night. After a minute, he set the paper aside and looked up. Sam saw it immediately. It was there in his eyes. Something was wrong—bad wrong.

"Gentlemen, in the last twenty-four hours, the North Vietnamese Army, along with numerous main-force Vietcong units, have gone on a major offensive, attacking every major city and military installation in South Vietnam. Apparently, they used the Tet Holiday cease-fire to position their forces and the results as of now are devastating. Our units there are fighting to regain control of the country.

"According to this dispatch, the cities seem to be their primary objectives. Several have been overrun including Saigon, Hue, and Quang Tri. The perimeter at Tan Son Nhut Airbase has been breached and there are enemy combatants inside our embassy in Saigon. I cannot overstate the significance of what is currently happening there in Vietnam."

The room was quiet as a crypt. The only sound Sam could hear was the ringing in his ears—something that had not gone away since November.

"For now, Third Brigade personnel are not restricted to base and there have been no orders issued for deployment, but the division commander in his own words 'in an abundance of caution' is ordering Third Brigade to begin preparations for a full alert. I will make this announcement at first formation this morning, but I will also make it clear to all of you and your men that no part of any of this communication is to be discussed with anyone outside of this unit. Obviously our families will know, but they too must be cautioned about discussing this with anyone.

"The company medics will begin reviewing shot records and supply will begin working on a requisition for additional tropical gear, as well as flak jackets and other equipment we may need should we deploy. Questions?"

"Sir," Hardrick said, "I myself am more than ready to go and do my duty, but most of my men have already served tours in Vietnam. Most have been back here less than a year, and they lack motivation. Can we get replacements for them?"

"Lieutenant Hardrick, we have no choice but to do as we are ordered. Hopefully, the situation over there in Nam will be rectified by the units already there and we will pass the month here at Fort Bragg, but that withstanding, it's our duty to be prepared.

"Gentlemen, I suggest you meet with your NCOs prior to first formation and brief them, but make certain they understand that we have *not* been put on alert and we are simply taking measures to ensure we are prepared should that happen. You are dismissed."

He pointed at Sam. "Lieutenant Walker, I want a moment to talk with you before you go. Lieutenant Stone, will you close the door on the way out, please?"

When the others were gone, the CO cleared his throat. "How are you feeling, Sam?"

"Fine, sir."

"Are you back to a hundred percent?"

"I'm getting there. Why are you asking?"

"I read the citations accompanying your Bronze and Silver Stars, and it sounds like you saw some pretty tough combat back in November. Technically, you're still on limited duty. I'm thinking of giving you a break should we deploy—a temporary medical deferment."

"Sir, I appreciate what you're suggesting, but I don't want to be separated from my men. If they have to go back, I want to go with them."

Captain Calvert nodded. "I thought you might say that, and I am damned proud to have an officer of your caliber in my command. Regardless, I'll expect you to be one hundred percent recovered before I put you back in the field. That means the doctors over at Womack will have to clear you for full duty. Is that clear?"

"Yes, sir."

February 12, 1968
Fort Bragg, North Carolina

It had taken nearly two weeks, but Sam had received his clearance for full duty. That same day the order had come down placing the Third Brigade of the 82nd Airborne Division on full alert status. All personnel were restricted to base and MPs were posted on all roads and gates in and out of Fort Bragg. Preparations began in earnest. As always, the exact reason for the alert was not announced, but when the company was marched down to the warehouse and issued flak jackets, jungle fatigues, and jungle boots along with new weapons, their destination was no longer in doubt. They were going to the Republic of Vietnam.

Three days later Sam and his Second Platoon along with Hardrick and Stone and their platoons were onboard a C-141 cargo jet somewhere over the Pacific and beyond the Alaskan coast. The headquarters group and weapons platoon were on board a second aircraft. Up to now, although everyone was pretty certain where they were going, their destination had not been officially announced.

Hardrick, being the ranking officer on the aircraft, had received the sealed envelope with a copy of the orders. Now that they were over international waters and bound for wherever they were going, it was his responsibility to open and read the orders aloud to all those aboard.

He stood and walked midway up the aisle where he ceremoniously opened the envelope. After unfolding the papers, he studied them carefully. A few moments later he raised his head, threw his fist in the air, and let out a crazed "Yeehaaa!" Sam found it somewhat reminiscent of Slim Pickens riding the H-bomb from the B-52 bomb bay in the old Dr. Strangelove movie.

"Chu Lai, Republic of Viet-fucking-*nam*!" Hardrick screamed in a shrill voice.

Most of the men, like Sam, simply stared at him with looks of incredulity. After a few moments, Hardrick seemed to find some sense of self-awareness and walked over to where Sam was sitting. "I suppose it's not so exciting for those of you who have already been there," Hardrick said. "I understand."

"No, Lieutenant, I don't think you do, but you will soon enough."

Hardrick's face flushed. "You don't have to be a dick about it, Walker, especially in front of these enlisted men."

Sam came to his feet. "You're the one they call Hard Dick Louie, and if you didn't want it said in front of my men, you shouldn't have brought it up. Now, get the fuck out of my face."

Hardrick raised his chin and stood rigid. "I can't believe you are speaking to a ranking officer in that manner."

"Let's get something straight, Lieutenant. You came over here and called me a 'dick' in front of my men. You may have gotten away with talking to underclassmen at the Academy that way, but I'm not a cadet and I'm not your subordinate. And don't try to fucking pull rank with me when you only outrank me by a few months."

Doug Stone scrambled over several wooden crates and pushed himself between Walker and Hardrick. "You guys need to tone it down. Louie, why don't you go back to the other side and rejoin your men? Oh, and do you mind if I take a look at our orders?"

After glancing down at the papers still clutched in his hand, Hardrick raised his chin and shoved them at Stone. "Knock yourself out. Not much there other than what I already announced."

Sam glanced around. Several of his men were still eyeing him. He'd blown it. He'd lost his cool. It was something that wouldn't have happened prior to Dak To, but now it was done.

"You okay?" Stone asked.

"No, Doug. I'm not. I acted like a damned fool."

Upon arrival at the Chu Lai Airbase, they were reunited with the headquarters group and weapons platoon. Several days of churning confusion, planning, and preparation ended with the battalion ordered northward to an LZ west of Hue. There they joined with elements of the 101st Airborne who were facing main-force VC and NVA units trying tenaciously to reach their comrades still entrenched in the city of Hue. Captain Calvert had said it best. This was going to be an up close and personal slugfest, and it was going to be a fight where the 82nd would lose some men.

The sky was overcast and the roads were a muddy mess, but the sweat dripped from the end of Sam's nose. His new rip-stop jungle fatigues were soaked with both the sweat and the rain. His platoon was gathered around him, glassy-eyed from lack of sleep, smoking cigarettes and fidgeting nervously.

"Gentlemen, many of you have already been here and you know the drill, but I'm going to talk about some things that I hope will help extend your life expectancy when we make contact—and have no doubts, the enemy is here in force, and we *will* be in contact very soon.

"Your reaction in the first few seconds of a firefight may well determine whether or not you and the men around you live. Going prone instantly and establishing well-directed suppressing fire are two things that must come automatically. Freeze up and the enemy will maintain and increase their fire superiority and you will eventually become a casualty."

Sam continued discussing fire and maneuver tactics, night contact, and the dozens of simple but not so obvious tricks of the trade he had learned from Sergeant Ingram and his men in the 173rd. Three weeks of continuous contact around Dak To had brought relevance to all his previous training and he did his best to communicate it now to his platoon.

The rain started again, and the men broke out their ponchos. Cigarette smoke streamed upward and hung in a foggy shroud above them. When he was done, Sam turned to the platoon sergeant. "Sergeant Evans, do you have anything you want to say?"

"Only that I've never heard an officer of any rank give such a clear and easy to understand lesson on combat tactics. You men best remember everything the lieutenant just said, and I want to add one more thing. When you see that NVA haversack lying there on the ground or that NVA helmet with the pretty red star, leave it the hell alone. Don't touch it—unless of course you want to die. They don't often leave things like that lying around unless doing so with a purpose, and that's so some dumbass American soldier will pick it up and blow himself away with the grenade that's beneath it."

It was late that evening and the men were settled in their NDP when Captain Calvert called the platoon leaders and their first sergeants together. The rains had stopped and there was a dank chill in the air as they gathered in the command tent. From somewhere in the distance came the constant *karoomphs* of heavy artillery. Sam had wrapped himself with a poncho liner. He and Sergeant Evans sat with the other platoon leaders and platoon sergeants while the CO briefed them on the next day's mission. He pointed to a series of villages and hamlets on the map.

"Tomorrow morning we'll convoy southwest from here and cross Highway One where we'll meet up with a company of ARVN Rangers and begin a RIF of these hamlets. S-2 says we should expect moderate to heavy resistance from at least one of two main-force VC companies in the area. We will move in platoon columns with a platoon as point column and the other two platoons trailing on either flank—"

"Sir, I can take First Platoon for that point column if you wish," Hardrick said.

The Coleman lantern hissed softly in the subsequent silence, its yellow light casting a pale glow on the men's faces. It seemed the CO might have been nonplussed, but he did a masterful job of remaining poker-faced. No one looked left or right and the captain continued with the briefing.

"...and deploy on line within five hundred meters of the first village, terrain permitting. First Platoon will be the point platoon. Second will be trailing oblique on the left and Third trailing oblique on the right. Weapons platoon will follow up the middle. As we approach and move through the villages, the ARVN forces will circle to the south to cut off escape routes. According to one of my counterparts from the One-Oh-One, we should search for and expect to find extensive tunnel complexes beneath the villages. Our ARVN translators will give anyone in the tunnels fair chance to surrender. After that, they're all fair game."

Maps were marked with points of origin and call signs assigned along with radio frequencies for medevac and friendly forces in the AO. The captain wished them well and Sam walked with Sergeant Evans back to the platoon CP. A thick mist hung in the stagnant night air and dripped from the surrounding trees and vegetation.

"What are your thoughts about tomorrow, Sergeant?"

"I'm worried that we're missing something," Evans said. "I mean, it's not something I can put my finger on, but..." His voice tapered off into silence and he didn't finish.

"I believe we've done all we can to prepare the men. And to your point: I'm not sure we can prepare for everything that might happen. We just have to be ready to adjust to whatever comes our way."

"I reckon you're right, LT."

They huddled beneath a palm tree and pulled their ponchos over their heads. The incessant whining of the mosquitoes guaranteed another miserable night. Sam sat awake and listened as his platoon sergeant began breathing heavily. Evans had started him thinking. Perhaps his platoon sergeant was right. Perhaps they *were* overlooking something, but what? After several hours Sam had gone through a hundred "what ifs" before finally drifting into a restless sleep.

The company had boarded trucks well before daylight and arrived at dawn. The men were now moving into position as the sun burned through the morning haze. Sam gazed skyward at two helicopter gunships circling beyond the village. Adrenaline did wonders for the tired body. He had gotten all of two hours' sleep that night, but his heartbeat was increasing as he signaled his squad leaders to bring the platoon on line.

Sam led Second Platoon, moving them up on the left side of the village. Lieutenant Hardrick's men were approaching the center of the village on his right, while Lieutenant Stone's platoon was somewhere over on the far right. The CO and his headquarters group along with weapons platoon were moving up behind Hardrick to deploy the recoilless rifle. Other than an occasional shout from the various squad leaders, all remained quiet. Sam hadn't done a lot of work around villages, but something didn't seem quite right.

First Platoon entered the village from the north while Sam skirted it on the east. Once in position, his men lined up and took a knee to protect the left flank. They smoked cigarettes and cast wary glances at one another while Sam listened to Hardrick on the radio. He was reporting to the captain that there was no livestock and only a few stragglers remaining in the village. It was quiet—too quiet. Sam's sixth sense was now on full alert. This was not good. Only one thing would have made the people flee their village—the enemy.

There was only a slight downward grade toward the village, and the surrounding terrain was dramatically different from the highlands around Dak To. Here, the land was mostly flat and other than a few bunches of palm trees there was little overhead cover. The circling choppers could easily spot any large numbers of the enemy moving to flank the company. If the enemy was still here, there was but one place they could be. The CO directed Hardrick to search for possible tunnels while the Vietnamese Special Police interrogated the few stragglers that remained in the village.

The sound of a jeep's engine came from somewhere behind them. He couldn't see it but Sam knew it was the weapons platoon jeep carrying the recoilless rifle. The sound ceased as it took up a position just outside the village. Other than the subdued voices of his men, there were only the occasional radio transmissions and the thumping of the helicopters circling in the distance. All remained quiet inside the village.

This should have been a good thing, but there was again that sixth sense that often spoke so clearly to him. This time it was telling him they were being sucked in. He eased over to talk with Evans. "Sarge, do you feel like the shit is about to hit the fan?" Sam asked in a subdued voice.

Evans gave him a grim nod. "Yeah, I do."

"Let's get the men down. Tell them to go prone, and let's turn one squad around to face back north," Sam said.

The platoon sergeant eased out toward the men and silently motioned them to get down. Not a word was spoken and the entire platoon quickly disappeared into the grass. Lieutenant Hardrick's voice came over the radio again as he called the captain. His men had found what appeared to be a tunnel opening inside a hooch at the center of the village.

Captain Calvert was talking on the radio when his voice was suddenly replaced by a blast of static. A moment later the sound of an explosion echoed from north of the village, followed by the rattle of automatic weapons fire.

"Shit! They're hitting the CO and weapons platoon," Evans said.

Sam listened. There were both AK-47s and M-16s firing.

"Let's turn the platoon and sweep back toward them," Sam said.

"Those damned tunnels probably have openings back that way outside the village."

They rushed the men on line and started them back toward weapons platoon. Out of instinct Sam glanced over his shoulder. An enemy soldier had just climbed from a tunnel opening hidden in the grass. He was less than twenty meters away. Sam shot him, ran back, and dropped a white phosphorus grenade in the hole.

Turning, he shouted at Evans. "Turn a squad around to face behind us and watch our rear. I'll take the rest of the men forward, but let's not get separated."

The sounds of more explosions and automatic weapons fire began coming from inside the village. Lieutenant Hardrick's First Platoon was now under attack. Only then did it occur to Sam that the radio was still streaming static. He grabbed Fergie by the shoulder and flipped the knob on the Prick-25 to the alternate frequency. Hardrick was screaming into his mic that he was taking fire from all sides.

Sam grabbed his radio handset. "Charlie-Blue-Six, this is Charlie-Whiskey-Six. We're moving toward Charlie-Six's pos, over."

Charlie-Blue-Six was Lieutenant Stone's call-sign. He answered immediately. "Roger, Whiskey-Six. I'll try to sweep toward Red-Six inside the 'ville."

Enemy soldiers were now streaming like hornets from out of the ground.

"Keep a squad on your flank, Doug. They're coming up everywhere around us."

"Roger that," Stone answered.

"Hurry up," Hardrick's voice shrieked over the radio. "I'm taking fire from the huts all around me." He sounded on the verge of panic.

Sam moved ahead with his men, watching as fire teams alternately rushed forward, while the next team provided cover fire. They moved like seasoned combat veterans, maintaining fire superiority. They had been here before and knew what it took to survive, and hunkering down in position wasn't the way. Hunkering down often seemed the safest response, but these men knew it would only pass the momentum over to the enemy.

When his men reached the weapons platoon, Sam saw the recoilless rifle on the jeep was cocked askew and unmanned. The bodies of several of the weapons platoon soldiers were sprawled about.

"Over here, LT," one of his men shouted. "It's the CO."

He ran that way. The company RTO was dead, but Captain Calvert, though unconscious, was still breathing. "Medic!" Sam shouted.

The automatic weapons fire and explosions from inside the village continued, but the enemy that attacked weapons platoon and the CO had already disappeared. That at least seemed to be the case for the moment. Sam cast a wild glance around.

"Fan out and form a perimeter," he shouted.

The entire operation had gone to shit as confusion reigned. Sam continued glancing about. *Had the enemy retreated, or were they regrouping to do again what they had done to weapons platoon?* And it occurred to him—the tunnels. He looked around and grabbed Sergeant Parks, his most experienced squad leader.

"Take your men and find the tunnel openings out here. Throw phosphorus grenades in them and leave a man on every opening."

Parks turned and motioned for his men to follow. Sam shook his head, trying to gain some sense of understanding in the fog of confusion that surrounded him. Sergeant Evans appeared, and it was as if an angel of God had come to his aid. "You okay, LT?"

Sam nodded. "The CO is down. I'm trying to get the men to form a perimeter and locate the tunnels out here."

"I'll take care of that, sir. You probably need to switch to the command net and get a medevac in here ASAP. We could use some more men, too, if there's another unit in the area."

His platoon sergeant was an experienced NCO with exceptional situational awareness. Evans was the rock Sam needed and despite the flood of adrenaline in his system, he felt his world coming back into focus. Fergie handed him the handset and changed the frequency on the radio. Immediately they heard the voice of the battalion commander.

"Charlie-Six, Charlie-Six, this is Sky-Ranger-Six, talk to me, Rob. What the hell is going on down there?"

Sam answered. "Sky-Ranger-Six, this is Charlie-Whiskey-Six, Charlie-Six is down and in need of immediate dust-off. We have multiple casualties and are working to establish a secure position north of the 'ville. Over."

For several long moments there were only the sounds of the firefight still raging inside the village and the sounds of the choppers high overhead.

The radio finally broke squelch. "Roger, Whiskey-Six. I'll get some dust-offs inbound to your pos. What else do you need?"

"Sky-Ranger-Six, we have what I believe is an extensive tunnel complex below us. As soon as we can get control of the village, we will need to start clearing it."

"Roger, Whiskey-Six. Let me know if you need anything. Out."

Sam looked around at Fergie and several of his other men. Red-faced, open-mouthed, and with bloodshot eyes they looked back at him. It was time to say something that sounded like calm leadership, but all he could think about was a conversation he'd had with another officer back at Bragg.

That lieutenant had told him about his tour in Nam and how they had gone for weeks on end with little more than crotch rot and an occasional booby-trap. This was his second tour and Sam was wondering where that crotch-rot war was, because both of his tours had now begun with outright slugfests with a determined enemy.

"Let's fan out and make sure we haven't overlooked any spider holes or tunnel openings, men. If you find one, don't look inside. Just call "fire-in-the-hole" and recon it with a frag or willy pete."

The men responded with wry smiles and nods.

"They like the way you think, LT," Fergie said.

By noon the village was secured, and the first men were sent down into the tunnels with flashlights and .45 automatics. It was less than fifteen minutes before Hardrick called over the radio saying his first tunnel rat had been killed and a second wounded. A few moments later Sam's own man scrambled back to the surface with a graze wound across his jaw and back. The enemy was still down there and not about to give up.

"Sergeant Evans, let's put CS canisters in every opening we can find out here. Move the men upwind and let's get to work."

Hardrick's voice came over the radio as he called for Sky-Ranger-Six. He wanted drums of gasoline to pour in the tunnels. Evans stopped and looked back at Sam. Lieutenant Hardrick was now the ranking officer on the ground.

"Go ahead, Sergeant, and do as I said," Sam said. "I'll call him on the radio as soon as we put the tear gas in the tunnels. He's not going to get any gasoline out here."

A few minutes later the colonel called for Hardrick. They agreed it was their lucky day. A Marine armor unit with a couple M67 "Zippo" Patton flamethrower tanks was escorting an engineer unit with Rome plows and bulldozers a few klicks away out on Highway One. Evans gave him a thumbs-up as the last of the CS canisters were tossed into the tunnel openings.

"Charlie-Red-Six, this is Charlie-Whiskey-Six, Over," Sam called for Lieutenant Hardrick over the radio.

"Go ahead, Whiskey-Six."

"Roger, Red-Six, we've dropped CS into all the openings out here. Be advised, you may get some residual down that way."

There was a pause before Hardrick answered. "Damned right we will! We're downwind and—" Hardrick had forgone all radio protocol, but his voice disappeared in an extended squelch of static. When the static ceased the colonel's voice could be heard, "...proper to use the CS first. If we don't flush out any of the enemy, we'll close the openings with the dozers. Over."

By early afternoon it was clear that the tear gas wasn't working, and the armor had arrived. After spraying most of the tunnel openings with the flamethrowers, the engineers set charges and blasted them closed. Afterward the Rome plows and dozers were brought up. Armored versions of the huge Caterpillar D7E bulldozer, the plows went to work leveling the village while the dozers pushed more dirt over the tunnel openings. With no air, it wouldn't take long for anyone below ground to die.

It seemed the ground for a thousand square meters was leveled and the remaining remnants of the village shoved into burning heaps by the dozers. The few enemy soldiers that stumbled to the surface were quickly shot, but mostly there was only the odor of burning gas, greasy black smoke, and the clanking of the plows and dozers. As the flames consumed the last of the hooches, a few of the men gave whoops of joy—no doubt, because they wouldn't have to search them or go into the tunnels to ferret out the enemy. By dusk the entire village, nearly a quarter-square-mile of thatched huts, was gone—replaced by mounds of smoking ashes.

October 2018
I-65 in Southern Alabama

"Are you still with me?" Sam asked.

Claire sat up and gave an involuntary shiver. "How could I not be after that?"

It was after midnight and Sam was growing sleepy as the green interstate highway signs passed by in a continual procession into the night. Only the big rigs were out now, and the traffic was relatively light for I-65.

"Did Captain Calvert die?"

"No. He lived. He returned to the States and made a full recovery."

"Well, at least y'all were able to…" she paused. "Survive…"

"Do you remember when I asked if you wanted to hear the ugly truth about the war?"

She looked over at him. Her face glowed in the dim dashboard lights, but she said nothing.

"This is one of those lessons. When you wonder why old veterans can't talk about the things they saw, you need to remember that surviving isn't necessarily the end of one's wartime experiences."

"What do you mean?"

"I suppose all of us wanted to survive in spite of the things we witnessed, but sometimes the better part of surviving is forgetting what happened back there. It's difficult to do."

Sam gritted his teeth. He had told no one, not even Caroline about this, but it was something he needed to talk about. And whether it was a mea culpa of sorts or simply a statement about the real meaning of war, he didn't know, but it was something people needed to hear if for no other reason than to know about the burden their fathers, brothers, and sons had to bear for having been a part of such an apocalyptic event.

"We never knew for sure where the people in that village had gone, and I've often wondered if they might have been held prisoner by the enemy down there in those tunnels. It's a possibility that's plagued me all my life."

Sam maintained his gaze ahead on the highway. Claire glanced over at him before quickly turning to also stare straight ahead. He watched her from the corner of his eye and after a long while she slowly turned back toward him. It was as if she wanted to say something, but was at a loss for words. Sam felt her eyes searching his face.

"Just remember this: There were shameful things done by some of our men during that war, but most of us weren't the wanton killers we've been made out to be. Regardless, we were damned sure there and have lived the rest of our lives with the fact that a lot of innocent people died on our watch."

"You really haven't said much about the Vietnamese people up to now. Is there a reason?"

"It's probably because my men and I had only minimal interaction with them. We went into maybe a half-dozen villages in the months after Tet '68, but it was always the same. They lied to us, some because they were Vietcong or Vietcong sympathizers. Others lied because if they didn't, the communists gutted them like pigs and had their heads mounted on stakes at the village gate. Like I've said before, the communists had a special way of influencing people. The people did what they had to do to survive.

"Hell, every time we went into a village they smiled at us, but you could see it clearly if you looked them in the eyes. They didn't smile because they were happy to see us. They smiled because it was their instinct—something bred by generations of ancestors who had suffered hordes of invaders over the centuries—the Chinese, the Japanese, the French. They smiled to survive the moment—all the while knowing another horde would eventually come along to take the current one's place."

Sam drove a while longer. Claire gazed into the night, seemingly lost in thought. Neither had slept, and they both needed rest.

"I can't stay awake much longer. I'm pulling into the next rest stop and catching a nap. Why don't you go ahead and try to get some sleep. We can drive on into Pensacola after daylight."

Claire nodded and curled up with her pillow.

CHAPTER TWELVE

Searching for Answers

October, 2018
I-65 Rest Stop south of Evergreen, Alabama

S am inhaled that familiar fragrance, the one he'd so grown to love over the years—the subtle but sensuous odor of Caroline's perfume. It was the only one she ever wore, and he'd experienced it on their first date. A scent with a maddening attraction, it was guaranteed to make any man act a fool, but he'd fought his every instinct that night, realizing he'd found a real lady.

She wore it every time they went on a date, and despite his best efforts, it finally took its toll. He succumbed. After that night Caroline had stolen his heart forever. And the next time he remembered it most was the first time he saw her after months in Vietnam, but now she was here with him again.

He felt her warmth as she rested her head against his shoulder. Gently caressing her hair, he opened his eyes. They were in his truck and the windows were fogged with condensation, but it was daylight outside. He blinked, disoriented and groggy, as he tried to regain some sense of awareness. Only then did he realize where he was and that it wasn't Caroline there sleeping with him.

Claire was lying against him in a deep drooling sleep. *Little*

Claire, my God in heaven. He exhaled with a deep sigh. She was indeed a beautifully attractive woman, but thank God he was now completely awake. She was wearing the same perfume that Caroline had always worn, and he was now fighting back the passion that arose during his dream. He studied her gentle face, but it came to him that she reminded him more of his granddaughter, Annie.

Back when he had taken Annie on a deer hunting trip, she had done the same thing. That evening on the way home she too had fallen asleep on his shoulder, only for him to realize his granddaughter had been wearing perfume she'd sampled from her grandmother's dresser. *It was no wonder they hadn't seen any deer that day. They had probably smelled them from a mile away, and the critters were probably laughing their little tails off at the perfumed hunters.*

Claire's deep sleep, however, unlike Annie's, was induced not by a day of fun, but by Sam's painful recollections of the war. A deep regret gripped him for putting her through what had to have been equally painful for her. No matter how mature she acted, she was still a kid and there was no way she could have prepared for the things he had told her that night. Although it had come as a second-hand report, she'd gotten a true glimpse of the dark side of mankind.

He closed his eyes, and by the time she stirred, the old wounds in his back and shoulder were aching. Her hand was wrapped around his right arm and he reached up and patted it lightly.

"You ready to get back on the road?" he said in a soft voice.

She sat up, rubbing her eyes.

"I need to run up to that restroom and freshen up, if you don't mind," she said.

"No problem. Go ahead. We'll stop down the road and get some coffee and a bag of donuts."

While she was gone, he searched his overnight bag for the

bottle of arthritis pills and thought about his close call. His thoughts and dreams had carried him someplace he would never go with this young woman. After all, in past years there had been many a young co-ed who tried it intentionally. Most suffered from infatuation while others more cynically did so seeking a passing grade. Despite all those temptations he had remained steadfastly anchored to his Caroline. She was all the woman a man could ever want.

When they reached I-10 in Pensacola, Sam glanced over at Claire. She had again slumped in her seat and was napping.

"Hey, sleepyhead, you never told me where you made our hotel reservations."

She sat up, stretched, and pulled her cell phone from her purse. "The Hilton, out near the airport. Hang on. I'm googling it now."

A few minutes later they pulled up out front.

"I suggest we get our rooms, rest and clean up and meet downstairs around noon. We can grab some lunch and head down to the Vet Center. I spoke with a counselor there this week. She's coming in today at 1:00 to talk with us. She promised to call around to the other Veterans' offices this week to see if she could get us any leads."

They walked through the automated doors into the hotel lobby. Sam carried his bag and one of Claire's. She trailed behind him, carrying the others along with her purse.

"Uh, there's just one thing," she said. Claire paused inside the door. Her lips were turned down at the corners.

Sam stopped and glanced back. "What's wrong?"

"I only reserved one room for us."

"You what? What the h—!" He caught himself and took a deep breath. "Why did you do that?"

"I saved you a ton of money, and it's not like we're sleeping in the same bed. I got a room with two queen beds. Besides, it was the last one they had available and I didn't think—"

"That's pretty damned obvious, young lady. Come on." Sam turned toward the front desk. "I can remedy that. Whose name did you put on the reservation?"

"Yours."

Sam stepped up to the desk. "I have a room reserved. Sam Walker. And I need to add a second room, please."

"I am sorry, Mister Walker, but we have no more rooms available. I'll be happy to call around for you and check for vacancies but I seriously doubt that with fall break you'll find another room anywhere in the area. Every room between Panama City Beach and Gulf Shores is probably booked by now."

Sam turned toward Claire, but she had turned away and pretended to gaze toward the front doors. Her feigned nonchalance was betrayed by cheeks that were burning crimson. Avoiding eye contact was probably best—at least for the moment. Even the brightest ones of this generation seemed prone to colossal misjudgments, and this was one situation that even a modicum of common sense could have prevented.

He turned back to the desk clerk. "If you have any last minute cancellations, I will take whatever room becomes available. I suppose I'll take the one room for now."

The ride up the elevator was one of stony silence. Sam could only think of his own granddaughter and how Annie had shown some of the same brash overconfidence and lack of judgment. Thank God she lived in California and he heard about it after the fact and second-hand from Caroline. It was tempting to lecture Claire, but they were both tired and he wanted to let his anger subside. He let them into the room.

"I'll take the bed nearest the restroom," he said. "It's an old man thing you'll understand later."

"You don't have to explain. I lived with Papa Pearle for a long time."

"Well, *I* am NOT your grandfather! I may be old, but I'm not dead, leastwise not yet, and I…"

Tears filled her eyes, and Sam tossed the bags on his bed and stepped forward, taking her by the hand. "Okay, I'm sorry, Claire. I shouldn't have shouted at you."

Despite her lack of judgement, he wondered if he wasn't angry more with himself than her.

"Sam, sometimes I just don't think, and I do stupid stuff, but—"

"It's okay. We'll talk more about it later. Just calm down."

"Well, don't you see? I mean, I know I've been stupid and thoughtless, and I'm sorry. It's just that I've never felt so alone as I have since Papa Pearle died. Mama's gone. Daddy's gone. I trust you, Sam, and I've known from the very beginning what kind of man you are. Please, don't be mad at me."

She leaned her head against his chest. "I'm sorry. I just wasn't thinking."

Sam gave her a gentle hug. "It's okay."

She looked up at him. "Do you know I haven't had anyone give me a real hug since Papa Pearle died? …and Brad's gropes don't count."

Sam looked down at her and smiled while smoothing her hair with his hand. "Okay. It's official. I will be your adopted grandfather, and hugs are free anytime. How's that?"

"Thank you, Sam."

"Just one thing, little lady. There's a caveat to our relationship."

She looked up at him in expectant silence. He thumbed a tear from beneath her eye. "The hugs may come with occasional lectures and even a mild scolding now and then."

She pulled her right arm free and extended her hand. "Deal," she said, and they shook hands.

"You get the bath first," Sam said. "I'm going to lie on the bed and nap for an hour or so. I'll get a shower when I get up."

After their meeting with the counselor at the Vet Center, Sam was somewhat encouraged. Claire's father had been picked up by the Pensacola Police down near Seville Square and released. He had also visited the American Legion on Intendencia Street at least one time. The south side of the city seemed to be his location of choice, but even if he was still in the area, there remained a lot of ground to cover.

"Let's get an early supper then start hitting the parks and the obvious places. What do you say?"

Claire seemed lost in thought as she slowly nodded. It was tempting to ask her what was on her mind, but Sam decided she would talk when she was ready. They drove around Pensacola, first to Lee Square, then Fort George. Next it was Plaza Ferdinand VII and Aragon Park. The daylight was fading to dusk when they arrived at Seville Square.

Sam parked the truck and strolled down the sidewalk beneath the live oaks. It was quiet in the park and the stroll would have been enjoyable except that his back and feet were beginning to ache, and it was only the first day. Old age was a bitch, but he wasn't complaining.

They came across a man lying on a bench, but their questions were fruitless. All day they had found one thing common among the homeless people they encountered. All of them remained tight-lipped and seemingly paranoid. If they knew anything, they weren't revealing it. Claire had come to tears with one young veteran who she was certain knew something, but it came to naught. Music floated through the park from a nearby bar as they made their way back to the truck.

"What now?" Claire asked in a faraway voice.

Despite his sore feet, aching back, and second thoughts, Sam gave her his best smile. "Buck up, sweet thang. This is only our first day. We still have a lot of ground to cover."

She looked over at him and took his hand, and Sam hoped he wasn't leading her on some quixotic quest where she would be met with the same rejection her mother had gotten the summer before. It was one of the most troublesome symptoms for those with traumatic brain injuries. They became easily agitated and irritable, often turning their anger on those closest to them.

"We'll head back to the hotel, have a beverage or two and hit the sack early. We've still got a lot of parks to search tomorrow."

It was only 8:30 that evening when Sam and Claire returned to their room, but Sam was pretty sure neither of them was feeling much pain. She had put away two glasses of white wine and he'd downed two doubles of Makers Mark. He pulled the sheet up and tossed his clothes out on the floor. Claire was still wearing her clothes and shoes as she sat on her bed watching him.

"Aren't you going to bed?" he asked. "You know us old folks need our beauty rest."

She shrugged. "Can I turn on my recorder and we talk for just a few minutes about that day at the village when you were in Vietnam?"

"You *are* driven, little lady, but since I am pleasantly inebriated, I am at your service."

Sam propped himself against the backboard knowing that if he didn't sit upright, he'd be gone in minutes. He thought again about that day in the village. It was one of those memories he had worked hard to bury forever, but it was now exhumed. He took a deep breath and exhaled.

"I'll continue with my story, but I don't want to talk about that village anymore—at least not now. I mean it's just—"

"It's okay. I understand."

Their eyes met and Sam nodded. She did understand, and that was what made all this seem worthwhile.

Republic of Vietnam
South of Hue, February 1968

The 82nd Airborne was in a tumultuous flux with many of the combat veterans from previous tours appealing to their congressmen back home. Most had returned to the States only within the last few months, and by right, they weren't supposed to be here again—at least not in such a short time. They deserved to go home or at least out of harm's way. Sam agreed. The majority of his men had already served their time in this hell hole, and this war was different in so many ways from other conflicts.

Enemy contact here in Vietnam was much more frequent than in other wars, and unlike their fathers' and grandfathers' wars, there were no front lines here. The helicopters were a nice means of transportation, but they were also a means for the top brass to rush them from one battle to the next almost continuously. And not the least of it was that indefinable apparition called the enemy that appeared in insurmountable numbers, inflicting gross numbers of casualties, only to melt away as soon as the Americans gained the advantage.

Fighting the Vietcong and the North Vietnamese was the equivalent of wrestling with smoke, and it had become deeply frustrating for the men as they watched their buddies day after day being blown to hell, maimed and killed by booby-traps. And there was the heavy artillery bombardments coming across the borders and the DMZ from areas they weren't allowed to touch. They were chin-deep in the reality of an oxymoron called "limited war." Wars for those who must fight them normally demand an all-out effort to seek victory, however it is defined. Sam's problem was he had no idea what victory in Vietnam would look like.

The company had been pulled back near the Perfume River just south of Hue to refit. Lieutenant DeGrass had lost half of his weapons platoon, seven of which were Killed In Action. Sam and Doug Stone had no KIAs, but had three men medevaced with wounds. Hardrick had lost three men KIA and seven WIA from First Platoon. The battalion commander brought in a new platoon leader for First Platoon, Lieutenant Jim Powell. By virtue of his time in rank, Hardrick was appointed acting company commander. None of the platoon leaders spoke a word when they got the news, but it wasn't necessary. Their eyes said to one another what words could not.

Upon reaching the staging area, Hardrick wasted no time bringing his officers together for the first time since the disastrous mission two days before at the village. Ponchos were stretched overhead as the rain-soaked officers knelt beneath the makeshift shelter in the wet grass. Smoking cigarettes and slapping mosquitoes, they waited in silence while Hardrick made a show of reviewing his notes. Flipping pages, he pressed his lips tightly together and nodded to no one in particular. Across the river in the city of Hue, the sounds of battle continued with the cracking and popping of small arms interspersed with the explosions of hand grenades and RPGs. Occasionally, there came the thundering boom of a tank's main gun.

"The first thing we're going to do is a self-critique of what we did wrong at the village the other day," Hardrick said. "I have to send my After Action Report to the Battalion Commander by 0900 tomorrow and I don't intend to make a lot of excuses for our poor performance."

The officers glanced around at one another while First Platoon's new second lieutenant, Powell, nodded as if he agreed. Hardrick seemed to take satisfaction from Powell's nod. Sam was pretty certain it was more of an unconscious response coming from a young officer who didn't know his ass from a hole in the ground. The only one who seemed to know less than this new guy was Hardrick.

"Lieutenant Degrass, let me ask you first. How did you fail to provide proper security for the headquarters group?"

Degrass's face turned to stone and flushed blood-red with anger, but he said nothing.

"Okay," Hardrick said, "The CO, his RTO and the entire recoilless rifle crew are taken out right at the start of the fight with an RPG. Come on. Tell me. How the hell did that happen? Where were you? Answer my question, Lieutenant. Did you learn anything from that fucking fiasco or is *my* headquarters group going to end up the same way?"

Sam was the only one of them with previous combat experience and he knew exactly how it happened. It happened because the enemy was on his home turf and had the area well prepared in advance of their arrival. The enemy was cunning and knew how to breach the very best defensive formation. Nothing short of a B-52 Arc Light strike would have prevented the ambush.

"Lieutenant Hardrick, the only thing that might have prevented what occurred would have been an Arc Light strike."

Hardrick slowly turned toward Sam with a vitriolic grin. "So, Lieutenant Walker, you would have called in the B-52s to destroy the entire village and slaughter all its inhabitants. Is that what you're saying?"

"I think you know damned well that's not what I'm saying, Lieutenant. What I—"

"Well, it sure sounded like it to me. I thought with your previous combat experience you could do better than that."

Sam took a deep breath and paused before he spoke. He had to keep himself in check. "Sir, I would like to help you, but I don't think we're going to see eye to eye on much of anything. I believe it will be best for both of us if you passed my request for reassignment up to the colonel."

Hardrick had to know this would be a poor reflection on him because of Sam's reputation. He gave a knowing nod. "So, you want to desert your men, right? Now that things have gotten a little hot, you want to leave them for greener pastures. Is that it? Do I hear you right, *Second* Lieutenant?"

Sam inhaled deeply from his cigarette, looked down and dropped it in the grass. He mashed it under his jungle boot. Hardrick was right. It *was* the easy way out and there was no telling what would become of his men with an egotistical idiot like Hardrick as company commander. Many of them might die needlessly.

"You know, on second thought, you make a good point, Lieutenant. I withdraw my request. I need to be here for them."

Hardrick seemed caught off-guard by Sam's sudden reversal. "Yes, well…" Despite a plastic smile, his eyes darted left and right as he glanced around at the other officers while he spoke. "I suppose we will see how that works out. You certainly took care of them the other day when you pulled back and exposed my left flank."

"Beg your pardon, sir," Doug Stone said, "but that was a plan we discussed over the radio for Walker to move back and relieve weapons platoon while I brought my platoon into the village to pull your bacon out of the fire."

Hardrick's smile faded and his eyes darted around at the other lieutenants. Only now did he seem to realize how much he had alienated them. Even his fellow Academy grad had called him out.

"All right, gentlemen, perhaps we got off on the wrong foot. Let's start over, but keep in mind that I am *not* Captain Calvert. I am going to run a tight and well-disciplined outfit. First, I want to spend a few days working with my old platoon and bring Lieutenant Powell up to speed. Meanwhile, I want the rest of you to ensure we have tight security on the perimeter and bring your replacements up to speed as well. Any questions?"

The patter of the rain continued on the ponchos hanging above their heads while across the river a firefight had ignited and raged with a distant but continuous roar.

"All right then. Except for you, Jim, you men are dismissed."

Sam lit a cigarette and trudged back through the rain toward Second Platoon. Behind him he heard the squishing of footsteps in the mud. It was Doug Stone.

"You all right?" Stone asked.

"Yeah."

"Sam, I have to tell you, I met some assholes while I was at the military academy, but I don't think I've ever met one as fucked up as Hardrick."

Sam sucked hard on his unfiltered Camel and exhaled into the misting rain. "Training can overcome only so much," he said. "I'm surprised the moron made it this far. We just need to keep an eye on him so he doesn't get a bunch of our people hurt."

Stone glanced over his shoulder. It was pretty obvious he didn't want to be overheard. "I agree, but don't you think Hard Dick acting like a mother hen with the new guy is a bit strange?"

Sam gave him a wry glance. "I would think it was a good thing if it weren't for the fact that it's the blind leading the blind. I'll try to help Powell when I can. He seems like a pretty bright guy."

———————————

Late April 1968
Firebase Birmingham, Republic of Vietnam

Sam's platoon was on point that morning. It was a rare day of actual sunshine, but with it came the heat. March and much of April had passed and it seemed the war gods were smiling down on them. For the last several weeks, the company had experienced only occasional light enemy contact while surrounding units were locked in firefights almost daily. Their time was coming, Sam had no doubt. No one in the company expected their luck to continue as they patrolled the hills southwest of Hue.

The lack of contact seemed especially fortunate since the company was experiencing a constant turnover in manpower. Many of the old heads who had served previous tours were given thirty-day leaves and some were allowed to return to the States permanently, including Sam's platoon sergeant, Evans. His replacement was a newly promoted buck sergeant, Dale Rainmaker. He was a diminutive guy, quiet and unassuming who for some reason, despite this, seemed to draw strong respect from the men.

Rainmaker had *some* combat experience and seemed competent but said little. The men liked him because he wasn't a bullshitter, and there was a calmness about him that led to a feeling of security amongst the others. Sam's gut told him Rainmaker was going to do well as an NCO.

More replacements were brought in and units were combined, but the influx of inexperienced men only created more sleepless nights for Sam and the other platoon leaders. Today after weeks beating the bush, they were moving to a new firebase on Highway 547 for a much-needed day or two of rest and resupply. Sam hoped to use the time to coach some of his newbies on the finer elements of surviving the shit.

Exhausted, dirty, bug-bitten and ragged, Sam's platoon led the way through the wire and up the red dirt hill into Firebase

Birmingham. The men of the 101st greeted them with the usual good-natured cat calls and insults while an officer pointed out their new digs. And they were "new digs" indeed—partially completed bunkers, some with no overhead cover. The firebase was still under construction. Below, on the south side of the firebase, was the Perfume River. The Vietnamese had other names for it, Sông Hương or Hương Giang, but given its strangely sweet odor, the anglicized name fit well.

The only positive thing about their entire situation was that the 101st would provide perimeter security while the men from the 82nd got new fatigues, socks, and ammunition, and also what Sam hoped would be a decent night's sleep. They needed it. He'd had little time to talk with his new men, and most still seemed lost despite some good coaching from Rainmaker and the old heads. A few good talks with them might help restore their morale.

The weeks of humping the bush seemed to have taken some of the fire and brimstone out of Hardrick, but Sam and the other platoon leaders continued regarding him with the cautious sentiments of miners handling dynamite. The first lieutenant was still trying to find his way as acting company commander and doing his best to impress the battalion commander. This led to the enlisted men mumbling to one another about his acid tongue and relentless quest for glory.

Sam's men were growing more sullen every day. All they cared about was surviving what seemed like a pointless war, but Hardrick had been volunteering them for every mission that came along—everything from extra patrols to night ambushes. They were tired, and their anger had the potential to grow into something much worse if someone didn't address their concerns.

Trying to reason with Hardrick was certain to be an exercise in futility. Sam hoped spending time with the men—listening and engaging them in conversation—would pre-empt anything foolhardy on their part.

Gathered around the sandbagged pit of an unfinished bunker that afternoon, the men were cleaning weapons when Sam joined them. He began cleaning his M-16 while smoking a cigarette. His new platoon RTO had already cleaned and reassembled his rifle and was now spooning the last of the ham and lima beans from a can of C-rations. It seemed PFC Chewy Lovejoy actually loved C-rations.

Chewy was from Alabama—lived on a hill in a trailer park. Said his mama's trailer was in the thirty-first row up the hill from the highway. She chain-smoked Marlboros and drank Pepsi, but Chewy wasn't sure which of her ex-boyfriends was his daddy. She signed his paper to enlist in the Army the day he turned seventeen. Chewy hadn't graduated from high school, but Sam had grown to trust his young radioman. He was a piece of work, but a good soldier who did his job and watched his back. A platoon leader couldn't ask for much more.

Sergeant Dale Rainmaker, the new platoon sergeant, was a full-blooded Cherokee from Sallisaw, Oklahoma. He clenched a Kool cigarette between his front teeth and squinted through the smoke, while studying Chewy. After a moment he pinched the cigarette from his mouth, set it aside on a sandbag and ran the cleaning rod down the barrel of his M-16.

"You see the date on that ration box, Chewy?" Rainmaker asked. He motioned to the empty cardboard case the C-rations had come in. "Those C-rats are damned near old as you."

Several of the men laughed. The year 1953 was clearly stamped on the discarded box.

"Sonsabitches were canned back during the Korean War," Fergie said. "I reckon we should be thankful Uncle Sam is so damned frugal with our tax dollars."

Sam had promoted and moved Fergie to a squad leader's position. He was a smart kid and only needed a little polishing as an NCO.

"Maybe so," Rainmaker said, "but in this case, I'm thinkin' the tightwad bastard could spend a few extra bucks and get us some lurp rations. Know what I mean?"

Chewy dropped the empty can in the dirt and crushed it with his boot. "These here Cs are pretty okay with me."

"A man with expedient, if not epicurean, taste," Sam said.

"What's that mean?" Chewy asked.

"Means you could sit on a gut pile and eat cheese," Fergie said.

Chewy wrinkled his top lip and squinted.

"Not really," Sam said, and he turned to Fergie as he spoke. "I think what Sergeant Ferguson means to say is you have the good taste for what's convenient—even under the conditions out here in the bush. Right, Fergie?"

"Uh, yes sir. I guess that's what I was trying to say."

Chewy grinned and fished his dog tag chain and P-38 out of his flak jacket. He began opening a can of ham and eggs.

"You *do* know they're bringing in a hot meal on the resupply chopper later, don't you?" Rainmaker asked.

"Don't matter," Chewy said. "Hell, I ate mayonnaise sandwiches on stale bread for two weeks one time when my mama left with one of her boyfriends. Nope, it don't get much better'n this."

The fifteen-year-old ham and eggs were gone in seconds and Chewy licked his plastic spoon before sticking it back in his shirt pocket.

"Anybody who likes C-rats that much just ain't right," Campanella said.

"Maybe that's why Chewy's breath always smells like dog shit," Tim Batters said. "Cs smell like a fresh fart to me every time I open one."

"Okay guys, let's cut my RTO some slack," Sam said. "How's everybody's feet? Any problems?"

"It's not my feet I'm worried about," Shanks said. "It's my ass."

Shanks, a black kid from Ohio, seldom said much, so he caught everyone's attention.

"I take it you're talking about something besides hemorrhoids or crotch-rot," Sam said.

"Damn right, I am," the young soldier muttered. "We keep getting volunteered to walk point for the battalion, and last week it was us who got sent into that village first. That Mickey Mouse motherfucker running this company is—"

"Shanks! Let me ask you something," Sam said.

Everyone was suddenly silent and gazing at the lieutenant.

"What really matters most to you here in Nam?"

"That's pretty fuckin' easy, LT. Getting my ass outta here and back to the world in one piece."

"Damned right," Campanella said. The others nodded in silent agreement.

Sam set his M-16 aside and took off his helmet. "I agree, and that is what I am going to do my best to help you accomplish, but I want you guys to listen to me. Most of us didn't choose to be here. Most of us would rather be almost anywhere besides here, but short of ruining our lives this is what we chose to do. We didn't dodge the draft or run off to Canada like a lot of the wusses back home. Hell, every one of us took it a step further. We became paratroopers. And it's important now that you don't do anything foolish that might ruin your life. I'd rather mine ended here in Nam than spend the rest of it in Leavenworth."

The men began shifting about uneasily and some gazed past him. Sam stood up. He had to drive his point home.

"I want you guys to keep one thing foremost in your minds. The best chance for us to get out of here alive is to stick together and look out for one another. As your platoon leader, I will always be out front and I will never ask you to do anything I won't do myself. I'll also do whatever I can to minimize our risks, and I will never ask you to take on more than your share of the load."

"Uh, sir," Chewy said.

Sam gazed down at him and Chewy motioned with his chin to Sam's rear. He turned to find Hardrick standing on the berm above him. He had his hands on his hips and was wearing his usual sideways grin. Sam knew now why the men had suddenly shifted about and gazed past him.

"Nice speech, Lieutenant," Hardrick said.

"It wasn't a speech, Lieutenant. It was…" Sam paused. "Would you like to say something to the men?"

"Sure," Hardrick said.

Sam's regret was immediate. Hungry wolves might howl in the night for full bellies, but the hearts of his men would remain empty for the likes of Hardrick, no matter how much he talked. He spread his feet apart, raised his chin and placed the heel of one hand on his holstered pistol. The melodramatic gesture didn't escape them as several of the men cut their eyes at one another and traded knowing grins. Hardrick, of course, was oblivious.

"Gentlemen," he began. "I have an announcement to make. So, listen up. We are the 82nd Airborne and tomorrow we're going to show these screaming chickens of the Hundred and First what real paratroopers look like. We will be air assaulting into an area north of here and setting up as a blocking force behind some villages. The one goal I want you to keep in mind is body-count. You hear me? *Body-count, body-count, body-count*—that is our goal. We made a name for ourselves back in March with an estimated hundred and ninety-five kills in that first village we assaulted."

Sam was stunned and couldn't help himself as he threw his head around and stared up at Hardrick. There were only eighteen confirmed enemy dead from that first battle. The other estimates were those accounting for the missing villagers—the ones they had likely buried in the underground tunnels.

Hardrick's face flushed as he pretended not to notice Sam's steadfast gaze.

"The old man wants more body-count and we're going to give it to him. You hear me? We are the Airborne. We are the best. We are going to be aggressive and show no quarter tomorrow. *Let me hear you. Airborne!*"

A couple of the cherries sounded off, "*All the way,*" but quickly looked around at the others who remained largely silent.

"Fine group of men you have here, Lieutenant Walker, but you might want to work on their morale. They seem a bit down."

Sam had found his best defense in situations such as this was to simply smile—which he did. "They will do their jobs when the time comes, Lieutenant. Be assured of that."

Hardrick pursed his lips and cocked his head back.

"Let's hope so."

October 2018
Pensacola, Florida

Other than the hum of the air-conditioning system, the room was quiet. Sam glanced over at Claire. She was sleeping soundly, but a small LED light indicated her recorder was still running. He got up, quietly pushed the Off button and set the recorder aside. Claire was lying on top of her blankets. He carefully removed her shoes and took a blanket from his bed. After gently laying it over her, he tucked her in and turned off the bedside lamp.

If nothing else, it seemed all this reminiscing and Claire's friendship were beginning to have a more positive effect on his psyche. It was as if the thick layers of protection he'd built over the years were not only being peeled away, but they were also no longer necessary. The nightmares had become somewhat less frequent the last few days. And it made him think again of just how much of a saving angel Caroline had been for him.

Since her death, he had begun once again to retreat inside himself, much as he had done immediately after returning from Nam. Now it was little Claire who had helped him see the path beyond the darkness.

He lay back on his bed and quickly slipped into a restful sleep.

CHAPTER THIRTEEN

No Safe Place

October 2018
Pensacola, Florida

S am's eyes opened and he stared disoriented at the ceiling for several seconds before realizing where he was. He had been dreaming again and it was much the same dream as the one he had at the rest stop when he dreamt of Caroline, except this time, he had also dreamt of Claire. He was a silly old fool, and there wasn't a chance in hell he would act on his dreams, but he planned to call the front desk as soon as she wasn't around to see if they had any cancellations.

Turning, he glanced over at the other bed. It was empty and tiny beams of sunshine were streaming in around the closed window drapes. He heard a sound and turned to find the bathroom door closed, but there was the wonderful scent of coffee brewing. A moment later the door opened.

"I fixed you some coffee," Claire said as she circled the bed. She set the cup on the bedside table and smiled. Her head was wrapped in the cone of a white towel. His granddaughter, Annie, was the one who often made his morning coffee when she came to visit, and he wanted to tell Claire how much she reminded him of her, but early morning conversations were no longer one of his strong suits. He sat up on the side of the bed and sipped the coffee.

"I'm going to sit on my bed and dry my hair, so the bathroom is all yours," she said.

"Thanks. I'll hurry so we can go down before they stop serving breakfast."

———————————

Sam and Claire found an alcove on one side of the breakfast area and sat quietly with the recorder running.

"Sorry. I didn't mean to fall asleep on you last night," she said.

"Don't worry. Your recorder got what you missed."

"Last thing I remember was y'all had reached a safe place on a firebase to rest for a couple days."

Sam gazed across the lobby of the hotel, and wondered if there was ever really such a thing as a "safe place." There was certainly no such thing in Vietnam.

"That 'safe place' thing is somewhat of a misconception. You see, danger was everywhere, and it was present almost every hour of every day. No place was truly safe. Never did we exhale and totally relax. Never could we entirely let down our guard, because no matter where we were, there was always the chance of an enemy attack.

"In the boonies we expected it to be that way—booby-traps, snipers, ambushes, and the random rocket and mortar attacks. Those things happened often, but there was also danger elsewhere—even in the cities. The VC bombed everything from bars and restaurants to USO shows. There simply were no true 'rear' areas.

"You know, we officers were not authorized to carry our sidearms when in so-called 'safe' areas like Saigon and other big cities, but we did. That's because the Vietcong were everywhere, in every city, town, and village, and they watched and waited for the careless individual who let down his guard. If a soldier got too much to drink in a bar or wandered too far off the main drag he could easily wake up starved, feverish, and dying in a bamboo cell somewhere in the jungle. It happened.

"It didn't matter if you were on the beach at Vung Tau, in a hotel in Saigon, or on a firebase surrounded with sandbags and barbed wire. A random rocket or mortar round could find you anywhere and send you into eternity as a fine red mist. A tour of duty in Nam was twelve months where you exhaled only when the blue waters of the South China Sea passed beneath your freedom bird. I believe that's why that war had such lasting effects on the men who served there."

Claire sat in silence while Sam sipped his coffee and studied her. If America was to have a worthwhile future, it would be because of young thinkers like her. She noticed his steadfast gaze and reached across the table, placing her hand over his.

"You never finished telling me about Caroline. When did y'all get married?"

"I didn't think I had told you we were married. Did I?"

"Sam, duh! You have a picture of her on your wall at home in a bikini. I don't think any self-respecting woman is going to let a man put a picture of another woman in a bikini on her wall—especially one of an ex-girlfriend."

Sam closed his eyes, grinned and shook his head. "Yeah, you're right. I suppose the glow of my one remaining brain cell is beginning to fade."

She patted the back of his hand. "Drink some more coffee. I'm sure it will start glowing in a minute or two. So, did you finally start answering her letters?"

"Yeah, I did. I got one from her one day after a pretty bad firefight. We had lost one of our men. I don't know exactly why, but something made me realize then that, whether I committed to her or not, things would be the same if I got killed. She refused to give up on me, so I wrote her a very long three-page letter telling her how much I loved her and how she had been with me every day since I arrived in Vietnam.

"She was graduating from Appalachian State by then and in her next letter she said she was coming to visit me. I don't know how she got that idea, but I had to write back and tell her that was impossible. They wouldn't allow her into the country."

"So there was no way of seeing her?"

"The army had a program for married personnel to go to Hawaii to meet their spouses on R&R, but since we weren't married, I wasn't sure I could qualify. I wrote her again later and told her I would try to get more information."

Sam reached across the table and punched off the recorder. "We have a lot of ground to cover today. Are you ready to get started?"

Despite the perplexed look on her face, Claire nodded. "Where are we going?"

"I thought we'd check some more places like the Waterfront Rescue Mission, Escambia County Jail, and maybe the local VFW. I think we should also go back to several of the parks and try to talk with some of those homeless people again. I just wish we had a recent photo of him."

Sam had to admit that back when he first turned seventy he realized he no longer had much stamina, and it didn't help that Claire had fixed him a waffle with butter and maple syrup for breakfast. No amount of coffee was going to overcome that. He tossed her the truck keys.

"You're the pilot today. I'm navigating for you."

"You still haven't fully recovered from that all-night drive, have you?"

He grinned. "If I doze off, wake me up."

———————

By midafternoon they had returned to the hotel. Despite hours of pounding sidewalks and conversations with dozens of strangers, the day had resulted in nothing new. Claire was difficult to read, and Sam wasn't sure if it was her disappointment or perhaps simply that she was tired after the day's search. Whatever it was, she was quieter than normal.

"You okay?" he asked.

"Yeah, sure. What's the plan?"

"Why don't we take your recorder and go to the beach, catch some sun and relax?"

For the first time that day her face lit up.

"Really?"

"Sure. You look like you could use a little rest. Did you bring something to wear on the beach?"

It was as if he'd thrown a switch and she came to life.

"I have some shorts and a tank top," she said as she ripped into her bag.

They drove across the causeway and out to the Gulf that afternoon. The heavy traffic should have been a tip-off, but Sam had neglected to think about one thing. It was fall break for almost every college kid in the South.

"Oh my—look at all the people," Claire said. "There must be hundreds—thousands."

Pensacola Beach was packed with college kids, and Sam wasn't sure his suggested beach visit was such a good idea after all. Volleyball nets, beach chairs, umbrellas, boogie boards and thousands of college students crammed the white sand beach east and west as far as he could see.

"Look at this," Claire said. Her eyes were wide with wonderment. "It's unbelievable. It's like one gigantic beach party."

"I didn't realize fall break was such a big deal down here," Sam said.

"I know. I thought spring break was the big attraction."

She lowered the window on her side and began taking photos with her cell phone. The blue-green waters of the Gulf of Mexico rose in gentle swells and the waves broke in crystalline white foam, sliding up the sand beach. It was inviting, but there was not a square inch of sand that wasn't already claimed with umbrellas, blankets, and chairs. Sam continued driving eastward down the beach highway.

"Do you want to join the beach party or try to find someplace that's not quite so crowded?"

"It's tempting, for sure," she said. Claire gazed out at the throngs. After a few moments she turned and smiled. "I think maybe we should try to find someplace that's not as crowded. I really want to work on my thesis some more."

Any kid who could turn her back on a beach party like that had to know herself and where she was going, but Sam worried. Claire seemed almost *too* driven.

"You sure? Looks like they're having a blast out there."

"Yeah. I like a good party, but I'd rather be with people I know or at least friends of friends. I'm going to pass."

Sam couldn't agree more, but she still needed to relax and let go for a few hours.

"According to a brochure I saw at the hotel, there's a state park somewhere down this way. It requires an entry fee, so I'm betting we'll find a quieter spot there. What about it?"

"Sounds good," she said.

With the windows down, the salty odor of the gulf filled the pickup and for a moment Sam thought back to that trip with Ausie to Hawaii—before all this began. It seemed a time far away and long ago, yet here he was, living it again. And this time, his Ausie was a twenty-one-year-old college co-ed named Claire. His life had indeed been an almost surreal journey that had awarded him with friends as dear to him as any member of his family.

They found a beach where a few like-minded people had fled the crowds. Walking with chairs and beach towels they crossed the dunes and followed the sound of the crashing surf to the shore. Sam sat in his chair, while Claire spread her beach towel and pulled the recorder from her canvas bag. She lay back on the towel and started the recorder.

"You are relentless, Claire my dear."

She looked up at him with disappointment and switched off the recorder. "I suppose you're right. It's just that I—"

"Turn it back on, but no sleeping this time."

Her eyes glowed. "I promise—no sleeping this time."

Sam gazed out at the distant gulf horizon a while before again finding himself lost in the memories of his time in Vietnam.

April 1968
Firebase Birmingham, Republic of Vietnam

"When they said 'one day of rest' they sure didn't lie," Chewy bitched.

"Come on, Chewy," Sam said. "Admit it. You were getting bored sitting around. Besides, it was actually two nights' sleep and one full day's rest."

"Shiiuut, LT, them damned howitzers woke me up three times last night, but I gotta admit I could'a spent the rest of this cotton-pickin' war sittin' on that hill if they let me."

The sun was rising in the east that morning as the company humped down to the low pad area north of the base to board choppers. They had a new mission involving an air assault into an area of occupied villages located west of Hue and south of

Highway One. Part of a joint task force under the command of the 101st, the company was once again on the hunt for Charlie.

The platoon sergeants were dividing their men into sticks, each of which would be assigned to the helicopters when they arrived. Hardrick was high strung and barking orders at men who already knew better than him what to do next. Sam wanted to tell him to lighten up and let the men do their jobs, but thought better of it. Doug Stone walked up behind him and placed his hand on his shoulder.

"We should send that sonofabitch to search for riser grease and canopy lights," Stone said.

Sam said nothing as he shook his head in resignation.

"Buck up, partner," Stone said. "I'm sure it'll get worse."

"Love your optimism, Doug."

Shortly after sunrise the choppers lifted skyward and thundered out across the hills toward the swampy lowlands to the north. The warm air on the ground was replaced by a cool wind blowing through the open cabin as Sam sat between Chewy and Fergie, their legs dangling from the Huey. He was aboard the lead chopper for the planned combat assault into a rice paddy area south of the villages.

Their mission was to hump westward from the LZ and set up as a blocking force for the Hundred and First troopers coming into the villages from Highway One to the north. S-2 had reported a large NVA force infiltrating the hamlets and villages there and making their way eastward toward Hue. Contact with the enemy was almost certain.

For the first time in two and a half months Sam was rested, dry, and wearing new fatigues, socks, and jungle boots. For a brief moment life was good, but he buckled his chin strap and checked his M-16. Up ahead vast stretches of rice paddies came into view. They sparkled in the morning sunlight. Beyond them were the clustered thatched roofs of the villages lining the highway for several kilometers. The enemy could be almost anywhere. They might be in the villages or hidden along the edges of the rice paddies, or in the hills back to the southwest.

The choppers began dropping closer to the treetops and the sunlight reflecting from the paddies became nearly blinding. Fergie tapped his shoulder and pointed ahead to a distant stream of green smoke drifting across one of the paddies. Sam gave him a thumbs-up. It seemed life had offered at least one small blessing today. Green smoke meant it was a cold LZ—at least for now.

Within minutes, Sam's new boots and fatigues were soaked with slimy muck while a salty sweat dripped from beneath his helmet as he directed his platoon to secure the south side of the LZ. So far, so good, and Lieutenant Powell was now arriving with First Platoon in the next wave. Sam watched from a nearby dike as the young lieutenant ran and squatted with several of his men in some palms near the LZ. Powell seemed disoriented while his new platoon sergeant and all his inexperienced squad leaders knelt, waiting and watching him for a signal.

"Sergeant Rainmaker," Sam said, "stay with the platoon while I cross over there and help Lieutenant Powell organize his platoon."

With that, Sam dropped his rucksack and sprinted across the LZ ahead of more inbound choppers. A few moments later he dropped to a knee beside Powell. The young lieutenant was holding his compass in the palm of his hand and studying a map.

"What's up, Jim?" Sam asked.

"Just trying to get my bearings here."

"Okay, the villages are out there," Sam said, pointing to the north. "See them? I believe the CO said the plan is for you to form your men up and move out over this way about two hundred meters."

Sam pointed to the west, and the red-faced Powell nodded rapidly. "Thanks, Sam."

Powell immediately signaled to his men along the LZ to spread out and move forward. Despite his inexperience, it seemed he would make a good platoon leader. Sam glanced back as the third flight of choppers landed and lifted off. Hardrick was coming his way as Sam started back across the LZ to his men.

"What are you doing over here? Why aren't you with your platoon?"

"I was helping Lieutenant Powell get his men organized, Lieutenant."

"You let *me* run my company, Lieutenant. Lieutenant Powell seems to have his men well under control. You need to get back over there with yours."

The company RTO and first sergeant turned away and Sam found himself gritting his teeth. Had the company not been in the middle of an air assault, he might have lost his temper.

"Sorry, sir—didn't mean to interfere."

Hardrick said nothing but stood with a fist on his hip staring as Sam turned and sprinted back across the LZ. After the last Slicks had delivered the rest of the company, Hardrick put Powell's First Platoon on the point and the company began the hump westward. The men from the Hundred and First weren't supposed to move into the villages until 1200 hours. It was 0845 hours. There was plenty of time to reach the objective and deploy, but Hardrick was standing atop a rice paddy dike pumping his fist in the air—signaling ahead for Powell to move faster.

Sergeant Rainmaker eased up beside Sam and motioned with his head. "He's in too much of a hurry. We need to be careful. These damned dikes are probably booby-trapped."

"I know. Tell Fergie, Blackie, and Mick to ignore him, stay off the dikes, and stay focused. If First Platoon gets too far ahead, I'll go over and have a word with him."

After an hour Sam realized his platoon was being left behind. With his men avoiding the dikes, they had become winded from fighting the muck in the rice paddies. They had less than a klick to go to reach their objective where the plan was to block the backside of the villages, but the company was strung out for several hundred meters and nearly exhausted.

He motioned to Chewy. "Give me the handset."

"Charlie-Six, this is Charlie-Whiskey-Six, Over."

"Go ahead Whiskey-Six," Hardrick answered.

"Roger, Charlie-Six, we're stretched out too much. Can we slow up and consolidate our position before we reach the objective? Over."

"Negative, Whiskey-Six. Keep moving, and I want you to come over here so we can talk."

"Roger, Charlie-Six. Out."

Sam motioned to Rainmaker and told him he was going to meet with the CO. Slogging across the paddy, he headed toward the dike three hundred meters to the north where Hardrick was walking with the headquarters group.

Sam caught up with Hardrick, who didn't acknowledge him for a minute or two. After what he was pretty sure was Hardrick's way of showing his dissatisfaction, the lieutenant addressed him while staring straight ahead. "Lieutenant Walker, why are you and your men lagging behind?"

"We are out there in the paddies. It's slow going in the muck. You have First Platoon and the headquarters group up here walking on this dike."

"And there's another dike down there along the base of those hills. Why aren't you using it?"

"Because it's too close to the wood-line and the higher ground. We'd be begging to get ambushed over there with no cover. Besides that, we've been lucky so far because these dikes are likely booby-trapped."

"Oh, really, Walker? You sound like you're afraid. Are you?"

"Damned right I am, and if you aren't you should be."

"There's no room for fear in a leader's mind, Walker. If you're afraid, maybe you shouldn't be leading a platoon."

"If you're not a little afraid, you're either lying or you're a—"

The crackle of M-16 fire erupted up at the point, and Lieutenant Powell's voice came over the radio. The radio broke squelch several times and the transmission was garbled. "...uniformed NVA crossing north to south...thousand meters to our front. We... taking them under fire."

"Roger, Charlie-Red-Six, move your men forward. Keep pressure on them. Push hard. We need to block them from leaving those villages."

Sam glanced to the north where Third Platoon should have been moving up on the right. He spotted two men struggling through a rice paddy three hundred yards away. It was Doug Stone's point and slack men. The rest of his platoon was strung out for several hundred meters back to the east.

"Lieutenant Hardrick," Sam shouted. "That's ill-advised. Third Platoon is stretched out even worse than my men are."

"Come on, Walker, show some courage. I don't have time for your whining right now. Get back over there and bring your men up fast. I'll take care of Stone myself."

He had to talk some sense into Hardrick. Otherwise, someone was going to get their ass in a bind.

"There's a big difference between having courage and being foolhardy, Lieutenant. You need to hold First Platoon in check till we get the other platoons up to support them, and you need to bring the sixties up as well. We need those guns."

"Walker, *I* will run my goddamned company, and I don't have time for your shit, right now. Do as I said and bring your men up!" Hardrick turned to his RTO. "Get Red-Leg-Two-Zero on the horn and tell them to prepare for a fire mission. Let's move up there with First Platoon. If we hurry, we can bring some real shit down on those gooks before they get away."

Sam started back across the rice paddy but stopped to look back. Hardrick and his RTO were running ahead down the dike. From somewhere beyond the palm trees up ahead came the blasts of impacting RPGs. That could mean only one thing. First Platoon had blundered into an enemy ambush.

October 2018
Pensacola Beach, Florida

The evening air chilled quickly as the sun dropped down in the west. Sam and Claire walked back to the pickup, leaving the sound of the pounding surf fading behind them as they hiked over the dunes. It had been a much-needed few hours of rest that relieved some of the ache in his old legs.

"This put me in the mood for fresh seafood," Sam said. "How about you?"

Claire's face was reddened slightly by the sun and her blue-gray eyes glowed in the dusky light. "Sounds good."

"After supper, I'd like to take a look at that folder with your grandfather's military papers, if you don't mind."

"Sure."

Sam was sitting at the desk in the room that evening going through Sergeant Pearle's documents, the first of which was his DD214. Something had caught his eye. Item #12, where the heading was "Last Duty Assignment and Major Command." Pearle, James Robert was in the 505th Infantry Regiment and the same battalion in which Sam had served. He looked at the dates and studied them.

Claire came out of the bathroom in her pajamas and walked up beside him.

"Sam, there's something I need to tell you."

He peered over his eyeglasses up at her.

"There are a couple letters in there I wish maybe you didn't read."

He was already caught off guard by the information on the DD214. The dates indicated they may have been there at the same time, but he had no memory of Sergeant Pearle. There had been a lot of turnover in those few weeks. New men came into the unit while others departed, and keeping up with every man in the company was difficult. Now, there was this strange request coming from Claire.

"Why?" he asked.

"Do you remember when you first told me that you were an officer?"

"Yes, I do. You seemed kind of...I don't know. Was it disappointed?"

"I guess I didn't hide it very well. You see, Papa Pearle, well, he really didn't like officers. He said it was his platoon leader and company commander that got him wounded and most of his men killed. He was pretty bitter about it, and he says as much in one of those letters."

Sam was light-headed as he looked back down at the documents on the desk. His heart raced, and he took Claire's hand and held it.

"Are you okay, Sam?"

He could only nod.

She put her hand on his back. "I didn't mean to sound—"

"It's okay. It's okay."

He looked up at her, but was having difficulty focusing. He had a strange feeling in his gut. It made him wonder if Claire had known something all along—something she hadn't told him. Nothing made sense. His head spun and it occurred to him that perhaps some sort of senility was setting in. This was all too strange.

She furrowed her brows. "What's the matter, Sam? What are you thinking?"

Sam took two more deep breaths to calm himself.

"Do any of these letters tell about the day your grandfather was wounded?"

"Yes. As a matter of fact that's the one I'm talking about. He wrote to his dad from the hospital in Japan. If I remember right it's pretty detailed, but I've read it only once a long time ago. It's really kind of sad."

"Okay, see if you can find it and hang on to it, but first I want to finish telling you about that firefight in the rice paddies we were talking about at the beach this afternoon."

Claire began shuffling through the letters.

CHAPTER FOURTEEN

From Bad to Worse

April 1968
West of Hue, Republic of Vietnam

Further up the dike and beyond a low growth of scrub and palms, Lieutenant Hardrick ran ahead toward the sounds of the gunfire, followed by his headquarters group. Sam slogged back across the rice paddy to Chewy, who was listening to the radio with Sergeant Rainmaker. Beyond the palms, the rapid pops of M-16 fire were now being trumped by the *karoomphs* of impacting enemy mortar rounds. Smoke and dust had begun rising into the air. Matters were going to hell in a handbasket and Sam was already second-guessing himself. *Had he done enough?*

The enemy rockets had likely claimed a number of casualties and the mortars were now adding to the toll. Young Lieutenant Powell knew no better, but Hardrick should have, and Sam could have stopped it all from happening, but his was not the ranking command. Hardrick was the officer in charge and Sam's duty was to follow his commanding officer's orders. At least that was what he had been trained to believe. His combat experience and his heart told him otherwise.

Kneeling beside him were Chewy and Rainmaker, both staring at him with questioning eyes. Sam was up to his knees in the muddy water as he fought to catch his breath while the firefight intensified.

"We heard the CO tell Lieutenant Stone that you refused to bring our platoon up to support him and that he needed him to double-time his men up," Rainmaker said.

Gasping for breath after the three-hundred-meter sprint through the muck, Sam rested his hands on his knees while he caught his wind. "That's not true, Sergeant. Go ahead and bring our men up, but send Fergie's squad south to protect our left flank. We need to move up and try to support those men."

"But, sir, I think First Platoon just walked into an ambush, At least that's what it sounds like."

"Don't worry. I'm not going to run into that damned kill zone. We'll move up to where we can give them support. Give me the handset, Chewy."

"Charlie-Blue-Six, Charlie-Whiskey-Six, give me a Sit-Rep, Over."

Doug Stone answered immediately. "Charlie-Whiskey-Six—" The radio broke squelch with a stream of static, but Stone's voice came back. "Sam, I'm bringing my men up and putting them on line to move forward, but they're all pretty winded. It's slow going."

Stone sounded like he was gasping for breath.

"Roger, Blue-Six. We're doing the same over here, but be careful when you move up. I believe Red-Six has walked into an ambush."

"Roger, Whiskey-Six—"

The huffing crack of bullets began passing around them. Sam and the others squatted deeper in the paddy as spouts of water shot into the air.

"Get down," Sam screamed. "Everybody down."

From the hills to the south came the dull *dut-dut-dut-dut* of an enemy machine gun. An RPG arced in from the hills and exploded in the paddy, sending muck and water skyward. A moment later, even larger fountains of water began erupting as mortar rounds impacted all around them, but the men were scattered and most were still strung out back to the east.

Fergie's men had dumped their rucks and were crawling toward the palms with only their helmets visible above the water. Sam looked back to the east and motioned the rest of the platoon toward the hills. It was their only reasonable option. The enemy fire was bound to intensify and staying out in the paddy was suicide. The world quickly became a confusing fog of zipping bullets, exploding mortar rounds, screams, and shouts. Sam tried to think, but his months of training had kicked in and his mind was on auto-pilot.

He pressed the handset to his ear. "Charlie-Lima-Six, this is Whiskey-Six. We're taking fire from the Sierra. Is there any way you can bring a gun up and give me some fire on those hills out there, Tom?"

Tom DeGrass answered. "Roger, Whiskey-Six. One of my guns is just now up. I have to send him forward. As soon as the next one gets here, we'll get at it. Tell your men we'll be firing over their heads. Over."

"Roger, Tom. Hurry up every chance you get. The shit's getting heavy out here."

The platoon was lying in the water of the rice paddy returning a heavy volume of fire, but they were too exposed. There was only one direction to go.

"Move," Sam shouted. "Stay down, but move forward to that dike next to the hills. Hold up, Chewy."

He reached over and twisted the knob on the PRC-25 to the command net frequency. It sounded like Hardrick's voice. "…Blackwood-Six, we have to have it, now." He was talking to the 101st colonel commanding the task force. There came the deafening *karoomphs* of heavy artillery rounds impacting just beyond the palms.

"Cease fire! Cease fire! Short rounds," came Hardrick's voice over the radio. "I don't know." His voice now sounded more distant. He was apparently holding his handset with the mic button still pressed and talking over the open net. "This damned map is soaked. I must have misread the coordinates. Can you see out there where First Pla—" The radio broke squelch and went silent.

"Charlie-Six, Blackwood-Six. Are you still with me, Lieutenant?"

"Roger, sir."

"Okay, I want you to remain calm. I have two Cobras inbound and I want you to pop smoke and shoot an azimuth to the enemy position. When we confirm your smoke I want you to give us the heading and the distance. Do you roger?"

"I roger, sir, but we're taking heavy fire from both the hills and the village, and I have multiple Whiskey India Alphas, over."

"My boys are already engaging the enemy in the village. Now go ahead and shoot the azimuth for the enemy positions in the hills to the south, roger?"

"Go, go," Sam shouted at Chewy. "We gotta move."

By the time they reached the dike along the edge of the hills, Sam could see the tracers from Fergie's squad slashing into the jungle undergrowth, and his grenadier was dropping M-79 rounds on target as well. Glancing back to the east, he spotted several men crossing the dike and running into the jungle. It was one of his squads. They were flanking the enemy. Despite their inexperience, his choice of squad leaders was paying off. They weren't slackers. They were taking the initiative without having to be told.

The radio cracked and popped, and the static of voices filled the handset, but it was all now becoming drowned out by the buzzing roar of the Cobra mini-guns as they flew back and forth raking the hillside jungle to a fine salad. Sam switched frequencies, called Tom DeGrass, and stopped his machine gun. For a moment there was silence. The enemy was gone. The battle had ended, but from the black pall of smoke beyond the palms where First Platoon had been ambushed came the desperate shouts of men and calls of "medic."

October 2018
Pensacola, Florida

Sam glanced at the bedside clock. It was after midnight. He sat propped against the pillows, but he couldn't go on. He had thought he was doing better, but the memories were once again overwhelming. Claire sat cross-legged on her bed, tablet in hand. She stopped writing and gazed his way, studying him carefully.

He'd had enough for one night, but his head still buzzed with the memories. After a few moments he swung his legs off the bed and went over to his overnight bag where he dug out his flask. He unscrewed the cap, tipped it up and drank. He drank until he'd emptied nearly half the container and recapped it.

"You okay?" she asked.

Sam swiped at his mouth while he tried to make sense of the "now" versus "then" and all that had happened since. It had been a surreal experience back then and after reading Sergeant Pearle's DD214, it was becoming surreal once again. He eyed the letter on Claire's nightstand. It was time.

"Open that now and let's read it."

She eyed him with unspoken questions as she reached across and picked up the envelope. Sam sat in the chair as she placed the open letter on the desk in front of him. It was faded and stained but still very readable. Sam smoothed the wrinkles with his hand and read.

May, 1968

Dear Dad,

I suppose by now the army has notified you that I got hit again. This time it's a lot worse, but the good news is I should make a full recovery. It's what they call the "million-dollar wound." I'm coming back to the world and I won't have to go back to Nam again. I'm at a hospital in Japan right now. I got hit in my upper chest, but the round was what they called T&T and didn't hit my heart or lungs. The medic, Tommy Dieter, was tying it with field dressings when there was a really huge explosion and a big piece of shrapnel glanced off my helmet. At least that's what they told me later because I don't remember none of it. It killed Tommy, and it was our own artillery that did it. None of this should have happened. I knew our new platoon leader, Lieutenant Powell, was screwing up when he told us to go after some NVA crossing up ahead of us, but the CO was yelling at him to chase after the gooks. It seemed way too much like a setup and it was. They blew their ambush on our left and killed Jack Simpson and a new guy right off. Almost all of Jack's squad was killed in the first minute, and.

Sorry, I had to stop writing for a while, but I'm back. A couple of our other guys from my squad who made it are here with me in the hospital and one of them says it was the CO, a guy named Hardeck, who screwed up the coordinates on the fire mission and dropped our own artillery on us. Our officers are incompetent and I'm starting to understand why some of the guys want to frag them. Half the platoon was new guys who didn't know anything before they were wounded or killed and this whole war is screwed up. They can take these new sergeant stripes and give them to somebody else. I'm glad I'm coming home, and I'll be getting out of this army as soon as they let me. Please don't worry about me. I'm really not feeling too awful bad, considering all that happened. I hope to see you and Mom soon.

Love,

Jimmy

Claire stood silently at his side for a long while after reading the letter. Neither of them moved. Neither spoke. Sam removed his glasses and set them atop the letter. Reaching up with his right hand, he took her hand in his and held it. She gripped it as if it were a life-line pulling her from oblivion.

"Claire, do you believe in Divine Providence?" he asked.

He heard her stifle a sob before she spoke in a near whisper. "You were sent to help me find my father, weren't you?"

A teardrop hit the back of his neck and he looked up at her. The crystalline tracks of her tears lined her face.

"I don't know. I'm pretty ancient and I've been alone in this world for a while now. Maybe it was *you* who was sent here for me."

Claire drew a quivering breath. "I know our families are from the same area, and you live there in Boone where I'm going to school, but it still defies logic that we are here together, trying to find my father. What I mean is it defies logic that you and Papa Pearle were in Vietnam together. I know people want to credit or blame God for the good and bad things that happen, but this is just too, I mean all of it, it just seems…"

Sam shoved his chair back, stood, and pulled her into his arms. "Claire, honey, dry your tears and let's not dwell on this too much right now. There are a lot of things in this world that I've never been able to explain, and we'll have plenty of time later to think about this one. Go get in your bed. Try to get some sleep. We will talk about it more tomorrow."

"Do you remember seeing Papa Pearle—I mean, after the battle?"

Even after fifty years, Sam found his officer training taking control as he maintained a steady countenance. This was a moment that demanded a façade of strong leadership. He drew a deep breath and exhaled.

"You know, I keep thinking about that, but I'm not sure. I don't think so. I mean, I saw a lot of wounded men that day, and he could have been any one of them, but recognizing any of them as having been your grandpa...well...that was a long time ago. War does strange things to a man's mind, and some aren't so bad because they help us forget."

And only now did he clearly understand what Claire was seeking. He pressed his lips together and gave her his best look of confidence—that of a man who could answer her questions and tell her something that would assuage her fears and doubts, and explain what the war in Iraq had done to her father. That was what she wanted most—to understand how war had changed him.

"Let's go to bed now. We can talk about it some more tomorrow while we look for your father."

CHAPTER FIFTEEN

Insubordination

October 2018
Pensacola, Florida

Back at it again, Sam and Claire drove the streets of Pensacola, talking to policemen, panhandlers, and people at boarding houses. Most were pleasant, but no one was able to provide them with any new information. By late afternoon they sat in the pickup at Wayside Park looking out at Pensacola Bay. Sea gulls flashed white against a cloudless blue sky and brown pelicans glided along the shore, but the two tired searchers sat in silence.

Sam remained determined, but doubt had begun creeping up on him. He hoped he hadn't led Claire on a wild goose chase. Pensacola was no small town, but they had searched everywhere and the thought plagued him that Claire's father could be anywhere in the country by now. He had to think. Somewhere there had to be something he had overlooked.

"What next?" she asked.

Her voice was quiet and there was a hint of the same desperation he was feeling.

"I don't know. Turn on your recorder and let's do that a while. Maybe something will come to me."

Although it had become an unpleasant task, the interview was at least a momentary distraction from what now seemed a futile search for her father.

April 1968
West of Hue, Republic of Vietnam

Blackwood-Six had called for medevac choppers and a company from the 101st was securing an LZ on the south side of the villages. So far there wasn't a single serious casualty in Second, Third or Weapons Platoons. Sam hoped to keep it that way, but he had to sweep forward where he expected to find the decimated remains of First Platoon.

He glanced over at his RTO. "Let's move out, Chewy. We've got work to do."

After deploying Fergie's squad on the left flank, he led the rest of the men forward through the low growth of scrub and palms. The dry ground beyond was obscured by a pall of smoke and dust, glowing orange from the blotted sun beyond. The chemical odors of spent explosives filled his nostrils along with that of dirt and rotted vegetation blown into the air as a fine dust.

From somewhere out in the surreal world of fog and smoke came the moans of the wounded, and someone calling for a medic. The only other sound came from the now distant clatter of the choppers still circling somewhere to the southwest. It was going to be a grim and dangerous task. He motioned his men forward and their forms grew ghost-like as they became lost in the haze of smoke and dust.

The radio broke squelch. "Charlie-Whiskey-Six, this is Charlie-Lima-Six, Over."

Chewy gave Sam the handset. It was Tom DeGrass. The last

Sam heard was when Tom was moving his guns up on line at the center with the rest of the company.

"Go ahead, Tom. What'cha got?" Sam said.

"I've found Charlie-Six. His radio is in-op and he wants you to report to his pos' ASAP. We're over here where the dike hits the dry ground on the other side of the palms."

Hardrick had survived, and Sam wasn't looking forward to dealing with him—not now, not with so many dead and wounded out there.

"Roger that."

He turned to his platoon sergeant. "Sergeant Rainmaker, continue forward with the men and let's try to get the wounded moved to the LZ as quickly as possible. Keep security out front and Fergie's squad out there on the left just in case."

Rainmaker's face was a grim mask of stoicism. He simply nodded. Sam weaved his way northward through the palms and scattered undergrowth. He half expected to find a body or two along the way, but there were none. The enemy had waited patiently and sucked First Platoon all the way in before springing the ambush. And all he could think of was what a fool Hardrick had been. He had gotten his coveted body-count, except they were all his own men.

Farther up he spotted Tom DeGrass standing with Doug Stone. As he approached he realized Lieutenant Hardrick was there too, kneeling beside his RTO who was bandaged around the head and arm.

"How bad is he hit?" Sam asked.

"He's going to make it, Lieutenant Walker," Hardrick said. "What I want to know is where in hell you and your men have been?"

"The enemy hit us on our left from those hills back there. We moved this way as soon as we could."

Hardrick turned to Stone. "What's *your* excuse, Lieutenant Stone?"

Sam found himself consumed with blind rage, and stepped between Hardrick and Stone. He had held his tongue far too long and it was time to rip the curtain open on this pompous ass.

"You blundered into this debacle yourself, Lieutenant Hardrick. Hell, I tried to warn you. Anyone but an idiot would have sensed it was an ambush, and you made it worse by calling in artillery on our own men. You got your body-count, Lieutenant. Unfortunately, it was your own men!"

"Sam!" Stone said. "Take it easy."

He turned to Stone. "I don't care anymore, Doug. The only thing dumber than a dumbass is a dumbass who thinks he's smart."

"You heard him," Hardrick says. "He's being disrespectful to a sup—"

"I didn't hear shit...*sir*," Stone said.

Hardrick turned to DeGrass. "Lieutenant DeGrass, I want you to make note of exactly what was said here."

"Duly noted, sir. What I heard Lieutenant Walker say was that he was engaged by the enemy on his left while Lieutenant Stone was doing everything possible to bring his winded platoon up from the rice paddy to your support. And despite the advice of your platoon leaders, you chose to proceed without their support by ordering First Platoon to pursue the enemy they encountered to our front. Anything else?"

Hardrick was speechless. His eyes flitted about like those of a panicked bird.

Sam turned to Lieutenant Stone. "Doug, if I might suggest—we need to get organized. How about taking your men up further and establishing security for us while my men gather the dead and wounded? Tom's men can help by transporting them to the LZ while we police the area for weapons and equipment."

He turned to Hardrick. "Of course, with your approval, Lieutenant."

Hardrick, who was staring down at his wounded RTO, slowly nodded. "Yes, of course. Go ahead," he said in a subdued voice.

———————

October 2018
Pensacola, Florida

Sam awoke that morning to the continuous ringing in his ears. After those first firefights around Dak To in 1967 it had lasted for days, then weeks. And even now, years afterward, it was still there, but there was something more beyond the tinnitus—something he sometimes heard even when he was awake. It was their voices— faint—sometimes almost indiscernible—lost in the ringing, but always there. It was the voices of those men whose distant shouts and muffled cries of "incoming" and "medic" had never ceased. Their voices returned again and again, reminding him that they had not made it back that day. Forever gone, they had never walked from the smoke and the haze of that distant battlefield.

He and the others who lived that day carried the bodies of the dead and wounded back to the LZ where they stood watching as the choppers thundered into the sky, taking them away. That was their battlefield requiem. They were good men, and they were now gone forever. And for those left behind, there remained only a feeling of helplessness. It had all been so unnecessary, and even fifty years later, the regret of not having done more to prevent it still burned in Sam's soul—a regret that burned with the fires of a hell he couldn't escape.

He heard a sound and it dawned on him—it was a new day. He opened his eyes as Claire walked from the bathroom. She had prepared what had become his ritual first cup of coffee. Sitting up on the side of his bed, he debated whether or not to stretch. He didn't want more strained muscles—no more than he wanted more regrets for not doing everything possible to find her father. Thinking and hoping for an answer, he gazed down into the swirling blackness of the coffee. They had searched everywhere that homeless people could be, and he had to rethink their strategy.

Claire, dressed in jeans and a T-shirt, stood with her head cocked to one side as she pulled a brush through her hair. "What are you thinking about now, Sam?"

His awareness surfaced from the subconscious depths of thought and he looked up at her.

"Nothing really, and I suppose everything. I keep asking myself if we've missed something—if we've done all we can do. I just don't know. Maybe your father headed farther south for the winter."

Claire stopped brushing her hair and stared back at him. "If he did, we might never find him."

"I've been racking my brain, but I can't think of anything else to do except keep looking."

"We've searched under every shrub in every park, and under every overpass in town. I didn't realize there were so many parks and so many homeless people out there. Where else could he be?"

"I don't know, but we're not giving up yet, little woman. We've got to stay at it. Go in there and smear on some lipstick or whatever and let me get dressed. We'll go down for some breakfast and get back out there."

Claire gave him a sideways grin. "You are so much my Papa Pearle made over. Do you mind if I bring the recorder?"

"Of course not. Why do you ask?"

"I could tell yesterday was kind of rough on you—the memories, I suppose."

Sam avoided making eye contact. She was right. The memories had kept him awake that night, and although some days it felt good to talk, yesterday hadn't been one of them. She didn't need to know that.

"Claire, darling, those old memories aren't all bad. You've brought back a lot of good ones, like those of my Caroline."

―――――――――

Sam sat in the passenger seat while Claire drove down 9th Avenue into the heart of Pensacola. Both had been silent since leaving the hotel, and Sam tried to think what it was that he might have missed. The person that was Jim Cunningham still wasn't clear in his mind. He had to learn more about Claire's father—perhaps something that would give him an idea of which way he should go next.

"Tell me more about your dad. You said he was a lieutenant. Did he and your Papa Pearle talk with one another about their military experiences?"

"Well, not really. They didn't exactly see eye to eye. I think Dad always felt intimidated by Papa and he seemed to resent him in some ways. I never heard Papa Pearle say or do anything that should have caused it, but I think Dad may have read some of Papa's old letters, and there was also a religious thing he held against him. Papa was a strong believer, but he didn't care for religions. I think because Mom and I had much the same beliefs and didn't go to church that often, Dad blamed Papa Pearle. You see, Dad was real religious, and he loved going to church."

"I don't know why I haven't thought of that," Sam said.

"Thought of what?"

"You said he was religious. We haven't tried any churches. Maybe we should go around to some today. What do you think?"

Claire shrugged. "Can't hurt. I'll pull over and let you drive while I look up some on my phone."

After taking the wheel, Sam drove to a parking lot near the Veterans' Memorial Park and waited while Claire searched her phone. The lot was nearly empty, and they sat for a long while before she looked up.

"I think I may have something. Go back up 9th Street to Gregory. We have to get on I-110 North."

"Where are we headed?"

"To a church that apparently has a pretty big homeless persons' ministry. They've got some information on here about homeless camps around town."

It was little more than fifteen minutes later when Sam turned down a narrow and cracked blacktop road. The neighborhood, a mix of small homes, old cars, and homegrown businesses, was in an area north of Interstate-10. He stopped the pickup adjacent to several weather-worn buildings. A sign out front, the only thing that didn't look ancient, said they had arrived at the Escambia First Baptist Church. The buildings, possibly from the World War II or Korean War era, had a fresh coat of paint, but they clearly had a previous life as a business of some sort.

"Well, they certainly have their priorities in line," Sam said.

"What do you mean?"

"They put their money into the community instead of a fancy church. Let's see if there's anyone around."

They walked around until finding an unlocked door at the back. Sam pushed it open. "Hello?" His voice echoed down a long hallway.

A man came walking up the shadowy hall toward them. "Can I help you?"

After explaining their situation, Sam and Claire were invited back to a small office where they sat with the man, Pastor Jerry Johnston. "As I explained, Miss Cunningham, the homeless camps can be somewhat fluid, but I'll be glad to show you on this map where two are located right now. As for knowing your father by name, that's a little problematic. We know most of them only on a first name basis, and none of them that go by Bill match your father's description."

"I think some of his army buddies used to call him BJ, too," Claire said.

The preacher looked up and his face brightened. "Well, now, I think I may know him after all. At least, I mean, I met a man named BJ a few weeks back. I believe he's staying at a camp down south of I-10, but he told me that he moves around a lot. It would still be worth a try. He seemed to be a good man, but a troubled one. A lot of the homeless veterans are that way."

He eyed Sam. "You're a vet, too, maybe, World War II or Korea?"

"I know I look pretty old, Reverend, but I'm a mere boy of seventy-three. My war was the one in Vietnam."

"Oh, my apologies, sir. I sure didn't mean to make you feel like a senior citizen."

The men laughed, and Claire shot a quick grin at Sam while Johnston ran his hand over the map. "Go out here to Pensacola Boulevard and head south. Do you know where the CSX railyards are?"

Sam and Claire wagged their heads in unison.

"That's okay. Look here and I'll show you. This is Pensacola Boulevard. It's also Highway 29."

The preacher followed the highway with his finger down the map, giving a detailed description of how to find a backroad leading along the edge of the railyards. He showed them where it ended at a dirt and sand trail leading into a large scope of woods.

"Most of the camps that I've seen have a dozen or more people living in them and they all have one thing in common. They help one another. So, be patient with them if at first they seem unwilling to tell you anything. They're afraid of law enforcement. The police can be a little rough on them at times. I believe if you tell them what you told me they will help you."

It wasn't even noon yet, and they were on a hot lead. At least it seemed so, and Sam hoped for Claire's sake it led them to her father. Despite all her denials, it was evident now that she not only wanted him but she needed him. The preacher's directions were good, and after a few turns, they drove under an overpass where the pavement ended. A train rumbled northward out of the railyard, streaming past with an artistic panorama of spray-painted graffiti on its cars. This was a different world—home of the disenfranchised.

Sam slowed the truck as he eased through potholes and around muddy sluices. Piles of trash lined the road, old refrigerators, mattresses, tires—the refuse uncaring litterers left for someone else to clean up. They reached the end of the road and there it was—the dirt path on which their hopes lay. They got out and glanced about. There was no one around.

"You ready?" Sam asked.

Claire nodded, but said nothing.

"Have you thought about what you want to say to your father if we find him?"

She stood staring at the narrow path winding back into the trees. Sam put his hand on her shoulder. Claire remained silent.

"It's okay. There's seldom a way to rehearse one's life. Let's go."

He took her hand and led her into the cool shadows of the woods, down the path, until they spotted a cluster of bright red, blue, and green tarps, tents, and makeshift shelters. The smoky odor of a wood fire drifted through the trees along with the low murmur of voices from the camp. A man with a brown, leathered face, wearing ragged jeans and a dirty T-shirt, sat on a plastic bucket beside a smoldering fire. He poked at it with a stick and avoided eye contact as Sam and Claire walked up.

"We're looking for this girl's father," Sam said. "The preacher at the church said he might be around here."

"He's a military veteran," Claire said, "and he has a traumatic brain injury from when he was in Iraq."

The old man cut his eyes up at them and nodded carefully. "What's his name?"

"Bill Cunningham. He goes by BJ," Claire said.

The old man pointed with the stick out toward the railyard. "He hitched a ride on a freight train out yonder early this morning. Said he was ridin' down to the Loaves & Fishes Soup Kitchen to get something to eat."

"Loaves and Fishes?" Sam said.

"Yeah, it's downtown under the One-Ten expressway—Lee Street, I think."

"Is there anything we can do for you?" Sam asked.

The old man gave him a sad smile and poked at the fire with his stick. "No. I don't reckon. I just hope you can find the girl's daddy. Good luck."

———————

Sam pulled the pickup into the parking lot of a large blue and white metal building beneath the One-Ten Expressway. The signs above the double entrances read "Loaves & Fishes" and "United Ministries." Claire's eyes were wide and her lips pressed firmly together as she stared up at the building. She hadn't spoken a word since leaving the homeless camp near the railyard.

"You okay?" he asked.

She nodded rapidly.

"Let's go inside and see if he's here?"

They walked in to find a motley group of the hungry homeless eating lunch. Claire's eyes searched desperately over the tables. Sam wrapped his arm across her shoulders and pulled her close.

"Do you see him?"

With lips still pressed firmly together, she wagged her head. "No."

"How can we help you folks?" a man asked. He wore pressed black slacks and a dark blue golf shirt.

"We're looking for someone," Sam said, "this young lady's father."

"I'm assuming you don't see him at any of the tables?"

Claire again slowly shook her head.

"A man at a homeless persons' camp said he was coming here this morning," Sam said.

"What's his name?"

"He goes by BJ," Claire said, "B.J. Cunningham."

"Yes, he was here early this morning. He had a good breakfast, but he said he was hitting the road for South Florida before it got cold here. He probably caught a freight train out there. That's what most of them do."

Claire turned toward Sam, but he refused to look her way. He didn't want her to see the canned poker face he was fighting to maintain. Nor did he want to see Claire's eyes, because they would be the same as Caroline's eyes had been when he told her he was leaving her before going to Vietnam.

"He's gone," Claire whispered. "We'll never find him now."

"I'm sorry," the man said. He gave Claire a napkin and she wiped her eyes. "I will pray for you and your father."

"We appreciate your prayers," Sam said.

Taking Claire by the hand, he led her to the door. "We can't give up."

"You're sweet, Sam, but we have to face the facts."

"This is not about being sweet, Claire. It's about never giving up." He opened the truck door for her.

"Sam!"

"Claire?"

"I'm just being realistic. We're wasting our time now. I think we need to go home."

She began buckling her seat belt as Sam closed her door. Perhaps she was right. They had failed, and he was just an old fool for leading her on this wild goose chase. As he climbed in on his side he noticed a man squatted against one of the highway support pillars further up the street. The homeless people were everywhere and they had talked to scores of them. Talking to even one more seemed a futile gesture.

He cranked the truck and reached for the gear shift but hesitated. Glancing again at the man who was several hundred feet away, he shrugged. He had never been a quitter, and he wasn't going to start this late in life. Twisting the key, he shut off the engine.

"What's wrong?" Claire asked.

"There's a guy up there under the freeway. Why don't we at least go talk with him and see if he knows where your father went? Come on. Let's go before he disappears."

They walked up the street to where the man was squatted with his back against the white concrete column. The traffic rumbled past on the expressway overhead. The man was bearded and his face was burned to a deep copper patina. Raising his head, he smiled.

The bum's eyes were a familiar bright blue-gray, and Sam found himself speechless. There was no doubt. It was him. He was staring down into the eyes of Claire's father.

The man cocked his head slightly and looked over at Claire. "Connie, what are you doing here?"

Claire dropped to her knees in front of him. "No, it's me, Daddy, Claire."

"No, Connie, it's you. Why did you come way down here?"

"I'm not Connie, Dad. It's me, Claire, your daughter."

Bill Cunningham's face became a jumbled wreck of confusion.

"Dad, Mom died last fall. She had a heart attack. She's gone."

"Connie? No. She can't..." His eyes darted left and right and he again looked up at her. "Claire?"

"Yes, Daddy. Mama's gone."

His haunches dropped to the ground and he let out a wail the likes of which Sam hadn't heard since Vietnam. "No. No. No. She can't be dead. No." Claire pulled her father close as his wailing sobs echoed beneath the interstate highway. She too was now crying. Sam stood with his hand on her shoulder and the man's sobs reminded him of that day in 1968 when they'd watched the choppers carrying away the men of First Platoon.

He wished he could have cried then. He wished he could have cried when Caroline died and he wished he could cry now, but his soul was seared and the emotions forever sealed within. He was an officer for life—one who wasn't allowed that luxury. He knelt beside Claire, wrapped his arm around her shoulders, and reached out with his other to her father.

"Let's go home, soldier."

Claire's father was taken back to a room for triage, and Sam and Claire waited nearly two hours before a doctor at the VA clinic came out to meet with them.

"I'm not sure who you know, Mr. Walker, but it must be someone well up the chain of command," she said. "We've been directed to give Mister Cunningham top priority."

"We appreciate your help, doctor. When will Claire be allowed to visit with her father?"

"Hopefully, by tomorrow, but you will have to drive to the VA hospital in Biloxi, Mississippi. That's where we are making arrangements to have him transported. Right now he's in a very confused and emotional state. We've already given him a strong sedative. He will be taken by ambulance to Biloxi and kept on a ward with restricted egress until we can do further evaluation."

"I understand," Sam said. "I believe it might be helpful for him if he can see his daughter as soon as tomorrow. He's been living on the street and it took us a long time to find him. They need to talk."

The doctor nodded. "I'll put that in my notes to the doctors at Biloxi."

"Thank you."

Sam took Claire by the hand and led her out through the glass doors. "There's nothing more we can do here tonight. Besides, it's getting late. We'll go get something to eat and head back to the hotel. You need to relax. Maybe I can tell you some more about my wonderful trip to Vietnam."

She gave him a sad smile. "I'm not quite sure I deserve a friend like you, Sam, but thank you. Thank you for being here for me."

It was after eight when they arrived back at the hotel that evening. Claire had purchased a bottle of Sauvignon Blanc and poured herself a generous glass as they sat down with the recorder. Sam resisted the urge to give her a grandfatherly lecture because there were times when a good drink took the edge off a lot of things. This was one of those occasions when a little more drink seemed appropriate. He poured himself a glass of Old Forester.

"You know," Claire said. "I think I'd like to try some of that hard stuff tonight. Do you mind?"

"Damned right, I do!" Sam said. "No granddaughter of mine adopted or otherwise, is going to drink whiskey on my watch. Now, drink your wine and behave."

Claire took a dainty sip of her wine and set the glass back on her bedside table.

"You know something, Sam?"

He glared at her. "What?"

"I love you."

Sam looked down into his drink, shaking his head and smiling. "I honest to God think you must have studied female dominance under my Caroline."

"So, did they fire your company commander for being so incompetent?"

"Hardrick?"

"Yeah. I mean—he got a lot of men killed and he was the one who got Papa Pearle wounded, wasn't he?"

Because she was actually talking common sense, Sam fought the urge to lead off with a tirade of four-letter words concerning military protocol. Problem was the army didn't often allow common sense to interfere with its way of doing business and the issue with Hardrick wasn't much different.

"Claire, little darling, I wish the reality of military command principles and politics were that simple."

"What do you mean?"

"What I mean is, it was more likely that *I* would be the one in trouble if Hardrick chose to make an issue of what happened that day, and he did."

"You mean you got in trouble and he didn't?"

Sam raised his eyebrows and nodded.

"Yup."

CHAPTER SIXTEEN

Hardrick's After Action Report

May 1968
3rd Brigade HQ, 82nd Airborne Division
Camp Eagle, Republic of Vietnam

The company had once again taken too many casualties and was pulled back to Camp Eagle for refit, while replacements were brought in and given in-country orientation. Several letters from Caroline awaited him and Sam lay back on his makeshift cot of empty ammo crates as he read each one again and again. He smiled as she described how her parents were against her idea, but how she had already begun packing her bags and only awaited his word to catch a flight to Hawaii. She was as irrepressibly stubborn as she was loveable. There was no stopping her.

"Sir?"

It was Chewy standing in the door of the hooch. Sam sat up and dropped his feet to the dirt floor. "What's up, Chewy?"

"Sergeant Rainmaker sent me. He said Lieutenant Hardrick wants you to report to the Brigade Commander ASAP."

"Crap," he muttered. "Okay, Chewy. Thanks."

The little worm didn't even have the balls to come give him the order himself, and Sam was pretty sure he wasn't being called to brigade for a beer-bust. Either word had gotten out or else Hardrick himself had made an issue of their clash. It really didn't matter now because Hardrick had likely already given his version of events that day, and being a graduate of the U.S. Military Academy would probably stack the chips in his favor. Sam searched his ruck for a clean pair of socks. If he was going before the brigade commander on charges of insubordination, it would at least be with dry feet.

He had no clean fatigues and his boots were scuffed to raw leather. He glanced into a piece of mirror tied to a nearby tent-post. A three-day growth of beard covered his face. Digging through his kit bag, he found his razor and wet his face with water from his canteen. If nothing else, he would also be clean-shaven.

When he was done, he dried his face, donned his helmet, and pulled on his flak jacket. Stepping out into the bright sunlight, he squinted as he gazed out at the fine yellow dust that hung in the air. *This was a really shitty war.* He started down the road toward Brigade HQ.

A large sandbagged tent had a makeshift sign hanging over the doorway that read: HQ 3rd Brigade, 82nd Airborne Div. Sam walked between the walls of sandbags and ducked through the doorway. Several men were inside, some standing to one side studying a map, others sitting at field desks. Radios scratched and squawked while multiple Coleman lanterns hung about, lighting the interior all the way back to a desk where the colonel sat. A young officer turned his way and Sam's mouth involuntarily gaped open.

"What the f...Ausie?"

His old friend seemed equally surprised. "Sam!"

The two men embraced, slapping one another's backs.

"I told you you'd be back, you bastard." Ausie was wearing a wide grin.

"Well, you can be assured it wasn't by choice. What are you doing here?"

"They sent me down to MACV in Saigon back in April, but a couple weeks ago they asked for volunteers to come up here to work staff admin with the 82nd. Man, I had to go for it—too much knuckle-dragging brass down there for me. I jumped on the first flight coming upcountry."

This "knuckle-dragging brass" reference was totally out of character for Ausie. Sam studied his face.

"What? I have a mosquito on my nose?"

Sam caught himself and laughed. "Oh, no. It's just that I'm surprised to see you."

"So, what are you doing here?" Ausie asked.

Sam bowed his head and slowly shook it side to side. "I'm not exactly sure, but it may be that I'm going on the carpet for a little run-in I had with my company commander."

"You? What happened?"

Sam noticed several of the men inside the tent looking their way. "Maybe I can tell you later. I think I better report for now."

"Get with me later," Ausie said.

"Will do."

The colonel's aide announced his arrival and Sam held his helmet under his left arm as he saluted the colonel. "Lieutenant Walker reporting as ordered, sir."

"At ease, Lieutenant."

The colonel stood. "Let's step outside so we can talk."

The colonel donned his helmet and they walked between the tents to a vacant area on a nearby hill. The sky over Camp Eagle held a strange, almost surreal yellow tint, something that seemed to fit the sickly feeling Sam now felt. He was pretty certain the colonel was about to rip him a new one and he would be lucky if that was all he did.

"Lieutenant Walker, your battalion commander is up to his ass in field operations at the moment, so I'm handling this matter. Tell me what happened between you and your CO, Lieutenant Hardrick, the other day."

"Sir, I voiced my concern to the lieutenant for his decision to pursue an enemy force that was passing to our front without first allowing our other platoons to move up in support. I suggested he deploy First Platoon on line and wait until we could bring up Second and Third Platoons as well as the guns from Weapons Platoon to support him. He stated that he would run the company and for me to get my men up. I explained that they were severely winded, but I would do my best."

"What happened then?"

"Lieutenant Hardrick ordered Lieutenant Powell to lead First Platoon in pursuit of the enemy soldiers that were spotted. My platoon subsequently came under heavy fire by a force hidden in the hills to our south. Fortunately, we were spread out and took no casualties. We engaged the enemy and were able to flank and rout them. By the time we moved up in support of First Platoon, they had already been ambushed and taken heavy casualties, both by the enemy and our own artillery that had been incorrectly called in."

The colonel slowly nodded. "I suppose you realize your statement differs substantially with Lieutenant Hardrick's AAR."

"I don't doubt that, sir."

"Did you and Lieutenant Hardrick have words afterward?"

"Yes, sir. He questioned my inability to get my platoon up to support his attack. I told him that this was my concern from the beginning and he should have known there was a strong potential for the enemy ambush that decimated First Platoon."

"Was there anyone else present during this exchange?"

"Lieutenants Stone and DeGrass, and we may have been overheard by a couple of enlisted men as well."

"Lieutenant, you have an exemplary record, but I'll have to investigate this matter further. Until then, I want you to go on

R&R. Get with my staff and they'll make arrangements. When you return, report back to me."

"Sir—" Sam paused to gather his thoughts. There was so much more he had to say, so much more that might save men's lives if Hardrick were held accountable and removed from command. Yet he was unable to speak. He was shackled by the chains of military propriety.

"Yes, Lieutenant?"

"Thank you, sir, for giving me the opportunity to explain myself."

The colonel's face became a wrinkled map of consternation, and it was pretty clear that he knew Sam was holding back, but he only nodded.

"You're dismissed, Lieutenant."

The Military Auxiliary Radio System (MARS) was a Department of Defense communication program that soldiers could use to make phone calls to their families. Often utilized by those wounded in action to talk with loved ones back home, it was also rationed when available to all soldiers to contact their families. A somewhat clumsy system, it was state of the art for the times, and the following morning Sam got in line for his call to Caroline. Once the necessary procedures were established, the phone began ringing. He waited.

Sam felt his throat swelling. He swallowed hard, fighting to remain calm—if only he could hear her soft feminine voice again. If there was to be a moment of relief from this war, that would be it—to hear Caroline's sweet voice over nine thousand miles away—a lifetime, possibly an eternity, away. Feedback resonated through the line along with the sleepy voice of a man answering at the other end. An operator somewhere in the chain of communication announced a call for Caroline Devereux.

"She's asleep," the man's voice said. "It's after midnight. Who did you say this was?"

He'd forgotten the time difference. Sam slammed his fist down. He was a dumbass.

"State your name, caller," an operator's voice said.

"Sam! Sam Walker. It's me, Mister Deveraux, Sam. I'm calling from Vietnam." He remembered the protocol. "Over."

The pause was probably no more than six or seven seconds, but it seemed an eternity.

"Wait. Wait. I'll get her."

Sam felt the lump knotted in his throat growing larger as he waited. Hollow sounds echoed over the line—static and the distant echoes of voices out there somewhere helping him to reach her.

"Please." And he realized he'd said it aloud.

The seconds ticked ever so slowly by.

"Hello? Hello. Sam, are you there?"

He wasn't sure if it was the result of the radio and land lines, but her voice seemed as if it were quivering and shaky.

"Yes. Yes, it's me, baby. I'm sorry to call so late, but I just found out that I have R&R. I couldn't get Hawaii. I'm sorry. The only thing available was Manila. I'm sorry. I'm going there maybe by tomorrow. I'm not sure. I tried, but...."

There was so much more he wanted to say.

"Over. Are you still there?" He could no longer talk.

More seconds ticked by.

"I'm here, Sam. I'm calling the airline as soon as they open in the morning. I already have a passport, and I'll meet you at the airport in Manila. I promise."

Another long pause filled with hollow electronic echoes ensued.

"Sam, Sam, I love you. I love you, Sam. It's going to be okay. I'll get there."

Caroline had heard it in his voice, the desperation, the loneliness, the loss of a world with meaning. That wasn't what he wanted. He drew a deep breath and forced himself to regain some sense of calm. He wanted to sound upbeat and tried to close the call with a lighter *Leave It to Beaver* Eddie Haskell-tone of voice.

"Don't forget that yellow bikini, Caroline." But as everyone did with Eddie Haskell, she saw through him. "It's okay, Sam. I'll be there soon."

The call ended all too quickly.

May 1968
R&R
Manila, Philippine Islands

By the following evening Sam had arrived in Manila, but the flight from the States arrived without Caroline. It was too soon. At best, it would be the next evening before she arrived—if she had been able to find a flight. He could only hope, and he didn't want to leave the airport—not till he saw Caroline. Instead, he found a bench in the corner of the arrival area where he sat and stared out at the nighttime lights of Manila.

It was already late night and after a while the exhaustion of months in the bush overcame him. There may have been a time when he would have bitched about sleeping in an airport terminal, but vowing to never again complain, he curled up on the bench and slept in what was almost decadent comfort compared to the boonies of Vietnam. He heard nothing. He felt nothing. It was nearly a sleep of death, until he awoke with a start.

There were people standing around him, staring down at him. He blinked his eyes and slowly sat upright, putting his feet on the floor. It was two military policemen along with a Filipino man in a business suit. There was a moment of disorientation before he realized he'd slept through the night. Outside the terminal, the sun was shining brightly on a new day.

"This gentleman is with the Philippine Airport Authority and he thinks you may be an American soldier," one of the MPs said.

Sam nodded. "I am. I was waiting for my girlfriend to arrive from the States and fell asleep."

"I need to see your military ID. Do you have orders?"

Sam produced both and the MPs studied them. "Have you registered at the hotel, sir?"

"Not yet."

"Why don't you let us take you over there? The next flight from the States doesn't arrive until later this evening. You can get some rest and a shower and come back then."

As much as he didn't want to leave here, it made sense and the MPs delivered him to the hotel where he was greeted by the R&R liaison. It seemed he was expected to require the services of a female escort for the week, and it took several attempts to explain his refusal before he was shown to his room. He spent the next two hours in the shower—his second in as many days.

With the water running as hot as he could stand, Sam soaped his body with a thick lather, pushing it between his toes, scouring his hair, and scrubbing his skin until it glowed red. Never had soap and hot water felt so wonderful. When he was done, he tugged the chain on the ceiling fan, lay back on the bed and again fell into another bottomless sleep.

He even dreamt of sleeping, taking it as one would a drug, refusing to relent to any threat of wakefulness, but from somewhere back in his dreams he heard a light tapping sound. He listened to it for a while. It didn't stop. It may have been woodcutters somewhere far back in the jungle, working with machetes and axes, but it sounded more like a quiet but incessant knocking—at a door perhaps.

Sam opened his eyes and realized the room was dark. A cold

realization struck him. Scrambling about he found his boxers. Someone was knocking at the door to his room. He pulled on the boxers and rubbed his eyes as he tried to focus on his army issue wristwatch. The fluorescent hands had to be wrong. It was late night.

He stumbled to the door and cracked it open. Squinting out into the hallway, he let the door swing open as a rush of adrenaline brought him fully awake. She was there—Caroline, her soft brown eyes gazed at him with a warmth that begged him to take her, but he was frozen. She dropped her bags and leapt into his arms, crushing his lips with hers. He held her close, and they remained in the room, lost to time for the next two days. Sam would have gladly spent the entire week there, but they decided later to explore the island instead.

Renting a car, he and Caroline drove southward and westward exploring small towns and remote tropical beaches day after day. They drove northward and explored the mountain jungles. Every day and every moment seemed to take him further from Vietnam and the terrible war that still churned only nine hundred miles away across the South China Sea. He never dreamed there could be a place more beautiful than the mountains of North Carolina, but he had found paradise here with Caroline in the Philippines.

For Sam, time had stopped these few days on this palm-treed island, walking along its pristine beaches, and wading through its blue-turquoise waters. Caroline was here with him and walking hand in hand, they explored the island, life, and themselves. It was a dream he never wanted to wake up from. Even the rusted and vine-shrouded hulk of a half-sunken Japanese tank abandoned at the jungle's edge seemed to have found a peaceful resting place. Vietnam seemed a lifetime ago as they explored this once Japanese-held stronghold, now a remote beach returned to nature with the calls of birds and the scent of flowers and the ocean.

Life was good again. He inhaled the clean salty air of the ocean, looked into Caroline's brown eyes, smiled, and glanced back at the tank. There came from somewhere back in the mountains the distant rumble of a thunderstorm. Sam stopped and stared again, first at the old Japanese tank, then up into the mountains beyond. It was a razor-sharp shred of shrapnel, a stray thought ripping through the moment, shattering it with the impending realization that he was soon going back to the war—perhaps forever. He heard the ticking of the clock.

"What's wrong?" Caroline asked.

"I'll be going back day after tomorrow."

She lowered her head. "Yes, I know, but let's make the best of the time we have left."

They walked hand in hand down the beach and found the shade of a palm tree where they spread a blanket.

"There's something I want to ask you," Sam said.

Caroline sat on the blanket and looked up at him with raised brows.

"What is it?"

"I want to know why?" he said.

"Why what?"

"Why do you love me? I mean, why do you still love me after I walked away from you when I enlisted?"

"You didn't walk away."

"Yes, I did."

"No. What you did was try to protect me, even though you knew you could lose me."

Sam sat down beside her. "How the hell did you know that?"

"Come on, Sam. You had a very noble intent, but you should know: Men are dogs and women are cats. You drool and we rule."

"Damn," he muttered. She had seen through him the entire time.

"Don't be so down about it. I'll take care of you no matter what happens. Just come home to me when this war is over."

"*You* take care of *me*? You *do* know *I* am the man, right?"

She patted him on the head. "That's okay, baby. I'll make an exception for that."

Sam tickled her bare abdomen. Caroline giggled and gasped as he gently pushed her back on the blanket. "I love you, Caroline."

"And you, dear boy, are my sunshine and the one and only love of my life. You'll never know how much I love you."

He gently pressed his lips against hers and found himself lost in a warmth like none he had ever experienced. If there was such a thing as salvation in this world, Caroline had given it to him. All he had to do now was survive Vietnam.

———————————

May 1968
Camp Eagle, 3rd Brigade HQ, 82nd Airborne Division

If he survived the war, Sam was now certain he had found a shelter to protect himself from a lifetime of bad memories. That was Caroline's heart. With her at his side, he could survive anything, unless of course he was killed first or sent to Leavenworth. Clean-shaven and wearing new fatigues and jungle boots, he reported back to the brigade commander the day he returned from R&R.

As he walked into the headquarters hooch that morning, Ausie met him with a grin and a wink before quickly turning away. Something was up. An aide showed him back to the colonel.

"Lieutenant Walker reporting, sir."

"Grab that chair, Lieutenant. Bring it over here and have a seat."

The colonel's demeanor had changed since their last meeting.

"After speaking with Lieutenants DeGrass and Stone, I met with Lieutenant Hardrick and pointed out some discrepancies in his AAR. I asked if he would like to correct them and consider dropping his complaint against you. Otherwise, if he wished, I told him I would continue with my investigation.

"He elected to rewrite his report and drop his complaint. Lieutenant Hardrick has been reassigned down at MACV. I'm sorry, Sam. I just don't have the time required to address all the issues that need my attention. Right now, this war and this brigade have one hundred percent of my attention. Hardrick is in a safe place with S4 there in Saigon where he will have little opportunity to do further harm."

Sam remained silent and simply nodded. The colonel drew a deep breath.

"I was also approached by Lieutenant Langston in our S-2 Section. He spoke highly of you—seems to think you were short-changed for your actions at Dak To and should have been awarded the Congressional Medal of Honor. In the short time he's been on my staff, I've grown to respect Langston. He's a damned sharp officer."

Sam again said nothing, but he agreed. Despite his trials early on, Ausie had grown and developed to his potential. All he had needed to do was listen to him and Ted. They were Ausie's two best and worst critics.

"Sam, I think you are a wasted talent in a line company. General Zais has taken command of the 101st and wants me to form a long-range reconnaissance platoon here in the 82nd. We need more eyes and ears on the ground back in those mountains. He was able to get the SF boys down at Phu Bai to give us twelve Montagnards from one of their CIDG outfits. They are supposed to be well trained and experienced working back in the highlands. I'd like for you to take them and recruit twelve of our own men to work with the Yards. I'm thinking it will take a rotation of two six-man teams with a twelve-man reaction team on standby to accomplish the mission. You will report directly to me. What do you think?"

Poking around out in the highlands with a six-man recon team was the last thing Sam wanted to do. It was a job for the suicidal-insane. Yet, here it was—no court martial, no reprimand, no Leavenworth, and something the colonel likely saw all too well—a chance for him to escape some of the idiocy and be his own boss for a while.

"Once I get all my men on board, it will take at least a couple weeks to get them squared away and ready to perform missions. How do we keep the line companies from sending us their problem children?"

"I'll take care of that."

"Can I go down to Phu Bai to meet with the Green Beanies and get the skinny on the Yards they're sending us?"

The colonel gave a chest-deep chuckle. "No problem with that, but I wouldn't call them green beanies if you like wearing your head on your shoulders."

"Believe me, I know, sir. I have several buddies from OCS who are with Special Forces. We share a mutual respect but they're real quick to tell you, 'they aren't a hat.' I only do it to screw with them."

"Go for it, then. Your group will be monitored here at the brigade TOC by my S2 group. Let me know what else you will need. My door will be open anytime you need to talk. I want an update by the end of the week. I should have you twelve volunteers by then. Any more questions?"

"No, sir."

"Oh, and your orders for promotion to First Lieutenant have been issued. Congratulations."

Sam stood rigid and saluted, "Thank you, sir."

CHAPTER SEVENTEEN

A Time of Fear and Hope

October 2018
Interstate-65 Southern Alabama

Sam drove northward toward home, fighting the sharp points of sunlight shimmering from the windshields of the southbound vehicles. Claire was leaned against the door on the passenger side of the truck. Lost in thought, her eyes remained unfocused as she rode in silence. They had departed Biloxi by noon that day, leaving behind the salty odors of the ocean, the scent of the pines, and her father at the VA hospital. His young protégée needed uplifting, but Sam hardly knew where to begin.

"You okay?"

Claire sat upright, but she didn't look his way.

"The doctor said that with Dad's brain injury, he will need someone to be with him most of the time. I'm just thinking about some hard choices I have to make."

"What do you mean?"

"If I can get him to come back home to Maggie Valley, I'll have to be there to take care of him. I mean—you saw him. He needs me."

"Well, yes, but there's a good VA Hospital there in Asheville. They can give him—"

"I know what they can do, but he still won't be able to stay at home alone, at least not for long periods. I need to be there."

Sam was taken aback by the hardened tone of her voice. He waited for her to say more, but she remained silent.

"You can't stay down in Maggie Valley and finish school. It's too far to commute every day."

"I know. I'm going to quit school for a while."

"Like hell, you will!"

"I *know* what I have to do," she shouted, "and I am going to take care of my father!"

"You can't shuck your dreams just like—"

"Sam! I am going to do what I have to do."

It was the first time they had clashed to this degree. Claire's jaw was set hard and fire blazed in her eyes. Sam's chest prickled with pain—nothing serious. He'd felt it before. The old ticker just didn't handle stress like it once did. Several minutes of silence ensued as they drove northward toward home. Claire had folded her arms across her chest and the only sound was the hum of the truck tires.

"Do me one favor," he said, calmer now.

"What's that?" The harsh tone of the stress-induced anger remained in her voice.

"The doctor said it would be at least a week, possibly two before we can pick him up and take him back home. Until then, keep doing your schoolwork and let's agree to talk about it when we aren't so tired."

Several long seconds elapsed before she finally nodded and glanced his way. "I'm sorry I yelled."

"It's okay. We'll work through this. Besides, I like a woman with spunk."

"Well, I'm sorry you had to find out I had it that way."

"Oh, I already knew."

She wrinkled her forehead. "How?"

"I realized you were my kind of woman that day we first met when you called Brad an idiot."

"Oh...I forgot about that."

"Why do you think I've tiptoed around you so carefully? I sure as heck didn't want to experience that wrath."

She leaned across the cab and gave him a playful punch on the shoulder. "You're not funny, Sam. I'm just worried and I don't know what to do."

"Lighten up, little lady. Everything will work out. Reach back there and get your recorder and let's get back to work."

———————————

May 1968
5th Special Forces Group (Airborne) Forward Operating Base
(FOB-1)
Phu Bai, Republic of Vietnam

The Special Forces team at FOB-1 greeted Sam with a hospitality that included a fat, medium-rare T-bone steak, ice cold beer, and enough harrowing tales to make him question again his decision to become the commander of a LRRP platoon. But it no longer mattered. He was now committed and decided to leave behind these second thoughts as useless worries.

He had to learn as much as possible as quickly as he could. A Special Forces captain named Benhauser, call-sign Howitzer, and a master sergeant named Mahoney sat with him at a picnic table in the shade. The captain opened another beer and handed it to him.

"Have you ever run any long-range recon missions, Lieutenant?" the captain asked.

"Not a one."

"What do you think about running a couple with my people—I mean if you want?"

"Hell yes!"

The captain grinned.

"We could take him out to Monkey Island," Sergeant Mahoney said.

"I think sending him up close to the fence with the Yards would be better."

Mahoney raised his brows and drew his lips down on one side. Whatever it was Howitzer was suggesting was apparently risky.

"The fence?" Sam said.

"The border—the Laotian border in this case. We call it 'crossing the fence' when we go over into Laos. You have the required clearance, but just so you know, it *is* top-secret shit, so I appreciate you treating this discussion as such."

"I hear you Lima Charlie, Captain."

"I think it'll be good for you to work with your CIDG people on ground they already know. That's the Civilian Irregular Defense Group—Montagnards in this case. They're by far the most loyal and dependable, but they can take some getting used to, especially in situations where you need to break contact."

"What do you mean?"

"Let's just say there ain't no 'quit' in some of 'em," the sergeant said.

"Sometimes," the captain said, "a fast retrograde movement from an AO is the better part of good judgement. Problem is some of our Bru brothers are a little stubborn, especially Khul and his men. They'd rather stay behind and kill NVA. I'm not sure exactly why Khul is that way, but I believe it has to do with his elders' refusal to relocate to a CIDG camp. They've remained in their village up in the highlands. I think Khul's logic is something like if he can kill enough of the NVA they won't find his village."

"But—"

"I know. I've talked to him about it and he tried to talk with his village elders, but they won't listen and he thinks he's protecting them. What he really wants is to go back to his village."

"So, I'm getting a bunch of Yards who really don't want to be here?"

"It wasn't my decision, Lieutenant—not even my idea. Let me offer a suggestion: talk to your higher-ups—see if you can arrange a visit to Khul's village. Take them some food, clothes, tools, medical. Know what I mean?"

"Do you think I can get them to come in to a CIDG camp?"

"We've tried everything. The best you can hope for is that Khul and his men will decide to stay with your recon group. They're damned good at what they do—guides, interpreters, scouts, trackers, and they're proficient as prisoner of war interrogators as well. I mean it. They're damned good."

"You mean until they get us into a firefight we can't win, right?"

"My people have run immediate action drills with him. He knows what to do. The problem is he's like a pit-bull. Sometimes he just won't turn loose. You'll have to work on that, Lieutenant. Get with Sergeant Mahoney here, and he'll introduce you to the Montagnards then get you geared up and briefed for the first training mission. Good luck."

The captain turned to the sergeant, "Andy, get one of those new CAR-15s from the arms room and give it to Lieutenant Walker."

He turned back to Sam. "We have an open tab with MACV S-4. It's a little gift you'll grow to appreciate later when you're humping those mountains."

Sam drank down his cup of hot coffee as if it was his last, and it was, at least for the next three days. He was with Special Forces Sergeant Mahoney preparing for his first recon mission along the Laotian border. Khul and his men sat along the edge of the acid pad as the whining pitch of the Hueys' turbines grew. The first three of his line company recruits from the 82nd had joined them and applied camo paint to their faces and hands while Mahoney gave out last minute instructions and inspected their equipment.

All the recruits, Allen Lowry, Frank Redden, and Robbie Knowlton were experienced NCOs. Redden packed the spare PRC-25 and worked with the Special Forces RTO, while Lowry, Knowlton, and Sam worked closely with Mahoney. After completing a detailed inspection of each man's equipment, Mahoney signaled the twelve-man team to mount up. Sam took a deep breath. He wasn't sure if Caroline would think him smart, brave, or simply dumb as a brick—mainly because he wasn't sure himself.

The choppers lifted out of the dense humid air of Phu Bai and swung westward toward the highlands. Sergeant Mahoney had explained how all missions were pre-planned with a fly-over to select the LZs and possible extraction sites. These had already been reconnoitered by previous visual recon flights and accepted as suitable sites. The air grew cool, almost cold, as Sam gazed out across miles of mountainous jungles and fog-filled valleys. It was a vast and desolate expanse in which a man could become lost forever.

It seemed the anti-war people back in America were right. He and all the other men in this war were being fed, a few at a time, into a giant meat grinder with no clear objective or path that might lead to victory. But who was he to question a nation like his? They surely knew what they were doing. As long as he did his duty, they would take this war to a successful conclusion. Hope was all he had, but the more he saw, the more his doubts grew. Perhaps the army was leading Khul and his men down the same primrose path to hell.

In all directions the mountains stretched endlessly to the horizon and it seemed they were in the middle of nowhere when Sam's ears popped as the chopper began descending. After several false insertions, the helicopters again dropped toward something that looked like a hole in the treetops. It was hardly large enough for a single chopper to land, much less two. This was a detail Mahoney had neglected to communicate. The LZ was a postage-stamp spot where only a fool would try to land a helicopter, but they continued their downward spiral.

Sam's heart thumped and he stopped breathing as the chopper descended through the trees, dropping as if it were plummeting into a well. Mere feet away in all directions, bits of leaves and limbs began shearing away from the surrounding trees. And the whap of the rotors grew to a thunder as the pilot pulled back on the collective and twisted the throttle for more power as he slowed their descent. That they could crash into this mountainous jungle and become more of the "missing in action" was something Sam had not seriously considered until now. The ground appeared below and the pilot slowed the chopper's descent to a hover.

Sam, Mahoney, the two RTOs, along with Khul and one of his men, Dak, leapt clear as the rotors again clacked and the chopper climbed vertically back up through the trees. Mahoney signaled the team to spread out and secure the LZ. Within moments the rotor wash of the second chopper churned in the trees overhead as it descended. The rest of the team leapt from the skids and the chopper immediately powered its way back up through the tunnel-like opening.

Trying not to appear bug-eyed, Sam glanced around at Mahoney, who shot him a thumbs-up. Despite his pounding heart and dry mouth, Sam nodded and forced an uneasy smile. *Damned Green Berets had kahunas big as bowling balls.*

The insertion had gone well—so far. The sounds of the helicopters quickly faded in the distance as the team waited and listened. After a few minutes it seemed they were alone and Mahoney gave a silent signal for the men to form up and begin making their way down the mountain. Khul was on point with

Robbie Knowlton walking slack, followed next by Mahoney and Sam. They descended a few hundred feet before turning northwestward around the mountain. Sam checked the sun and shot an azimuth with his compass.

Other than the ringing in his ears that had never gone away after Dak To, there was only silence. This lack of sound was as much a part of the boonies as was the odor of decayed vegetation, except there were normally birds calling and monkeys howling. Today there were none. This wasn't good. In the silence that surrounded them, the thunder and roar of battle never seemed so far away as it did now, because there was as much, if not more, danger here in this quiet jungle.

Moving at a slow and deliberate pace, they covered several klicks down and around the mountain. Still the jungle remained eerily silent. Sam wiped the sweat from his face with an olive drab towel. Hour by hour he was growing more confident, but he cradled his new CAR-15 in the crook of his arm with his right thumb resting on the selector switch. His eyes constantly picked apart the jungle shadows.

It seemed things were going well, when Khul raised a hand and the entire team simultaneously dropped to one knee. It was as if the jungle had swallowed them, leaving an inch or two of a buttstock visible here or the top portion of a rucksack visible there, but it all blended in near invisible harmony with the jungle. The men were statues, unmoving, rigid, alert. Only Khul was still barely visible at the head of the patrol as he pointed to his ear and tapped his thumb and fingers together, signaling he had heard voices. No one moved.

Sam cut his eyes toward Mahoney. The sergeant's thumb was slowly turning the selector switch on his CAR-15. A minute passed and another. Ten more minutes elapsed before Khul slowly turned his head and locked eyes with Mahoney. The sergeant eased forward and knelt beside the young Montagnard. A bead of sweat rolled into Sam's eye, but he remained motionless. Twenty minutes later the two men stood. Khul moved ahead. Mahoney motioned for Knowlton to follow. Sam exhaled as Mahoney signaled him and the others to begin moving once again.

When he reached Mahoney, Sam stopped, and the team leader pressed his mouth close to his ear and whispered, "NVA patrol, one hundred meters." He pointed down the mountain. There was nothing there but a wall of green. Mahoney motioned him ahead.

Sam had not seen nor heard them, but not another word was spoken as the team moved silently onward. When they stopped for a lunch that afternoon they communicated with whispered phrases while eating cold rations and discussing their next move. They were getting close to the objective, a small mountain valley that extended out into the main valley to the northeast.

Aerial reconnaissance had located a redball road that looked well-used. It led from the A Shau Valley and disappeared beneath the triple-canopied jungle into this smaller valley. The enemy was apparently using it only at night and obliterating whatever tracks they made before daylight the following day. The speculation was it led to an NVA base camp, but exactly where and how large were details Sergeant Mahoney and Sam were expected to determine.

By dusk they reached a finger-like ridge that extended down the mountain along a small valley. There they moved into a night defensive position and contacted the X-ray radio relay team with a situation report. The jungle remained unusually quiet—no birds, no monkeys—only the sounds of insects and a soft mountain breeze stirring in the treetops far above. This could mean only one thing. They weren't the only people out here.

Sam expected nothing about this mission to be easy, but his primal instincts were screaming in his subconscious, telling him they were treading close to the precipice. The birds and monkeys remained silent for one reason. There were enemy troops, lots of them, somewhere close. The day faded to black.

The total absence of light could be disconcerting to some, but Sam had grown accustomed to the opaque wall of black caused by the moonless Vietnam nights. It wasn't the darkness that troubled him, and perhaps he was overreacting to the silence, but he remained on edge. He felt for his CAR-15, pulled it closer, and wrapped his poncho liner around his head and upper torso to thwart the ravaging hordes of mosquitoes. His thoughts took him to Caroline and that day in Manila when he'd taken her to a jewelry store. After a few days together it had become a foregone conclusion for them both. They hoped to marry when he got back to the States. Sam purchased a ring to make it official.

He saw her eyes again, there before him in the darkness, glowing as they had that day when he slipped the ring on her finger. His only hope now was to complete her dream by returning home alive and in one piece. He slipped into a light sleep, rolled and turned, still gripping the poncho liner to keep his face covered as he dreamt a strange dream of trucks on a highway. He could hear their engines revving and groaning as if they were caught in a traffic jam and he searched for them in his mind's eye, only to realize he wasn't asleep. The sounds were not those of a dream.

Snatching the poncho from around his head, Sam sat upright. He sensed a presence close beside him in the darkness. "NVA vehicles." It was Mahoney. His whisper came from mere inches away.

They listened to the sounds of revving engines rising up from the valley below and Sam realized every man on the team was now awake and listening. Barely two kilometers below he spotted dim lights—vanilla, almost candle-like—jerking and drifting about beneath the trees. There also came a rapid and rhythmic *clanking* from below, and Sam couldn't believe what he was hearing. *Tracked vehicles? Surely not.*

"Tanks?" he whispered.

"That'd be my guess," Mahoney answered. "Russian PT-76s

like they used up at Lang Vei. That's probably the same bastards that overran our boys up there—the NVA 198th Tank Battalion."

"Shiiuuutt," Sam muttered.

He watched the lights burning like scores of fireflies in the trees below, and after a while he noticed something new. The vehicles were not going anywhere, but merely circling at each end of the valley and returning to a staging area to be parked. They'd hit a jackpot—a major NVA truck park. The engines began shutting down, one, two at a time, as the vehicles were parked, until the sounds dissipated entirely.

From somewhere close by came another whisper, "Jeeeessuuus!"

"Noise discipline," Mahoney whispered. "If it ain't necessary, don't say it."

Sam didn't recognize the other voice, but it was one of his men. This was something he would have to work on. He had to know his men, even in the pitch black of the nighttime jungle.

———————

Dawn broke after a number of sleepless hours. A dripping rain was filtering through from the trees above. The team huddled together after sending a sit-rep to the X-ray team, reporting the coordinates for the huge concentration of enemy vehicles. An hour later the X-ray team relayed a message from the operations center. "Exit the area. Move to the primary extraction point." The team ate cold rations as they prepared to move out. Sam rolled his already soaked poncho liner and stuffed it in his ruck.

The rain was a leveler. Its sound-masking patter hid anything that wasn't visible—except for one thing. He glanced around to see if one of the team was squatting and emptying his bowels, but all were still eating their rations. He decided someone must have blown a terrible fart, but there was another odor as well—one of rotting fish.

It made no sense. Khul and his men were required to eat either plain rice or the same rations as the Americans—not without purpose. It was the same reason no one smoked, made hot coffee or used mosquito repellant—odor control. Yet the odors were strong.

The drift of the wind changed and the odors faded. Sam glanced at Mahoney. The sergeant was locked in earnest conversation with Khul as they whispered back and forth. Sam walked over and sat beside them. Khul silently signaled for one of his men to follow and they eased out into the jungle, disappearing down the ridge.

"We have an enemy camp somewhere close, and Khul thinks he may have heard voices during the night," Mahoney said.

"I know. I smelled it," Sam said.

Mahoney gave him a tight-lipped nod. "You're a fast learner, Lieutenant. What did you smell?"

"A latrine, maybe, but rotted fish?"

"Nước mắm. It's a fermented fish sauce they put on their rice and such. Tastes better than it smells."

"You've actually eaten something that smells like that?"

Mahoney smiled. The rain had intensified by the time Khul returned. Sam listened while the Montagnard briefed Mahoney.

"Beaucoup NVA," he said. "Hunred, maybe more. Beaucoup, many bunker, too. Big gun, twenty-three millimeter, very close. There." He pointed into the jungle as if he were looking directly at the anti-aircraft gun he was describing.

Mahoney turned to Sam and whispered, "It looks like we spent the night in their backyard. We need to get the hell out of Dodge, so tell me how you would get your team out of here?"

Sam turned to Khul. "Which way do we go?"

Mahoney grinned. "Good move."

Khul pointed back up the mountain. "That way, Đại-úy."

"But that's Laos," Sam said.

"Better listen to him if you want to get out of here. They can't extract us if we're all dead or locked up in bamboo cages."

Sam nodded to Khul and the young Montagnard started up the ridge through the dense undergrowth. Robbie Knowlton followed, and Mahoney signaled for the rest to fall in line behind them. The primary extraction point was out in the main valley, in the opposite direction from which they were going, but that way was blocked by the enemy base camp. The team would probably make a wide circle and....

From behind came a shout and another—the excited voices of enemy soldiers. Sam's gut went cold as he looked toward Mahoney, but the sergeant had stopped and was gazing skyward. The rain had dissipated and there was the distant buzz of a small aircraft somewhere high overhead. The stuttering roar of an anti-aircraft gun exploded only a few meters away, shattering the silence and shaking a shower of raindrops from the trees overhead. Sam heard the clanking of the empty brass casings striking together as they fell to the ground. The gun was close—too damned close.

"Move!" Mahoney hissed. "Go, go, go."

Weaving through the wet undergrowth the team climbed the mountain toward Laos. They were moving fast, too fast, and Sam realized Mahoney was taking a calculated risk to get them out of the area. An hour later, after moving several klicks, Khul brought them to a stop and signaled Mahoney up to the point. Sam followed.

They'd come up on a well-worn trail coming over the mountain from Laos. It led to the little valley below. The thin mountain air had the men breathing heavily and a hot vapor rose from the backs of their rain-soaked fatigues. The muddy trail was filled with hundreds of fresh footprints. Mahoney motioned in silence for the men to begin crossing the trail one at a time, but he held Sam back.

When the last man had crossed, he quietly showed him how to obliterate their tracks by sweeping the trail with a palm frond. By midafternoon they turned southeastward and reached another steep mountain valley where they began climbing the next ridge. They had moved non-stop for seven hours, and several times throughout the day, the RTO had tried to raise the x-ray team without success. On a signal from Mahoney, Khul led them into a thicket of palms and ferns where the men dropped to the ground in near exhaustion.

"We'll move up as high on this ridge as we can before dark," Mahoney said. "We've missed every scheduled sit-rep today, so I expect they'll send a Bird Dog out to try and locate us."

"What was that plane doing up there this morning?" Sam asked.

"My guess is it was an Air Force Bird Dog doing reconnaissance for an Arc Light strike on that valley."

"Dude has some big kahunas flying in these mountains in the rain."

"Yeah, it was pretty risky, but he probably took off within a few minutes after our sit-rep this morning. They don't waste time when we make a find like that. We'll move out in one-five."

Dusk was rapidly approaching when they formed their NDP that evening. The men ate their first rations since breakfast. Sam thought he heard a scratch on one of the PRC-25 handsets. Redden and the Special Forces RTO grabbed them, shoved them against their ears and listened.

"Roger, Bravo-Delta-Niner-Niner, this is Sierra-Mike-One-Four. Wait one," Redden whispered. He gave the handset to Mahoney. "It's a Bird Dog trying to find us."

For nearly two minutes Mahoney talked on the radio as the sound of the little Cessna drew closer and it began flying back and forth across the mountainside. The plane approached again and when it finally passed directly overhead Mahoney whispered, "Bingo," into the handset.

There was another pause before the team leader ended the transmission. "Roger, Bravo-Delta-Niner-Niner, will do. Thanks. Out," he said.

The team gathered close. "The Bird Dog spotted a pretty good place we can use for extraction just up the ridge from here. If the weather holds, there'll be a pink team in here after daylight to get us out."

"What's a pink team?" Sam asked.

"It's an extraction package—a C&C ship and a Cobra gunship that'll escort two or three Slicks to the PZ."

"Sounds like a good homecoming committee," Knowlton said.

"Just pray we don't need the gunship," Mahoney said. "Things may not be going too good if we do."

A series of brilliant flashes appeared in the evening sky to the northwest. The surrounding hills were momentarily lit like daylight as the flashes reflected in the men's faces. Mahoney came to his feet and stared out that way. Sam and the others did the same. Several seconds later tremendous thundering booms echoed through the mountains and the ground trembled beneath their feet.

"What the fuck?" Lowry whispered.

"That's an Arc Light strike," Mahoney said.

"But I didn't hear any jets."

The flashing light, trembling ground, and rumbling roar lasted another ten or twelve seconds before silence returned to the nighttime jungle. Mahoney turned to Lowry. "The B-52s dropping those bombs are six miles up. You can't see 'em or hear 'em, but they don't miss their targets. I'm pretty sure all those tanks and vehicles we saw back there in that valley are scrap iron by now, and that NVA base camp is nothing but a big hole in the ground."

"Jeeessssuuus!" Lowry hissed.

Sam slapped his back. "Just be thankful you weren't over there in that valley. I'm thinking the enemy KIAs must be numbering in the hundreds right now."

"That's the beauty of the LRRPs," Mahoney said, "minimal risks for big payoffs. Now, let's minimize *our* risks and mind our noise discipline."

CHAPTER EIGHTEEN

A Mighty Fine Wine

October 2018
Boone, North Carolina

It was after midnight when Sam pulled the pickup into his driveway. Claire was sleeping soundly with her head resting on a pillow against the door. She didn't stir when he switched off the engine. His muscles were stiff and sore, but it felt good to be home. The trip from Biloxi had taken twelve hours. He smoothed her hair with the palm of his hand and she smiled, but her eyes remained closed.

"Hey, wake up, sleepyhead. We're back."

She sat up, blinking and staring out as if she were disoriented.

"I'm putting you up in the spare bedroom tonight. I'll take you back to the dorm after breakfast in the morning."

He retrieved two of her bags from the back seat and gave her the key to open the door.

"I was having a dream," she said. "You and Papa Pearle were in it. Y'all were mad at me because I was quitting school."

"Stop worrying about that. The last few hours while you were sleeping I've been thinking. I may have a solution."

"What's that?"

She unlocked the back door. Sam followed her in, and after setting her bags in the middle of the kitchen floor, he flipped on the light. The air in the house was stale.

"Let's get you situated back there in the spare bedroom. Let me think on it some more and we'll talk about it over breakfast in the morning."

The sun had risen, and Sam had lain awake for an hour, but there wasn't a sound in the house. They had stopped for hamburgers and fries the afternoon before and Claire hadn't had anything to eat since then. *Perhaps breakfast would be the best way to wake her.* He went to work and the aromas of the sizzling sausage and baking waffles wafted through the house. Still not a sound.

Shuffling down the hallway, he peeked into the spare bedroom. Claire was buried beneath a pile of blankets. He gave a soft whistle. She didn't move.

"Hey, sleepyhead, wake up," he said in a soft voice.

There came a groan and she rolled on her back, throwing away the blankets. "God, Sam, is this basic training or what?"

Sam couldn't help but laugh. "It's almost nine o'clock, sweetheart—time to fall out for first formation."

"Uuuuuhhhhgg. I can't believe school starts back tomorrow."

"Come on. Your waffle is almost ready."

Sam spooned dollops of butter on the waffle and set the maple syrup beside her plate. Claire shuffled in, wrapped in a blanket.

"Are you cold?" he asked.

"No. I forgot the bathrobe you bought me and left it in the closet at the hotel."

"Oh. I'll call and have them mail it to you."

"This waffle smells like heaven."

"Have at it."

Sam poured her coffee.

"You sure know how to spoil a person, don't you?"

He smiled. "I try. Caroline and I used to take turns making breakfast just to see who could outdo the other. She won the competition the morning she fixed me a fried oyster omelet."

"Sounds gross."

"It's better than you might think. And thinking about Caroline has reminded me of something else. Did you know there's a full moon on the twenty-fourth and the fall colors will be peaking? We should ride up to one of the overlooks."

"Sam." She paused and sipped her coffee. "Tell me what you think is going to happen—I mean with us, and with Dad. I just don't see a way out."

"What do you think about letting him come here to live with me?"

"Really?"

"I mean, you can too. I have that other bedroom upstairs, but it's full of junk. We'll have to clean it out—maybe have a yard sale or something."

"Sam…"

"Just think about it, Claire."

"But there's no way we can carry our load. Other than the house in Maggie Valley and the trust fund money Papa Pearle left me, we're practically penniless."

"The money is irrelevant, dear girl. I have the means. And I would never admit it to my daughter and granddaughter but it's been a very lonely time for me since Caroline passed away. Oh, they come to visit every summer and sometimes around Christmas, but they have families and lives of their own. They have asked me to come live with them, but it's not what I want. It's not their fault, but this is my home and I'm not jerking up my roots this late in life. Besides, this is where Caroline is buried."

"But, Sam, I don't think I can ever repay you unless I become a millionaire or something."

"Fact is you already have repaid me. I have never felt so lonesome as I did before we met, but you gave me not only friendship, but a purpose again. Besides, you can't take care of your father alone. So, that's that. Eat your waffle."

"I just don't know what to say. Without you, I would never have been able to save my dad."

"Don't get ahead of yourself. We aren't there yet. We still have a ways to go with your father and there are no guarantees. Together we'll do our best, but for now, can we agree that you should stay focused on your studies?"

"Yes, sir."

"Good."

"We'll work on the interview for a couple hours after breakfast. Then I'm dropping you off at your dorm. You settle in there, get some rest, or go out and do something with your friends. Have some fun...and call me when you're ready to get back to work. Sound like a plan?"

Claire's cheeks bulged from a mouth full of waffle. She gave him a thumbs-up.

May 1968
5th Special Forces Group (Airborne) Forward Operating Base (FOB-1)
Phu Bai, Republic of Vietnam

Sam and his team members sat with Captain Benhauser and Sergeant Mahoney for a mission debriefing. The extraction had gone off without a hitch and everyone returned safely. Consensus was that considering they had spent a night no more than a stone's-throw from a massive NVA basecamp, they had been lucky. It was a tale no one at FOB-1 wanted to believe until Khul told his version.

He had walked less than fifty meters down the ridge when he realized he was standing between two bunkers. The NVA soldiers were apparently inside avoiding the rain and didn't see him. He and Dak dropped to the ground and crawled out, only to run into the anti-aircraft gun halfway back up the ridge. That was when an NVA soldier walked by within five meters of them and used a latrine while they waited for him to leave.

After Khul's story began circulating, the entire post began coming by to shake their hands, slap their backs, and check out the cherry recon group from the 82nd that had spent the night in an NVA base camp.

"We'll work on some rapid reaction drills day after tomorrow and have Sergeant Mahoney pull one more mission to iron out any wrinkles that come up. After that, you'll be on your own," Benhauser said.

"Y'all did damned good," Mahoney said, "but you'll see later that there's a lot more to learn."

Sam had no doubt the sergeant was right, and a few days later they completed their second training mission. Although not exactly a dry hole, the second patrol had gone far better. Sam and his men were now preparing to go back to Camp Eagle. Captain Benhauser bid him good luck and said if there was any equipment he needed and couldn't get, to contact him. His open tab with MACV would remain available to Sam's group as well. It was an offer Sam assured him he might take him up on.

June 1968
Camp Eagle, Republic of Vietnam

Two days later Sam and his men returned to Camp Eagle where they were assigned a sandbagged hooch near brigade headquarters.

Khul and the Montagnards were housed in an adjacent one while the platoon continued training. With his new recon platoon now up to strength, they were nearly ready for their first mission. Sam hammered home drills and fire discipline and made certain his men understood the Montagnards were to be treated as equals.

"Your lives might hinge on that someday," he had said. "Those men will fight, not only for you, but also to protect you, but they must know you respect them." Their first mission came a week later.

The Marines to the north, along with several ARVN battalions and the Hundred and First, were trying to choke off the supply lines leading to the coastal areas from the highlands. The problem was they would plug one hole only to have another spring open elsewhere. An immense web of roads and trails led around and through the mountains and valleys, but they were hidden beneath the jungle canopy. The only way to find which were the most heavily used was with ground reconnaissance. The LRRPs from the 101st were stretched thin, and Sam's infant recon platoon was ordered to field two teams ASAP.

His first mission was a straightforward order. After a fly-over, he was to insert two teams for ground reconnaissance in the vicinity of the Rao Trang and Song Bo Rivers in Thau Thien Province. The only problem he had encountered so far was that Khul was the only one of the Montagnards who spoke enough English to get by. This meant the Yards had to be kept together on a single team until Khul worked with Dak enough to improve his language skills. Sam put Robbie Knowlton in charge of that team. Brick Ireland led the other.

Sam decided to insert Knowlton's Montagnard team Romeo-Bravo first that day, and when they were safely on the ground, he would insert Ireland's team. He waited back at Camp Eagle with Ireland's Romeo-Charlie team and a twelve-man reserve group listening to the radio. The Huey carrying Romeo-Bravo had just completed its first false insertion and was climbing out when the call came. Heavy ground fire had struck the chopper and they were taking evasive action. A moment later all contact was lost.

The second chopper was already powered-up on the pad and Sam told Ireland to get his team extra ammo and get loaded ASAP. He changed frequencies to the command net and notified the brigade TOC. Ausie, who was on TOC watch, agreed that it had already become a hell of an inaugural mission.

Sam signaled the second chopper pilot to take off as he crawled in beside Ireland. As soon as they were airborne, he pressed the radio handset to his ear and called for Romeo-Bravo. He heard Robbie's distant voice in the scratchy static of the radio. "Roger...forced down in...I...one Kilo India Alpha...two...contact with...Over."

"Romeo-Bravo-One your transmission is garbled. I have Romeo-Charlie coming your way."

He switched to the command net. Brigade had already requested assistance from the 101st. As the second chopper approached the confluence of the two rivers, Sam craned his neck to look out at the hills beyond. This was where the first of the two false insertions was to have occurred. He saw nothing. The crew chief tapped his shoulder and pointed out to the north as the pilot banked the chopper. Curling black smoke rose from the trees on a hillside a half-mile away. He switched back to the ops frequency.

"Romeo-Bravo. Give me a sit-rep, Robbie."

"Heavy contact. We have too many Whiskey India Alphas to break away. Estimate we're engaged with at least a platoon-size November Victor Alpha too close for arty or TAC. We need the cavalry pretty quick or this isn't going to end well. Over."

"Is that your chopper burning black smoke?"

"That's a Roger. It's down and burning."

"We have you. There's a Lima Zebra at eighty-five degrees, five hundred meters from your pos. We're going in there. Over."

"Roger, stay away from those hills to the west. They have heavy Alpha-Alpha over there somewhere. Over."

"Roger."

It would have already been too late had they flown to the west and gotten within range of the anti-aircraft guns, because the chopper was already flaring. Sam gave the handset to the RTO. Within seconds he was on the ground with Ireland and his six men. They knelt and listened as the chopper climbed away and turned out to the northeast. The constant crackling of small arms and the booms of grenades came from the ridge only a few hundred meters to the west.

Sam grabbed Brick Ireland by the shoulder. "Okay, if they saw us come in, there'll be a welcoming party waiting for us up that ridge. Let's cross down along the river and swing up behind them." He turned to Redden. "Call Knowlton and tell him what we're doing. Let's go."

The seven men plowed through the undergrowth with Sam only a few feet behind the point man. When they reached a position just south of the firefight, the team turned up the hill under the jungle canopy. The sounds of automatic weapons and exploding grenades echoed all around them. Sam pulled the team together.

"Spread out on line, but try to keep the men on your left and right in sight. Watch me for a signal. When I tell you to move out, don't shoot until you have a target and don't stop till we reach our people."

It took only seconds before Sam gave the signal to move out, and within thirty meters they made contact. The enemy had been so intent on overrunning the recon team from the downed chopper, they were taken by total surprise. An enemy soldier rolled on his back and raised his rifle, but Sam shot first. Several more were still firing up the hill toward Knowlton's team and never saw the advancing line. As the team pushed forward, more fire began coming from the flanks. Sam shouted for Ireland to move to the right with two men, while he took Redden and another man and turned to the left.

Several enemy soldiers sprang from cover and ran down the hill. Sam and Redden fired, knocking two to the ground. Screams of pain, shouts, and grenade explosions came from every direction. Sam pushed past a clot of palms to find Khul and one of his men in a hand-to-hand death struggle with several NVA regulars.

Khul was bleeding and pinned to the ground by an enemy soldier while another raised his rifle into the air and was about to plunge his bayonet into the little Montagnard. Sam riddled the enemy soldier with several rounds. The second soldier holding Khul turned just in time to catch Sam's boot full in his face. A third released the other Montagnard, pointed his SKS at Sam, and fired. That one died a moment later when the Montagnard he had been holding split his skull with a machete.

Certain he had been shot, Sam looked down at his torso, but there was nothing there—no hole, no blood, not even a scratch. He sucked in a breath just to make sure his lungs still worked. The enemy soldier had missed him at near point-blank range. Khul stumbled to his feet, retrieved his weapon, and gazed at Sam. All around them the sound of the firefight was rapidly diminishing. The enemy soldier Sam had kicked in the head rolled over and groaned. Khul raised his rifle.

"No!" Sam shouted. "Take him prisoner." He pulled the towel from around his neck, stepped forward and wiped the blood from Khul's head. It was a cut, but a few stitches would close it. "Let's move up the hill toward the downed chopper. Blindfold that fucker and tie his wrists."

Within hours, a battalion-size NVA force in the hills to the west was being engaged on three sides by elements of the 82nd, the 101st, and the ARVN Rangers. The black smoke of a napalm strike blanketed the enemy position while Sam's recon teams were flown back to Camp Eagle. Four of the Lurps were wounded, including Khul. They were being treated at the army hospital in Phu Bai. One of the helicopter pilots had been killed prior to the chopper going down and the other was injured in the hard landing. The door gunner had detached his M-60 from its mount and worked with the team to hold the enemy at bay until the second recon team arrived.

It wasn't exactly the start Sam had envisioned, but the higher-ups were ecstatic. They had found and stopped a major enemy force attempting to infiltrate the area. For Sam, the net effect was none of his men received permanently disabling injuries and they gained invaluable experience, albeit at the cost of some severely frayed nerves. The colonel, after reading Sam's AAR the next morning, sent word for him to report to brigade HQ.

"So," the colonel said, "let me see if I understand this correctly. You took a six-man recon team and led an assault on what your other team said was at least a platoon-size enemy force attacking them. Is that correct?"

"I know it seems brash, sir, but had we hesitated, my men would have been overrun. I figured if we could flank the enemy and catch them by surprise, we might have a chance. I suppose God and luck were on our side because it worked."

The colonel set two shot glasses out on his field table and pulled a flask from his pocket.

"Word is you're a bourbon man."

"Yes, sir, but if you don't mind me asking, where did you hear that?"

The colonel poured the amber liquid to the rim of each shot glass.

"You've got a big fan here in S-2, Lieutenant Langston. He came to me again yesterday—said he spoke with one of your team leaders, Sergeant Ireland. I'll cut to the chase. I'm submitting you for a Distinguished Service Cross, Sam."

He handed a glass across the table.

"And here's to show my appreciation for a real leader."

The men touched glasses and threw back their drinks.

"Thank you, sir. I appreciate your recognition, but I would trade that medal in a heartbeat for each of my men to receive a Bronze Star with a V device, a steak dinner, and a shot of this bourbon."

"Ask and thou shalt receive," the brigade commander said, "but promise me one thing."

Sam raised his eyebrows.

"I want you and your men to be front and center day after tomorrow—ready to go back in the field."

"You have my word, sir."

"Sergeant Major," the colonel called out. "Let's get a case of that bourbon from the Conex and give it to Lieutenant Walker. And don't tell me how you do it, but wrangle up about twenty-six steaks medium rare in mermite cans along with potatoes, rolls and whatever else you can get. Have it delivered to the recon hooch by 1800 hundred hours. Can you do that?"

"Can do, sir."

———————————

Late that afternoon, Khul and two of the wounded Montagnards returned from the hospital. The third man, one of Sergeant Ireland's team who had taken a round in the thigh, was destined for a longer-term recovery. Sam studied their faces. The Montagnards were people ridiculed and held in low regard by the ethnic Vietnamese, but they had every right, if not more, to their claim on this land. A simple mountain people, whose name came from the

French, the Montagnards were not only tenacious fighters, but furiously loyal.

After a debriefing with Khul translating, Sam gave them the news about the steaks and whiskey. Their faces fell, and Sam listened while Khul explained.

"But, Đại-úy," he said, "It is we who should give wine. You are brave and we live now because of you."

He hoped he wasn't violating some sacred Montagnard tradition with his ignorance, but Sam insisted. "Tonight, Khul, the wine is on me. Next time we drink your wine, okay?"

The Montagnard reached out with his fingers and touched Sam's face. Sam remained rigid and did not move or flinch. "We drink your wine today, okay," Khul said.

Khul bowed and stepped back.

"One thing, Khul. My drink is bourbon. You know? It's, ah… beaucoup strong, much more than Montagnard wine. Do you understand?"

"We understand. We drink *rất ít* bourbon."

"Rất ít?" Sam said.

"Yes. We drink only little of bourbon."

"No! You can drink all you want. Just be careful. Yours is a mighty fine wine, but mine will make you beaucoup *điên cái đầu.*" Sam cuffed the side of his own head and rolled his eyes. "It's beaucoup strong."

The Montagnard warrior nodded knowingly and translated it for the others. His men laughed and giggled almost like children. Such furious warriors, yet they had a certain innocence about them— much like children.

Late that night after consuming steaks, potatoes, and more whiskey than he cared to think about, Sam sat with the Montagnards in their hooch. The candles and Coleman lanterns were burning low, and they gazed across at him—their glassy eyes, like those of disciples, burned with loyalty. The men cast somber smiles at him, and he at them.

He was pretty well demolished but Sam poured more whiskey into his glass and passed the bottle. He waited and watched as each man added more bourbon to his cup, and only then Sam raised his glass for one final toast. He held it out with a surprisingly steady hand and waited until every last man had raised his cup. Their eyes were all locked on his and a sudden realization struck him. It was the weight of responsibility, the weight of being an officer leading these men. They were fighting for so much more than politics or whatever it was the Americans were fighting for. These men were battling for their survival and the survival of their families and their homelands.

"Here's to the trust and understanding that makes us brothers."

Khul translated to his men. They drank and Sam felt he had reached a place no military rank could take a man. These men looked to him with reverence—something he probably didn't deserve but a responsibility he could not ignore. The waters of war were still tonight, but there would be more turbulent days soon to come.

Sam had but one hope: that he, his men, and these brave mountain men of Vietnam would survive. It was a good night to be drunk, because he was consumed by the dread that they would all be gone before this war was ended.

CHAPTER NINETEEN

Another Trip to the Emerald Forest

October 24, 2018
Boone, North Carolina

C laire had received a call from the VA hospital in Biloxi, Mississippi. The doctor there wanted her to come down and do a co-counselling session with her father. Sam agreed to take her, but when he said he would make reservations for their hotel rooms, she objected.

"No," she said. "I don't want to stay in a room alone."

Age had given him something he had experienced only for a few years after returning from Nam—a much shorter fuse, but Sam didn't react. Instead, he took a deep breath and said nothing. It still bothered him, the way this girl acted, but hers was a generation many times removed from his. He made the reservation for a single room with queen beds and they went that night to the Thunder Hill Overlook.

Together they gazed out from where he and Caroline had sat many times over the years. It was across the parkway on the rock above the overlook. Far across the Carolina hills, the harvest moon had risen above the eastern horizon and Claire was pouring herself a glass of wine. Sam was already sipping his bourbon.

She rested her elbows on her knees and held the wine glass entwined in her fingers as she stared out at the full moon.

"Did you make the room reservation?" she asked.

"Yes, missy, just as you requested—one room, two queen beds."

Reading the disapproval in his voice she turned to him. "It's okay being old-fashioned, Sam, but really, you need to lighten up and stop worrying about it."

He turned and gazed into Claire's eyes, now a soft gray with the full moon reflecting in them. A woman with the naïve innocence of a child, she could easily be called just another confused millennial, but she was trying desperately to find herself and a purpose in a world of loneliness. And there was that special something that set her apart from, if not above, most of those in her generation. She might never find the limelight of history as a poet or a general, but Sam felt certain she was one with that potential.

"A little bit of the right kind of worry might serve you well one day."

"I'll take that under advisement," she said.

Sam refused to laugh at her quick wit. Dropping his head instead, he shook it in resignation.

"What time are we leaving tomorrow?" she asked.

"I'll pick you up at the dorm at six in the morning. We'll run by The Local Lion for coffee and a donut then hit the road."

"You military dudes have this thing about getting up at the butt-crack of dawn, don't you?"

Sam fought back a laugh. "I do believe the full moon and that wine have freed you of your inhibitions, little woman."

"No, it's just you, Sam. You make me feel totally free, totally safe and relaxed. I just wish I could find a guy my age that makes me feel the way you do."

"Don't worry. Someday you will, and he'll be the luckiest man alive."

She hugged his arm and rested her head on his shoulder.

Sam and Claire walked into the coffee shop the following morning where the barista greeted them. "You're dating 'em mighty young nowadays, professor."

Sam glared at him. "I believe you're making an incorrect assumption, young man, and you're not showing this lady the respect she deserves."

The look of incredulity on Claire's face made Sam realize he was overreacting. "It's okay, Sam. I'm sure he was just kidding."

The young man too seemed taken aback. "Sorry, professor. I was…kidding, that is. How about having coffee on me this morning?"

All his life Sam had prided himself on his ability to mask his feelings, but he felt a growing pressure to help Claire make the right decisions in her life.

"I'm sorry. I'm just being a grumpy old man."

"We all have our days," the barista said.

Sam was still thinking about the evening before when he and Claire had gone up to the overlook to watch the moon rise. It was supposed to have been an enjoyable excursion, but he was beginning to have second thoughts about giving her so many of his opinions about the war. They were truths to him, but her trust was nearly blind and there were so many other opinions that she needed to consider as a part of her thesis.

Yes, the Vietnam War was incubated in an ocean of lies, deceit, and wrongfully exploited good intentions. And as is often the case with good intentions, those pertaining to the war had only paved its path to a debacle of historical proportions. But his current problem was with the alternative history of the war—a history that was made up of lies no different from the ones that caused it. Some of the very political entities that led the country into the war were now using it as a means of damning the country as a war-mongering nation.

They left The Local Lion that morning before seven and were on their way to Biloxi. Claire pulled the recorder from the bag and opened her spiral notebook.

"It's going to be a long day. Are you ready to get back to work?" she asked.

"Sure," Sam said.

The morning sunlight reflected against the fluttering leaves on the mountainsides and the fall colors flamed with magnificence beneath a cobalt blue sky. He would rather have driven along in peace and enjoyed the scenery, but Claire was unrelenting with this thesis.

"First tell me what that word meant that Khul was calling you— đại-úy."

"That's Vietnamese for 'captain.' I didn't want to confuse matters by telling him I was just a lieutenant, so…." Sam shrugged.

Claire laughed and he again began telling his story.

June 1968
3rd Brigade, 82nd Airborne, Tactical Operations Center
Camp Eagle, Republic of Vietnam

Sam brought along his two team leaders, Sergeants Robbie Knowlton and Brick Ireland, that morning as they met with Ausie for an intelligence briefing. Ausie had taken it upon himself to become the primary TOC and S-2 contact for the LRRP platoon—something Sam found reassuring. There would be no guesstimates and no bullshit with Ausie—just facts.

"The colonel wants you to put three teams in these mountains here." Ausie pointed to a topo map hanging on the wall. "They're about ten kilometers further west of where you guys went in the last time. Some of the peaks up there are four to six thousand feet, so it won't be a fun place to navigate. These two blue lines north and south of the AO are tributaries of the Song Bo."

"What about enemy activity?" Sam asked.

"Do you want me to tell you what we know?"

"I suppose, but I think I already know."

"Yeah. Bottom line is we don't know shit, Sam. We have over a dozen reported sightings—everything from three or four men crossing a river to a nearly mile-long column of flashlights coming around the mountain one night. We don't know if they're transiting or if there's a base camp up there. That's where you and your men come in. We need to know what's on that mountain."

"I'll need you back here at the TOC in my place, Ausie. I have to run one of the teams because I just don't have a third man who is ready to lead one yet."

"I already made arrangements for that. I'll be your primary contact back here, and we'll have a company from the 505th on standby if you need them."

"A company—really?"

Ausie smiled and whispered. "I think the colonel likes you."

"Can I take a look at those reports?"

"Here's the target folder." Aussie shoved a green file folder across the table. "Not much there, but help yourself."

Sam thumbed through the papers for several minutes before looking up at Ausie. "I'll do my first flyovers this afternoon with my team leaders. I need a favor."

Ausie raised an eyebrow.

"I put in a requisition for eight 120-foot ropes and sixteen McGuire rigs. Can you check with your S-4 counterpart and get me an update on the requisition?"

"I heard them talking with the colonel about it yesterday. I wasn't going to tell you, but a certain asshole down at MACV S-4 in Saigon said it'll be at least a week or two, maybe longer before we get the rigs."

Ausie seemed to be referring to someone in particular.

"And you know who this certain someone is, I assume," Sam said.

"Yes, I suppose so."

"Okay, so stop the bullshit. Who is it?"

"Look, Sam—"

"It's that asshole Hardrick. Isn't it?"

"Sam, it doesn't—"

"Sonofabitch! If I lose a single fucking man because of that asshole, I'll go down to Saigon personally and stomp the life out of that piece of—"

"Sam!"

"What!?"

Thankfully, it was late and the only witnesses were Knowlton, Ireland, and the duty officer.

"I already spoke with the colonel. He's going to handle it as soon as he returns from the field."

"Never mind," Sam said. "I have my own means."

He hated to do it so soon, but Sam had to contact Captain Benhauser down at FOB-1. It was time to take him up on his offer. Howitzer was a man of his word and would no doubt deliver.

"I want you to contact a Special Forces Captain named Benhauser down at the Special Forces Base in Phu Bai. Tell him I need those McGuire rigs and ropes and ask him how long it will take to get them."

"Sure. I've got you covered."

———————————

Sam, his two team leaders and Khul sat in the open door of a Huey helicopter as it circled high above the mountains. The air was thin and cold, and despite his field jacket, Sam shivered as he pointed out possible LZs for inserting and extracting the teams. Five klicks to the southwest, beyond the highest peaks, was the A Shau Valley. A place of awe and mysterious reverence for those who faced the possibility of combat there, it was nearly lost in the haze and clouds.

This was a vast, rugged, and remote area of the Annamite Range—towering mountains draped with double- and triple-canopied jungles. Beneath them the NVA hid, moved about, and waited for the perfect moment to pounce and annihilate American units. This was a tiger Sam didn't wish to feed, but he had his job to do. He was going there into the tiger's jungle realm.

Upon their return to Camp Eagle, they sat with Ausie and went over their notes. The insertion and extraction sites were chosen as well as alternatives for any unforeseen events that might have the teams scrambling and possibly fleeing for their lives. Maps were marked with red and blue ink, indicating points of origin, recon areas, and other pertinent data. The mission would begin with the teams patrolling around the base of the mountain in search of trails, roads, and other sign that might indicate the enemy's presence. Once these were found—and Sam had no doubt they would be—the teams would remain in place for up to five days recording traffic and counting men, weapons, and equipment.

"This just doesn't look good to me," Knowlton said. "We're going way out on a limb and there are way too many opportunities for us to get our butts in a crack."

"Nothing we will ever do in this business is going to look good, but it's what we've been asked to do," Sam said. "Let's just try to figure how we can get in there and get out with the least amount of risk."

"What if one of the teams is in contact and can't get to an extraction point—then what?" Ireland asked.

Sam glanced at Ausie. "Did you talk with Captain Benhauser?"

"He's sending you eight ropes with McGuire rigs—said that was all he could muster on short notice. They'll be coming up by chopper in the morning."

"Good enough. I want each of you to have your men familiarize themselves with the rigs and be able to get in one while lying prone. Work with Khul and make sure his men know how to use them as well. Those rigs will enable us to be extracted from wherever we are."

"I'll see that we have a couple of the Hueys with the McGuire rigs," Ausie said.

Khul had remained silent the entire time. Sam glanced over at him. "Khul, do you have any ideas or suggestions?"

"Why not we can bring more helicopter—confuse enemy?"

They had planned for the false insertions with the Slicks carrying the teams, but it made sense to have others doing the same thing. Sam nodded at Ausie and exhaled. "It's not a bad idea. Do you think you could stir up a couple extra birds just to fly up and down the river valley and draw attention away from the actual insertions?"

"I'll get with the colonel. I'm not sure he'll risk them, but if we can't get more choppers, we might use the gunships."

Sam dismissed his men and sat studying the map. When he looked up, Ausie was still staring at him. The look on his face was strange—vexed perhaps and a little worried. "What is it?" Sam asked.

Ausie glanced around to make sure no one was listening. "Look, Sam. You need to be careful out there. I don't mean to sound like a wussy, but I'm beginning to think there's no end to any of this shit. It's just not something worth dying for."

"I agree, my friend. I think our civilian leaders have led us down that proverbial primrose path. Don't worry. I won't take any chances that I don't have to take." With that he stood and they shook hands.

Sam glanced back as they parted. Ausie's statement, given his military academy training, was totally out of character. He had let his personal feelings show. Yet he was right. It was eminently clear that they were in a fight with no clear end, no clear goals, no clear anything. What the politicians in Washington hoped to achieve was known only to them—something that wasn't giving Sam the warm-fuzzies. On the contrary, he had grown rather cynical about the futures of both his country and The Republic of Vietnam.

Six choppers were warming up on the LZ that morning. Three were loaded to maximum capacity with the LRRP teams and their equipment. Three more were gunships that would act as decoys and perform additional false insertions in the area, but they were also armed with rockets and mini-guns to provide close air support if needed. The Slick pilots increased their RPMs and the choppers began lumbering slowly across the LZ to achieve lift. One by one they labored skyward, their rotors thundering as they began a slow turn westward toward the mountains.

Sam gazed out at the horizon. The mountains ahead were dark gray shadows looming in the morning mist. The villages and coastal lowlands quickly disappeared as the choppers climbed into the hills. Below, luminescent pools of fog, tinged with the orange morning sunlight, filled every crevice and valley. The weather was supposed to hold for at least two or three days, but the morning fog seemed to never go away. The gunships passed the slower moving Slicks, and disappeared up ahead. They were on their way to begin making the false insertions.

The plan was for each team to be inserted from twenty to thirty minutes apart in case someone made contact. This would allow an orderly execution of contingency plans if any of them were forced to abort. Sam's Romeo-Alpha team, which included RTO Allen Lowry and the most inexperienced six men in the platoon, went in first high on the mountain where they raised the long-distance antenna and established communication with a radio relay team. Knowlton along with his RTO Frank Redden, Khul, and four Montagnards made up Romeo-Bravo and went in next, near the southwest base of the mountain.

Thirty minutes later, Brick Ireland's Romeo-Charlie team, which included RTO Charley Conway, Dak, and four more Montagnards, was inserted on the northeastern side of the mountain. The choppers flew across the face of the mountain making several more false insertions before disappearing back to the east.

It was suddenly quiet and no one moved as they remained in place and listened for the first thirty minutes. The jungle remained still. The silence was almost spooky. A nearly indiscernible scratch of static came from the radio as Knowlton called in and reported Romeo-Bravo moving out.

Their plan was to patrol down to the blue line to the southwest, circle, and come back up the mountain until the terrain became too steep. Ireland called in next as he began his movement down to the blue line on the northern slope of the mountain. Sam was fairly certain they would find roads or trails, and the plan was to check them for sign. If a trail looked productive, they would set up and watch it that night and the next day.

"Romeo-Alpha-One, Romeo-Bravo-One, Over." The call came in from Robbie Knowlton barely thirty minutes after he started down the mountain.

"Go ahead Romeo-Bravo," Sam whispered.

"I've found the New Jersey Turnpike down here, sir. Over."

"Roger, Romeo-Bravo. Go ahead and send Red-Leg-Carentan your Papa-Tango-Delta. I'll listen in. If you have trouble with the transmission, I'll help. Over."

By nightfall both teams were in their overnight positions. Romeo-Charlie had already circled back toward the mountain in what appeared was going to be a dry hole. Ireland and his team had found nothing. Sam would determine what to do with them the following morning. In the meantime, everyone would wait and listen.

Sam felt his own heartbeat. And there was the sixth sense that told him the enemy was here. They were here in overwhelming numbers all over this mountain, and he and his men were now nestled amongst them. It would be a proverbial lethal game of cat and mouse—his teams ghosting about, sending back reports and hoping the big NVA cat didn't catch them. The strangest part of all of this was his continual thoughts of how much he didn't want to disappoint Caroline by not coming home.

CHAPTER TWENTY

The Fog of War

October 2018
Biloxi, Mississippi

C laire and her father had their first joint counseling session with the doctor that morning while Sam sat in the waiting room. All had gone well, and the doctor suggested Claire spend another hour with her father later that afternoon in a more casual setting. She insisted that Sam be there as well. Bill Cunningham had shaved and his face was no longer gaunt and sunburned. The three of them sat on a bench beside the fountain near the hospital entrance as she introduced the two men.

"Daddy, this is Sam Walker. He's the man who was with me the day we found you in Pensacola. He was a lieutenant in the Army, too."

Claire's father stared at him with an inscrutable countenance, and Sam extended his hand. "Pleased to meet you, again, sir."

Cunningham didn't offer his hand. "When were you in?" he asked. His question carried the tone of a cross-examination.

"1967 and '68."

Cunningham studied him. "Did you see combat in Vietnam?"

Sam nodded. "Yeah. I was an infantry platoon leader with the 173rd Airborne in '67 and the 82nd Airborne in '68."

"Did you lose any of your men over there?"

Cunningham's eyes searched Sam's, and Sam saw reflected there his own pain—the pain he had compartmentalized and buried so deeply over the years. It had been the two new kids, Tommy Mooney and Mike Razura killed that first day along with Calvin Castleman, and later Darrell Washington, one of his squad leaders, had died in his arms. And then there was Billy Baker, the freckle-faced RTO they called Glasspack, who followed faithfully in his footsteps until that day on Hill 875. More of them passed through his mind's eye. You never forgot them—good men who trusted you but who never came home.

"There are damned few of us who led men into combat that didn't lose some," Sam said.

"I lost my platoon sergeant, a squad leader, and one of my drivers all in one day," Cunningham said.

The unrequited loss of those men was imprinted deep within Cunningham's eyes. Words would make little difference, but Sam had to try. "I understand how you feel. Our men, both those who survived and the ones who didn't, become a part of our lives for as long as we live, but I believe it's so they won't be forgotten."

"I sure as hell never forgot mine," Cunningham said.

Sam glanced over at Claire. Her eyes seemed lost in the unfocused thought of something deep within, and he realized then that this conversation had likely provided some of the understanding she had sought when they first met. This was knowledge that a thesis or a thousand words of any kind could never impart. It was something only those with that experience could describe.

Cunningham turned to Claire. "Connie, you know your daddy was in the 82nd Airborne. When you get back home, you should ask him if he remembers Sam."

Claire took her father's hand. "Daddy, I'm Claire—your daughter."

He reached over and clumsily patted her head. "I know, baby. I just get a little confused now and then. You should ask Mama. Papa Pearle was a paratrooper like Sam here, and they were in the same outfit."

A tear trickled down her cheek and she quickly wiped it away. "It's okay, Daddy. I will always take care of you."

Cunningham cast a nervous glance Sam's way and their eyes met. Sam saw there what he already suspected. Cunningham knew he was wandering about in a tilted world—one spinning as a mad carousel that had lost its center. The two veterans gazed into one another's eyes for several seconds until the younger man gave a slight nod. It seemed like one of ambivalent trust. Despite the bond that existed between them as combat veterans, Sam realized it would take time to overcome Cunningham's paranoia.

"I suppose combat leaves us all with a few scars," Sam said.

Cunningham nodded. "And sometimes that 'fog of war' never goes away. Some days I wake up and I feel like I'm a thousand miles from home and I don't know where I am. It's like I'll never see it again."

His eyes faded into the unfocused stare of a veteran who had seen one too many days of combat.

After the meeting with her father that afternoon Claire was quiet and lost in thought as they rode back to the hotel. The visits with her father and their future together had to be weighing heavily on her mind, but there was something Sam wanted to discuss with her and he didn't want it to wait. He reasoned that it might actually be a needed distraction. At least he hoped so, because he could see the stress on his young protégée's face.

"Let's go to the Half Shell Oyster House for supper. What do you say?"

"Oyster house?"

"Yeah. They have oysters cooked more ways than you can imagine."

Claire wrinkled her nose.

"What's wrong?" he asked.

"I've never had oysters."

"You're kidding."

"No."

"Never?"

"Never."

"Well, unwrinkle your nose, little woman. I am going to treat you to one of the true delicacies of the sea."

"Brad and his buddies talked about eating them raw when they went down to Myrtle Beach this summer. I'm not sure I can eat a raw one."

"Honey child, stick with me. I'll make you a shellfish connoisseur of the first degree."

"Don't they fix them some way other than raw?"

Sam scratched his chin. "Well, let me see. I believe they have charbroiled oysters, Oysters Orleans, Oysters Bienville, Oysters Rockefeller, fried oysters, oyster poor-boys and, of course, if you really get brave there is always my favorite, raw oysters."

"I may have to pass on the raw ones, but let's give it a try," she said. "Let me go in the bathroom to freshen up and put on something more comfortable."

A few minutes later the bathroom door opened and Sam sat up on the bed. He glanced at Claire and did a double-take.

"You ready?" she asked.

"Well, yeah," Sam said, "but did you forget something?"

Claire stepped in front of the mirror and looked herself up and down. "What?"

"Your britches, maybe?"

"My what?"

"Surely you aren't going out to eat wearing only those black pantyhose?"

Sarah turned with a laugh. "You can't be serious. These are yoga pants."

Sam knew what they were, and he'd seen women wearing them everywhere, the malls, the grocery store, parks, and even restaurants.

"I know what they are."

"So, they're the style now. Everyone wears them, and see," she turned about, "my T-shirt comes down far enough to…well…to make me look respectable."

"Respectable? Hell, there's not much left to the imagination. Besides, I can see the bottom of your butt cheeks."

She snatched at the T-shirt, stretching it downward.

"Okay, Claire. Do you remember what I said when we agreed you were to be my adopted granddaughter?"

"Yeeessss," she moaned. "You said it came with lectures and whatnot."

"Look, you are probably one of the four or five percent of women who actually has a figure for that kind of *dress*, if that's what you want to call it, but that *still* doesn't make it decent. Hell, most of those lumpy-butted old heifers would look better wearing ponchos."

Claire laughed. "One thing is for sure," she said. "Political correctness is *not* one of your stronger traits."

Sam had spoken his mind and decided enough had been said. She was an adult. He stood and pulled on his jacket.

"Oh heck," she said. "Just hang on a minute." Walking to the closet she took a pair of khaki pants off a hanger and held them up. "How about these?"

"No," Sam said. "You're an adult, and I'm not dictating to you what you can wear. It was only my opinion."

Claire pushed open the bathroom door. "And I respect that. It's a two-way street. If you aren't comfortable with me going out in yoga pants then I'm not going to wear them."

———————————

They had been served their drinks and their first sampler plate of a dozen oysters prepared three ways had arrived, when Sam decided to discuss what was on his mind.

"It's probably not very good timing right now given what you're going through with your dad, but there's something I want to talk about."

Sam paused to gather his thoughts. Claire said nothing as she stared back at him, seeming to sense his uneasiness.

"We've been working on this thesis now for several weeks, and I've been giving you my opinions on the war. I will likely give you more, but I'm just not sure… I mean… I think…you should take what I say and compare it."

Her brows furrowed. "What do you mean? Compare it to what?"

"When I give you my opinions about the Vietnam War and the politics surrounding it, they are all things that I truly believe. I just don't want you to accept everything I say blindly. You have to present it in a neutral manner and, if necessary, justify why it has merit when you write your paper."

She sucked her drink through a straw until it was dry and held up the empty glass for the waiter to see.

"You better go easy on that liquor, girl."

"Sam, there are many points of views, and I've already heard most of the alternative ones from my history professors, but I can't think of a better source than a man who actually lived it. I trust your opinions more than I do some professor who never did much more than burn his draft card and participate in campus protests when he was a student. Besides, I'm making no pretense of an unbiased presentation. My tentative title is 'A Veteran's Perspective.'"

The waiter delivered another tray of oysters and fresh drinks. Claire plucked the cherry and orange slice from hers, ate them and sucked down half the glass. By the time they were on their third tray of oysters, Sam figured she was feeling very little pain.

"I take it you've become an oyster fan."

She looked up with a broad grin that remained fixed on her face, and even with eyes that were riddled with red roadmaps, she was a beautiful sight.

"You have a severe case of perma-grin, little lady."

"It's you, Sam. You make me happy. Of course it's possible these drinks are making a contribution as well."

"Well, you've had oysters fixed every way possible, except one."

"I missed one?"

"Yes, but if you don't slow down on the liquor you're going to be sick."

"Which one did I miss?"

It seemed her usual quick wit had failed her. "We need to order something for dessert. How does a half-dozen raw oysters sound?"

Claire's perma-grin shriveled to a doubtful frown and Sam laughed.

"I'm just kidding. I'll ask for the check and we'll head back to the hotel."

"No! I'm in. I'm all in. I want to try them."

"Are you sure?"

"Order them."

Claire was not her usual pleasant self the next morning when they departed Biloxi. Saying little, she put on her sunglasses and curled up in the seat. They hadn't yet reached Mobile, Alabama, and she was already sleeping soundly on her pillow against the truck door. Sam decided to avoid giving her a temperance lecture—opting instead to let her sleep it off. Her hangover was a small price to pay for the relief she'd gotten after an emotional day with her father, and it was also a good lesson for her. At least he hoped it was. It might keep her from developing a bad habit—something he would at least mention when she felt better.

October 1968
Boone, North Carolina

"So what's the verdict?" Sam asked.

They had been back for two days, and he and Claire were sitting in The Local Lion coffee shop sipping coffee and looking out at a drizzling gray rain. It was Tuesday.

"The verdict?"

"Yeah—on the oysters."

She gave him an embarrassed smile and looked down into her coffee cup. "They were fantastic. I just wish I hadn't drunk so much. I didn't know they put so much liquor in mixed drinks."

"Stick with your occasional white wine, little lady, and you'll be better off."

"I believe that! I've been eating ibuprofen like candy for two days. Oh, and I talked with the doctor down at Biloxi. I told him about your offer and he wants the three of us to meet together with Daddy this Friday—I mean if you don't mind. If all goes well and Dad agrees to live with you, the doctor is going to release him and transfer his records to the VA in Asheville."

"That *is* good news. We need to go over to the house later and get the bedroom ready for him. Crank up your recorder and let's get to work."

"Okay, but first I want to ask you some questions."

"Sure."

"When we went out to eat that night, you seemed apologetic for giving me your opinions, but you have actually said very little. I've read a lot about how the war came about, but what's your opinion on it? Did it have to happen or was it avoidable?"

"That's a question those currently writing our history books have chosen to answer as 'no, it didn't have to happen,' but the consequences—had we followed that belief—will never be known. You see, Uncle Ho—Ho Chi Minh that is—was our ally whom we supported while fighting the Japanese during World War II, but he turned to the Communists when we supported France taking over his country. He kicked the French out in 1954, and then, in the name of stopping Communist world domination, we got involved. Yeah, it was a mess, and our leaders made some fundamental mistakes—ones that proved monumental in later years."

"What were those?"

"Let me say this first. There have been volumes written on these questions, so what I say here is very narrow in scope. Let's just say these are the same opinions we talked about over supper the other night.

"The first mistake made was by Harry Truman, allowing France to maintain its hold on Indochina after World War II. The Vietnamese had already announced their intent to be self-governing. Our government backing French colonialism went against our every tenet as a free nation. We sold our souls to the devil to appease the French, whom we had just bailed out for the second time in Europe."

"What's another mistake we made?"

"Have you ever heard the quote 'never fight a land war in Asia?'"

"Yes, when we studied modern European history, the professor said Napoleon and Hitler both tried it and failed."

"Yes, and we, the Americans, did it in Vietnam. You see, a few weeks after John F. Kennedy was assassinated, Lyndon Johnson called the Joint Chiefs of Staff to the White House and asked them what military options we had for dealing with the Vietnam issue and the probability of success for each. They gave him three: One was a limited response with only gradually increasing troop involvement. Their prediction was that this course of action would lead to absolute certain and total failure. The second option was to go all in with the entire strength of the American military. Their prediction on that one was still a rather weak fifty-fifty chance of success. The third option, and believe it or not the one they recommended, was to get out entirely and let Vietnam decide its own destiny. They predicted that after a brief conflict, South Vietnam would fall to Communist North Vietnam."

"And we went with the first and the worst one. Why?"

"That's another debated question."

"The LBJ fan club said he wanted to avoid a full-blown conflict with China, but a deeper study of government records has proven almost every decision he made pertaining to the war in Vietnam was based on political expediency. He knew we were bound to fail and even said as much, but he didn't want to go down in history as the first president to lose a war, and he wanted to get re-elected in 1964. To go for all-out war or to get out entirely meant he would likely lose that presidential election. Our leader was playing politics with men's lives not only to win an election, but because he didn't trust his own military leaders' opinions.

"LBJ had no intention of either fully engaging or else getting the hell out. Hell, he trusted a bean-counter from Ford named McNamara, and together they lied to the joint chiefs, they lied to congress, and they lied to the American people. That's what we didn't know at the time."

"And it wasn't only the Americans who lost. We gave the South Vietnamese people false hope. And many of those loyal to us lost everything. Khul and his men lost their families when their village was wiped out by the Communists."

Claire sat staring through him, lost in thought as her coffee grew cold.

Sam added, "My only question now and always will be, 'What idiot in the White House decided to make decisions and establish policies regarding Vietnam without having read *Street Without Joy*? Have you read it yet?"

"Not yet. It's next on the list."

"When it was published in the early 1960s, it should have been required reading for every politician in Washington. It chronicles the French involvement in Indochina and how General Giap and the Viet-Minh slowly overwhelmed them, eventually crushing them at Dien Bien Phu.

"Many of our military leaders had read it, and they understood what such a war would look like for Americans. That's why the joint chiefs recommended we stay home. The politicians, though, had other ideas that involved smoke and mirrors and votes and careers. Everything else, including the lives of thousands of American soldiers, was inconsequential and subverted to the advancement of those purposes."

Claire remained silent and seemingly lost in thought.

Sam was again feeling a little sheepish. Perhaps he had gotten a little carried away. He knew he was right, but wondered if she was really listening and understanding what he was trying to tell her. Dissecting the war, its history, causes, and effects was akin to separating the ingredients for spaghetti sauce after it was cooked. Her thesis was a bold undertaking and he didn't envy her.

"Okay, let's finish my part in this story. We can talk more on the politics later if you want."

She looked up at him. Her lips were firmly set and her brows wrinkled as she slowly nodded, but her eyes again lost focus and faded into thought. Debacles on the scale of the Vietnam War are never easily understood, even years after the fact. And it was obvious Claire was trying to sort through these things, but there was no simple right and wrong, no simple good and bad. He wanted to tell her that it was a bad time and most of his generation had done what they thought was right, but that was something she would now have to decide for herself.

CHAPTER TWENTY-ONE

Escape & Evasion on the Mountain

June 1968
Highlands Northeast of the A Shau Valley

Robbie Knowlton's Romeo-Bravo team reported two large NVA patrols that night moving in opposite directions on the trail he called the Jersey Turnpike. Or was it the same patrol that returned later? If so, this could mean the enemy was searching for them.

After sunup, Romeo-Bravo remained in place while Sam sent Brick Ireland's Romeo-Charlie team southeastward to see if he could find where the road crossed into the Song Bo River Valley. He wanted to get a better picture of where these enemy patrols were coming from and where they were going.

By late afternoon, Ireland and his team had circled the base of the mountain and found the road, but it didn't have near the signs and usage as what Knowlton had reported from his position up the mountain. The more he thought about it, the more Sam realized that the enemy patrols, as well as the ruts and other signs of traffic on the road, must have originated from a place somewhere on the eastern slope between his and Ireland's positions. It was likely an enemy base camp.

The sun would set soon, and Sam was preoccupied

contemplating the next day's plan when he suddenly realized something had changed. He stopped and listened. It was a fluctuation in the sounds of the jungle further down the mountain. He glanced over his shoulder. Although the sun was about to set, its misty beams still filtered down the mountain. It was still too early for the birds to have roosted. He cocked his head and continued straining to hear more.

There were voices, but they were too close. Sam turned to see two of his new men lying side by side talking. With several quick steps, he slipped down the slope and wedged himself between them. Glaring first at one then the other he said nothing. Their eyes were wide. They knew they had screwed up, and Sam left it at that, because it wasn't them that had caused the sudden change in the jungle sounds down below. There was no doubt in his mind. Something was down there.

The last orange beams of sunlight had faded to darkness when Sam slipped back up to where Allen Lowry sat with the radio. Knowlton had called in saying another NVA patrol had come up the Jersey Turnpike, but just after reporting them, he called again and said they had returned and gone back the way they came. He also reported one man carrying a radio with an odd circular antenna attached.

Sam studied the luminous hands on his wristwatch. The next sit-rep with the TOC was due at 2000 hours. The jungle was quiet tonight, definitely quieter than normal. Something was out of place. A bright flash lit the night sky, silhouetting the treetops above. It could have been another Arc Light strike, but it wasn't. It was lightning. The first fat raindrops thudded down through the jungle canopy and heaven's artillery rumbled down the mountainside reverberating with hollow booms against the far slopes. A storm had come over the mountain.

Sam crawled around to his men and whispered in each one's ear to be ready. As soon as the 2000 report was done, the team was going to relocate. A night move was risky, but his every instinct was telling him they had been compromised. They were no longer the hunters but the hunted.

At 2000 hours sharp, Sam switched on the radio and whispered into the handset. The X-ray team answered instantly. "Romeo-Alpha-one, Tango-Oscar-Charlie sends 'Punt the ball, now. Repeat, Punt the ball, now.' Over."

It was the prearranged signal for all the teams to move immediately to their planned extraction points. Problem was it was pitch dark and for whatever the reason the TOC had not sent the expected words "at first light."

"Roger, Romeo-X-ray, 'Punt the ball, now.'" Sam answered. "Romeo-Bravo and Romeo-Charlie, do you Roger? Over."

"Romeo-Bravo, Roger, Punt the ball, now. Over," Knowlton called.

"Romeo-Charlie, Roger, Punt the ball, now. Over," Ireland called.

"Romeo-Charlie, alternate in-zone. Over." Sam was redirecting Romeo-Charlie because their primary extraction point was straight up the eastern slope of the mountain where he suspected the NVA base camp might be located.

"Romeo-Charlie, Roger, alternate in-zone. Over," Ireland answered.

"Romeo-X-ray, report Tango-Oscar-Charlie, Romeo-Alpha and Romeo-Charlie, alternate in-zone. Over."

"Roger, Romeo-Alpha and Romeo-Charlie, alternate in-zone. Over."

Sam signed off and signaled for parachute cord to be stretched down the line from the point man to the tail-gunner. The wind, thunder, and pouring rain masked the sounds as the team moved out and struggled through the darkness, moving across the slope toward the south. Slipping and sliding, they crossed a series of rugged ravines and small valleys. Most were running knee-deep with muddy water.

The parachute cord suddenly stretched taut and popped back in Sam's face. He stopped. The rain deadened all sound, but he thought he heard a thud. Neither his point man nor his slack man was still holding the line. His mind ran amuck with the possibilities.

"Max, Ronny, you there?" he called in a low voice.

He took a careful step forward while reaching out into the darkness. He felt nothing but open air—not even any undergrowth. Lightning flickered and danced through the jungle canopy and Sam realized he was standing at the edge of an abyss. He had also gotten a snapshot glance of his two men sprawled on the jungle floor some twenty or thirty feet below.

"What's up?" Lowry whispered.

"We're on a ledge. Max and Ronny fell. Tell Semmes to pass the big rope up to the front."

After shedding his gear, Sam tied off the climbing rope and lowered himself into the ravine. When his feet touched the ground, he called their names again, "Max, Ronny?"

"I think we're okay." It was Max's voice coming from only a foot or two away. He sounded groggy.

"No, we're not," Ronny said. "I think my damned leg is broke."

They were forced to turn eastward down the mountain to get out of the ravine and climb back up the mountain again to regain their line of travel. By daylight the team was muddy and exhausted, but the rain had stopped. Broken clouds scuttled across the sky and the wind worked in their favor masking all sound. Each man had taken his turn carrying either Ronny or his equipment, and Sam was giving them a few minutes of much-needed rest. He studied the slope of the far ridge searching for the clearing that was the extraction point.

He had seen it one time from several thousand feet up during his aerial recon, but the terrain was beginning to all look the same. They had traveled the five klicks necessary to get there, but with the rugged ridges and valleys and misdirected line of travel, Sam was uncertain if they were in the right place. The clearing was a rock slide at the top edge of a large bowl-shaped valley two-thirds of the way up the mountain. All indications were that the team was in the right place, but the clearing wasn't visible.

Sam glanced at his watch. It was time to break radio silence. He switched on the radio and immediately heard Brick Ireland sign off, saying his Romeo-Charlie team was clear and Eagle bound. Sam was about to key the mic and acknowledge Ireland, but another voice broke in, "Roger, Romeo-Bravo, I confirm your banana and I'm inbound." It was the second extraction chopper confirming yellow smoke and going in to pick up Robbie Knowlton's team.

The original plan was for Sam's team to be the last one off the mountain, and intentionally or otherwise, it seemed things were going as planned. Sam's only problem was he couldn't find the alternate LZ, and his pink team would be inbound in the next twenty minutes.

He studied the map—trying to match the gridlines with the surrounding terrain. The map matched the slope above. He had to be in the right place. Perhaps he had to climb higher before he could see the clearing. Folding the map, he stuffed it in a cargo pocket and stood up.

"We've got company," Lowry whispered. The sergeant pointed out across the valley.

Sam searched the far slope and spotted movement nearly twelve hundred meters away. "I see them. Let's watch and see if we can tell which way they're going." It was an NVA patrol of at least twenty, perhaps twenty-five men, strung out along the far ridge.

A faint scratch came from the radio handset. Lowry pushed it to his ear and listened. "It's Papa-Tango-Three. They're inbound."

Sam continued watching the enemy patrol moving along the ridge. "Go ahead and roger them. Tell them we're still trying to reach the extraction point, but we have an enemy patrol in the area."

As soon as Lowry began his transmission to the inbound pink team, the enemy patrol came to a halt. They stood like statues, except for one who held some type of metal contraption above his head, moving it back and forth.

"Shit," Sam muttered. "They're using a directional antenna to locate us."

The soldier holding the antenna pointed out across the valley directly toward where Sam and his team were hidden.

"Tell them we have a platoon-size enemy patrol with a directional antenna locked in on us. We're going to limit our radio transmissions for now and turn to the west in case there are more of them following us that we haven't seen yet."

Sam watched the line of soldiers while Lowry sent the transmission. The enemy patrol began moving at a trot down the ridge toward him and his team.

"They're coming fast," he said. "Let's move."

The LRRPs started westward up the mountain, but Mackey, the man carrying Ronny, would have to set the pace. They'd gone only two or three hundred meters when Mackey stumbled and fell. The team gathered around and Sam glanced back down the ridge. The enemy patrol would continue moving in the direction of the last radio transmission. This would buy them some time, but not much.

"What's your plan, LT?" Lowry whispered. The thin mountain air had his team panting and red-faced, and everything was on his shoulders now as Sam realized whatever he did could mean life or death for his men.

"It's too thick in here. We need to keep moving up this ridge till we find the right place to pull an ambush. Y'all swap out carrying Ronny, and let's get going."

"We're outnumbered more than three to one, sir," Lowry said. "We'll have to get that ambush right the first time, or we'll be in deep shit."

Sam nodded. "I know. Let's get moving."

The clatter of the circling choppers echoed off the mountainside as the team moved another three hundred meters before Sam found the place he wanted. It wasn't an ideal set-up, but two steep and narrow ravines came up on either side of the ridge. These would likely slow the enemy's efforts to flank them.

"I want a man over on each flank with a Claymore," Sam said. "Two more will set up right here on either side of this trail. The two here will blow their Claymores on my signal. You two men on the flanks will wait. The enemy will try to flank us. If you can see them out in front, blow the mine. If you can't see through the cover, give it one minute, no less, no more. Use your watch and blow your mine. Everyone will empty one magazine and reload. You guys on the flanks will head back to a rally point a hundred meters up this trail. Tucker, you go ahead and carry Ronny up the trail. Move! We don't have much time."

Sam turned to Lowry. "When I give you the word, contact the pink team. Tell them to locate the LZ for us and as soon as we blow the ambush we'll pop smoke. Tell them to give us an azimuth and distance. The enemy is probably not far down there and as soon as you start the radio transmission they'll be coming our way."

"Sir," Lowry said, "why don't we just let the gunships handle them?"

"Because they'll split up and keep coming. This way, we bust them in the chops while they're all together. After that we run and let the choppers do their thing."

Lowry radioed the pink team and it was only a matter of minutes before a line of uniformed NVA came trotting up the trail. They were almost too close when Sam gave the signal and the two

Claymores at the center exploded. The first four or five enemy soldiers in line disappeared in a shower of smoke, dust, vegetation, and fourteen hundred ball-bearing-sized steel pellets. Darting figures went left and right in the jungle below while the men fired their M-16s. Green tracers began zipping past. A minute later the two Claymores on the flanks exploded. Sam popped a red smoke grenade and motioned for the others to fall back.

Swapping magazines, he backed away up the hill. Everyone was there unscathed at the rally-point when he arrived. *For once in this damned war things seemed to be going right.* Lowry was studying his compass.

"Where's the LZ?" Sam asked.

The sergeant looked up and pointed out into the valley. "Out that way—three hundred and fifty meters, but I still can't see anything but more trees."

"Tell the gunships to light up the area around our red smoke in two minutes."

"Already done, sir. They should—"

The *whoosh* of a half-dozen incoming rockets was followed by explosions down the ridge.

"They didn't wait. Let's move out."

The team moved at a trot down the ridge and out into the valley until they stumbled out onto the rockslide. They had made it and a Slick was hovering into position. Within minutes the team piled into the cabin of the chopper while the gunships swept across the mountain searching for targets. Sweating, winded, and exhausted, Sam and his men lay in silence as the chopper rose forever so slowly from the jungle. When he cleared the trees, the pilot dropped the nose and the helicopter dove down the mountain toward the Song Bo River Valley. It had been a textbook extraction under fire.

CHAPTER TWENTY-TWO

Give Something Back

November 2018
En Route to Biloxi, Mississippi

Thursday after her last class, Claire was waiting outside her dorm. It was going to be another long drive. Sam got out of the truck and after helping her load her bags, he tossed her the keys.

"You have first shift. It's an old dude thing. I'm going to be lazy and nap for an hour or two."

"No problem," she said.

A cold front had passed through during the night, and it was cloudy and cool. The leaves, red, yellow, and brown, showered down everywhere on the roadway as they drove southward through the mountains. He turned on the radio.

"What kind of music is it going to be today, sweet thing?" he asked.

"Put that playlist on with the old rock love songs."

He punched the buttons on his phone until an old Mamas and Papas tune began playing.

All the leaves are brown
And the sky is grey
I've been for a walk
On a winter's day

Claire had that killer smile on her face—the one she always got when she was on top of things. "That's pretty appropriate. Did you mean to start with that one?"

Sam cracked his window to let in some air. "I've become a high-tech redneck since I met you, dearie. Keep her between the ditches. I'm taking my nap now." Closing his eyes, he lay back in his seat, felt the cool wind in his face and inhaled the sweet crisp odors of another Carolina autumn.

When he cracked open one eye, Sam realized he had slept for more than an hour and Claire was singing along with an old Skyliners tune.

I don't have plans and schemes
And I don't have hopes and dreams
I-I-I don't have anything
Since I don't have you

He had never heard her sing and was surprised at the tone and subtle vibrato of her voice. *But why should he be surprised?* This young woman had already set herself apart in so many ways. Opening his eyes, he sat up and stretched. Claire stopped singing.

"Why did you stop?"

She blushed. "I don't know. Did I wake you up?"

"Well, if you did, I can't think of a better way to wake up from an afternoon nap. Where did you learn to sing like that?"

"Mama and I used to sing along with all these old songs. I think it was her way of dealing with the loneliness when Daddy was deployed."

"Pull over next chance you get. I'll drive while we get to work on the interview."

A few minutes later, after changing seats, Sam pulled the pickup back onto the highway. Claire punched on the recorder and sat ready with her spiral notebook in her lap.

"So, where did we leave off?" he asked.

She nibbled the eraser on her pencil and glanced at her notes. "Let's see. Yesterday, you said y'all completed a 'textbook' extraction under fire."

"Oh, yeah. That was good. Matter of fact it was *real* good, but it was also about the last thing that went right before I left Vietnam. A week or so after we got back to Camp Eagle, Khul came to me wanting to take his men back to their village in the highlands. I discussed it with the colonel and suggested that I take one of my team leaders and a medic and go along with them. We requisitioned some food and medical supplies for the people in the village. We hoped the gesture might change Khul's mind and once he saw his people were safe, he would return to Camp Eagle with us. The colonel agreed."

Sam began telling Claire about that day when they found Khul's entire village murdered by the North Vietnamese. It had been one of his worst days of the entire war, and Sam found himself driving down the interstate highway lost in a long pause.

"Why did the North Vietnamese kill all the people in his village?"

"You should read some books on Stalin or the Khmer Rouge. Hell, read what's written about any of the Socialist-Communist regimes. The only way they gain and hold control over their people is through death and intimidation. My best guess would be that the NVA killed their families so Khul and his men would give up and stop fighting."

"Did they?"

"That night after we left their village, Khul and his men were like lost children. I discussed our options with Robbie and Lee. We could hear the enemy patrols out there searching for us with their tracker dogs and things weren't looking so good. Remembering what Captain Benhauser told me about the Montagnards, I was worried that they might react and go off hunting on their own. We needed them to help us get to the extraction point, because it was dangerous terrain to navigate in the dark."

July, 1968
Central Highlands, Republic of Vietnam

It was another moonless night and moving through mountainous terrain with cliffs and rocky ledges would be risky, but Sam had a decision to make. He crawled back into the center of the bamboo thicket where Khul and his men were huddled. They had been whispering amongst themselves but stopped as he crawled into their midst. He could hear them breathing, but more importantly he could feel their grief and their anger.

"We talk, Đại-úy." It was Khul's voice.

"Do we move now, or do we stay put?" Sam asked.

Khul remained silent.

"Can you take us through this jungle at night?"

"I am here all my life. I play here when child."

"Then I think we should move before those bastards get any closer."

Again Khul said nothing.

"Do you agree?"

"My men, we take you to LZ. Then we go back."

"Go back? Where?"

"We go back kill communists."

It was Sam's turn to remain silent as he tried to figure a way to reason with Khul.

"You may well kill some communists, but there are too many of them. You will all end up dead like your families."

"Yes. Our spirits will be with theirs."

From somewhere on a nearby ridge came the bark of another tracker dog. Sam would try to reason with Khul later. It was time to move. With Khul in the lead, the patrol moved down the narrow mountain valley. Lee Miller salted the back-trail with powdered CS. After an hour Sam ordered Khul to make a ninety-degree turn, and after another hour he ordered a second turn. The navigational calculations were becoming progressively more difficult, and Sam feared he was becoming disoriented. A few hours after midnight he brought the team to a halt. He had lost his bearings.

"Which way, Khul?" he whispered.

"I take you to best numba one place," he said. "Not far. It close to LZ."

The team moved for several more hours, and just before dawn they were making their way along the base of a steep ridge. Khul led them as he turned and began climbing up the ridge. About a hundred feet up, he doubled back along the slope. It didn't make sense. *Was he zig-zagging to lose the enemy?* The little Montagnard brought the team to a stop.

Sam eased up beside him and whispered in his ear. "Where are you going?"

"It is here we wait for day to come. Then we move to LZ that way downstream, close. Put Claymore mine on trail down there. Wind come down valley from mountain. Dog not smell us."

It suddenly made sense. Khul had thought of everything. He had come along the base of the ridge several hundred meters before turning, climbing higher, and doubling back. The wind direction would keep the NVA from being forewarned by their dogs if they were on their trail. They were now in a perfect place to ambush them if they showed up. A line of Claymores was set out along the trail and two more were faced directly up the trail. The men circled back up the ridge and threw up what cover they could scrape together.

"Okay," Sam said. "As soon as we blow the ambush, everyone will di di mau. We'll go straight to the LZ for extraction."

Khul nodded and turned as he translated Sam's order to his men. The Montagnards usually remained silent and simply nodded, except this time he heard several quiet whispers amongst them. Sam couldn't help but wonder exactly what Khul had said, except there wasn't much he could do about it at this point. His only hope was that the ambush wouldn't be necessary. If it was, it would be a crapshoot no matter how well the initial attack was executed. The NVA would have multiple patrols in the area and they would close quickly to the contact.

───────────

A milky fog hung stagnant around them as the first gray light of day revealed the thick undergrowth on the ridge. The trail below was barely visible, and the jungle dripped with condensation. Sam was damp, sore, and jittery from lack of sleep. He looked about at the men. Most were face-down sleeping, except for Khul and Dak. Like faithful guard dogs they sat motionless studying the jungle below. From somewhere high above came the distant buzz of a small aircraft. A quiet scratch of squelch came from the radio and Robbie pushed the handset against his ear.

"It's a Bird Dog, LT," he whispered. "He wants a sit-rep."

"Tell him we're about one klick from the extraction point and to bring in the pink team ASAP. Tell him we have enemy patrols in the—"

Sam spotted movement below as Knowlton began whispering

into the handset. Ghostlike apparitions in the fog were moving along the trail below—NVA soldiers. They were walking slowly, quietly, taking their time. Without moving his head, Sam cut his eyes as he looked down the line to where his men were sleeping. It was as if some mysterious spirit had shaken every one of them awake.

With their heads raised, all were alert as they readied their weapons and aimed them at the enemy patrol below. Afraid to move more than his fingers, Sam flipped the safety from the Claymore's detonator. His men were all doing the same.

He paused, waiting until every man had flipped the safety from his detonator. All were ready. Sam nodded to the others and snapped the clacker between his thumb and fingers twice. His Claymore detonated with a flash and a roar. A moment later five more exploded, roaring almost simultaneously up and down the trail. The plan was for everyone to empty one magazine, reload, and move out. Coming to his feet in a crouch, Sam motioned for the others to follow, but only then did he realize Khul and his men were charging down the ridge.

He glanced over at Robbie. "I should have known."

The Montagnards disappeared into the foggy jungle below. Screams of agony and single gunshots continued as the Yards wiped out the entire enemy patrol. Robbie began talking into the radio handset, while Sam and Lee listened and waited.

"Roger, Bravo-Delta-Seven. Tell them to hurry. We've got a lot of company down here and it's getting pretty ugly."

Robbie shoved the handset into his pocket and stood up.

"Bird Dog said the TOC already had the pink team on standby—estimates maybe forty-five minutes."

"Did you tell him we were in heavy contact?"

"Yeah, he said for us to standby. The officer back at the TOC is calling around to see if he can get us some TAC air in here any faster."

"That's my boy, Ausie. He has our backs."

There came the shuffling sounds of men running along the ridge above them.

"Shit! That's got to be another NVA patrol. They're flanking us."

Grabbing a grenade, Sam pulled the pin and threw it in a high arc up the ridge toward the sounds.

"Come on. Let's move down toward Khul and his men and tell them just how screwed we are now."

With the grenade's explosion the running sounds had ceased, but a torrent of automatic weapons fire now streamed down the ridge. The three men ran, stumbled, and tumbled down the hillside toward the trail. Most of the enemy rounds were snapping past above their heads, and they had nearly reached Khul and his men when an RPG exploded in the trees above. Robbie staggered and pitched face down. He quickly regained his feet, but stood gazing about. He was stunned.

"Are you hit?"

Robbie's boonie hat was gone, and it quickly became evident he'd been struck by shrapnel in several places. He bent over and picked up his rifle. "Yeah, but I'm okay. We can't stop now."

Khul and several of his men ran out of the fog and passed the three Americans, as they charged back up the hill toward the second enemy patrol. The Montagnards' eyes were ablaze with a fiery determination to destroy the people who had slain their families. Mahoney's warnings were coming true. Khul and his men were not stopping, but this time, Sam couldn't blame them. He would have done the same thing. Still, he had to regain control.

"Khul," Sam shouted. "Let's make a run for it. Go to the LZ and set up a defensive perimeter."

Khul stopped and looked back. "You go, Đại-úy. We stay, kill communists." With that he turned and followed his men up the ridge.

Sam turned to Robbie. "Can you make it?"

"I'll carry the radio," Lee said. "Let me look at your head."

"We don't have time," Robbie said. "I'll keep up."

The medic looked toward Sam. "We'll follow you, and I'll stay behind him."

"Let's go," Sam said.

After only a hundred meters Sam realized Robbie wasn't keeping up. Blood flowed steadily from a gash in his head. They stopped and Lee wrapped it with a dressing. Robbie was growing groggy. The firefight continued behind them, but it now seemed to be getting closer. Khul and his men were apparently fighting a delaying action as they too fell back toward the LZ.

"It sounds like they've decided their damned banzai charge wasn't the best idea," Robbie muttered.

"Can you make it now?" Lee asked as he tightened Robbie's bandages.

"Yeah, I'm good. Let's go."

They stumbled down the widening mountain valley, arriving exhausted at the LZ. The extraction point was a wide, partially dry creek bed with gravel, piles of driftwood, and multiple channels. A few larger boulders would offer some cover if needed. Sam called for the pink team on the radio as the running gunfight up the valley drew closer.

The Bird Dog answered. "Romeo-Tango-One, this is Bravo-Delta-Seven-Seven. Papa-Tango-Two says they're still about 15 mikes out. Over."

"Roger, Bravo-Delta, tell them it's going to be a hot one. I'll pop smoke for confirmation and give them target data when they get closer."

A few moments later Sam spotted a Montagnard carrying another on his shoulders. The man was picking his way down the dry creek bed. The sounds of the firefight were now echoing off the surrounding ridges. Robbie had curled against a rock with his eyes shut.

"You still with me?" Lee asked.

Robbie's eyes remained closed, but he nodded. Sam shed the radio and gave Lee the handset and a red smoke canister.

"I'm going out there and help them with the wounded. The heading is roughly zero-eight degrees up that valley. If I'm not back when the pink team gets here, pop the smoke and give them the heading."

The medic nodded and Sam ran back up the creek bed toward the approaching firefight. As he drew closer, he realized it was Khul being carried by one of his men. Both had been wounded, but Khul was bleeding heavily from both legs.

Stopping them, Sam stuffed wads of gauze into the worst wounds and quickly cinched them tight with dressings. Khul watched stoically with hard brown eyes. Occasional rounds were now ricocheting from the surrounding rocks as Sam pointed out where Robbie and Lee were hidden and told them to go.

Back up the creek bed he spotted four more of the Montagnards coming his way. He motioned to them. It was Dak who immediately pulled the magazine from his weapon and held it up. "No bullet," he shouted, and pointed around to the others as well.

Only Dak and two others had M-16s that shot the same 5.56 millimeter round as Sam's AR-15. He began pulling loaded magazines from his bandolier, giving one to each of the men. He had four frags left in his grenade pouch and gave them those as well. It was none too soon as a clot of NVA regulars sprinted from around a bend upstream. They were coming toward them down the creek bed.

Sam aimed carefully at the one waving his arms and shouting orders at the others. He squeezed off the round and the enemy soldier fell. The others scattered and took cover as Dak and his men followed Sam's example and began carefully picking targets. Four of his twelve-man team were still unaccounted for, but he had to make the call. Sam motioned for the others to fall back, while he waited. The rest were likely dead, but he could provide cover if any of them showed up.

A sudden and thunderous roar sent Sam diving into the gravel as a helicopter shot past close overhead. The buzz of its Vulcan machine guns and the whooshing sounds of multiple rockets filled the sky as the gunship flew up the creek bed at treetop level, raking the approaching enemy. Farther up the valley it pulled skyward, followed by thousands of green streaks—enemy tracer rounds. The chopper climbed out and turned back to the east.

"Jesus," Sam muttered as he came to his feet. It looked as if the whole damned North Vietnamese Army was shooting at the chopper. He shouted to Dak. "Let's go."

Lee had popped the red smoke and a Slick was approaching as it dropped down the side of the mountain nearly a half-mile away. Sam glanced back up the valley. The first gunship had begun smoking and was limping away over the far ridge. An RPG exploded fifty meters away sending a shower of rocks skyward. Sam sprayed suppressing fire up the creek bed as rock shards and gravel rattled down around him.

A C&C ship and second Slick had arrived and were circling in the distance. The second gunship began its run on the approaching enemy soldiers while the first Slick's main rotor popped loudly as it hovered and landed on a gravel bar to their rear. Sam motioned for Lee and the Yards to help Robbie, while he ran to help the man carrying Khul. More enemy rounds began striking the rocks, and the man carrying Khul stumbled and fell. Sam ran to them, but Khul insisted he take his wounded man first.

After carrying the first man to the chopper, Sam went back for Khul. Scooping up the Montagnard warrior, he turned and ran toward the chopper. More RPGs exploded all around as the chopper's turbine whined and the RPMs increased. It had to be overloaded, but the crew chief was waving them aboard as the chopper began growing light on its skids.

CHAPTER TWENTY-THREE

Coming Home

November, 2018
Biloxi, Mississippi

S am was past tired when he and Claire arrived at the hotel in Biloxi. It was already past two-thirty in the morning and Claire went to the bathroom to brush her teeth and put on her pajamas. Sam figured he would slip into his while she was in there. All he wanted for now was to get some sleep. The door closed and he quickly slipped off his shirt and undershirt.

"I forgot to get my—" Claire gasped in what nearly became a scream as she stood staring at Sam's shirtless back. He had not heard her come back out of the bathroom.

"Damned! Sorry," he said. "I thought you—"

She hurried toward him. "No. Your back. What happened? I mean....I know you said you were wounded, but I never imagined...." She delicately ran her fingers over the deep scars crisscrossing his shoulders and lower back.

"Well, I didn't exactly finish the last part of the story I was telling you earlier. When I was running back to the helicopter with Khul that day, one of those damned RPGs blew up right behind me. Other than that big diagonal scar you're touching now, the rest came from that RPG. It messed me up pretty bad. I don't remember much after that. They said Lee and the Yards jumped out and carried us both back to the chopper, and we got out of there okay.

"The next thing I remember was waking up in the hospital at Phu Bai with a nurse picking shrapnel and rock shards out of my back. That's when I found the second Purple Heart pinned to my pillow and also when I found this on my wrist."

He held up his arm for her to see the copper bracelet he always wore.

"I wondered what that was."

"It's a Montagnard bracelet—something they give only to their special friends."

"Do the scars still hurt?"

"Not so much anymore, but they did for a lot of years because bits of shrapnel would work their way out and had to be removed."

"I just—I just never imagined—I mean...."

"It's okay. Most people don't, and it's because of those stupid bastards in Hollywood. Do you remember that old TV series back in the eighties called *The A-Team* where Mister T and his buddies got into these big shoot-outs with automatic weapons, grenades and such? At the end of every show they would stand around shucking and jiving and wearing arm slings and little gauze wraps on their heads. That bullshit drove me crazy. I mean...it just doesn't happen that way. People don't shoot one another with automatic weapons and—"

"Sam!"

He stopped. "What?"

"I wasn't even born back then, but I get the idea."

He felt his face burning with embarrassment. He had been on another rant.

"Sorry," he said. "At least Hollywood began adding a little realism to their movies."

"No reason to be sorry. I just didn't like seeing you so upset, but you're right. I didn't fully understand what getting a Purple

Heart really meant till I saw your back. I mean Daddy's scars don't look nearly as bad as yours."

"Make no mistake, Claire darling. Not all battle scars are visible. The ones you can't see on your father are far worse than any of mine. Now, go get ready for bed and we'll talk more about it tomorrow."

She nodded, retrieved something from her bag and turned toward the bathroom but stopped. "What about Khul and his men, and Robbie? What happened to them?"

"Robbie actually recovered from his wounds and finished his tour of duty. I was flown out of the country and a few weeks later ended up at Womack Army Hospital again. I stayed pretty drugged-up most of the time, but I had the same question about Khul and his men, and sent a letter to my brigade commander back at Camp Eagle. He checked with the army hospital in Phu Bai but the Montagnards had been transferred to another medical facility and he couldn't track them down.

"I then sent a letter to Sergeant Mahoney, my old Special Forces mentor. It was early 1969 before I got an answer from him. He wrote saying he had exhausted every possible lead searching for them, but promised to keep looking."

"It just doesn't seem fair," Claire said.

"Nothing about life is fair. We take the hand we're dealt and play it as well as we can. Regardless, it's like that Frenchman, La Bruyere, said, 'Life is a tragedy for those who feel, and a comedy for those who think.' Go get your pajamas on, honey. I'll tell you more later. Right now, it's going on three a.m. and we need to get some sleep before we go to our counseling session this afternoon."

The counselling session went well and though he seemed reluctant at first, Claire's father agreed to live with Sam. He was released in

Biloxi and the next morning rode with them back to North Carolina. It was clear that Bill Cunningham suffered from a number of major issues, but the trip home had nevertheless left Sam feeling unsettled. Cunningham seemed paranoid about him. He and his daughter had shared most of the conversation, with Cunningham directing only an occasional question toward Sam. It was probably to be expected, and Sam shrugged it off till they reached the college that evening.

When they dropped Claire off at the dormitory, her father had walked with her to the door while Sam waited in the truck. It was when they reached the steps there that he watched Claire spin toward her father with a scowl and shake her head adamantly. They were arguing. Afterward very little was said as Sam drove to his house and showed Cunningham the bedroom.

"If you need anything, my room is down at the end of the hall. Don't hesitate to come down there any time during the night."

Sam began pulling the door shut when Cunningham spoke. "Wait." He paused for several seconds. "Look, Sam, I don't mean to look in the horse's mouth, but why are you doing this? What's in it for you?"

It was a fair question.

"Only the reward of knowing I am giving something back for what Claire has done for me."

Cunningham remained silent while staring at him.

Sam shrugged. "That's it."

"Really? Is that all there is to it?"

Sam felt a twinge of anxiety. It was the tone of his voice. Cunningham was obviously insinuating there were nefarious purposes for his generosity. "What do you mean?"

"You're having sex with my daughter. Aren't you?"

The twinge of anxiety turned to full-blown anger. "You can't be serious! No way you can think I—" Sam stopped talking and stepped back into the bedroom. He was fighting to restrain himself.

"Well, why is she so damned infatuated with you?"

He wanted to slap some sense into Cunningham, but assaulting a fellow disabled vet would not go over well with anyone, especially Claire. "You don't know just what kind of woman you have for a daughter, do you?"

"Look, Sam. Frankly, the problem is already solved. When we dropped her off at the dorm I told her we're moving home to Maggie Valley as soon as we can."

Sam saw it immediately. This really wasn't about Claire. It was more of Bill Cunningham running away instead of facing reality. It was more about his wants than Claire's, but confronting him now would only make matters worse. Sam decided to bide his time and discuss it with Claire before acting.

"Bill, it's good that you are putting your daughter's interests ahead of your own. I will help you however I can. Get some sleep and we'll make whatever arrangements as soon as we can."

November, 2018
Boone, North Carolina

Sam lay awake that night, thinking about the months of surgeries and recovery he had gone through at the VA Hospital in Asheville. Bill Cunningham faced an even more difficult type of recovery, if one could be had, and Claire was the key. She had many of the same traits as Caroline, and he had to find a way for Claire to do for her father what Caroline had done for him. It seemed like only yesterday when he was there with her at the VA, trying to get past another surgery.

Caroline pulled his right arm across his chest while Sam sat upright on the stool. The pain was not so horrendous as it had been in the first months of his recovery, but it was still painful. The therapist had trained her to keep stretching the back muscles, and after months of therapy and multiple surgeries Sam felt himself getting better—at least physically. He still worried about those he had left behind in Vietnam.

Ausie and Ted should have rotated back to the States by now, but they were both still there. Ted had taken a command over a security unit attached to a mobile army surgical unit while Ausie had taken a company commander's position with the 101st. Ausie was still in the thick of it, fighting up in the A Shau Valley, while Ted was seeing the worst of the wounded that arrived almost daily. The war, it seemed, was never going to end. He grimaced as Caroline gently pulled his arm, stretching his shoulder and back muscles.

"You received another letter today from the Department of the Army," Caroline said. "I opened it. Your brigade commander with the 82nd put you in for another commendation and it was appr—"

"I don't give a shit about any more commendations. When you get home you can throw it in the trash."

"Give me your left arm, and let's stretch it now," she said.

Her patience with him was unsettling. How could this woman tolerate him? Hell, he could hardly stand himself. They clasped hands and she began a slow pull of his arm across his chest. Again, pain radiated across his knotted back muscles as they reluctantly yielded to her gentle pressure.

"You know you will get better sooner if you try to focus on the positive. Being angry isn't going to change things."

Caroline was right. She was always right, and her soft words soothed his raw feelings, but the anger remained nearly overwhelming. He was bitter, but he had every reason to be.

"I just wish there was more I had done."

"By the looks of your back and arm, I'd say you have done enough. Besides, I want a husband healthy enough to do all those things you talked about the other day while you were in recovery after the surgery."

"What kinds of things?"

"Well, let's see. One involved something about us taking a blanket and hiking up to a high mountain pasture this summer and, well, it wouldn't be very ladylike for me to say what you said, but—"

"No! You know me better than that. I wouldn't say any—"

She raised her brows and cocked her head to one side. "Oh, yes, you did."

"Were there any doctors or nurses in the room?"

"Just one nurse."

"Oh, shit! I hope I didn't embarrass you. What'd she say?"

"She said she was jealous but hoped you weren't all talk like some men. I assured her that you had already proven yourself in Manila."

"Is that what you young women talk about nowadays?"

"You were the one who was doing the talking. Better get well, so you can hold up your end of the bargain."

And Sam realized at that moment how deftly she had changed the subject and raised his spirits. Someone up above was definitely looking after him. If there was going to be a decent life after Vietnam, it was because of Caroline. She was the one holding the door open for him to see the sunshine.

———————

Claire called him late that Sunday night from her dorm and told Sam about the argument with her father. He went to meet with her the next afternoon. They sipped their tea while trying to come up with a plan. He had not told her about her father's accusation because it would be hurtful and possibly create a serious rift in their relationship.

"I believe he's just uncomfortable taking help," Sam said.

"No, it's more than that," she countered.

"Like what?"

"I'm not sure, but I get the distinct impression he's jealous because you've been looking after me the last couple months. When you went to the restroom at that restaurant on the way home, I told him about how you put Mama's pickup in the shop and bought me liability insurance. He kind of freaked out and wanted to know why I was taking all these gifts from you."

"Claire, you've got to understand that he comes from that proud Appalachian mountain stock, plus he has that traumatic brain injury. He can't think clearly and doesn't really mean much of what he says, but you can't let him ruin your life."

"We've already been down that road together, Sam. I've got to do something. What do you suggest?"

"I'd open a can of whoop-ass on him."

"What do you mean?"

"You know, back when I went through OCS one of the things they drilled into us from the first moment was respect for our superiors. Your father went through that, but since OCS he's pretty much been the man in charge of his family and his platoon. I think you need to get into his face and tell him in no uncertain terms that in his absence you have taken on those duties and that you intend to hold your family together on your terms. Tell him you won't tolerate him hurting himself anymore or running away. And tell him you won't let him keep you from finishing school."

"Sam, I don't know if I can talk to my father that way. I mean he is my—"

"Hang on. Do you remember when you called Brad an idiot, and when you shouted me down when we disagreed? You have it in you. I would say it doesn't matter that he's your father, but it *does,* because he is the most important person in your life right now and he needs you, but it has to be on your terms. He is the reason you need to get tough and do what it takes to make this arrangement work."

"Why can't you tell him these things?"

"He needs to hear it from you, but I'll tell you what I'll do. The three of us can meet together and I'll try to reason with him. I'll do my best, but if it doesn't work, you're going to have to step up and get tough with him."

Sam waited while Claire fidgeted with her teacup. After a few seconds, she looked up at him. "When do you want to meet with him?"

"How about right now? We can go by the house, pick him up and drive up to Howard's Knob. It's not far from the house and there's not likely to be anyone up there in the middle of the week."

CHAPTER TWENTY-FOUR

The Thanksgiving Day Guests

November 2018
Boone, North Carolina

C laire, her father, and Sam wore sweaters and jackets as they sat on a rock outcropping high up on Howard's Knob. A single red-tailed hawk sailed silently across the slope farther down the mountain while the threesome gazed down on Boone and the Appalachian State University campus a mile below. The school marching band was practicing in the stadium, making geometric patterns on what appeared to be a postage-stamp-size football field. It was not without purpose that Sam had chosen this place to talk.

Bill Cunningham had a choice to make. Did he want to call this place home? More importantly, his eyes would be led to see the world around him on a broader scale, hopefully turning his attention outward toward others and less toward himself. Sam had always found that focus a better approach for overcoming his wartime memories.

Claire's father sat with his arms folded, staring out across the town far below. "If you two think you're going to change my mind, you're wrong."

"Just hear me out, Dad."

Sam glanced at Claire, surprised by her quick engagement.

"Let's just talk a while. We don't have to make any decisions today," she said.

Sam stared out over Booneville and let Claire take the lead. The doctors in Biloxi had said that her father seemed more rational some days than others. He hoped today would be one of the better ones.

"The first thing I want to make clear is that Sam has our best interests foremost in mind."

"Oh for the love of—"

"Dad!"

Claire had nearly shouted. Her jaw was clenched and she stared at him with fire in her eyes. Sam held up what he hoped was a calming hand.

"Okay, let's just stay calm," he said. "Bill, I think you should give it a few weeks before making any final decisions. Let's go to a couple of our veterans' meetings down at the VA in Asheville. I don't see what harm there is in that. Then if—"

"Oh, yeah, so you can exercise more of your influence over my daughter and—"

Claire scrambled to her feet and spun to face him. "Dad, shut the fuck up!"

Cunningham's mouth fell open as he stared up at her with the look of a new boot in front of a drill instructor. Sam found himself not wanting to say anything either.

"When Mama died, you weren't here. I had to bury her, and I took on the duties of trying to put our family back together. Now that I've got you back here, I'm not going to tolerate any more of your running away. You are going to those meetings, and I am going to finish college. And you should damned well be thankful to Mister Sam, because he is the one who made all of this possible."

There came only the quiet whisper of a mild breeze across the mountain below. Cunningham's eyes fell to an unfocused stare.

Claire sat back down beside him and put her arm across his shoulders.

"We can still have a good life, Dad, but you have to trust me and you have to trust Sam."

Tears began streaming from his eyes, and Claire kissed his cheek.

"We can do this, Dad. We just have to stick together."

The Saturday morning before Thanksgiving, Sam had driven down to the VA in Asheville with Bill Cunningham. They were gathered with several other vets in a meeting room to discuss their issues with post-traumatic stress. The moderator introduced himself and asked that all the others do so as well. Afterward, he prompted several men to talk about their recent issues. Nearly an hour elapsed before he turned to Sam and Bill.

"Bill, Sam, I know this is your first time here. That's why we went around the room and let some of the others speak first. We'd like to hear a little from each of you. Tell me what you would like to get out of these meetings. Which of you wants to go first?"

Sam cut his eyes to Bill. He sat stone-faced staring straight ahead. It was pretty obvious he wasn't going to say anything. "I'll go first," Sam said. "I was in Vietnam back in the sixties. My saving grace when I returned from the war was my wife, Caroline. I never quite realized just how much till she died three years ago. That's when things changed. I retired and turned inside myself. Besides losing my Caroline, I didn't realize there was something else hanging over me, until this young college student asked to interview me for her senior thesis. The title of her thesis was The Vietnam War Experience, A Veteran's Perspective.

"During the course of our interviews, she was able to help me come to terms with my memories of the war, and I also discovered this young woman's father had received a severe traumatic brain injury while in Iraq and had left home. He was living on the street somewhere, but she didn't know where. I also learned that she wasn't simply writing her senior thesis, but was trying to gain a better understanding of a combat veteran's mind so she could help her father."

Sam cut his eyes over to Cunningham. His face glowed fire red.

"Because this girl had brought me out of a dark place, I was committed to helping her find her father and bring him home. That man is Bill here."

Bill Cunningham choked out a loud sob and dropped his head into his lap, where he cried. Sam and another vet rubbed his back.

Thanksgiving Day, 2018
Boone, North Carolina

Sam and Claire had been cooking for two days and the house was filled with the aromas of roasted turkey, sage dressing, baked bread, and sweet potato pie. Claire had used her mother's recipes for most of the cooking and Sam acted as chief 'gofer.' She had also decorated the house with fall colors and set the table for eight. And when all was done, she went to shower and don her best fall dress to meet the surprise guests that Sam said were coming. Sam watched her and knew she was a godsend—very much the same as his Caroline had been.

When she returned, Claire curtsied and Sam stood spellbound at the center of the family room, gazing at her.

"What's wrong?" she said. She looked down at her dress.

"Nothing," he said. "Nothing. I mean, it just hit me that this is the first Thanksgiving that I've actually celebrated since Caroline died, and you did almost everything—just like her. You cooked. You decorated. You—" Sam found himself choked with emotion as Claire stepped into his arms and they embraced. The doorbell rang.

His guests were arriving and despite Claire's repeated attempts to get their names, all he had told her was that they were old army buddies, and one was the person who helped him find her father.

Sam regained his composure and drew a deep breath. "Are you ready to meet some of my old friends?"

Claire brushed her hand down her dress. "Do I look okay?"

"Okay? My god, child, you look fantastic. Someday you will be the woman of some man's dreams. Now stop stressing."

Sam opened the door and Claire stood beside him, her hands clasped together in a nervous fist. An elderly man and a woman were there, smiling. Sam and the man embraced, slapping one another's backs.

"It's about time you showed up again," Sam said. "What was it—the offer of a free meal?"

"Why the hell else would I come down here, you old derelict?" the man said.

Sam stepped back and put his hand behind Claire's arm. "Claire, I want you to meet the man who carried me off Hill 875. This is Doctor Ted Salter, and his wife, Doctor Angie Salter."

Ted reached to shake her hand. "Sam has told me a lot about you and your father. He says you're his adopted granddaughter."

She gazed at him and smiled. Ted smiled back.

"Ted is with the Veterans Administration, and he was my contact who helped us find your dad."

Claire blushed as she stared at Sam then Ted. "Oh. Oh my," she said. "I didn't realize…" She stepped forward and wrapped her arms around Ted's neck. "I really appreciate your help, Doctor Salter. I'm not sure what else to say except, 'thank you.'"

"Oh my! Please call me Ted. If I had known I was going to get a hug from such a pretty woman—"

"Down, boy," his wife said.

"Awww, Mama, you know it's still fun to bark up a tree once in a while."

"Still incorrigible after all these years," Sam said.

Angie nodded. "Yep."

"Y'all come on in."

"Speaking of incorrigible," Ted said, "is our retired three-star buddy going to be here?"

"No. Ausie couldn't make it. He's spending this Thanksgiving with his family," Sam said. "How was the drive down from D.C.?"

"Not too bad. Man, that food smells good."

"Claire is one heck of a good cook," Sam said. "Check out the spread in the dining room. She fixed most all of it."

Bill Cunningham walked into the room. Sam stepped back as Claire went to him and took his hand. "Daddy, this is the man who helped us find you. He and Sam served together in Vietnam and he is with the office of Veterans' Affairs in Washington. This is Doctor Ted Salter and this is his wife, Doctor Angie Salter."

Cunningham released her hand and walked up to Ted. Both men gazed at one another in what seemed an interminable silence. Ted's wife glanced at him and then at Sam, but Sam knew better. He would let it play out. Claire fidgeted a moment and started to step forward but Sam caught her arm. She turned and Sam's eyes met hers as he pulled her close and put his arm around her waist.

"So you were in Vietnam and fought beside Sam here?" Cunningham said.

Ted nodded. "Yup. Long time ago. We were cherry lieutenants together."

Cunningham stepped forward and wrapped his arm around Ted's neck. "Thanks for bringing me home, sir."

Salter's eyes grew red as his wife patted his back. He returned Cunningham's hug, stepped back, and gave him a salute. "It was the least I could do for a brother."

Cunningham's eyes too had grown red with the weight of

emotion as he returned Ted's salute. Sam glanced at Claire. She was smiling. It was indeed a day for thanksgiving.

"Why don't we adjourn to the family room for drinks until our other guests arrive?" Sam said.

A few minutes later the doorbell rang again. Claire was in the hallway helping her father with his tie while Sam greeted the next guests. When she finished, Sam introduced the new arrivals. He saw her furrowed brows as she studied the two little brown men and one tall white man.

"These are my friends," Sam said. "This is Khul and this is Dak. They were two of the brave Montagnard warriors I served with in Vietnam."

Claire bowed respectfully, but Sam was suddenly feeling very old as the two aging Montagnards stood before him, bright-eyed but withered as raisins and leaning on walking canes. The moment was a little overwhelming. He turned and shook hands with his old Special Forces mentor. "And this is retired Sergeant Major Andrew Mahoney. Good to see you, Andy."

The three men traded hugs and Claire shook their hands while casting a quizzical glance at Sam.

"Okay. Let me explain," he said. "Sergeant Mahoney gave me a call out of the blue one day about nine or ten years after the war ended. He wanted me to go to Thailand with him. When the war ended, the State Department made us leave behind most all of our Montagnard brothers. The communists went to work destroying them and their culture. It was a pretty sad time for everyone, especially after they had fought side by side with the Green Berets and remained so loyal for all those years.

"In 1986 the Green Berets established a non-profit charity called 'Save the Montagnard People,' and a few years after that Andy got word that Khul and Dak had made their way to Thailand. That's when he called me. We flew to Bangkok, eventually found them, and made arrangements to bring them back here.

"You see, along with the help of the State Department, human rights groups, and churches, the Green Berets sponsor eight to nine thousand Montagnards. They settled them in an area here in North Carolina near Asheboro. There are only 600,000 left world-wide and the Green Berets have never forgotten how the Montagnards helped them during the Vietnam War.

"They're still doing their best to reciprocate. I make the birdhouses and sell them to help out. They aren't much, and I *do* make alterations on them occasionally, like the one with the school colors, but most remain true in appearance to the Montagnard homes back in the highlands of Vietnam. Like one of my team members, Robbie Knowlton, said one time, 'They look like birdhouses on stilts.'"

Sam cast a glance at Khul. The little man's eyes were glowing with happiness—something no doubt spawned by their reunion. Khul raised his cane in the air. "Are you going to talk all day, Đại-úy, or you going to pour me a glass of your bourbon?"

If you enjoyed this story

Please leave your written review of
The Birdhouse Man now at
www.amazon.com/review/create-review?asin=B086LKMDS1.
The author and other readers will appreciate your comments. Post
your review now and tell others what you liked about this book.

Glossary

.45: Forty-Five automatic pistol, the standard American sidearm

AAR: After Action Report (Usually filed by the commanding officer)

Airborne: Paratroop Units—82nd Airborne, 101st Airborne, 173rd Airborne

AK-47: Russian Kalashnikov automatic rifle used by enemy troops

AO: Area of Operation

AR-15: light-weight version of the M-16 automatic rifle

Arc Light: The code name for massive B-52 bomb strikes on enemy positions

Article-15: Army disciplinary action usually ranging from extra duty to loss of stripe

ARVN: Army of the Republic of Vietnam (The South Vietnamese Army)

Bird Dog: A single-engine light reconnaissance aircraft

Blue Line: Jargon referencing rivers and creeks on topographical maps

CAR-15: Lightweight carbine version of the M-16 rifle

C&C Ship: Command & Control helicopter flown above an operations area

Chieu Hoi: Amnesty program for VC defectors (individuals referred to as Chieu Hois)

CIDG: Civilian Irregular Defense Group (indigenous forces)

Claymore: A command-detonated directional mine that fires 700 steel pellets

CO: Commanding Officer

CP: Command Post

CS: Tear Gas comes in various forms including powder and canisters

DD-214: Military Record Form

Dai-uy: Vietnamese for "Captain"

Di Di Mau: Vietnamese for "move quickly" (literally, travel quickly)

Dust-off: A medical evacuation helicopter

E&E: Escape & Evasion

Extraction Point: Predetermined location recon teams are picked up by helicopter

Gunship: Support helicopter armed with rockets, mini-guns and machine guns.

Huey: Nickname for the UH-1 Helicopter

IED: Improvised Explosive Device

Insertion Point: Location where recon teams are inserted into the area of operation

KIA: Kilo India Alpha, Killed In Action

Klick: One kilometer, one thousand meters, one grid on a topo map

LBJ: Long Binh Jail, army stockade located at Long Binh, Republic of Vietnam

LRRP: Long Range Reconnaissance Patrol

LT: Short for "Lieutenant"

LZ: Landing Zone for helicopters

M-79: American grenade launcher, also fired shotgun-like flechette rounds

MACV: U.S. Military Assistance Command, Vietnam

Medevac: Medical Evacuation helicopter, or verb: to evacuate for medical treatment

Mermite Can: Insulated metal container military used to transport hot food to troops

Mikes: Military jargon for Minutes

Montagnard/Yard: Indigenous highland people who fought with the Americans

NCO: Non-Commissioned Officer (A Sergeant)

NDP: Night Defensive Position

Nuoc mam: A highly "aromatic" sauce made of fermented fish

NVA: North Vietnamese Army, well-armed uniformed communist troops

OCS: Officer Candidate School (six-month training school for officers)

Pink Team: Helicopter group used to retrieve recon teams from the field

Point Man: The man who walks at the head of a patrol

Pos': Jargon for "position"

PRC-25: Standard military backpack radio (sometimes called Prick-25)

PX: Post Exchange (army post businesses)

Redball: A hard-packed red clay and sand road

RIF: Recon In Force

RPG: Rocket Propelled Grenade

R&R: Rest and Recuperation leave

RTO: Radio Telephone Operator (The guy who carries the radio)

S-2 Section: The military intelligence group

S-4 Section: The military supply group

Sit-Rep: Short for "Situation Report"

Slack Man: The man who walks directly behind the point man

Slick: Troop-carrying helicopter with no armaments, except a door gunner

Spider hole: A very small one-man foxhole usually hidden by cover

TAC: Tactical Air Cover, provided by aircraft

TOC : Tactical Operations Center that monitors field operations

T&T: Through & through referring to a projectile that enters and exits the body

VC: Viet Cong, communist guerrillas

WIA: Whisky India Alpha, wounded in action

XO: Executive Officer (second in command)

X-Ray Team: Radio relay team deployed to assist communications in remote areas.

Rick DeStefanis lives in northern Mississippi with his wife, Janet, four cats and a male yellow lab named Blondie. Although many of his novels cross genre lines that include military fiction, southern fiction and historical western fiction, he utilizes his military expertise to produce the Vietnam War Series. *Melody Hill* (*Book #1*) is the prequel to his award-winning novel *The Gomorrah Principle*, both of which draw from his experiences as a paratrooper with the 82nd Airborne Division from 1970 to 1972.

Learn more about DeStefanis and his books online at www.rickdestefanis.com/, or you can visit him on Facebook at www.facebook.com/RickDeStefanisAuthor/.